A Copperhead Summer

A Camp Itawa Mystery

Books by Mark Warren

Moon of the White Tears
Indigo Heaven
A Tale Twice Told
Last of the Pistoleers
Song of the Horseman
Two Winters in a Tipi
Wyatt Earp, an American Odyssey (a trilogy)
The Long Road to Legend
Born to the Badge
A Law Unto Himself
Secrets of the Forest (4 volumes)
Wild Plants & Survival Lore
Fire-making, Storytelling, & Ceremony
Stalking, Tracking, & Playing Games in the Wild
Archery, Projectiles & Canoeing
Librarians of the West
The Westering Trail Travesties
A Last Serenade for Billy Bonney

The Camp Itawa Mysteries
Book One: A Copperhead Summer

Coming Soon!
The Camp Itawa Mysteries
Book Two: The Last Real Place
Book Three: A Dance in the Devil's Rain

For more information
visit: www.SpeakingVolumes.us

A Copperhead Summer

A Camp Itawa Mystery

Mark Warren

SPEAKING VOLUMES, LLC
NAPLES, FLORIDA
2024

A Copperhead Summer

Copyright © 2024 by Mark Warren

All rights reserved. No part of this book may be reproduced or transmitted in any form or by any means without written permission.

ISBN 979-8-89022-116-2

For Nathan Roark

Chapter One

The first time I saw Tyler Raintree, his head was tilted against the last window in the back of the first camp bus of the 1984 season. An oval section of his dark hair was pressed flat to the glass like a wet spot. His limp body jounced with the bumps in the dirt drive, but his eyes remained unfocused, dead. He reminded me of a prisoner of war who had seen the last of his homeland.

As the bus came grinding up the drive from the gate, he didn't see me in the shadow of the giant white pine. I was leaning back into the top rail of the fence, counting the number of seasons I had watched new faces roll into Camp Itawa. In that tally I included those years when it had been me struggling up this same old hill in this same old bus. This was year eleven for me—a reminder that I was in the last months of my teen years. Come December, I would hit the big two-O.

Almost everyone was reminding me of that lately . . . that and the seemingly aimless plan for my life. I was the only head counselor at Camp Itawa who didn't disappear into college life for the off-season. For two years now, high school had been behind me, and my summer counseling and handyman job at Itawa had become my sole, year-round livelihood. I smiled. I was probably the most content nineteen-year-old on the planet.

Before the bus passed me, several of my old campers gave me big toothy grins as they crawled over each other to ratchet down the windows. They looked like paratroopers scrambling to see who could first bail out of a C-47. I heard my name ripple down the aisle of the bus in a chain reaction. I held the smile, but my eyes were pulled back to Tyler by that same palpable allure that makes people gawk at an accident on the highway.

Tyler's tragic eyes angled out to the green sprawling grounds of the camp and then rolled up to take in the walls of the steep mountain valley that had just swallowed him. He was inorganic—part of the upholstery—while the other kids were manic, gathering their belongings after the long ride from Atlanta.

I saw lots of faces I knew: eleven-, twelve-, and thirteen-year-old veterans standing in the aisle, pointing at the cabins, staking claims to their old bunks from a distance. One bed was like every other, as all the campers well knew, but the ritual was one way to show the newcomers that they knew the ropes at Itawa.

The old camp bus growled like a wounded mastodon and crept toward the front of the Lodge. Tyler's face floated past me like a lost soul trapped in Dante's dream. I had seen that look too many times. It wasn't boredom or disinterest, though he probably would have settled for either. It was a kind of contained fear that the camper had brought from home. Already, I knew he would be my project. There was always one.

There was no day quite like the first day of camp. By early June, spring had already retreated from the asphalt maze of Atlanta, but in the mountain coves of Appalachia the season lingered for an extra month. Mountain laurels were still in flower, dropping petals in snowy pink carpets along the creek. A phoebe was busy shoring up her nest under the eave of the Lodge, and the clean brisk mountain air was like an elixir promising adventure for all who would sign up for my classes. With the April and May rains, the river was up . . . but not so much to make running the Narrows dangerous.

Strong and renewed from a perfect winter, I had finished my log cabin on the far side of the lake and watched it nestle like a newborn into the hemlock forest when the first snows came. Sleeping in it that first December night was like falling into a parallel universe that had waited for me all my life. By February, I had moved in my piano, which was, to me, like breaking a champagne bottle across the bow of a new ship. It was the baby grand my grandmother had left me, and it knew more about me than any other entity on earth—except, of course, Bobby Whitehorse.

For the sake of the piano, I had mastered the art of fine-tuning the cabin's temperature with a wood stove. Even in June I still lit a fire in the late evenings and felt the heart inside my new home renew its steady beat.

I had read somewhere that Aaron Copland had originally composed *Appalachian Spring* under some other title, completely unrelated to these mountains. But I couldn't give it up. I was whistling its theme softly through my teeth as I gazed up at the mountain peaks that made a perfect ring around the camp. Each one of these ancient hills had written a healing chapter for my own troubled youth. And now each mountain waited for my return—along with the kids who would sign up for Outriders. That was the name of my group. We weren't just "special" for the adventures we undertook. We were "legendary."

The Outriders were to Itawa what Special Forces are to the military. Our agenda was more primitive than the rest of camp, preparing us for more autonomy in wilderness. Periodically, we struck out for days in search of a world that had existed centuries ago. We ate wild sochani greens and greenbrier shoots and the core of cattail stems—whatever was in season. We speared fish and cooked them on handmade spits. We dug into logs and earth for beetle larvae, which we cooked on heated rocks oiled with the skins of the fish. We boiled crayfish, raided yellow jacket nests at night, and converted pine inner bark to pasta.

On our excursions, our cooking fires were spun from dead wood, Indian-style. No one wore a watch. We set our rhythms to sun and moon and weather. We worked as a tribe even as each Outrider took on secret quests that tested his or her heart in personal and private ways. Everything we did benefited the group, because if a camper learned new things about himself, that camper became a more effective part of the whole.

At night, gathered around our fire in a remote section of wilderness, we talked about things like honor and courage, fear and need. Or perhaps we did not talk. Either way was respected. No one belittled. No one judged. With this kind of trust, every Outrider knew that he could depend on every other Outrider. Not just during the camp session . . . but for life.

Bobby Whitehorse eased up behind me and leaned against the fence on his thickly muscled forearms. I smelled him before I saw or heard him. His scent was a mix of salt and horse and soaped leather. We were quiet as we watched the second bus climb the hill.

"Here we go," Bobby said, softening his voice with that same sandy whisper he used with the horses. His natural conversational voice was a chasm, humming with a power you could feel like faraway thunder prowling distant mountains. He knew when to use it. And when not to. Like a bright morning in June with children who had left home, perhaps for the first time.

"You see him?" Bobby said in his off-handed way.

I pivoted my head enough to show the question on my face, but I knew exactly what he'd meant. Bobby appeared to be looking at nothing . . . and at everything. I turned back to watch the unloading of the buses.

"Yeah," I said. "I saw him."

The third bus—the one from North Carolina—pulled past us and stopped in the turnaround, taking its place in line under the grandfather hemlock that would greet over two hundred city kids this summer. When the engine sputtered out, we could hear the driver barking her final orders before allowing the campers to exit.

"Divorce within the last month," Bobby said. "I'd bet the farm." He knew I would still be thinking about the mute boy in the back of the first bus.

I nodded. "Maybe." I didn't have to look back again. Bobby's mouth would be curled into a false smile, a grim salute to the ravages of divorce we had seen in too many children. Like so many times, he and I would be thinking the same thoughts with no need to voice them.

"War is hell, Stoney," he said.

At that I turned and gave him a look. Bobby Whitehorse was a few inches over five feet tall in his wrinkled cowboy boots, a full-blooded Cherokee, and timeless. I knew he had done a tour in Vietnam, but few could have guessed it by the youthful clarity of his eyes. His beat-up Stetson was the only part of him that aged. Square-shouldered and thick, Bobby was big the way a sofa is big in a living room, not taking up so much space—not among these Georgia mountains—but you wouldn't want to have to move him by yourself.

He wore his hair long, pulled back and braided into a ponytail that glistened like a black king snake hanging down between his shoulder blades. But it was his hands I always lingered on. They were massive entities that glided at his sides just above his knees when he walked. Even relaxed, they looked capable of crushing stones into powder.

His given name was Robert Steals-the-White-Man's-Horse—a surname passed down from an enterprising ancestor, but the unhyphenated alteration had proved more resilient in the white world. I had never seen him run or swim or touch a barbell by choice, but I had once seen him lift a toppled tractor off of Boyd Justus' bleeding legs while I pulled Boyd free. And the year Tony DeLantes took a rattlesnake bite on the calf up on Standing Bear Dome, Bobby Whitehorse had lived up to his name, saddled Tony on his back, and jogged out the six miles of rough mountain terrain in under an hour.

Bobby had carried his abridged name long before I had met him, when it was my turn to come bouncing into Itawa on that bus for the first time. There were times when I pulled out his proper name and gave it back to him when the occasion called for it. It was like a shot of adrenaline, magnifying the horsepower of his warrior spirit. But I did this selectively. One must be mindful of what one unleashes.

" 'War is hell'?" I said, lowering my chin so that I looked up at him—not an easy maneuver considering Bobby's height.

Bobby Whitehorse had probably seen every Western ever filmed, and he owned most of them on video and DVD. He was famous for his quotes from these movies . . . not from Union generals. Although he could hold his own in conversations with tenured professors on Shakespeare or Stephen Hawking, Nietzsche or Thomas Moore, most of what Bobby ever said came from *Shane* or *Gunfight at the O.K. Corral* or *One-Eyed Jacks* . . . or any other movie that involved horses and holsters. Bobby shrugged, and I turned back around.

I could hear the last bus—the one from Gainesville—about a half mile down the dirt road. I shrugged too. I couldn't think of a good divorce line from a Western either.

"He remind you of anybody?" Bobby said.

I turned a little too quickly. This time his eyes were like lights clicked on over the open book of my life. I may have been the most miserable, messed-up kid ever to pass through Itawa's gate. The warzone in my father's house had tied me into a tight knot, and my tongue had been knife-edge sharp to prove how tough I was. At eight years old, I'd been ready to fight anyone who presumed authority over me, choosing my victims as surrogate punching bags for my father's scowling disapproval.

Bobby smiled as though he were reading my thoughts. With his big, blocky hand he gently squeezed my upper arm and moved off toward the Lodge in his slow, steady march that always reminded me of a victorious warrior quietly walking off the field of battle.

When the last bus had unloaded, we herded the campers onto the flagstone amphitheater behind the Lodge. I sat down on the retaining wall that made a little private niche by the door and looked out over the grounds. Broad spears of light slanted through the evergreens onto the dark oval of the lake then ricocheted off its surface to the dining hall. Unless you knew where to look, you couldn't see my cabin in the black bath of shadow across the water. But I could make out the pattern of notched logs and a blue wisp of smoke, and I felt the little prayer of thanks rise inside me like morning mist lifting off the lake. Itawa had been my full-time place of residence for several years, but now I had a *home*.

Trying to take a read on the summer, I watched the counselors muster the kids into some semblance of order. Some of the veteran staff faces that filed by were reassuring, some inspiring. Other counselors had come simply for a job. They needed to earn money somewhere, and summer camp was as good a place as any.

But there were campers here we should have paid to come to Itawa. Like Troy and Amanda. They taught more by example than some of the counselors ever would with the entire Peterson Field Guide series stuffed into their backpacks.

Then there was Stephen Beasley, the twelve-year-old serial "stripper," who, last year in the lake, had yanked swimsuits off his male enemies, which were legion. So far, he had left the girls alone, but broadening his victim base to another gender might be in his plans. Even if it wasn't, I didn't like thinking about his career as an underwater voyeur. This would be the year, I had determined, that Stephen's energy would be redirected toward loftier goals.

Amy Littlefield was back as master clique organizer and trendsetter. She might never break a boy's heart, but with her power of exclusion, she had wounded many a girl's soul.

Big Ben Souther marched past me like a walking side of beef. Last year, under the guise of a soccer game, he had run over a camper from New Jersey and broken two of the boy's ribs. Rumor had it that Ben didn't like the way Yankees talked. Ben was back at Itawa with the understanding that the signatures at Appomattox still stood.

And, of course, Bill Columbine—the "skunkman of cabin four"—was back to consume as many beans as humanly possible to shatter the night with his legendary one-man brass section. We hated him, and we loved him. Now that I was in my own cabin on the other side of the lake, I was safe from fall-out, if not the thunder.

There were some new counselors this year—the most visible being a supple blonde with the feline beauty of a young Kim Bassinger. Her name was Gwendolyn, and she was a sophomore at the University of Georgia majoring in recreation. She was assigned to teach girls' sports and needed no more qualifications than her long, magazine-cover legs and deep tan. God had certainly created her for tennis or swimming or empowering the dreams of boys—not necessarily in that order.

Right behind her was golden-haired, blue-eyed Justin Kent. He was almost perfectly proportioned. I had always assumed this to be a product of genetics, because I could not imagine him breaking a sweat unless it was in the throes of sexual passion, which he might have been approaching as he followed in Gwendolyn's wake. He was drinking in her scent like a bloodhound. His eyes roved freely over the flex of muscle in her calves, thighs, and buttocks. In Gwendolyn he had his mission set for this camp session. Last year it had been Trish Manus, who was, notably, *not* back at Itawa.

Bobby Whitehorse stepped over the wall from behind and lowered himself by his arms to sit beside me. His lips were pursed as he chewed on a green stem of grass that gave off the scent of anise.

"All right, people! Listen up! I'm Justin Kent . . . head-counselor. That means I'm in charge, okay?" Justin stood at the center of the stone matrix, pulled off his Georgia Tech baseball cap, shook his silky hair, and see-sawed the hat back in place with the brim settled just above his eyebrows. He held the same clipboard that I had carried last year. For me it had served as a reminder of the thousand details that a camp director had to juggle. In Justin's hands it was a prop—a scepter he waved with each official decree. It was my guess that most of what was written on that paper was to be delivered with Gwendolyn in mind.

"We've got a few things to talk about before you get squared away in your cabins and start activities." Justin's voice was a well-oiled purr as he read off a list of camp activities and how to sign up.

Bobby Whitehorse leaned toward me and spoke in a low tone out of the side of his mouth. "I was in the office waiting for Old Bill this morning. Justin was in the bathroom practicing this oration at the mirror. I heard him through the wall. Heard him try that 'I'm-in-charge' line in three different voices." He nudged me with his elbow. "Shouldn't a' given up that clipboard, Stoney. Ought to be you up there."

I shook my head. "I'm away from camp too much with the Outriders. Needs to be someone more present."

Bobby remained leaning next to my ear but was quiet for several seconds. "Justin may be leaving soon."

I turned to him and frowned. Bobby gave me his deadpan face that always preceded a piece of his wry wit.

"If his head gets any bigger with hot air, he should be floating away by lunchtime."

Bobby nudged me again and straightened when Old Bill came out of the office. Justin saw Old Bill too, and his orientation voice lost some of its martial command by taking on the melody of friendly authority.

Old Bill was ramrod straight, white-haired, and as soft-hearted as a mama panda. He stood at the edge of the crowd with the lesser-known staff. Old Bill had everybody on the payroll come out for this introduction: cooks, maintenance, drivers, nurse, Mrs. Old Bill, and T-Bone, the old camp dog of more than a decade.

Camp Itawa was a family, and Old Bill wanted the new campers to see this from the start. His philosophy was that everybody in the family was a key player and deserved the same degree of respect. There was no hierarchy of importance, except that he made the final decision on anything up for debate.

I doubt that anyone—outside of Bobby—knew that I had any part in these decisions. On one level, Old Bill was the father I'd never had; on another level, we were peers separated by half a century. We had burned a lot of midnight oil together and developed a camp like none other. Itawa had magic. The kids recognized it and came back each year to be re-anointed. In time, if a spot opened up, they became counselors. We did very little advertising. We didn't need to. Itawa was Camelot.

With Trish Manus gone, we had someone new to head up the girls' camp, and I was interested to see how she would handle it. I had met her briefly in December when she came to interview. "Abby" something. She had driven down on Christmas break from the high school in North Carolina where she was a rookie English teacher. She had scored a point just for showing up, because a major snowstorm had passed through the day before. I was so tied up clearing the damage at the riding trails that I had barely gotten to talk to her. But she seemed like a sensible lady—thoughtful and quiet by nature. I had seen that last quality work against others in her role. I was betting that, for her, it would work.

"Abby Parrish is our new director of the girls' camp," Justin announced, carving out a majestic arc in the air with the clipboard. "She'll be meeting with all you girls right here for cabin assignments when we break up. Boys will meet with me on the sports field. By the way, if any of you girls need help with your gear, we've got plenty of muscle here. Right, guys?"

The boys groaned a collective complaint. I looked at Abby. Her eyes lowered to the stones between her feet, and I thought I could see a smile pull at the corners of her mouth. Bobby Whitehorse let out a long slow breath and looked off to the trees.

I was still watching Abby. There was a self-possessed serenity in her face that I had seen before. Where was it? I kept looking at her until it came to me. It was a painting of Joan of Arc chained to the stake, her beatific face encircled by a nimbus of golden light. As Justin resumed his introductory duties, Abby rose in a smooth, unhurried motion and waited. When her presence caught Justin's eye, he stopped in mid-sentence.

"Thank you, Justin," Abby said with a benign smile. "And any of you boys who might need help with your gear, please don't hesitate to ask the girls for assistance."

There was a vacuum of dead silence as Justin tried to decipher what had just happened. His eyes darted to Gwendolyn, then to his clipboard, in case it contained the answer to the riddle of the Sphinx. The boys sat poised to follow his lead with a groan or a laugh as they endured a few giggles from the girls.

"Right," Justin said with a nervous laugh. "It goes both ways, guys."

Bobby chuckled under his breath, plucked the chewed grass stem from his mouth, and stuck it in his hatband. His raspy whisper took on a syrupy Southern drawl.

"I'm ya huckleberry," he said, putting in a word for Abby's spunk.

I looked at him and waited. Bobby always gave me at least ten seconds for my best guess, but this time he was staring at Abby with blatant admiration glowing in his eyes. "*Tombstone*," he said out of the corner of his mouth. "Val Kilmer to Michael Biehn."

I nodded at my hazy memory of the movie he had forced upon me. My eyes remained fixed on Abby Parrish, too. She sat down and assumed her attentive pose, as if she were enjoying a lecture on the folk art of Appalachia. Several of the older girls angled their eyes to study Abby's profile—just like I was doing. I could see no hidden message in the polite smile she wore. She had been direct. I liked that. And she had delivered her message without emotion, allowing the rest of us some flexibility in interpreting her meaning.

I knew my name appeared last on the list, right before Old Bill's, but Justin read it off halfway through introductions—a ploy, I guessed, to bury me inside the crowd, to distance me from the camp owner and any notion of status he imagined for me. By way of introduction, when he read my name, I raised my hand and stood just like everyone else had. Then I returned to my perch next to Bobby Whitehorse.

A few of last year's Outriders kept their eyes on me, giving me that indefinable look that was the symbol of our bond. I nodded to each of them, but my eyes kept returning to the miserable boy I would come to know as Tyler Raintree. He was staring out over the lake, probably painting a picture in his mind of a place he'd rather be.

"Stoney," Justin continued, raising the clipboard in my direction, "for those who don't know, is a counselor, but he's also part of the maintenance crew. So, if you have any problems in your cabin . . . like an overflowing toilet, a leaky roof, or something like that . . . be sure to let Stoney know, and he'll get right on it." Everyone turned to look at the toilet repairman. "And if Stoney can't fix it," Justin pressed on, "we'll send T-Bone. That's that skin-and-bones hound lying back there. He's the only other staffer with that kind of time on his hands."

Oblivious to his share of the insult, T-Bone lay on the stones below Bobby and me as he witnessed the kickoff of another camp season. Even though Justin bestowed upon me his famous smile—the one that check-marked boyish dimples into his smooth cheeks—I knew his remarks were intended not so much for me as for Gwendolyn. Justin was narrowing the field. I had been relegated to the unambitious blue-collar work force. There was no mention of "Outriders." Justin, on the other hand, held the clipboard, the floor, and the keys to the kingdom.

I could hear the reels of Western films turning inside Bobby Whitehorse's head. I waited. When finally he spoke, his voice emerged deep and velvety from his chest.

" 'It's a fine life, ain't it? Just waiting to get knocked off by some tough kid . . . like the kind of kid I was.' "

I smiled at Bobby's ability to nail an actor's voice. "Gregory Peck," I said without hesitation. "I don't remember the name of the movie." I turned to him. "Was it *The Gunfighter*?"

"Very good, Gray Eyes," he whispered like a song of praise.

That was what he called me most of the time—"Gray Eyes." He had never told me why, but it obviously had little to do with my eyes, which were, as my mother had once told me, Coca-Cola brown from being born in Atlanta.

"That was a great hat," Bobby reminisced.

"What hat?"

"Peck's," he said.

I looked at the well-worn haberdashery perched atop Bobby's broad head." "Better than that one?" I said, nodding toward his old Stetson.

He shrugged again and tapped his blocky fist against my thigh. "You're getting better with the Silver Screen quotes." He smiled proudly, the grand master acknowledging the work of his apprentice.

"Well, it helps that you can sound exactly like Gregory Peck," I said and cocked my head to one side. "Now would you please come back to the East and join us at Camp Itawa?"

Bobby gave me his innocent look and then shared a short communique with T-Bone about a life unappreciated. To his credit, T-Bone remained neutral and said nothing.

As the staff introductions continued, I could not help remembering the time I had sat on these stones and sulked through my first orientation. In those days, Old Bill did all the talking and made us feel at home from the first time his smiling eyes sent a sunburst of crinkles across his temples and into his snow-white hair. It was eleven years ago to the day since I had first met him.

I looked over the crowd and inventoried the few faces that had been present then. Some of these counselors had been campers. Now they were salaried instructors. T-Bone and I had started off together that year. The whites of his eyes flashed when he rolled his big brown irises my way. I was glad now I had not voiced my comeback to Justin's comparison of me to the dog. I could have mentioned that I had a high school diploma and T-Bone did not. There was no need to embarrass T-Bone in front of everyone.

Eleven years ago, Old Bill had a secretary whose name was Barbie Lalyre. This was three years before he'd married for the second and last time. It must have been a crisis period for him, because Barbie had very few work skills. She looked like she had stepped out of a *Playboy* centerfold and then relaxed her fitness standards for a dozen years.

Barbie had a small voice like a baby bird's, and walked as if she were on an invisible treadmill, hardly getting anywhere with all the swish and bounce. The day I got off that bus the first time, Barbie left her indelible mark on me by the way she had written my name on the roster. A single sentence from her pen looked like a Rococo-period vine rambling across a fence rail. If there was an *i* to dot or a *period* to close a sentence, she drew a little curlicue circle with a hollow center. This idiosyncrasy of penmanship gave me an unforgettable moment of embarrassment and a name that has stuck to this day.

Apparently, Old Bill had not yet gotten accustomed to her writing. So, he stumbled a bit as he read off the names in alphabetical order. At eight years old, I was already self-conscious about "St. Ney." I'd gotten enough grief in school about being saintly that the subject was like a blister from an ill-fitting shoe. While waiting to hear how my name would roll off Old Bill's tongue, someone didn't answer up. Old

Bill called out "Stoney" over and over until everybody was looking around the amphitheater for the idiot who didn't know his own name.

Old Bill didn't figure out the mistake until the roll call was over. He roared with laughter when he deciphered the pregnant period Barbie had planted in my name, but from that day on I was Stoney St. Ney. I guess it grew on me, because now it seems to fit me just fine.

Chapter Two

Nervous and barefooted, the campers tiptoed in single file out onto the boardwalk, wearing their towels like last-minute heat wraps for the dreaded plunge into the icy abyss of Lake Itawa. I smiled at their antics. The lake on a summer afternoon was a luxury to me. Unless there was a crust of ice on the water, I swam every morning of the year right after dawn.

This morning at first light before the campers had arrived, I had followed my routine of going for a run on the old logging road behind the stables. As always, Old Bill's light had been on, and I knew Bobby Whitehorse was stirring somewhere on the grounds. But the woods were mine. Mine and the deer, the boar, the bear and an ecumenical choir of birds to usher in the dawn.

Along the way I had stations for my workout. There were three big white pines spaced out along the trail, each with a perfect whorl of dead, broken limbs eight feet off the ground. The three-foot remnants of the limbs were strong, looking like the spokes of giant rimless wheels. On the way out from camp, I pumped out a set of pull-ups at each tree. On the way back, I switched to chin-ups.

When I returned, Bobby was at the barn tending to the horses, but we didn't speak as I jogged quietly past. He liked to use the dawn to bond with the horses as he scooped grain and touched them with the flat of his hand and breathed into their nostrils. Their language was silence. There was a way he moved among these big animals that reminded me of a powerful dancer holding back his strength, channeling all his energy into the simplest moves, like the bend of a knee . . . or the turn of a wrist.

Back at my cabin, I had pumped out a hundred push-ups, speared into the lake at a run, and sprinted to the canoe dock and back, all the while imagining that, if I swam hard enough, I could keep an envelope of warmth hovering around me.

By the time I had dried off and dressed, Bobby had clopped down the lake trail on whatever horse needed extra work that day. Even though we had repeated this ritual every morning since the cabin was completed, Bobby would not dismount for the coffee that I bought just for him until I came out and asked him in.

He never quoted a Western line in my home. It was as if this morning time was somehow sacred to us . . . to our friendship. By the open door of the wood stove, he sipped coffee and I worked on my mint tea as we talked quietly about subjects that were important to us: animals we had encountered in the wild, women we had loved, rivers we had paddled, or common friends that we respected . . . like Old Bill.

I loved the smell of Bobby's coffee. Wherever I smelled coffee now it connected me to these gentle mornings with him. But I never drank it, never acquired the taste. The odor had once repulsed me, conjuring up the instant image of my father's cold face brooding behind his morning newspaper. Bobby Whitehorse had changed that for me. He had changed a lot of things.

Now at midafternoon, the sun beat down on Lake Itawa and warmed the top several inches of water sufficient to dupe anyone dabbing a toe at the surface. The first immersion was an annual tradition, and now all seventy-two campers were lined up at the edge of the boardwalk and dock to make the jump together. It was meant to be a synchronized ritual, but it never quite worked out.

Justin built the moment into high drama and then finally blew a short chirp from his whistle. The new arrivals, who had just moments before balked at the idea of stepping off, were pushed in by the veterans. No rookie was spared. This was as close as Itawa came to an initiation rite. Then, everyone left standing high and dry on the boardwalk jumped in, laughing and screaming like crazed monkeys.

Tyler Raintree squirmed out of the water onto the sun-bleached boards to sit on the bench where he had left his towel. He had met the lake-jumping obligation and was now ready to disappear again inside his misery. Draping a huge Snoopy towel around his back, he wrapped into a cocoon and did not move.

Just before covering himself, I caught a brief glimpse of a dark blotch between his shoulder blades. I assumed it to be a birthmark. His back slouched forward like an old man's. Below him were girls treading water, talking in a fast, trebly chatter . . . and boys screaming too loud, declaring water-wars, splashing then diving like dolphins to escape. Tyler looked like a kid all alone in a room watching the only program he could get on his TV.

I strolled down the gray boards past him and stood looking out at the mayhem with my hands in the pockets of my jeans. Stephen Beasley, the so-called "reformed" swimsuit ripper, cruised by like a predatory shark, the water cutting a V at the bridge of his nose. Our eyes met for an instant, and he changed course, angling away into uninhabited waters, suggesting that the talk we had had an hour earlier might have taken effect.

At the end of the boardwalk, where it widened into a square dock, Justin and a few other counselors in swimsuits stood talking. Gwendolyn was there in a raspberry-colored one-piece—the kind of suit that cut high above the pelvis and only about one percent of the female population can successfully wear. Gwendolyn could wear that swimsuit just like Cinderella could wear her glass slipper. She looked like she had just stolen fire from the gods and dropped down to Itawa to share her golden-brown tan with us mortals.

She wore a thin chain necklace with an oval pendant engraved with "Theta Chi." The pendant fell right above the smooth valley formed by her breasts. She was giving this postcard setting of breathtaking mountains a run for its money. I was considering jumping in the lake, too.

On the raised platform above her, two of the waterfront staff sat in green nylon fold-up chairs and moved their heads like cannon turrets, scanning the roped-off area for problems. I could feel Tyler's eyes on my back as I pulled the piece of cane from my back pocket and unsheathed my knife. I had started the flute last summer but put it aside when work on my cabin became full-time. Twisting the tip of my blade gently inside the holes I had burned along the top of the cane, I scraped off a fine powder of black char and blew it away. I did this for three of the holes, and then I turned to sit on the bench three feet away from him.

"Hi," I said.

Tyler's mouth was already open. It didn't seem to move, but an unintelligible sound cracked from his throat as if I had taken him by surprise. I gave him his space and began working on the fourth hole. By the sixth hole he still hadn't looked at me.

During lunch I had gone into the office to check his records. The application form showed his parents as Mr. and Mrs. Beau Raintree on Randall Mill Road in Atlanta. There was only one address and one telephone number, which, from my knowledge of that neighborhood, had to be a home and not a business. Still, I didn't rule out Bobby Whitehorse's prognosis. Some estranged couples did not advertise their separations if it wasn't necessary. And then again, the parents could still be together, and *that* could be the problem. Or, for all I knew, Tyler could be the problem. But it never did me any good to start with that premise.

On the form, under the heading "interests," written in what had to be Tyler's own hand, three words were scrawled: "computers," "video-games," and "music." My inroad to him defaulted immediately to the last entry, although "music" *could* mean he was a devotee to a heavy metal band named after a veterinary disease.

I looked at my cane flute. It felt hopelessly light in my hands when I imagined Tyler wearing earphones plugged into something akin to the crash of planets. With my knife I made one more pass at the embrasure to make sure the receiving edge was sharp. If ever I needed a dulcet tone from an instrument, this was the moment.

I raised the cane to my mouth and blew hard to clear the flute of any dust. As I knew it would, the hollow sound brought his head around. Then I tightened my lips and funneled a soft jet of air across the blowhole. The first note was sweet, reminding me of a barred owl's rich nocturnal call. I tested each note then settled into one of the themes from *Appalachian Spring.*

"What's that?" Tyler said.

I finished the piece and lowered the flute, keeping my eyes on the smooth finish of the cane so as not to scare him off. "It's a melody by Aaron Copland."

I looked at Tyler, but he was frowning out at the lake. "No . . . what's *that*?" he said, guardedly lifting his hand and pointing. His frown stretched into a grimace, and his eyes showed a lot of white. I followed his line of vision and saw the weaving S that glided across the water toward the rope and buoys of the swim area. The colors were unmistakable; but I stood up, unbelieving, and stepped toward the edge of the boardwalk. *What the hell*, I almost said out loud.

It should have been a midland water snake or a queen snake, but it wasn't. It was a copperhead. I could see the bronze hourglass patterns saddled across its back. It slithered over the rope, heading directly toward a cluster of five swimmers.

I yelled up to the waterfront deck. "Three whistles! Now!" There was enough edge to my voice that no one questioned it. Two lifeguards blew in unison and every head turned.

In the sudden noiseless vacuum, I cupped my hands around my mouth and yelled to the swimmers. "If you can dive down to colder water and swim underwater to the dock with one breath right now you'll get an extra dessert tonight." Then I raised both arms and screamed like the starter at a race. "Go!" I swept both hands downward and watched the copperhead angle right for the group of campers.

Seventy heads disappeared in surface dives, and bare feet kicked the air until finding purchase in the water. I looked at Justin and pointed to the snake wending its way across the swim area. The swimming staff was coming down the steps with rope and life buoys in hand. Justin peered out toward the snake and then looked back at me and raised his hands palms up from his sides.

Some of the kids were already up for air, but there was good distance now between them and the danger. The counselors poked fingers in the air counting heads. Breathless voices were claiming victory at the edge of the dock, while other voices were raised in protest, claiming to have witnessed secret second-breaths. Mimi Dawes, in her white nylon pullover with a dozen water-safety patches, walked toward me chewing on the inside of her lip. Her eyes were hidden behind dark glasses, but I knew they were narrowed into a question.

"What's up, Stoney?"

I stepped closer and spoke quietly. "That was a copperhead that crossed the rope into the swim area."

Mimi turned in profile to me and studied the lake for several seconds. I knew part of her wanted to ask, *Are you sure?* But she wouldn't ask. We had known each other for four years. She knew what she knew about water safety. I knew what I knew about nature. It was a proven mutual trust.

"That's never happened before out here, has it?" she said scanning the water.

"Not that I know of. I've seen them cross the river in the hottest part of summer, but—" With my eyes I followed the faint, shimmering path of the snake to mark where it beached on the far side of the lake.

"Good call, Stoney," Mimi said.

I turned and raised my flute toward Tyler, almost forgetting and calling him by name. "You can thank this young man here. He spotted it."

The copperhead reached the shore unseen, but I could follow its path by the twitch of weeds and grasses. It was about forty yards away as the trout swims, probably six times that far by land.

"Mimi, can you get everybody up and over the hill real fast and get them preoccupied so they won't be looking back down here?"

She stared at me for three heartbeats. "I shouldn't ask, should I?"

I shook my head, keeping my eyes on the weeds across the lake. I had a special stake in this now. My cabin was a short slither from that spot.

I didn't have a swimsuit, and I knew my loose boxer shorts would never make the sprint across the lake. I held out the flute to Tyler.

"Would you hang on to that for me?"

Tyler finally looked me squarely in the eye. "Do I have to swim out there anymore?"

I looked at Mimi for a little help on that one and walked against the flow of campers, who were being herded off the boardwalk. When I passed Justin, his face was glowing with exasperation.

"Christ, Stoney, it's just a water snake." Gwendolyn was right behind him staring at me as if I might begin speaking in tongues.

"Hurry everybody up, will you, Justin. I've got to get over there."

He glanced at my jeans then bored into my eyes as if reading my mind. Coming to some private conclusion, he put a hand on Gwendolyn's elbow.

"Come on, Gwen," he sighed. "Ever so often, Tarzan here has to answer the call of the wild."

Gwen. Justin was removing the parts of her name at the rate of one syllable per hour.

As the crowd was cresting the hill, I saw Tyler watching me as he stood off to the side holding my flute next to his thigh. I tried to spot more of the snake's movements at the shore but could make out nothing. I couldn't wait any longer.

I stripped and dove off the dock. Before I hit the water my mind reconstructed an image from my peripheral memory. Gwendolyn had stepped up beside Tyler and together they had stood very still. A goddess and a mute munchkin witnessing the unfolding of a scene somewhere between Odyssean and quixotic. All I needed was a bowie knife clinched between my teeth. Or maybe a beanie with a propeller on top.

The cool water washed everything from my mind but my mission. I *was* going to catch that copper intruder and relocate him a few miles down the road. I would have to let my success at this balance the fact that I had semi-publically stripped buck-naked on the first day of the first session of camp.

With its screened upper walls, the dining hall was cool enough at twilight that almost everybody came to supper in long sleeves this early in the season. A few wore sweaters, and one very thin girl sported a fiber-fill jacket. There were no katydids ratcheting from the trees yet, so the overall static of conversation was comparatively mild. By second session the nocturnal insect chatter would be so invasive that the children's voices would sound like the rapids crashing through the Narrows.

I walked into the dining room and looked at the counselor table where Justin was telling a story with lots of hand gestures. Gwendolyn sat across from him in a man's white dress shirt. Somehow, she made that rectangular table into a circle, and she was at its hub. When she smiled, the color coordination of shirt and teeth was striking. Everyone seemed to be slightly leaning toward her in case she were to speak.

"Did you catch it, Stoney?" one of my Outriders, Troy Peyton, asked from a nearby table. I nodded, and he gave me a thumbs-up. "Was it a copperhead?"

"Yeah." The kids at his table stopped chewing and stared at me. "We're averaging one copperhead in the lake every thirty-eight years. Old Bill said it happened once before in the second year of camp. That means we'll be due another in the latter half of this century." They laughed, but there was no real relief in it. Their fragile eyes remained glued to me. I looked around until I saw Tyler. "Tyler can tell you," I said, just loud enough to carry to his table. "It swam the whole width of the lake and never even tried to get near anyone. It wasn't looking for trouble. Just doing what snakes do."

"Did you kill it?" Amy Littlefield's face was a stony amalgam of sarcasm and disapproval. She already knew my answer. I smiled at her and shook my head.

Troy turned toward Amy. "Stoney never kills 'em. He takes 'em away and lets 'em go."

Amy made a disgusted face, stared deeply into my eyes, and let her lips part a quarter of an inch. It was the kind of face you would never want to see among a jury of your peers.

"I would've killed it," she said flatly. There was a light spray of freckles across her nose and cheeks. It spread horizontally midway across her face and always made me think of the Milky Way.

Quite a few campers had turned in their seats now, listening to our conversation. Amy jabbed meatloaf into her mouth and chewed with a defiant, mechanical rhythm. A tall, black girl named Darcy raised her hand politely. She had started at Itawa last year and was an accomplished equestrian.

"Why don't you kill them, Stoney?"

It was one of those questions so easily answered inside my own head, without words. To explain it, my first impulse was always to try to take some measure of the sacredness of life and deliver it in an indelible revelation. But those kinds of abstractions were not useful with these kids, who were too far away from mortality. I wanted to say that it was just too beautiful to kill, but I also knew how that would go over.

Since more than half the room was poised for my answer, I went ahead and called for everybody's attention. The room quieted, and I felt the future of the snake kingdom riding on my shoulders. The only movement in the room was Justin casually rattling the ice cubes in his glass.

"Well," I said, "we all know we had a special event today that's got everybody's attention."

"Right," Justin mumbled, like an actor in a play delivering an "aside" meant to be heard by everyone. "Like a counselor skinny-dipping in front of the whole camp."

Everyone laughed. I couldn't argue it. I pictured my bare white derriere streaking across the lake. I lowered my head, smiled, and nodded.

"Okay," I said, "let's talk straight about this. You guys know that we counselors are not in the habit of swimming nude before the camp. That's why you were moved over the hill." Justin cleared his throat, but I ignored him. "The counselors are dedicated to keeping you safe. Thanks to Tyler there, we knew we had a copperhead where it shouldn't be. If I'd made the run around the lake, it might still be out there. I couldn't swim in my jeans. And since I seem to be the designated snake-catcher around here, I did what I thought needed to be done."

"So why didn't you kill it?" Amy said in her grating monotone.

I looked around the room and saw the same question on lots of faces, so I injected a little mystery into my voice and looked at Amy. "*That* is the secret I shall reveal to you at the fire circle tonight."

Their expectant faces showed only mild curiosity. I could see it wasn't enough.

"Don't forget, double desserts tonight." And with that bribe, all the snakes of the world slithered safely back into their holes.

I always sat with the campers at meals. I knew my reputation suffered for it in the hands of Justin, who may have actually believed I thought I was too good to eat with my peers. But I had yet to lose sleep over Justin's opinions of me.

When I sat down and started eating, I saw Abby Parrish at the next table with her back to me. She was surrounded by campers, engaged in several conversations at once. When she turned her head to the person next to her, I could just hear her voice—patient and personal. Then, she took the next question in turn and quietly dealt with another rapt face.

I was swamped in snake questions. *How big was it? Was it a male or female? Wouldn't there be others nearby? Where did it live? Did it strike at you? How did you catch it? Have you ever been bitten before? What's the secret you're gonna tell?*

Abby Parrish turned around and caught my eye. She smiled that Joan of Arc smile again and nodded once.

"That was quick thinking," she said.

"What . . . the dessert?"

Her smile graduated from Joan of Arc to Emmy Lou Harris. "No, the underwater race to the dock. I take it copperheads don't go under? How did you learn that?"

I shrugged. "It's not a rule. More a gut feeling from watching them and trying to figure them out. Water snakes will dive. They have to . . . to catch fish. All the others seem to want to stay as dry as possible. They even swim higher on the water."

"How do they do that?"

"Vent their ribs and bloat themselves with air. Their whole bodies swim on top. Water snakes just keep their heads above the surface."

Abby pushed her lower lip forward and cocked her head thoughtfully. When some of the kids at her table began tugging at her shirt, Abby gave me a wry smile that signaled a return to the zone of a million questions. I watched the back of her head for a while as she gave her attention to the kids. Her hair was short and silky, the color of chocolate. Through that rich, dark brown, I could still see her eyes in my mind. They were the color of dusty blue slate.

After dinner, while I was waiting for the kids to settle into the hexagon of log benches around the fire-ring, Justin strolled over to where I was assembling my fire kit. When he knelt down beside me, I looked at his face and knew that something was up. There were two other male counselors hovering right behind him, doing their best to hide flickering smiles. I spun the dried stalk of yucca between my palms and felt it take a pleasing bite into the slab of basswood that I held down with my foot.

"Actually, it was a pretty good idea to go after that snake naked like that, Stoney." Justin glanced at his cronies and then turned back to me with his poker face. "Kind of like fighting fire with fire, right?"

I didn't catch it at first. I thought he might be referring to the fire that I was about to make. I glanced past him and saw Gwendolyn glowing from her bench like a white candle flame. Justin cleared his throat and glanced at his buddies again.

"So . . . how did that copperhead react to the little snake you dangled in front of it?"

Justin's audience of two sputtered and choked with muffled laughs and turned away quickly. I looked at Justin and kept my face neutral. I had at least two killer retorts for him that would have turned the tables, but I scrapped them both. He didn't need lessons in how to be a smart-ass.

"Thanks for getting the kids up the hill so fast, Justin," I said, derailing his insult. "A minute later and I would have lost the copperhead."

Justin held a tight, V-shaped smile on his face, but I could see he didn't know how to handle my reply. If I had an angel—and I was pretty sure I did—she would have laid a hand on my shoulder just then and gently squeezed. With a self-satisfied grin, Justin stood and swaggered to the empty seat next to Gwendolyn.

A hand pressed down lightly on my shoulder and gently squeezed. So close to my ear, Bobby Whitehorse's voice was like a whisper of wind blowing through evergreen needles.

"A man can make a fool of himself only so many times before he dies. Life's too short." There was a definite Western twang to his words, but I had no idea whose voice he was imitating. Losing the cowboy inflection, Bobby said, "*Rim Rock Trail*. William Boyd to Brian Donlevy.

"Who is William Boyd?" I said.

He canted his head in regret. "Hopalong Cassidy . . . before your time."

The campers got quiet when I raised my fire kit above my head. Their silence was so complete that the distant slap of the office's screen door reverberated across the lake like a firecracker. I made the prayer of thanks to the plants and knelt to my fire kit. Every little sound—the stretch of fabric in my jeans, the tap of wood on wood, the chafing of my hands as I rubbed them together to distribute saliva—was like one side of a conversation to which the audience was rapt. I twirled the yucca spindle for a dozen passes, blew the hot ash into a red coal and created fire as the Cherokees had in this same valley centuries ago. In this one act, I knew I had planted a spark inside the hearts of at least a few awestruck campers, who would come to me tomorrow asking about Outriders. It always began this way.

As the flames built, Justin made some announcements for the boys, and then Abby did the same for the girls. When the floor was mine, Bobby Whitehorse leaned against the rock wall behind the benches, folded his arms over his wide chest and became an unmoving shadow. As the crowd got quiet again, I began stirring up the recipe for the story I'd thrown together over dinner.

Chapter Three

"This story will be a circle," I prefaced, "because it will begin and end with the same words."

I let that sink in for a moment as I laid two more logs on the fire. The logs were of tulip tree and would make a lot of light and shadow for the story. I watched the wood catch and then raised my index finger as a signal that I was beginning the story.

"No one knows how this works . . . and perhaps no one ever will. But what if?" To include everyone, I turned in a slow half circle holding the finger before me like a lighted candle. In my rotation, I glanced at Bobby, whose expectant eyes were as big as the campers'.

"There is a place behind the stars where you can find all the spirits of all the plants and animals that will ever be. They are lined up in a chain longer than you can imagine. Longer than all the rivers and creeks and branches of the world attached end to end. Receiving this line of souls there is a gray dog with a scruffy tail holding a clipboard." A little laughter here. "Up there he is called 'God's Dog.' Down here we would call him 'Coyote.' Every hundredth of a second, he calls out to the next spirit standing in line. What you have to understand is that, up there, what would be a hundredth of a second to us is more like a minute to God's Dog."

Amy Littlefield raised her hand—a courteous gesture that did not match the smirk on her mouth. "So, what's a live dog doing up there with all those . . . like . . . un-live spirits? How did *he* get there?"

I gave her an incredulous expression, as though she had missed one of the more obvious facts of the universe. "He's God's Dog," I explained, freezing my shrug with my palms open to the sky. "He's the one who assigns spirits to bodies." I gave Amy a look that hopefully informed her that questions of logic would not serve her well in this story.

"So," I continued. "God's Dog calls out, 'Next!' And the new soul at the head of the long line approaches him. God's Dog checks his clipboard and says, 'A wild horse in Madagascar is giving birth in the next instant. Ready? Go!' There is a loud *whoosh!*"

For sound effects, I expelled a rush of air through my teeth.

"That soul streaks down to Earth just off the African coast to enter the body of a newborn filly. At the very moment that the spirit inhabits the body, the baby horse takes its first breath."

At this point I attempted a falsetto whinny that inspired a lot of smiles from the campers. Before anyone could laugh, I quickly continued.

"God's Dog says 'Next, next, next, next, next, next . . .' " I ran the words together like an out-of-control sewing machine—which wasn't easy. ". . . Until he has said it ninety-eight times. Ninety-eight souls rush forward for their assignment. God's Dog looks at his clipboard and says, 'A wolf spider in Mexico has an egg sac about to burst open with new life. There will be ninety-eight baby spiders. Ready? Go!' *Whoosh, whoosh, whoosh, whoosh, whoosh*—! Ninety-eight whooshes in all!"

I went through variations on this theme three more times: once for a dandelion seed in Paris; another for a bear cub in the Ukraine; and last for an acorn in Canada. The campers started looking at each other with smiles and side-comments. Bobby Whitehorse had not moved. Just like the kids, he was wanting more. The only face I could see out there that was not swept up in the story was Tyler Raintree's. He looked numb. And Justin, of course, who was anything but numb. His radar was locked in on Gwendolyn, who was waving him quiet as she waited for the story to resume.

"God's Dog looks at his clipboard. 'Next, next, next . . .' " Again, I said the words as fast as I could until I had reached somewhere around thirty. The kids were rocking in their seats, guessing at the next animal to give birth. "He studies his clipboard again to double check, and he reads, 'A copperhead is about to bear twenty-eight babies in the Chattahoochee National Forest near a place called 'Itawa.' "

The campers started smiling broader and talking louder—as if they might know of such a place. I looked at Tyler. His eyes were fixed on the dark woods beyond the lake, straining to see the evils of the world waiting for him beyond the firelight.

"God's Dog says, 'Ready?' "

I got all wound up as though I were about to launch a barrel-full of copperhead spirits through space . . . and then I froze.

" 'Whoa!' God's Dog exclaims. 'Wait a minute! I've just been informed that a human has gone into labor earlier than expected. We're going to have to pre-empt that snake-birth. You! Come here!' "

"The first snake spirit in line moves forward, and God's Dog says, 'You're not going to be a copperhead after all. You'll be a little girl in Greenville and live in a yellow house near a big lake!' "

Amy Littlefield's eyes fixed on me as if I had divulged her deepest secrets.

"WHOOSH!" I said, surprising her—and everyone else—with the volume of my onomatopoetic soundtrack.

As I waited for the group to settle down from the chortling and chatter, I flattened my hand like a hat brim above my eyes, as if I were watching Amy Littlefield's spirit being borne down to Earth to join the human race. When everyone got quiet to see what I was doing, I cupped one hand beside my mouth and quietly pretended to yell after her.

"Watch out for all the stardust! You'll get freckles!"

In that pose I waited for the laughter to yield to complete silence. Then I turned to Amy. Through the camp records and the Outrider intelligence network, I had found out that she lived in Greenville, South Carolina in a yellow house by a lake. Her mouth formed a dark O, and her eyes were like bright quarters in the firelight.

"If that was you," I whispered, "you were almost a copperhead."

For ten heartbeats, Amy and I stared at one another. Then I dropped my storytelling pose, straightened, and talked in my normal voice.

"No one knows how this works . . . and perhaps no one ever will . . . but what if?"

As I walked through the applause, Justin took my place at center stage and tried to quiet everyone for his announcements. When I sat next to Bobby, a *basso profundo* John Wayne voice hummed in my ear.

"Amen, Parson."

I smiled and waited for him to cite his source.

"*The Searchers*. John Wayne to Hank Worden."

After Justin's end-of-the-day reminders, the campers milled about in their typical pre-bedtime chaos. As I watched Justin try unsuccessfully to organize the cabin groups, I felt a little tap on my elbow. Tyler Raintree stood quietly looking up at me with dead eyes. He held out my flute. I bent to him with my hands propped on my knees.

"Would you like to keep it a while? Maybe learn how to play it?"

He shook his head and continued to hold out the flute. "I guess I was standing in the wrong place in line," he muttered.

I was pretty sure I had heard the words right, but I didn't follow his meaning.

"What?" I said and lowered to a knee to get eye to eye with him.

He turned his attention to the children who were finally being corralled into their groups by the rookie counselors, who would sleep with them. I stared at the side of Tyler's face and watched him pull in his lips, making his mouth look like a thin incision on his face.

"I wish I'd been born a copperhead," he said.

Chapter Four

"*Nvda etsvgatiya disgitsislanedi atsila dogadanvdvi si saquo eyuwati.*"

Bobby Whitehorse's voice was rich and resonant, carrying out to the hills in the east from our mountaintop like the deep soft notes of a drum thumped from stretched rawhide. He raised his head again and repeated the prayer, translating for my benefit. "We are waiting for you, sun, to be born again into the day."

We stood very still as the yellow rim of the sun broke over Standing Bear Dome and floated upward like a hot-air balloon rising from the edge of the Earth. The soft rays touched my face with the weightless hands of a blind child and began the warming of the world. Behind us our small fire pushed heat through my jeans to the backs of my calves. The only sounds were wind on the ridge, vireos in the valley, and an occasional lazy nicker from the horses, where we had tied them at the edge of the clearing.

Crumbling the brittle leaves he had dried for this ceremony, Bobby raised both arms over his hatless head. He spoke again in Cherokee and rubbed his hands together like a man slowly lathering up with a bar of soap. The wind carried the tobacco behind us, sprinkling flakes and leaf dust toward camp, as if the air currents had chosen to aid in our ritual.

Raising empty palms toward the sky, Bobby spoke again. "Maker of All Things, we carry Your glowing coal inside our hearts. Breathe it into a flame for us one more time, so that we may set these children upon the true path."

Since we had arrived at our prayer place, I'd been thinking about Tyler Raintree, but now I broadened my thoughts to include all the faces around last night's fire. Sometimes the idea sobered me like a sneak punch to the solar plexus: that these were the children who would inherit the Earth. Bobby and I—and Mimi and Dorian and Andy and all the other counselors—had them for only a brief moment in time. But to understand the power of that small window in time, all I had to do was think back to my own days as a camper to remember that this fleeting chapter in their lives could be a pivotal one.

I had seen proof of it too many times to doubt it. Grown men and women—Itawa veteran campers who had climbed these mountains and canoed the Narrows when it had been just Old Bill, Bobby, and a handful of counselors teaching classes—returned from time to time in their business suits to walk the camp's grounds and reminisce. By the way they talked, I knew they still walked the true path and silently taught those around them in their chosen fields as CEO's, physicians, and land developers.

When Bobby closed his invocation to the new season, I rubbed hemlock needles into the bare shaft of the arrow I had made when I was twelve years old. Then I set it to string. In the dawn light the white markings of the hawk feather fletching glowed like clean scraps of paper on which this year's camp history would be written. I raised the medicine arrow to an angle that would send it deep into the valley—the valley Bobby had named "First Arrow"—and then I drew back the string of my bow.

With any luck, the Outriders would find this arrow just as they had every year past. We would build a small cairn of stones to mark the occasion and then scratch the year into a flat stone to be perched on top like a grave-marker with its meaning reversed. Later we would return the ceremonial arrow to its place above the front door of the Lodge, where it would slumber on display for another year and wait for the next new camp season.

When I released the string, I imagined the hawk leaping into the soul of the arrow, reclaiming its feathers, revisiting the freedom known only to the wingeds and soaring once again over its mountain kingdom. And I thought of Tyler. I wished for him some of that freedom. When the arrow had made its long arc and slipped through the canopy of trees without a sound, Bobby put on his hat and nodded, and then we left.

No one was stirring when we walked our horses past the boys' cabins. Out of respect for our annual rite, Bobby and I had not spoken since leaving the ridge, but now our silence took on a pragmatic theme among our sleeping campers. We led the horses into the paddock, poured grain for them, and rubbed them down as they ate.

Over my horse's back, I watched Bobby stroke his thick fingers along the soft velvet between his horse's nostrils. "You want coffee?" I said.

He shook his head. "I'll be by tomorrow at the usual time," he said. He slipped the hackamore from his horse's muzzle and waited for me to do the same. "That was a good story last night, Gray Eyes. I like that idea. You never know what you almost were."

"Yeah," I said. "It makes you think. Reminds you that everything is a somebody."

Bobby carried the hackamore toward the bridle pegs but stopped walking and looked at me with a blank expression. "Hell, I might have been a six-foot-two cowboy," he said.

"Or a four-foot-two cow," I countered.

Bobby pushed up the brim of his hat, pursed his lips, and looked up toward the roof of the barn with thoughtful contemplation working in his eyes. I knew he was running through his catalogue of Western quotes. When he had it, he turned his dark eyes on me.

"Moo," he said, delivering the word flatly and without expression.

" 'Moo'?" I said. "That's it?"

We stared at each other. For ten seconds the barn and woods and camp were so quiet, we might have dropped out of time.

"*Dodge City*," Bobby said straight-faced. "Texas longhorn to Errol Flynn."

As we left the barn and walked beside the lake toward the dining hall, voices began to drift from the girls' cabins. Then a loud shriek of laughter echoed across the valley from one of the boys' cabins. By the sadistic tone of it, I could tell that the summer's first prank had been a success. My money was on the Beez.

"Where did you take the copperhead?" Bobby asked.

"I drove up to that road the forest service gave over to the motorcycle crowd. Walked him in maybe a half mile."

Bobby nodded without looking at me. "Good place," he said.

A clatter of pots spilled out from the kitchen, where the cooks had been at work for hours. The salty smell of bacon tightened my stomach.

"I remember the other time that happened," Bobby said. We walked several more paces before he continued. "First day of camp. Copperhead swam through the swim area with the whole camp out in the water. Just like yesterday."

"What happened?"

Bobby shrugged his head to one side. "On that day . . . nothing. But I won't likely forget that year. That was 'the copperhead summer.' "

We kept walking. I looked at him for more, but Bobby just gazed out over the lake, lost in the memory.

"Were there a lot of copperheads that year?" I asked.

He pursed his lips and frowned. "No, I think that was the only one. But there was a lot of other stuff that year. Problems. Campers, counselors, parents . . . you name it. Nothing seemed to go right." Bobby stopped walking and studied the lake again. "Where did yours cross yesterday?"

I pointed and traced the route for him. "He hit land about thirty yards to the left of my cabin . . . near those alders." Bobby was quiet, his eyebrows pushed low. I looked toward the alders again. "Are you saying that that copperhead years ago was . . . what . . . an omen?"

Bobby shrugged. "Don't know beans about omens. Don't really believe in them. But that was one bad-luck camp season, and I always thought of it as 'the copperhead summer.' "

I looked out over the water as if the Lady of the Lake might break the surface and divine our future for this camp session. "I don't believe in omens either," I said.

Neither of us spoke for a time. As we stood and watched the morning rays of light angle down on the lake, I kept hearing my last words, wondering if they were true. The reflection in Lake Itawa was like an inverted photograph laid at the foot of the mountain that soared upward behind my cabin.

"Where did your snake cross the lake?" I asked.

Bobby pointed with his chin. "Same place. Got out the same place, too."

I looked at those alders again. "Did you catch it, or did it get away?"

Bobby inhaled and let out the air slowly through his nose. "Killed it," he said keeping his eyes on the lake. "That's what Old Bill did in those days." He turned his head to me. "Back then it was just me speaking for the animals. This was before there was you *and* me."

"Maybe that's why things went haywire," I said. "Because he killed it."

Bobby's face wrinkled, and he swiveled his head away an inch without breaking eye contact with me. "I thought you didn't believe in omens."

"I don't. I think that would fall under the heading of a curse."

"You believe in curses then?" he said.

"Nope."

Bobby stood stock-still and stared at me with a blank expression on his face. Then he dropped low and feinted an uppercut to my solar plexus. I didn't move. I'd known it was coming.

"I'm hungry," he said. "Let's go beg for a biscuit."

At the kitchen we got our biscuits—but not without a price. Bobby and I hauled out all the food platters to the tables, something close to torture with the warm aroma of eggs and bacon teasing us all the way.

When Mrs. Old Bill rang the bell, the first wave of campers trickled in. They knew they would have to wait for the others, but they seemed willing to settle for inhaling the scents filling the room.

When the second bell clanged, the stragglers hustled into the dining hall and filled the empty seats. Tyler Raintree had not shown up. Five minutes later I spooned eggs into a biscuit, broke a strip of crisp bacon in two, laid the halves over the eggs, and closed up the sandwich. I ate as I walked to Tyler's cabin.

Standing below the door, I finished the biscuit and listened. The cabin was quiet. I took the stairs slowly and hesitated at the door. Through the screen I saw Tyler sitting in the empty room on a lower bunk. The slump in his back was a portrait of misery.

I know he heard me open the rust-tuned door, but he didn't turn. Lined up neatly on the floor next to him was all of his gear, probably never unpacked. He was wearing the same clothes I had seen him in yesterday. The Snoopy towel hung off the bed frame drying. I walked past him to the next bunk and sat down facing him slightly cattycornered. His eyes remained glued to the floor.

"Hungry?" I asked quietly to match his mood. Tyler was beyond the "joy therapy" of an upbeat counselor. As an answer, his head moved a quarter inch each way as his eyes remained dedicated to the old worn floorboards. I looked at the floor, too, and drifted back to my first morning at Itawa, remembering the cold reality of a severed umbilical. I was coming around to Bobby's guess about a Raintree divorce. I wondered which parent he was thinking about. Decades ago, I had been this quiet, too, but it was my dog that I'd missed.

"I see you're all packed up. Where're you headed?"

"Home." The word came out quickly as if he had been waiting for the question so that he could ambush me with his answer.

"Did you get a call? Is something wrong?"

Tyler fixed me with a testy stare, as if I had questioned the law of gravity. His mouth tightened into a sneer, and his shoulders shook once as he made a sound through his teeth like a leak from an air hose. Then he returned his attention to the floor.

"Good breakfast this morning," I said. "Why don't we go get something to eat?"

The silence drew out, and his head made the minimal shake again. "I'm not hungry." The fact that he answered at all meant this was not a standoff of raw insolence. He clamped the edge of the mattress with white fists and leaned forward on his arms for a better view of the floor.

"Is this about the snake?" I asked.

He shook his head again, this time with more animation. Then he stole a glance at me to see if I was looking at him.

"You didn't want to come to camp, did you, Tyler?" He made the barely perceptible headshake again. Even though he wasn't looking at me, I nodded. "Parents make you?"

Though Tyler was not moving at all, he seemed to become even more still, as if the question had caused the blood to freeze in his veins. I could see he was struggling with how much of this he was going to let out. He didn't know me yet, but maybe I was the closest thing he had to a friend here. He nodded. Not wanting to rush things, I leaned back on the mattress on one elbow.

"How come they wanted you to come to camp?" I asked.

His eyes flashed up quickly to catch me in some pretense of being interested, but he must have seen something that reassured him. His gaze dropped to the floor again.

"My mom had to get rid of me for a while . . . while she divorces my father."

I hadn't been ready for that. Tyler could be very direct. A bright tear welled in each of his eyes, and he wiped at one with the back of his wrist. Then he maneuvered to the other eye with a little sleight of hand, pretending he was scratching his nose. Like every other ten-year-old child, he could be very indirect, too.

"What do you mean 'get rid of you'?"

He turned his face from me and sniffed. "So my father can't find me."

I wasn't quite getting all this. I looked at his bags so neatly arranged on the floor. Even his bed was made, wrinkle-free with a tight tuck under the mattress. It was the only one in the cabin like that.

"So, are you expecting your mother?" He shook his head, this time in a slow generous arc. "Your father?" He nodded. "Did you call him?"

He looked up quickly, his face distorted by the absurdity of the question. "No!"

"But you said your mother was putting you in a place where you can't be found. So how can he come get you?"

Tyler presented a mirthless smile that suggested how little I knew. "He'll find me."

A kingfisher made its dry rattling call from the mouth of the creek. I looked through the screened upper half of the cabin at the sunlit details of the trees beyond the lake. The gray mountains in the distance rose like a fortress wall. This valley seemed a long way from the kind of complications that can bring such ruin to a little boy's face.

"Will your mother tell him where you are?"

Headshake again.

"Do you want him to find you?" He gave me the incredulous look again. I sat up and propped my elbows on my knees so that my face was level with his. "Then he won't find you," I said.

"You don't know him," he shot back.

I was beginning to wonder about Beau Raintree. Somehow, I did not doubt Tyler's assessment of his father's powers.

"Tyler, did your mother warn Old Bill about all this?"

He shrugged. "I doubt it."

"Would you mind if I talked to Old Bill about it . . . maybe talk to your mom, too?"

He looked up and locked eyes with me. "What for?"

"I'd just like to see exactly how things stand. We need to know to turn away certain people who come looking for you. What's your mother's name?"

He wanted to believe I could protect him—that Itawa could be his safe harbor. I could see his eyes searching for hope in the cracks between the floorboards.

"Pat," he said. After saying his mother's name out loud, he swallowed.

Remembering the lone phone number on his camp application, I wondered how complete the paper had been. "Do you know your mother's cell phone number, Tyler?"

He shook his head. "She doesn't have one. My father won't let her."

I wanted to ask *why* but decided to let that one alone. "What about the number on your camp application? Is that your father's?"

He shrugged again. "It's just our regular phone. It's on the wall in our kitchen. There's another in their bedroom. My father has a cell phone, but I don't know the number."

I nodded and waited for him to look at me, but his sad eyes gazed at the floor with the eerie tenacity of a hara-kiri ritual. "Tyler, I won't let anyone take you away from here who is not supposed to."

His head came up, and he began to study me: my arms, my hands, and my shoulders. Apparently, he was appraising me for the job. I could have guessed a thousand times what was running through his head, and a thousand times I would have been wrong. He slanted his eyebrows into a peak that wrinkled his forehead and softened his voice to a whisper. It was a scene to break your heart but for the content of his words.

"Do you have a gun?"

In the block of silence that followed, we stared at each other through an intimacy I had rarely encountered with a camper so new. The voices drifting across the lawn from the dining hall seemed almost mocking with irrelevance. From this quiet introverted boy, I felt I had been handed the secret journal of his life in that one question. Then I remembered that discoloration on the center of his back that I had seen at the lake.

"Tyler, does your father hurt you?" His gaze lowered to the floor again, and he shut down. "Does he hurt your mother?" He shrugged. I thought this might be as much as he had ever conceded to anyone, so I decided not to push it. "Okay . . . look, I'm taking the Outriders on a day hike to Rainbow Falls today. I'd like you to go. If you want, we can talk more about this. If you don't want to talk, we won't."

"Outriders?"

He didn't look at me, but there was a faint ring of interest in his voice. His bags, I realized, were laid out like the foundation of a bunker. I tried to imagine the cloud of fear that must be suffocating him. He needed to breathe the fine mist swirling off the rocks below Rainbow Falls.

"It's a special group. Only certain people join up. We go out into the wilderness sometimes for a week . . . places where nobody knows where we are."

His forehead wrinkled, and he finally looked at me. "What if something happened?"

"Like what?"

"What if somebody got sick or hurt or something?"

"Well, we stop what we're doing and help them get well. We use the same medicines the Indians used."

"What do you mean? What kind of medicine?" He was with me now. The questions were popping out like any other ten-year-old boy.

"The Cherokees got all their medicines from the forest, Tyler. It's all still out there."

"Does that Indian go with you?"

"Bobby Whitehorse?" I paused, wondering if Bobby somehow frightened Tyler. "Usually."

Tyler squinted at me. "He said you were more Indian than he was."

Inside I smiled. I could hear that conversation as if a tape were playing in my head.

"Bobby is Cherokee, Tyler. His parents and grandparents and all before them were Cherokee. I'm like you. Just a good-looking white guy." I gave him my goofy smile.

Tyler's expression did not change. "I'm part-Indian," he said.

I felt my smile dissolve. "Really?"

"My father said we're part-Seneca."

I pushed out my lower lip and nodded. "Okay, I guess *I'm* the only good-looking white guy around here. You and Bobby are the good-looking Indians."

Tyler's expression remained grim. He opened his hands like a book and stared at his palms. There was still a little moist glimmer in each eye, but he was not crying. His skin and bone structure showed no evidence that he was descended from Native Americans, but I had wondered about his name: *Raintree*.

"Today's hike is sort of a try-out to see who might like the kind of stuff we do. But it's six miles in and six miles back. You're going to need some food in that belly. No self-respecting Seneca would take off on a journey without it." I stood up and slapped the flat of my stomach. "Come on. I'll eat everything on your tray that you don't want."

After a few seconds of complete stillness, he stood, and I felt the sun rise again inside me.

The dining hall was a beehive. Nobody paid much attention to Tyler and me as we came in late. It was just too loud for anyone to bother with a question anyway. Even with this ocean of voices and the loud clack of trays and the clink of silverware, still the dominant sound in my head was five words I couldn't shake.

Do you have a gun?

Chapter Five

"Morning," I said from the office doorway.

Old Bill turned from the glow of his computer screen and lowered his chin to look at me over his wire-rimmed glasses. His fingers gripped the sides of his keyboard as if he were considering ripping it away from the monitor and sailing it through the window. He dropped the scowl just long enough to greet me.

"Stoney." His voice cascaded pleasantly with its rusty Doppler effect just as it had when I was eight years old. He looked again at the computer, made a quick, dismissive shake of his head, and spun his chair to face me. Glad for a diversion, he slapped the arms of the chair. "What's up?"

"Problems with the electronic monster?" I asked.

He frowned at the screen and blew a flutter of air through his lips. I glanced out the window at the campers en route to their activities.

"Bill, any of those kids out there could run your computer in his sleep. Why don't you get one of them to help you with it sometime?"

His frown deepened, but I could see that he was considering it. "Well, the next time a camper goes astray, send 'im in here for his punishment. We'll see what an old dog can learn."

I smiled, imagining Stephen Beasley's face lighting up at the prospect of an afternoon with a glowing screen. "It wouldn't be punishment to them, Bill. They'd love to play with your computer."

Old Bill shook his head at the mysteries of the new generation of campers and reached for his coffee mug. "World's gone to hell in a hard-drive, Stoney."

"Except here at Itawa," I said, ". . . the last real place."

I saw him smile before the mug covered his mouth. He was proud of what we had, but I knew he would not talk about it. He sipped coffee and sat back in his chair. His white hair looked as soft as spider's silk. Against his leathery skin, his eyes were sky-blue and ingenuous, never disguising what was on his mind. His silence was my cue to talk.

"I'm taking the Outriders to Rainbow Falls today. I want to ask you about one of the boys going with us. Tyler Raintree."

Old Bill pursed his lips and nodded slowly. Balancing the coffee in one hand, he turned back to the computer and clicked the mouse a few times. His head bobbed like a bird's from screen to keyboard as he pecked keys with one finger. Then he waited.

"Raintree, Tyler. Ten years old. Atlanta. Goes to Pace Academy." Old Bill looked at me and waited.

"Did you remember talking to his parents, Bill?"

He leaned back to the screen and read for several seconds. "Looks like I talked to his mother back in—" He sat up straighter and became more animated. "Oh, yeah, I remember her. She called just a few weeks ago. Only reason he got into camp was because Billy Bauer decided to go with his school band to Europe."

I sat down on the arm of the big red leather chair. "Any special instructions about Tyler?"

"Like what?"

"Like what we should do if a father comes here and tries to take him back."

Old Bill lowered his eyebrows and his coffee mug simultaneously. "No."

"Tyler says it's a strong possibility."

He brought the mug to his lips again and stared at me over the rim. His eyes hardened with the liability side of running a summer camp.

"What did Tyler say?"

I stared at him for five seconds, preparing him by the expression on my face. "He asked if I owned a gun."

Old Bill became so still I could hear the second-hand on the wall clock *tick* like a time bomb. He filled his chest with a deep breath and set the coffee aside.

"We need to give his mother a call, Bill. I want to know who might show up at our gate looking for him. Tyler says his mother is hiding him from his father."

He laced his fingers over his skin-and-bones stomach and stared out the front window through the green lattice of the big hemlock. "Let's call 'er," he said. He wrote down the number from the screen, reached for the old rotary-dial telephone on his desk, and, using a pencil, spun through the numbers.

Outside on the dirt drive Dorian Saxe led her horseback group toward the front entrance. The horses' shoes *clopped* and *clacked* a pleasing, random rhythm that could have been the soundtrack of the old homestead that had stood here two centuries ago.

The campers were capped in black riding helmets that lent a sense of security to the excursion. Most of these kids stared at their horses' ears and balanced tentatively on their mounts like humble servants praying to the mass of muscle beneath them. Darcy Greyfield brought up the rear, sitting her horse with a grace born of equine devotion. Sandwiched between Dorian and Darcy, the group ambled down the road, blinking in and out of shadows like a string of Christmas lights.

"I think we ought to talk to our lawyer, too," I said, "so we know where we stand if someone shows up to claim Tyler."

Bill held the receiver to his ear and nodded. "Mrs. Raintree?" His brow lowered as he listened, and then he widened his eyes with surprise. "Hello?" He straightened his back and frowned. "Is Mrs. Raintree at home, please?" There was none of his usual down-home warmth in the greeting, just a stilted cordiality. Bill's eyes fixed on mine. I could hear a man's curt voice from the receiver. Bill's disapproving expression said volumes about the man's rudeness. Old Bill's eyes angled away from mine as he composed a lie. "This is the main branch of the library. Her book is in. She asked us to call."

The muffled voice rattled off a few terse words, and then all went quiet. Bill pulled the receiver from his ear and held it out as if he were showing me proof of the man's rudeness.

"Damned reprobate hung up on me."

"I hope you had a book title ready."

Old Bill ignored me. He focused on one thing at a time, and he wasn't through feeling incensed at the man's rudeness. He held the receiver by two fingers and let it fall the last half inch into the cradle, the way you might dispose of a dead rat by its tail.

"Was it Mister Raintree?" I asked.

"How the hell would I know?" Bill growled. "A woman answered with a Spanish accent. Then the jackass who hung up on me butted in." He paused, waiting to hear what I might say, but then, seeing my expression, he raised both palms toward me. "I know, I know. I can't yell at him, so I'm yelling at you." He picked up his coffee and took an angry gulp.

"If he's screening her calls," I suggested, "maybe we need a female voice on this end. Might seem more personal that way."

I stood and walked to the back window. On the sloped lawn between the dining hall and the upper playing field, a group of kids crowded around Gwendolyn. With a soccer ball wedged under one arm against the curve of her hip, she mustered out teams for a game. Her back was to me, and I could see two stylish braids of hair woven into one at the back. On her feet were regulation soccer shoes. They were cracked and worn, suggesting a history. Bobby Whitehorse had said she probably owned bulletproof bracelets and a tiara, too.

I held up an index finger to Old Bill. "I'll be right back."

Since I didn't know Gwendolyn well, I hoped to find another female for the task, but the junior counselor helping her had a cartoonish voice that could never pull off what we needed. I stood to one side, waiting for the final division of teams. Then I approached Gwendolyn.

"Could we borrow you in the office for a minute, Gwendolyn?"

Her face transitioned from surprise to alarm to guardedness. Then I thought I saw a flicker of fear. Words having failed her, she stared at me as if I were a disease.

"It's nothing to do with venomous snakes," I added. "I promise."

She glanced at the kids who were starting to mill around. "I guess Brittany could take them to the field." She looked back at me and frowned. "Is something wrong?"

"Nope. We just need your help. Ever take any drama classes?"

Her blue eyes took on a sharp intensity. "Drama?"

I started back toward the office, but I had to stop twice before she would follow. There was something preordained in her reaction to me, as though she had been coached to be wary. When I held the door open for her, she stopped several yards away and peered across the threshold.

"Is Mr. Wellborne in there?" she asked. By the way she stood her ground six feet away, I finally caught on. This was Justin's propaganda at work. Here was a forewarned fly gazing into the spider's parlor.

"Old Bill is in here," I said in the same soothing voice I might tell a new camper that there was no such thing as a fang-toothed cave rat living under the shower house, no matter what Stephen Beasley said. Gwendolyn did not budge. I smiled. "We'll be in the office when you're ready," I said and walked through the door.

In a little less than a minute, I heard the door open and then ease shut. Gwendolyn peered around the corner from the hallway. When she saw us waiting, her tanned face flushed red.

"Gwendolyn," Bill said. He combed his fingers back through his hair—his standard gesture of deference when addressing someone he admired. Female beauty was a virtue to Old Bill. She looked at me, and I did my best to appear neutral. If she turned any redder, I would have to ask Bobby Whitehorse about adopting her into the Cherokee tribe.

"We've gotta little problem that you might help us with," Old Bill explained. "I know you have things to do, but we have a camper in a very unusual situation." Bill turned to me. "You wanna explain this?"

I looked out the back window and saw Justin standing on the sports field yelling to the campers who were playing keep-away with the soccer ball. Several times he turned to frown at the office window, though I knew he couldn't see us through the glare. I figured if Gwendolyn was going to do this for us, she had a right to all the information we had.

"Well," I began, "the camper is on a legal fence being pulled by both parents who are divorcing, so I'm told. If one of them comes up here to take him home, we're not sure which side we're supposed to support for legal purposes. We've been told by the camper that the father is not supposed to know his son is here at Itawa. We need to verify that by talking first to the mother. We called but couldn't get past the father. We thought a female stood a better chance of getting through."

Old Bill leaned forward and folded his arms on his desk. "Now we don't want you to do this if you're not comfortable with it."

She stood before us in her perfect body on her perfect legs, her thoughts fairly transparent behind the angles of her Scandinavian face. Finally, she answered Old Bill like any other young employee would in her first year.

"What should I say?" she asked, looking first at Bill and then at me.

Old Bill raised his eyebrows at me, and I felt the burden of creative deception fall my way. "How about 'Is Pat there?'" I said.

Old Bill shook his head. "He's screening her calls. He'll ask Gwendolyn something for sure."

I nodded and looked out the window. Justin's fists were propped on his hips, elbows bent outward as he stared at the office window.

"Okay," I said. "How about this: 'This is Dr. Chandler's office calling for Mrs. Raintree.' If he gets pushy, you can say it's personal—maybe gynecological—and imperative that you speak to her."

"That's good," Bill said. "Can you do that, Gwendolyn?"

She made a face as though she detected an offensive smell in the air. "Dr. Chandler?"

"Use any name you want," I said. As Old Bill went through the dialing with his pencil, I stepped closer to Gwendolyn and lowered my voice to a whisper. "Make it 'Dr. Camp' instead. That way if he doesn't let you through but mentions it to her, maybe she'll know to call us."

"Okay," she said, trying hard to pass this test for the Itawa family. She took the phone and turned her back to us. Directly in her line of vision was Justin pacing the edge of the field, watching the campers scramble in their game. He turned his head toward the office, and Gwendolyn did an automatic quarter turn to face the filing cabinet.

The first thing we heard her say was, "Oh." Bill and I looked at each other, then back at Gwendolyn's golden-fleece braids. "Is this Pat?" She turned to look at us. "Hold, please." She covered the phone and whispered, "It's her. I didn't know what to say."

Old Bill took the telephone, and Gwendolyn backed away a few steps toward the door. I held up a finger for her to wait until I could see how things would go in the conversation. She didn't know if she should be listening, so she put her hands in her pockets, pivoted on a cleated shoe, and began to browse around the far side of the room. She stopped at the big fireplace and looked at the row of memorabilia on the mantle, part of which was my canoeing and archery awards that Old Bill had displayed there. She put a foot on the stone hearth and leaned close to read the inscriptions.

The trophies would have been anonymous except that Bill had framed the newspaper articles that accompanied each award. On each clipping was a photograph of Old Bill and me standing at the camp entrance with the big Itawa sign behind us. *Itawa Counselor Wins Southeastern Archery Title,* it read. The one next to it was for canoeing. Second place in the nationals.

The turn she made toward me seemed involuntary. Her expression was so flat, it looked like the muscles in her face had been injected with lidocaine. Her lips parted slightly, but nothing came out. From what I could hear, Old Bill had made the connection with Tyler's mother. I took two steps toward Gwendolyn and made an "okay" sign with my thumb and index.

"You did great. Go have fun with the kids. And thanks."

She looked hard at me, as if she were checking the bone structure in my face. Wearing a tight-lipped smile that showed no teeth, she backed to the door.

I heard Bill mention Tyler's name. I tried to listen to him and watch Gwendolyn at the same time, which was not easy. She got as far as the threshold and paused. Turning, she graced me with a timid smile, and I had the sense that I had shed the mantle of camp lecher. When she walked out, I stepped back to Bill and leaned to put my mouth close to his ear.

"Ask her about her divorce status," I whispered, "so we'll know what to ask our lawyer."

Bill looked annoyed at having to listen to two people at once. He turned away from me and stared at the computer screen.

"Let me put Stoney on the phone," he said, "since he's the one who—" I reached for the phone, but he pressed a palm over the mouthpiece. "I think someone just picked up on an extension," he whispered.

I took the phone from him, stretching the coiled cord from the desk. Holding the phone down by my leg, I gazed out the back window. Eighty miles away Tyler's mother probably stood petrified inside her hostile home—afraid to hang up, afraid not to. For all she knew, her son might have had an accident . . . or run away. If Beau Raintree was listening in, I didn't know how to handle this without creating a problem on her end. Actually, I wasn't sure how to handle it even if Pat Raintree and I were seated on top of Standing Bear Dome. I decided directness was my only option.

"Mrs. Raintree," I said, "this is Stoney. Can we talk or is this a bad time?"

There was a three-second delay before a quiet voice floated through the line. "The latter." I could hear a trace of fear in her voice, making the words tremble.

"Everything is fine here . . . but we need to talk. Call me," I said and hung up.

I sat in the leather chair, and, as a cheer rose and faded on the sports field, Bill and I just stared at one another. "What did you find out about the divorce status?" I asked.

"I didn't," he said, scowling. "Didn't have time."

Hoping for a call, we waited five minutes, Bill sipping coffee and staring out the front window, I replaying Tyler's five words that had stuck in my head. The phone remained stubbornly quiet, and I didn't like thinking about what might be going on in the Raintree house at that moment. I could see by the set of Old Bill's jaw that he was no more pleased by this situation than I.

"Something's wrong in that house," I said, breaking the silence. Old Bill stared blindly at the computer screen. I stood, walked to the back window, and watched the campers go through Gwendolyn's orderly soccer drills. "The thing is . . . I don't know if she's okay or not." I turned to Bill. "Do you think we should call the police?"

Old Bill shook his head. "Family problems are tricky. She didn't call us for help. And for Tyler's sake, we can't get our name into it." He frowned and thought for a moment. "What if we called the police anonymously?" he said.

I shook my head. "You can't call the police anonymously anymore." Hearing my own words, I felt my blood stop cold. I looked at the old rotary dial phone sitting on Bill's desk. "You can't call *anybody* anonymously anymore. Everybody's got 'caller ID' . . . except us." I closed my eyes and shook my head. "I wasn't thinking. We should have borrowed someone's cell phone."

When I opened my eyes, Old Bill's forehead had tightened into a furrowed field, and his eyes bored into mine. "What does that 'ID' gadget do?"

I leaned against the door frame and crossed my arms over my chest. "If the Raintrees have 'caller ID'—and it's almost certain they do—our name and number showed up on a little screen on their phone."

Bill tapped his pencil three times on the circular dial of his outdated telephone. Then he checked the wall clock and frowned at me.

"So, if he saw 'Camp Itawa' and our number, why didn't he call back? Maybe they don't have this 'ID' thing." His eyes fixed on me, and he seesawed the pencil between two fingers, the movement so fast it made a yellow blur.

"He knows who we are now," I mumbled. "He has no need to call. He can find us."

Bill looked south toward Atlanta. "Well, damn-nation." He threw the pencil onto his desk, took in a lot of air, and let it out in a huff. "Go to Rainbow Falls, Stoney. I'll let you know if she calls."

I was halfway down the grassy slope by the dining hall when I heard my name called behind me. Gwendolyn walked toward me, her head bowed in thought. Her golden hair shone brilliant in the sun. Watching her sun-browned legs make long, graceful strides down the lawn and hearing her cleats grip the sod with a tear of precision, I could believe that at night she transformed into some kind of panther woman and ran the woods in pursuit of the swiftest deer. She stopped two yards from me, jammed her hands into the pockets of her shorts, and looked down at the grass.

"I feel like an idiot," she said.

I waited, knowing not to touch that. She checked my face then resumed her study of the grass.

"I thought you—" She stopped and cracked a bitter smile. "I was told that you . . . well . . . to be careful of you." She swallowed and looked at her feet. I looked at her feet, too. No panther claws there. She took a deep breath and continued. "I just talked to Mimi. She said you weren't . . . well . . . she said I had been misinformed." She shook her head with two little jerks, as if she had just surfaced from a stagnant swamp and was flinging foul water from her face. Over the rise of the hill, the heads of the soccer players scattered like marbles. Someone yelled over and over that he was open for a pass. Justin appeared at the edge of the field and looked down at us. He looked impatient or nervous or on the verge of rut.

"You're not the idiot, Gwendolyn," I said, still gazing up the hill.

She shook her head again. "I thought you were getting me to go in the office for—"

"Don't apologize," I interrupted. "Caution is never a bad idea."

When Justin called out, Gwendolyn looked obediently up the hill. He waved her up and then turned away smartly as if duty called. "Yeah," she sighed, eyeing the spot where Justin had stood. "You're probably not any of those things he said."

I said nothing. She opened up the full force of her cerulean eyes.

"He said you were expelled from high school."

I shook my head. "Not true."

"But you didn't go to college?"

"True. Not yet, anyway."

"Because you couldn't get in?"

"Because I didn't apply."

She cocked her head to one side, daring me to answer even before she asked the next question. "Why not?"

"I wouldn't be happy there."

Her head retracted an inch as she winced. "At a college?" She glanced out at the lake and laughed with the weight of her freshman-year experience. "There's a party any night you want. No parents. Where else would you want to be?"

"Here," I said.

She let her eyes rove across the camp as though really seeing it for the first time. "This is all you want to do for the rest of your life?"

"This is what I want to do right now. Everything I want to learn is right here at Itawa."

Her eyebrows slanted to a peak. "What do you 'want to learn'?"

My eyes came to rest on the rock outcrop near the top of Standing Bear Dome. "The real world," I said. "The one that's always been here." When the wrinkles in her forehead would not relax, I added, "Bobby Whitehorse is my teacher."

Gwendolyn squinted at me. "That's the little Indian man?"

I smiled. "Yeah."

She let her head tilt to one side and tried to repress a smile. "What . . . is he a shaman or something?"

I smiled again and shook my head. I could see a list of questions building inside her.

"How old are you?" she demanded.

I told her. She looked me over as if checking my face for a lie.

"Justin said you've been married twice."

This time I laughed. Justin was pulling out all the stops.

"Have you been married?" she said.

I shook my head and watched the campers' heads charge around the field as if a swarm of bees was after them.

"When did you win the canoeing nationals?"

"I didn't win. I got second. It was three years ago."

Talking about sports, she seemed to relax a little and grow serious at the same time. "You would have been what . . . a junior in high school? And you got second . . . in the nation?"

"Gwendolyn, I've got to go catch up with the Outriders. I'm late."

When I turned to leave, she said, "You don't know what you're missing at college, Stoney."

I let my eyes angle off toward the hemlocks on the other side of the lake. "Maybe one day," I said. "There's time."

She seemed troubled by my answer. "But you want to be young enough to enjoy it, Stoney."

"I'll try and stay young," I said and jogged off down the trail.

Chapter Six

As I entered the clearing in the woods, the Outriders were a little too quiet . . . and a little too attentive to me. It was more than my being late. The silence was electric. I tried to read their eyes for what was up, but even Troy would not meet my gaze. When Bobby Whitehorse moved, it was like a figure had magically become animated in a photograph. He slipped on his daypack and brought over my green one, holding it in one hand by a strap.

"I've got the first aid," he said. "There's a lunch in here for you." Bobby's eyes were stone-cold dead in his broad face.

I took the pack and immediately felt the half dozen or so grapefruit-sized rocks. It was a strain for one arm, but I pretended not to notice.

"Why the big *wait*?" he said, delivering the homonymic pun with a poker face. "We were beginning to wonder if you would show."

I swung the pack over my shoulder and felt the rocks bunch into my lower spine. "I had a *ton* of stuff to do in the office," I said straight-faced. I could play poker, too. As I started up the trail. I tried to look as happy as the seventh dwarf bouncing off to work. *Heigh-ho*.

"Rainbow Falls or bust," I said.

Every camper was bug-eyed, holding his breath, a blink away from bursting into laughter, but Bobby's somber face held them in check. I did my best to walk in a normal gait with the extra fifty pounds. No one else moved. The stones in my pack grated and rumbled like shifting continents. I could only hope that my lunch was on top.

We hiked for ten minutes that way—I in the lead of a chain of snickers and giggles, and Bobby in the rear, no doubt sporting that twinkling star in his eye that I knew so well. I tried to think of the experience as weight-training . . . or practice in resisting torture from the enemy . . . but mostly I was imagining unpleasant scenes in an MRI.

Our trail climbed to a grand view overlooking the Etowah River. It was a place we always stopped to admire the valley. Here, there was nothing in sight connected to humans: no water tank, no power lines, no building or road. To the southeast the town of Dahlonega was nestled just over the third ridge, but here the eye saw exactly what people had seen six hundred years ago.

The Etowah was an interrupted silver ribbon snaking in and out of the trees where the hills stacked one behind the other and folded like alternating ribs against the spine of the river. A constant sibilant static rose from the valley, a long raspy breath that had been exhaled from the beginning of time.

"Long Man," Bobby said quietly, naming the river by its Cherokee metaphor.

The kids turned to him. He had a way of saying a thing that made you want to see his face when he said it. One by one, the kids followed his gaze back to the river. Where the sun's rays reached the dew-painted rocks on the slopes, wispy tongues of steam plumed upward and dissolved in the clear mountain air. It would be easy to believe we were looking down on the campfires of ancient tribes. My imagination usually bent in that direction.

Like every other square mile of the planet, this piece of land, I knew, was mapped on paper, crisscrossed by a numbered grid, and curling with concentric patterns of topographical contour lines. Still, I felt the Cherokees' presence here and a vast sense of the unknown. This valley could be any adventure we wanted it to be.

"What's 'Etowah' mean, Bobby Whitehorse?" asked P.J., one of the veteran campers. It was her first time with us. I'd been trying to talk her into Outriders for two years.

Bobby nodded as he always did at a good question. "Long ago, there was a Cherokee town on this river. It was called 'I-ta`-wa.' No one knows what it means anymore. The white man changed the word to fit his tongue: 'Etowah.' And later changed it again to 'Hightower.' That's Hightower Mountain there." He pointed.

"But the camp still uses the old name. How come?"

While Bobby explained, I maneuvered to the rear where Tyler sat. Without looking at him I bent to tie a bootlace and whispered.

"Want to help me return these rocks to their rightful owner?" Tyler checked my face and must have read mischief there. He returned his stoic gaze to the valley and nodded. We made our plan in less than a minute.

After we had been walking again for five minutes, I heard a thud behind me, and Bobby called out my name. I hurried back to find Tyler lying on his back on the ground with the crook of his arm bent across his eyes, his teeth bared in a grimace.

"What's the matter?" I said, slipping out of my heavy pack and setting it down gently to minimize the clatter of stones.

Bobby's face was hard. "He said something about his medicine. Is he diabetic?"

I gave Bobby a dead-serious look, and then, ignoring his question, I knelt. "Tyler," I said as quietly as a doctor beside a deathbed, "it's Stoney. Is it your disease?"

Tyler's head rocked up, then down. The others gathered around us, unnerved not only by the prostrate boy but by the way Bobby and I talked in hushed tones.

Tyler opened his mouth and inhaled repeatedly without exhaling. Then his voice wheezed out of his chest as if a giant oak had fallen across his body.

"The camp nurse said my medicine was in my lunch bag. It's not there."

I looked up at Bobby. "I don't have his medicine. Do you?"

"No," he said taking off his pack to double check. "What's he got?"

For the second time, I ignored his question and addressed the campers. "Everybody check your lunch bag! See if the nurse got it mixed up!"

While brown bags crackled, I touched Bobby's elbow and led him ten yards up the trail. Over his shoulder I called out instructions for the Outriders.

"You guys keep an eye on Tyler. Whatever he needs, see if you can help him out." I kept Bobby about a minute with his back to the group. I spoke quickly, running my syllables together in a blur, describing Tyler's malady as 'Reverse-legerdemain-syndrome.'

" 'Reverse' what?" he said.

I leaned to look over his shoulder as if making sure no one could hear me. Some of the kids were gawking at me with huge grins while others watched Tyler, Troy and P.J. quietly switch the stones from my pack to Bobby's.

I leaned back to Bobby and spoke in a low, confidential tone. "We'll have to carry him back to camp. Lucky for us we're not too far into this hike. Let's try not to alarm the kids with this . . . even though it's contagious."

"Contagious!" Bobby said and scowled.

We both knew that no child could come to Itawa with anything that could infect other campers, but the urgency of our situation seemed to carry the moment. When Bobby turned his head part way back toward the cluster of hikers, I touched his elbow again to bring his eyes back to me.

"Bobby, this is a disease that should be handled with a lot of gravity." This was a line I would be sure to remind him later. "I've already been around him a lot today, so I'll carry him. No sense in both of us getting exposed. Okay?"

I walked away from the question on Bobby's face and joined the others. "How is he?"

Amanda answered for everybody. "He looks a little better, Stoney." She delivered the line with Academy Award written all over it. Best supporting actress in a sham. I would remember her for future performances.

"Tyler?" I said kneeling beside him again. "How bad is it?"

"I think it's all passed now," he said. I didn't know if the double entendre was intentional, but I clamped my molars together, locking the laughter inside my chest.

I helped him get to his feet, swept up my now ultra-light pack, and pulled Tyler along with me. "Rainbow Falls or bust," I repeated, this time with emphasis on the "bust."

Bobby stood very still as I walked past him. Only his eyes moved, sliding like a snake under his half-closed lids, following Tyler and me as we walked carefree along the trail. I felt as light as a feather drifting on a breeze.

Several yards down the trail I turned around and walked backward to watch the double-cross drama play out. All the kids passed Bobby keeping their eyes straight ahead, fighting the smiles that twitched on their faces. Finally, unable to resist, we all stopped and watched Bobby pick up his pack and load it on his back like a truckload of bricks. As he started after us, I heard the pleasing rumble of rocks.

"Indian giver," he mumbled.

Everyone laughed openly now, and our spirits ran as high as the ridge we were traversing. Every few minutes I heard a loud thump behind me followed by tumbling and crashing sounds down the slope. Now my thoughts turned to preventative medicine—namely double-reverse-legerdemain-syndrome. I could almost smell the smoke rising from the fire that Trickster Rabbit kept smoldering in the head of Bobby Whitehorse. I would definitely not lose sight of my pack for the rest of this trip.

We didn't make it to the falls for lunch. Instead, we chose a flat slab of stone that shelved out over the river ten feet above an emerald pool. The campers pillaged their paper bags and ate cookies first. They were, of course, "starving." I took apart my sandwich and laid the pieces on top of the wrapping and started checking the shoreline for condiments.

One of the new kids was first to announce his disappointment at his lunch. "Hey, don't we get mayonnaise or anything?"

Like everyone else's sandwich, his was two pieces of dry bread and a thin slab of ham. He was looking right at me when he made his complaint, but I waited to let some of the veterans explain.

"Lizard skin!" Amanda yelled from the water's edge. All the new kids gathered around her and watched. I felt a little squeeze in my chest as she lightly rested her hand on the mat of scaly liverwort. She spoke the words that embraced the spirit of Outriders, and she said the prayer in such a way that caught everyone's attention—quietly as if she were talking casually to a friend.

"In a sacred manner we ask for a part of you to become part of us."

Even with the river purling by—the crash of rapids upstream and down—a blanket of silence dropped around us. Without talking, the others reached down and took their portions and copied Amanda as she washed away dirt and sand that clung to the plant's roots.

Troy harvested two pale green shoots from a stand of cattails emerging from a muddy shallow. When he returned, nine little hands spoked toward him as he cut dime-sized slivers from the core with his sheath knife. He dropped two succulent disks into each waiting hand.

When Tyler walked away from the crowd staring at the morsels cupped in his palm, I called him over to the floodplain where I was wandering through the beeches and oaks looking for toothwort. I told him the plant's story—how the white knobby roots reminded ancient people of a row of teeth and suggested a remedy for tooth problems.

"Did it work?" he asked.

"Nope, but it got them experimenting." I knelt by a healthy patch.

Tyler's face wrinkled like a twisted rag. "Isn't that poison ivy?"

I shook my head. "Toothwort." I pointed at the rounded teeth of the leaflets.

"So, that's how they learned about stuff?" he asked. "By guessing what it looked like?"

"Mostly the Indians knew what they knew by instinct, just like wild animals still do."

Tyler frowned as he digested that information. "Then how come they used the other way of guessing?"

I singled out one of the plants, cupping a hand under a leaf and straddling the stalk with my fingers. Tyler leaned in close to see.

"All cultures lose their instincts as their language develops," I explained. "They were probably trying to get those instincts back."

As he stared at the toothwort, one of his cheeks bulged from the push of his tongue. I could see I had piqued his interest.

"Tyler," I said, "this root is one heck of a sandwich spice, and you and I are about to become the Lewis and Clark of lunchtime discoveries." Still gently cradling the plant in my hand, I offered my prayer of thanks. "Little toothwort, may we use a part of you to nourish us? I will leave some of your root behind to grow another plant."

Tyler wrinkled his nose at me. "How come you talk to it that way?"

I tried for the kind of Joan of Arc smile I had seen on Abby's face in the dining hall. "Have you never said a blessing at a meal?"

He shrugged. "I guess. But I wasn't talking to a plant."

"Who were you talking to?"

His eyes lowered in embarrassment. "I don't know. God, I guess."

I nodded and decided to say no more. Digging into the sandy soil with my finger, I pried up a root. Tyler leaned in closer to see the so-called dental structure as I broke part of the root free. I tamped earth back over what I had left and asked Tyler to harvest one more plant. He looked down at the little colony of toothworts for a time, then turned away and gazed toward the river with his brow pinched. I stood and ambled away to give him some space. With my back to him, I gently brushed away the dirt clinging to the roots.

"Do I have to . . . like . . . say all that stuff you did?" he mumbled.

I turned my head only partway. "Only if it feels right to you. Say anything you want. Or not. Only remember . . . this little plant might have been standing in line behind you when God's Dog called you out."

I casually peeked back at him. With his nose wrinkled up, he turned so I could not see his face. He murmured something that might have been "Thanks-a-lot" and dug out a root.

After washing our plants at the water's edge, I cut a sample of root into my open palm and sniffed it. "Want to try it?" I offered.

Reluctantly, he plucked it from my hand and then stared at it for several seconds. "What does it taste like?" he mumbled and turned his frown on me.

I lifted my eyebrows. "It's a surprise. That's all I can tell you."

After studying it again, he held the sliver before his face, looked at me again, and then cautiously inserted it into his mouth. At his third chew, his eyes widened.

"Wow!" he said with ten-year-old abandon. As far as I knew, it was Tyler's first "wow" at Camp Itawa. And his was not to be the only "wow" of the day. He made a beeline to the group and dispensed sections of root to each Outrider. When he started to throw away the greenery, I called his name, and he froze with his arm cocked.

"I'll take that, if you don't want it!"

He frowned at the three green leaflets. "Can you eat this part, too?"

"Perfect for a sandwich," I informed him. "You keep that one."

We all spread out on the flat boulder for our meal. Several hundred yards downstream, Beaver Tooth Shoals roared like a distant sports arena. In two weeks, we would be back here in canoes, looking up at this rock, remembering this day when we had been an integral part of this valley, foraging for its gifts.

When that day came, a mile past Beaver Tooth, the kids would question that bond as we scouted the Narrows. There they would learn that life was not a free ride . . . that they had to make their way . . . by the skills they had acquired on Lake Itawa. And once they were at the bottom of the Narrows, with its white dash and splash behind them, they would have earned the right to carve a notch into their self-esteem.

On the other hand, if they capsized and swam, they would have learned something about accountability, motivation, and challenge, because we'd be back again in two more weeks to try it one more time.

Less than an hour after lunch, we hopped the big boulders at Beaver Tooth and turned up Panther Town Creek. The overhead canopy of rhododendron closed off the sky, and cool air coursed down the dark valley like springwater pouring into our faces. Behind me I felt the hikers gain momentum as the crash of the falls ahead grew louder. The trail opened into a wide flat area where giant hemlocks rose up like dark columns supporting the oval of blue sky above.

Here, the mist from the falls swirled like a wind made visible. The shattering of the water in the pool below made a shearing sound that filled this forest room. It seemed as if every molecule of air was spinning in a collective whisper, enveloping us in a thick gauze of static. We stood in awe of the sheet of falling water until some could no longer wait, and the assault on Rainbow Falls began. Packs hit the ground and swimsuits were dug out. Kids and water. I still felt it, too.

"Boys up the hill, girls back down the trail," I yelled over the roar. The boys hustled up the hill like they had hit the beaches at Normandy. The girls quietly dissolved into the shadows of the rhododendron. Bobby Whitehorse and I stood together looking up at the falls. At the lip of the rock ledge, the water made a smooth sagging line where it plummeted as a translucent curtain, breaking apart on the rock shelf below, sending up a shower of mist over a perfect swimming hole. I could never look at it without remembering my first time here when Bobby had taught me its secret.

In summer, when the sun was at the right angle, the light and water produced a rare phenomenon that still drew me like a magnet. After shedding down to my swimsuit, I swam out to the exploding water and helped the swimming campers up onto the narrow ledge behind the waterfall. As instructed, they stretched their necks through the cold curtain of water to peer into the mist over the pool. A rainbow formed a multi-colored circle around us. It was the only perfect halo I'd ever seen.

An hour later Tyler and I were sitting on a log brushing sand off our feet. It felt good to be clean and dry and dressed again. The invigoration of the cold water still hummed through my body, as if I had drunk a magic elixir to renew the soul. Tyler tugged at a shoelace, then paused looking up at the endless sheet of falling water.

"I've been thinking about the toothwort thing," he said in a dreamy voice. "About language getting in the way of instincts. How does that work exactly?"

I looked at the wonder in his face as it caught the flutter of light reflecting off the water. We had walked in only six miles, but for Tyler it was like crossing a continent. He was a long way from divorce right now.

"I've been thinking about that, too," I said. "You know that thing people have on their phone to let them know in advance who's calling?"

"'Caller ID'?" he said.

"Yeah. What if every time you picked up your phone you glanced at your 'caller ID' screen first and you knew exactly who was calling. Then after a year of this, say the screen stopped working. You might realize how heavily you had come to depend on it and lost the knack for recognizing people's voices."

"So . . . the 'caller ID' is like a language?" he said. "And using it might mean losing something else?"

I nodded, impressed by his agile mind. He stared some more at the falls as I drew a lazy arc in the sand between my feet.

"Do you have it at home?" I asked. "The 'caller ID' thing."

"Nuh-uh," he answered without hesitation. "We have an old phone without it."

I curved the line back on itself into a circle and touched my finger to its center like an arrow finding a bull's eye. I closed my eyes, let my cheeks balloon with air, and then released it in a slow seep under the cover of the thundering water.

Chapter Seven

The dining hall was intoxicating with the heavy aroma of meat and herbs and spices. It was Mrs. Old Bill's spaghetti night, strategically timed as the cure-all for any lingering cases of homesickness. When I thought of the sandwiches we had eaten at the river . . . the *oohs* and *ahs* of the Outriders as they devoured lunch . . . I smiled at the thought of Mrs. Old Bill showing up at our table rock with a pot of this spaghetti.

Miles of hiking and the taste of mountain air do wonders for the reputation of cattails and toothwort, but I would never want to compete with her homemade sauce. Each had its place. I loved the wild foods, but I would not want to live in a world without Mrs. Old Bill's spaghetti.

The Outriders did not eat together but mixed with the other campers, eager to relate the details of an epic journey, of freezing waters, ghostly rainbows, and grown men who traded fifty pounds of stones as a running joke. I sat down at a table that was all girls, most of whom I did not know. Many of them must have spent the day with Dorian and Darcy, because I heard a lot of equestrian talk.

We quickly reached some common ground when I told them secrets about their horses. I rode all the horses through the fall, winter, and spring and knew their individual quirks. Bobby Whitehorse had taught me the best ways to deal with them, and I put a few of these nuggets of wisdom out on the table and became, for a moment, almost as interesting to these girls as their equine soulmates.

Abby Parrish was at a different table, too, systematically making the rounds just like I did. P.J. was talking non-stop to her, forking gobs of noodles into her mouth without a lapse in the story. Abby politely nodded and ate, seemingly undaunted by P.J.'s predatory style.

The counselor table seemed sedate, somehow lacking in luminosity. Justin leaned over his plate and shoveled food single-mindedly—his corner of the room now a refueling station rather than a social event.

On the far side of the room the golden glow of Gwendolyn was centered in a new solar system of campers. She had removed herself from her table of peers to be a player in the bigger picture. I watched her smile and exchange lines with Stephen Beasley for half a minute, noting how Stephen eyed her breasts each time she looked away.

Old Bill emerged from the kitchen eating from a bowl. His eyes scanned the room, but I knew he wasn't seeing anything. When he ate, he was as dedicated as a 'possum to a trashcan. I had learned never to discuss anything of importance with him if blood was running to his stomach.

When he finished, he placed the bowl inside the clean-up window and then scanned the room again with new life in his eyes. When he saw me, he pointed toward the side door and walked that way, stopping to talk to every child who called his name. I swabbed my plate with a scrap of bread and downed it as I got up with my tray.

Gwendolyn, wearing a lavender blouse and white jeans, intersected with me at the tray-return window with the precision of an air-traffic controller. I slowed to give her first at the window.

"Hi," she said. Her smile stretched so wide that her eyes narrowed to slits and her pristine white teeth glowed against her tanned face like sun-bleached seashells laid out in a perfect row. Radiating a warmth I had not before seen in her, she slid her tray through the window and spun back to me, hooking her thumbs into the waistband of her jeans, one leg bending in classic contrapposto.

"Hello, Gwendolyn."

Her head tilted. "Oh, you can call me 'Gwen,'" she said.

I pushed my mouth to one side and shook my head. "I don't think I could do that." Her cerulean eyes could not settle on mine. They jittered in a nervous little dance. She tried to hold on to her smile. I doubt she had been denied much by my gender.

"Why not?" she laughed.

I looked down at my clean plate. "Well, I've never known a Gwendolyn before. It's kind of Arthurian. I'd hate to not use it." I stepped past her and pushed my tray through the window.

Mrs. Old Bill called from the kitchen. "Any need to wash that one, Stoney?"

"No, ma'am," I said. "Already done that."

She laughed and shook her head as she always did. She was round and kind and radiant with the secrets of the hearth.

"Dessert will be out in a minute," she said. I inflated my cheeks, clapped a hand to my stomach, and did a slow, comical about-face for her benefit. She laughed again.

Gwendolyn stood awkwardly, something I had thought her incapable of doing. She plunged both hands into her front jeans pockets and straightened her arms, which made her shoulders rise to her ears. She looked like a kid about to ask her father for an advance on her allowance.

"So did everything work out with that parent this morning?"

"Not sure. I'm hoping she called back today." I nodded toward the side porch. "I was just going to ask Old Bill about that."

Gwendolyn twisted at the waist and saw Old Bill waiting for me. Then she swung back to me.

"Well, just let me know if there is any way I can help."

"Thanks," I said.

She twisted the other way and checked the status of her table. All was quiet. Stephen Beasley smiled at Gwendolyn. Or, more probably, at Gwen. Or, even more probably, at Gwen's breasts. She twisted back again to Old Bill and sighed.

"Well," she said. If she twisted again, I thought about cinching her waspish waist between my hands, lifting her over my head to a horizontal position, dropping to one knee, and yelling *Viva la samba!*

"Are you going to have dessert?" she said.

"Depends on what it is. I need to talk to Bill first." I smiled and started past her.

"Stoney?" she said, almost stepping into my path.

I stopped, and she took half a step toward me and lowered her voice. "Thanks for this morning . . . your words, I mean. You know . . . your advice."

"You're welcome," I said.

"It's just, you know, I didn't think there would be a lot to do socially here and . . . well, I guess I sort of . . . like . . . jumped at the first chance."

"Are you kidding? Itawa is the epicenter of social events. We go to a folk dance in Sautee each session. We even have a movie. Do you like movies?"

"Sure," she chirped. She looked ready to grab her car keys.

The movie, *Survival on Blood Mountain,* was filmed in the '50s on location by some of Old Bill's canoeing cronies. He had shown it on the old sixteen-millimeter projector every year since I had known him. It was terrible cinema, but he considered it more important than Fellini or Bergman.

"Well, Gwendolyn, take heart. You are invited to the movies. It will be an experience you'll never forget."

When she smiled, the wattage boost in her teeth overflowed to the whites of her eyes. "Okay!" she said. "Sure! Thanks!"

"You may not want to thank me yet. Better wait till you've seen the film." I smiled and eased away. She raised her hand like a witness taking an oath, and she waved by bending her fingers over her palm.

At the nearest table, I caught Troy staring at me with a tight grin screwed onto his face. He raised his hand and waved exactly as Gwendolyn had. I gave him a pseudo-glare and went out on the porch.

The night air was pleasantly cool, still smelling of freshly cut grass. The sliver of first-quarter moon was already falling into the pines, hovering just high enough to bathe the lawn in a surreal glow of lunar green. T-Bone was stretched out on the planks next to Bill's feet. The old hound pushed himself up one leg at a time and walked to me for a scratch behind the ear but then seemed more interested in the spaghetti scents on my hands.

"Mrs. Raintree never called back," Old Bill said.

We stared at each other, sharing the weight of that piece of news. T-Bone ambled back to the screen door, where he could better intercept spaghetti fumes. Flopping down on his belly, he lowered his head over one front paw. I turned to face the lake and gripped both hands to the railing and leaned forward.

"Not good," I said staring at the stillness of the lake.

Bill stepped beside me and leaned on the railing, too, as if, since we were both connecting to the same problem, we had better look at it together from the same angle. The lake was so black, it might have been a crater that had opened up to swallow the light of day. It was probably the way the world looked to a ten-year-old boy whose parents were leaving each other.

"Bill, if we can't get a parent to contact us . . . we've got to consider that we might be in a pretty fragile position. Not to mention Tyler's position."

Old Bill nodded. "If we can't find out the status of their divorce or custody or whatever, I don't even know what to ask our lawyer."

"Maybe we'll need to talk to her lawyer," I suggested.

He exhaled a long, whistling sigh through his nose. "Maybe."

The screech owl that serenaded my cabin each night was getting cranked up. It was an eerie tremolo that I loved. This little bird of prey presided so regally over his dark domain that I always heard his nocturne as a writ of *habeas corpus* for me. He seemed to be asking me to come outside and state my reason for boxing myself up for the night inside four walls and a roof. He kept me thinking of going feral.

"Tyler told me they don't have 'caller ID'."

Bill turned his head to me. "Well, that's a good thing, right?"

"After this morning, Mr. Raintree might acquire caller ID." We were both quiet as we mulled over that possibility.

Finally, Bill made the little grunt deep in his chest that meant he had reached some decision. "You'd better go into Atlanta Saturday and call her from a phone down there," he said.

"I'd better go down there before Saturday. That's the day the Outriders are leaving for the Standing Bear trip. Might be better to catch her on a weekday anyway."

"All right. What'd you have planned for Friday?"

"My regular classes, packing food and gear for the trip . . . map study. Troy and Amanda can take my classes. Bobby Whitehorse can do the rest."

"All right. I guess if you can't get through to her you'll have to go by her house."

"And do what?"

"I don't know. Just do whatever you have to do to get this resolved."

"Okay," I said. "I'll go down Thursday night before supper. But if I have to engage in some clandestine activity—like finding her without engaging Mr. Raintree—I'll need something besides my truck. Something that won't look too out of place on Randall Mill Road. That's probably the richest neighborhood in Atlanta."

"What about one of the counselors? Justin has a pretty snazzy car."

I turned to stare at Old Bill's silhouette and wondered yet again how he could not know the true face of Justin Kent. I had about as much chance of using Justin's Corvette as I did fitting into Bobby Whitehorse's tiny boots. And I might have to sleep in the car. If I tried that in Justin's sleek phallic-mobile, I might never walk again.

"Too snazzy," I said. "That would draw attention, too."

He nodded. "Well, ask around, and I'll do the same. We'll come up with something."

The moon's thin smile was broken up in the black filigree of pines, and the lunar glow off the grass had dulled to a luteus gray. Old Bill dropped his elbows to the railing and sniffed, one of the many readable semaphores of his body language: This mission was set, and the conversation had come to a close.

"What's for dessert?" I said.

"Apple cobbler."

I pushed off the rail and straightened. "Duty calls." Bill made a token smile and nodded. I knew he was still tied up in the complications of the Raintree problem. "You gonna have some?" I said.

"Already did," he said. Neither rain nor sleet nor snow nor parental problem could stay us from our appointed confluence with Mrs. Old Bill's apple cobbler.

"You're the camp owner, Bill. You can have all you want."

He gave me a sidewise look. "I may be the camp owner, but Mrs. Old Bill runs my show."

T-Bone's eyes followed the edge of the door as I slowly hinged it over his muzzle to within a quarter inch of his brow. Otherwise, he did not move. I had to slip through the opening sideways. He either had unconditional trust in me or knew that cobblers and pies would eventually be my downfall. Maybe he was trying to save me. Or maybe he was just lazy. Through the screen I promised him some scrapped spaghetti from the garbage can. Still no movement. Complete motor control to achieve absolute passivity. Maybe T-Bone had a lot to teach me. He could be my inspiration if I had to stake out the Raintree house.

Working on my cobbler, I sat down with Amanda to talk about the upcoming trip to Standing Bear. The Outriders would not meet tomorrow as a group, and I needed her to do a little preparatory work, while I would be tied up with canoeing and archery.

P.J. approached with a strange look on her face. She set her empty bowl on our table and sat down next to me. Troy was right behind her. P.J. squinted at me as if my face was the Rosetta Stone.

"Stoney, why would a counselor call you a sissy for pulling that rock trick on Bobby Whitehorse? You carried those rocks a lot farther than he did."

I looked around for Bobby, wondering what he was up to. "He and I were just have fun with each other, P.J. Bobby is not serious. He's probably plotting revenge for me, and you're playing some innocent part in his diabolical plan."

"No," P.J. said, "it wasn't Bobby who said it." My head came up automatically to the counselor table. Justin was slumped back in his chair listening to Jimmy Dale Vickers' monotonic presentation on, no doubt, anything that touched on motorcycles. "It was the new lady who's in charge of the girls," P.J. said.

My head came back around, and I stared at P.J. "Abby?"

P.J. shrugged. "That's what she said."

I looked at the back of Abby Parrish's head. As I did, she turned in profile to answer a question from the little girl next to her. Abby's expression was calm and confiding. The camper was probably talking about problems with her bunkmate, but Abby listened as if they were discussing peace talks in the Middle East. I wondered what in the world Abby might have heard about the rock incident. I was surprised at the urgency I felt to correct her assessment of me. *Sissy?*

"That's not what she said, P.J.," Troy corrected. He made a sheepish smile and glanced obliquely at me before leaning to within a couple of inches of my ear. "I think she might have said something about syphilis," he whispered.

I felt my face tighten, and I stared at the back of Abby's head again. *Where had this come from?* I couldn't even imagine the word coming out of Abby's mouth . . . not in the presence of campers. Bobby Whitehorse sat down across from me with two bowls of cobbler. Without looking at any of us, he started in on one bowl.

"How'd you get two?" Troy asked.

Bobby's eyes were black marbles but for the little spark of humor about to ignite. He stopped chewing and waited a beat.

"Legerdemain," he said, not without some degree of satisfaction. He savored another spoonful as he kept his eyes on me. "Don't take it so hard, Gray Eyes." He bobbed his spoon toward his desserts. "One day—under my tutelage—you'll be able to pull off this sleight of hand."

I turned my attention back to Troy. The sissy-syphilis problem easily trumped my quest for extra cobbler.

"What exactly did Abby say?"

Troy's face colored as he wrestled with getting the words right. "She said you and Bobby must have some—" He lowered his voice again. ". . . Some syphilis in you."

Bobby's spoon stopped halfway to his mouth. He began chuckling silently from deep in his belly until he was laughing so hard that tears made their way to the slant of his cheekbones and clung there like beads of glass.

"That's funny?" I asked.

He let his eyes rove over the room as if taking his bearings on how to present to me the benefit of his insight. Then his thespian proclivities took over and he laid down his spoon.

"A man's reputation with his shooter is sometimes all he's got." He waited ten seconds and winked. "*Stand Tall with a Gun.* Glenn Ford to Lee J. Cobb." He took another bite and spoke around the cobbler. "Sisyphus," he said smiling. He wiped his napkin across his mouth without disturbing his smile. "From mythology. That's what Abby said."

I dropped my forehead into the cradle of my hand and laughed quietly. My vanity sank back into the dark core of me like a scolded dog.

"What's Sisyphus?" Troy said.

Bobby moved the cobbler around in his bowl with the spoon and began to chuckle again. "Not 'what' but 'who,' " Bobby began. "From Greek mythology. Old Sisyphus was always playing tricks on people, but he played one too many and was given the punishment of rolling a big rock up to the top of a hill. Every time he got near the top, the rock—by preordained retribution—would slip from his grasp and roll back down the hill. Then he would have to start over." Bobby pointed his index at me and then his thumb at himself. "We got some Sisyphus in us all right."

When I looked back at Abby she was still in rapt conversation with her wide-eyed friend. She was steadily accruing positive marks with me. First spunk, then compassion, and now literacy. I had to give her three gold stars. I watched her cross the room. She was wearing a pair of faded Western Carolina gym shorts. She had been wearing jeans on the first day of camp, so this was my first view of her legs. They were lean and shapely and toasty-brown. She looked strong. As my eyes tracked her across the room I didn't blink once. Maybe four gold stars.

Chapter Eight

Early Wednesday morning, flaming with wisps of steam after my run, I dove into the lake and sprinted to the canoe dock and back and muscled up onto my tiny landing—planting both feet at once just to see if I could do it. I stood there dripping, breathing like a racehorse and enjoying the subtle edge I always felt at getting a jump on the day at first light. The eastern sky had lost its violet blush and was now washed out into the transitional gray that would, in minutes, brighten to cornflower blue.

In the grainy light I saw movement on the lawn between the office and dining hall. Someone was running across the slope toward the sports field. When the runner hit the top of the hill he broke into a walk. It took two more seconds to see that *he* was a *she*. Abby Parrish disappeared over the horizon line on her way to her cabin. She had probably been running on the dirt road. Judging by the smooth stride I'd seen, I knew it was something she did on a regular basis.

Over coffee and cocoa, Bobby Whitehorse and I sat in my cabin and discussed preparations for the Standing Bear trip. When we got around to talking about my upcoming mission in Atlanta, Bobby set his cup on the table and tapped his finger on the rim like a metronome.

"Works better with two," he said. "One to keep an eye on the big picture while the other goes in close. We could use those walkie-talkies Old Bill got last winter."

"If this takes two nights that leaves no one to take the Outriders to Standing Bear. And if things go badly, I might be able to talk my way out of it. A full-blooded Cherokee built like a sack of concrete might not fare as well in a Buckhead neighborhood."

Bobby looked at me long and hard. "When you were eleven, in spite of your belligerent exterior, no camper I had ever known had given his eye to tracking as you did . . . and no leg to stalking. And you only got better through the years. Some people are born to it. You are one of those, Gray Eyes. All you needed was to lose the chip on your shoulder."

I sat very still, holding my cup with both hands, looking down at the dregs of my cocoa. Bobby Whitehorse seldom chained so many sentences together at any one time.

"When you were twelve," he continued, "you tracked me to the top of Hogback Mountain. At thirteen, on a bet, you stalked with scissors in hand into the male staff cabin and returned with a lock of hair from that sadistic bodybuilder. What was his name?"

"Roger Nuttycombe," I said. I pictured the mini-scalp that still hung above my archery plaque in the office. I remembered when Old Bill had finally noticed it and said to me, "I think I'll not ask about that one."

"By fourteen," Bobby went on, "you were hunting rabbit with a throwing stick. And on it went. But through those years you still wore that chip."

I nodded, remembering that version of myself. It had taken me a long time to come around, to rise above the history of my father's abuse. To have been nestled under the wing of Bobby Whitehorse was like a lost snarling puppy being toted off by the scruff of his neck by a charitable wolf. And if Bobby hadn't done it, I would have gone right off the edge of the mountain of trouble I was heaping up for myself.

"What are you getting at, Bobby?"

He finished his coffee and carried his cup to my wash basin. When he walked back, he remained standing above me, studying my face.

"Remember what it took to get where you are, Gray Eyes. Keep yourself sharp. Listen to everything around you."

I looked up into the intensity of his dark eyes. "I will."

I, too, knew it would be best if we both went to Atlanta. Bobby enjoyed a kind of underground reputation in Lumpkin County. Sheriffs Cantrell, Beck, and Canaday all had hired him as a tracker, but at Bobby's request they had never revealed his name to the newspapers.

When I was sixteen, during the time Bobby had served eleven months in Alto, Old Bill had sent me alone when the sheriff needed help. No one could have filled Bobby's boots in the intuitive part of tracking, but I had gotten pretty good with subtle signs. Together we were "the ultimate tracking team"—his words, not mine. After he came back from prison we took all tracking assignments as a team, and we simply never quit until we reached the "bingo track"—Bobby's phrase for a footprint with the foot still inside it.

We walked outside where he had tethered a big yellow sorrel named Custard to a crooked laurel trunk. The soaped saddle leather croaked like a bullfrog when he stood in the stirrup. He eased his free leg over and sat his horse with a dignity I had never seen equaled—as though the horse elevated Bobby to the rightful stature that nature had not afforded him. Looking straight ahead, he arranged the reins loosely between two thick fingers and spoke with quiet conviction.

"Enter it like it is more than it is," he said. Then he looked me squarely in the eye. "You never know."

It was the tracker's adage that could not be voiced too many times. "You never know," I repeated.

When he leaned, horse and rider turned as one to weave through the trees. Bobby's broad back shifted rhythmically with the horse's gait, rays of light from the sun blinking on him like a vintage film. And a Western, at that.

Last winter we had tracked a fourteen-year-old boy lost from a family outing on the Appalachian Trail. Bobby and I had followed his signs from the top of Blood Mountain to the headwaters of Frogtown Creek, where the "lost" boy opened fire on us with a .22 automatic pistol. The boy's parents had not told us he was a runaway. Nor had they mentioned a gun.

No one was hurt, and I was able to talk him out of his hiding place, but Bobby and I talked about that incident over several campfires. We'd had no idea we were tracking someone armed and dangerous. From that experience, we'd made a pledge. We would always enter a tracking scenario as if it were more than it was.

You never knew.

I had pressed Tyler to sign up for one of my classes today, archery or whitewater canoeing. Not only did I want to introduce his imprisoned spirit to the grace of a canoe gliding over water or the burst of freedom in an arrow's flight, but also I had an ulterior motive. I needed to learn all I could about his home and environs.

Good fortune was with me. He signed up for both classes.

I needed to find out as much as I could about where I would be skulking around to contact Tyler's mother. On the lake, I found more ways than I would have thought possible to draw analogies between a canoe and an expensive home in Atlanta.

"If you hear water rippling at the bow," I said to the class of tandem boaters, "get more weight to the stern and the boat will glide better. This rippling sound is like an alarm letting you know that something is wrong." Then with hardly a pause I said, "Kind of like a security system in a house. How many of you have alarm systems at home?"

In my peripheral vision, I saw most of the kids raise their hands, but I paid attention only to Tyler. When he did not raise his hand, I breathed a little sigh of relief.

Tyler was like most beginner paddlers, sitting up too straight in the boat, angling the paddle out too far like an oar, using too much arm rather than torso. I pulled alongside his boat.

"I've got a few tricks to show you that will help your boat to move faster with less effort."

Tyler's partner, Jamal, was a strong, twelve-year-old African American who had taken canoeing from me last year. This year he had taken the step into Outriders.

"After I show you these tricks," I said to Tyler, "then Jamal can help you perfect them." I looked back at Jamal for confirmation. He smiled broadly and nodded.

When I had finished a barrage of seven or eight fine points, both boys looked like they had stumbled out of a seminar on quantum physics.

"I don't know if I can remember all that," Tyler said.

"I *know* I can't," Jamal murmured under his breath.

I nodded thoughtfully. "Okay, let's do a memory exercise first, then we'll go over it all again." Tyler looked straight ahead and sighed. Jamal stared at me as if I had suggested we diagram all our sentences and translate them into Arabic.

I gave them clipboards and sat them on the edge of the dock with their backs to me. They looked so innocent and attentive, I almost felt guilty for doing this. But then I thought: *Enter it like it is more than it is*. I could rationalize with the best of them.

"Pretend you are a bird looking down on your house with the roof removed. Draw the shape of your house. Best way to do that is to put the rooms together like the pieces of a puzzle."

Jamal twisted around, his face earnest. "I'm supposed to pretend I'm a bird and draw a picture?"

"An artistic bird," I said and motioned him around to start working.

Tyler started pushing a slow, meticulous line across the paper, like a first grader attempting to follow a line underneath his tracing paper. Jamal peeked to see if I was serious. I gave him a reassuring nod.

"Which floor?" Jamal said.

"Ground floor," I instructed. Tyler stopped his pencil, stared at his mark, then turned the pencil around and erased all he had drawn. "Start with the room that has your television."

"Which one?" Jamal said.

"Which one *what*?" I said.

"Which television?"

"The one downstairs," I said.

"Yeah, I know but . . . like . . . which one?"

I closed my eyes and inhaled deeply. "The biggest TV, Jamal."

He leaned over his clipboard with new enthusiasm. I walked them through each room then had them flip the page over for the second floor. I learned from Tyler that a Hispanic woman named Maya cleaned their house. She lived in the downstairs bedroom but left on weekends to be with her own family. By now Tyler and Jamal were so involved in their maps that any relevance to canoeing was out of mind.

"What about your yards?" I said. Tyler's head came up with a blank expression. "Put a small circle outside the house everywhere you remember a tree. The size of the circle should represent the size of the tree trunk." In minutes Tyler's paper was polka-dotted with circles on one side of his house. "Looks like you've got some woods there, Tyler." With his face inches from his paper, he continued the pattern around the back to the other side of the house. Leaning over his shoulder, I felt my hopes rise. "Looks like you guys have big yards. Do either of you have a dog?"

Jamal turned to me and beamed. "I got a Welsh corgi named 'Shorty.'"

"How about you, Tyler?" I probed casually.

"I don't have a dog," he mumbled. I lifted a grateful smile to the mountains. "But my father keeps a Rottweiler chained in the backyard." I kept looking at the mountains and felt my face sag. I mouthed the word "Rottweiler."

The archery range was right next to the sports area, the arrow backstop a huge hydro-seeded slope carved out of the mountain when the sports field had been leveled by dozers. Lined up at the base of the slope were three colorful targets on tripod stands that Bobby and I had nailed together from treated two-by-fours.

Our esoteric weaponry always lured some of the sports class to the yellow rope that cordoned off the range. As usual, Justin stayed busy shooing his campers back like voyeurs caught in the act, shaming them for slipping down the hierarchy of jock-dom from manly ball-sports to shooting arrows.

Amanda, my paragon of the archer's string release, was helping me with the class as I talked to Tyler about dog behavior, family habits, meals, bedtimes, chores, and things of that sort. My clandestine investigation continued to fare well. I doubt that anyone had ever paid this much attention to the life of Tyler Raintree. After a handful of shy, laconic answers at the lake, now he was giving me paragraphs, then chapters, and I had to stop him if we were to get through the fundamentals of the bow and arrow today.

When the period ended and the sports class had disbanded, I asked my archers to stay behind a couple of minutes before going to lunch. I walked them diagonally across the empty sports field where we gathered into a semi-circle with me and my bow at its center.

"About a thousand years ago, the shot you are about to see was very useful," I said as I loaded. "See if you can guess how." I stopped Amanda with my eyes before she could answer. Settling into a wide stance with my torso partially reclined, I raised the bow until my arrow angled up so high it must have looked like I was shooting at the sun. Carefully, so as not to break from my line of aim, I drew the string.

When I released the string, the feathers whined, and the arrow soared gracefully to an apex some three hundred feet above the field. As it slowed and tilted back to earth, I stole a peek at the campers. Every mouth was open, every eye trained on the falling arrow, and all breathing suspended. Baby birds in a nest. The arrow picked up speed and dropped neatly behind the center target.

"Cool!" someone squealed. Everyone was squirming, bug-eyed, dying to shoot more.

"Is that how the Indians got eagle feathers?" P.J. asked.

Before I could answer, Tyler said, "What about shooting into castles?" They all looked at him. They knew a good answer when they heard one. Amanda was smiling and nodding.

"Of all the shots you will learn, the clout shot is the most difficult for accuracy. There is so much room for error. You'll be trying it in a few days after you get down the direct shot." As it did every year, the seed took root inside their eager souls.

"So why use it if it's so inaccurate?" Stephen Beasley said.

"Imagine an army of archers . . . say a hundred men shooting at once. That's a hundred arrows raining down on a castle at the same time. Pretty demoralizing."

"Yeah, but why use it if so many are going to miss?" the Beez argued. "Nobody could hit anything from that far anyway, no matter how you shot it." Since Stephen had everyone's attention, naturally he pushed it to the edge. "I mean, what if a guy was mooning you from the castle wall?" Some of the campers giggled. Then, as the Beez assumed the mooning position and smiled at us upside down between his legs, a few boys doubled up laughing.

"Stoney could!" Amanda yelled over the laughter. Even I stopped breathing. I had never heard anything louder from her than a clipped monotone. "He could with a direct shot," she explained.

"Let's see you!" the Beez dared me.

Amanda's eyes begged me to prove her right.

"Can you really hit a target from here, Stoney?" Tyler said.

There was more purpose glowing in his face in that moment than I had seen in the past two and a half days combined. I had been bombarding him with questions all morning. Now he had asked me *one*. The other faces in the crowd were a picture of anticipation. And that was when I saw Abby. She had joined our group and was standing quietly in the back. She gave me the Joan of Arc smile. I took in a breath and looked downfield at the target some eighty yards away. If I *couldn't* do this shot, then I wasn't who they thought I was . . . or, more importantly, who *I* thought I was.

I drew an arrow from my quiver and settled into my stance. Just before I blocked out all sound and ambient distractions, I heard the chatter of expectation swell and Amanda's peremptory *"Shhh!"* which stilled the crowd.

The wind touched the right side of my face. The center target came into clear focus, and the rest of the world blurred into irrelevance. I engaged the abstract appraisal of distance—not in yards or in feet, but in the arcane terms that I could never explain to anyone who asked. With my arrow point I etched a vertical line up into the grassy bevel until the target was completely hidden by my hand holding the bow.

When my string hand relaxed and the arrow leapt out into space, the gears of the universe seemed to lock into an immediate stillness for the time it took the shaft to complete its elegant arc. Our group stood at the edge of the world, looking down at something we had dropped to see where it would land. But I already knew. The moment of release always tells me when I have a true shot. The shallow curve of the arrow's flight seemed preordained to intersect with the distant target.

As we watched, the multi-colored concentric rings of the cloth target face shuttered and rippled with shadow just before we heard the report. I heard the cheers behind me suddenly, as if someone had turned the sound back on in the middle of a TV game show. I looked at Amanda. She smiled a smile that I would have walked to the top of Standing Bear Dome to see. Tyler stared at me as if I had just pulled a buffalo out of a fedora. Abby held fast to Joan of Arc and made a little bow with her head. The Beez was prostrate and screaming, no doubt seeing a mooning Norman sentry writhing on the castle wall with an arrow protruding from his backside.

"Go get lunch, everybody," I said and motioned with my bow toward the Beez. "And take this wounded hyena with you."

They left the field walking as quickly as they chattered—the Beez louder than all the rest. Abby walked over to me and smiled.

"That was impressive," she said.

"It helps for them to see it. Now, when I teach them, they'll listen."

She tilted her head and raised her eyebrows in the same rhythm. "Wow," she said. "Something in this world still works on merit."

Actually, most things in my life worked on merit—which was one reason I was still a camp counselor. But I knew exactly what she meant. Outside Itawa's gate there was another set of rules I didn't care to engage. Out there, it was not what-you-did . . . but whom-you-knew and what-they-could-do-for-you. At least, that was my take on it.

"How are your classes going, Abby?"

She thought for a moment. "Good. I like Itawa."

I nodded. "Me, too." Then I looked at her and squinted one eye. "I guess it's a leap going from a high school English class to a mob of pre-teens at a summer camp?"

She seesawed her head from side to side. "In some ways it's easier. These kids' minds are still open to new ideas, and they aren't yet obsessed with what they wear and how they look."

I pursed my lips and nodded, remembering what I had disliked about my high school years.

"On the other hand," she added with a laugh, "I didn't have to listen to quite so much bathroom humor in my English classes.".

Abby looked different to me every time I saw her. I knew she wasn't visibly making changes. She was simply one of those people who did not present herself all at once. The only way to get to know her was slowly. And in each increment, as I learned something new about her, her appearance seemed to alter, making the lines of her face more and more interesting.

I pointed to the targets. "I need to go down and get a couple of arrows. Want to walk?"

We had covered half the distance when she broke the comfortable bubble of silence that had surrounded us. "Gwendolyn said you were some kind of national champion in archery." She pointed to my arrow in the target. "I can believe it."

I almost explained that my archery championship had been regional, covering six states, but the distinction felt too petty to voice with Abby. My back was to her as I pulled the arrow from the target. I closed my eyes, laughed quietly, and shook my head. I couldn't remember reacting like this to anyone since I was in the eighth grade and wanted Mary Lou Deschene—a senior—to notice me. Maybe I should hunt up my old report cards from high school and show them to Abby. I had, after all, gotten mostly A's in English.

"Not quite that impressive," I said.

I walked behind the target and retrieved the clout shot. When I came back to her I noticed the sunlight on her cheek made a soft healthy glow. She had on a sleeveless T-shirt, revealing her shoulders and arms, which looked strong without being overly muscular. Abby Parrish, I realized, was very nice to look at.

"Mr. Wellborne told me you might need to borrow my car tomorrow?"

A little wave of disappointment passed through me, and the feeling took me a little by surprise. I had to let go of the idea that Abby had come out on the field on a social call.

"What kind of car do you have?"

"It's a fifteen-year-old Volvo."

I felt my eyebrows float up. An old Volvo just might pass for something vintage among Buckhead's elite. For Abby it was a safe car with a protective frame. For a north Atlantan to the manor born, it might be a grassroots statement—sort of a Great Gatsby look for arriving at the tennis courts or taking a jaunt to the store for Perrier.

"Have you had lunch yet?" I asked. She shook her head. I swept a hand toward the dining hall. "I know a great place close by. Do you like really noisy kids and food fights?"

As we walked off together, she narrowed her eyes and nodded. "I think I know this place."

The dining hall was in full-carnage-tilt when Abby and I asked for two late trays. We sat at a table near the door where we might have a semblance of privacy. Just after spreading my napkin in my lap, I looked over Abby's shoulder and saw Troy giving me a Cheshire cat grin while doing the little Gwendolyn wave with his fingers. This time I smiled and waved back.

"Fan club?" Abby said, her eyes twinkling.

I shook my head. "Chaperone."

Abby knitted her eyebrows, turned, and caught Troy off guard. He suddenly became interested in the texture of his bread.

"I like Troy," she said.

Troy would not have looked back at me now if I'd set myself on fire. "He's been an Outrider for two years and fast becoming my right hand. He's teaching *me* now."

"According to him," Abby said, "ninety-nine per cent of everything he knows—that is worth knowing—he learned from you."

I chuckled. "He probably knows ninety-nine per cent of everything I know."

"What will you do when he gets the other one per cent?"

"Start making stuff up, I guess."

This time I got the Emmy Lou Harris smile, which I liked a lot. Abby's slate gray eyes brightened when she smiled, radiant and fragile all at the same time, like a thin flake of mica. I watched the smile linger as she tilted her head and removed the processed cheese from her sandwich. She laid it to one side of her tray.

I was again amazed at the evolution of her appearance as I got to know her better. There was a strength in her that she carried quietly, but that strength did not get in the way of her kindness. I imagined her in the lead role of a story Bobby Whitehorse had once told me about an Indian maiden who returned a bear cub to its mother by walking confidently into the she-bear's cave. It was easy to see Abby walking out of that dark recess wearing the same serene expression she wore as she reassembled her sandwich. She was very comfortable with herself. I was very comfortable with herself, too.

With my sheath knife I sliced a red dome from my apple and ate it, as I scanned the room for Tyler. He was sitting at the table where the Beez was holding court. I cut a wedge of apple and offered it to Abby. She glanced at her own apple and hesitated.

"Is this payback for the Garden of Eden?" she said.

I shook my head. "Tastes better when you cut it with a knife." She slipped it off the blade and popped it into her mouth. "We have a camper whose parents have put us in a tight spot. They're divorcing, and apparently the mother is hiding the son here from his father. Not only do we not want to get in the middle of this, but the boy thinks his father may be dangerous. So, we need to know what to do if he shows up."

She took a bite of her sandwich and looked into my eyes, the full force of her attention on me—just like those times I had seen her conversing with campers. She was genuine and non-patronizing, and I knew in that moment that, in Abby Parrish, Itawa had added another jewel to its crown.

"Hadn't you better speak with their lawyers to know how it really stands?" she said. "You seldom get the whole story from one side."

"Yeah, but the catch is . . . the boy is afraid of his father. And legal or not, I don't want to hand him over to a dangerous situation."

Abby put down her sandwich. "There's not much you can do about that. You can't stand between the boy and either parent until the court rules on custody."

"That doesn't help the boy if his father is abusive. Mostly I want to talk to *her* lawyer."

"Why can't you just call him or her?"

I started in on my sandwich and reminded myself not to talk while chewing. Abby reached for my knife and made a first incision into her apple.

"We don't know who the lawyer is. We aren't having any luck calling the mother. The father screens the calls. The one time I got through to her, somebody else picked up on the line so I asked her to call me back. It's been over twenty-four hours now, and we haven't heard a thing. Old Bill wants me to go down to Atlanta and find a way to have a talk with her."

"Maybe I should go," Abby suggested. "Being a female, I might be better received at the door."

I paused with my sandwich before my mouth and considered the offer. I didn't doubt that Abby would be better at a parley with Mrs. Raintree than I would. But Tyler's father worried me. I put down my sandwich and lowered my voice.

"The thing is, Abby . . . the camper thinks I should have a gun."

Abby stopped chewing. Her eyes bored into me like ten penny nails.

"The reason we are looking for a car is that I may need to sit on their street a while to figure out how to get to her. It's the rich side of town. If I used my truck, it would stand out in the neighborhood. It might even get picked up by the city sanitation service."

Abby didn't smile. Over her shoulder I saw Tyler approach us in a hesitant shuffle. I took a bite out of my sandwich and waved him over. He approached and stared at the side of Abby's face. When she smiled and greeted him, he looked down at his feet. Abby narrowed her eyes at me and took a bite of her sandwich.

"Troy said you are having another archery class after lunch," Tyler mumbled. "Can I come to it again . . . instead of riflery?"

A wave of gratitude spread through my chest. The arc of a soaring arrow had spoken to this boy, maybe the same way it had spoken to me when I was his age.

"Sure. Tell Justin I said it was okay." The sun rose in Tyler's face. He looked at Abby as if she had witnessed a wonderful turning point in the course of human affairs. She smiled and patted the bench next to her leg, and Tyler eagerly climbed through and sat down.

"Stoney, how did you get so good with a bow and arrow?" he asked.

I thought about that a while, trying to gauge my words for a little boy just taking up a new skill. "Well, first of all, I had Bobby Whitehorse. He taught me what had been handed down to him by his grandfather. Now it'll all be handed down to you."

Tyler's face screwed up with a question. "But Bobby Whitehorse said you were the best archer he'd ever seen. He said he learned some things from you." When I laughed, Tyler looked at me as though I were an abstract painting in a museum. He seemed to have forgotten that Abby was there. "What's your real job, Stoney?"

I laughed again and looked at Abby, who was obviously enjoying her anonymity and front row seat in this impromptu interview. I stacked my forearms on the tabletop and ducked my head to Tyler's level.

"This is it. Being a counselor at Itawa is what I do."

"But what about when it's not summer?"

"I still work here . . . repairing things, building things, clearing trails, cutting firewood. And I teach an occasional nature class over at New Horizons . . . that school for juvenile delinquents—which, of course, helps me get ready for all you guys." I smiled, but I think the joke was lost on him.

Tyler's face registered mild shock. "You mean you don't go somewhere and . . . you know . . . like . . . work?"

I sat back and held his gaze. His expression was dead earnest.

"Troy said you work for the sheriff sometimes . . . tracking people."

"Well, that's sort of community work . . . volunteer stuff."

Now he looked at Abby for corroboration. She had finished her sandwich and was cradling her chin in her hand, her elbow propped on the table. She lifted her eyebrows, smiled at Tyler, and canted her head toward me.

"*I* believe him."

He thought about that until the next question popped out. "Do you have a suit?"

In my peripheral vision, I saw Abby shift her face in her hand so that her palm covered her mouth. "I have two," I said. He seemed interested in that. I let it stand for a few seconds before I elaborated. "My swimsuit and my birthday suit. I think you've seen both of them."

"On that note—" said Abby, rising from the table.

Tyler wasn't going anywhere. I could see at least six more questions in his eyes.

"I'll see you, Abby," I said. "I'll talk to you later about the car." She shook her head and carried her tray to the window. I wondered what that headshake meant. Maybe Abby didn't want her car mixed up in something that could turn testy. I didn't blame her. She hardly knew me. She was probably imagining her Volvo riddled with bullet holes.

"Before you did this, did you used to have a job where you wore a suit?"

"Tyler, what is all this about 'a suit'?"

Abby appeared again and stood next to Tyler as he continued his interview with a suit-less man. He kept his eyes trained on me.

"Are you really older than all the other counselors?"

"I'm closing in on twenty."

His eyes roamed over my face and hair and torso. "You don't look that old."

"Tyler, I'll give you three little gems about the secrets of life." I splayed my hands on the tabletop and leaned closer to him. He leaned on his forearms like my mirror image. "One, every guy doesn't need a suit. Two, guys generally like to look older than they really are." I leaned closer. "But you should reverse that for females."

Tyler stared at me with his mouth open as he nodded.

"And three, if you want to stay forever young, choose a career you love."

I felt something metallic slide under my left palm. When I broke from Tyler's gaze, I looked up to see Abby walking toward the door. I knew what was under my hand and slid it back to the edge of the table without a sound.

"We'd better get to archery class," I reminded.

He stood when I did. "Will you do another one of those high shots?"

"Sure." I picked up my tray. "Why don't you go on up and help Troy set up. This class is full of last year's archers. Everyone will be shooting this time."

His eyes showed a ring of white fire around each iris. "Me, too?"

When I nodded, he made a beeline for the door. It was the first time I had seen him run. Andy, who was on dining hall duty, leveled a finger at him to slow down. Tyler shifted to a fast walk, hardly losing any speed.

On the front porch, I opened up my hand and looked at Abby's key. It was an ordinary silver car key with the word "Volvo" raised on the flat head. But I couldn't shake the feeling that there was more than a piece of metal here. The key seemed to possess some private resonation of Abby's concern. *Be careful,* it said.

I put the key in the little coin pocket in the front of my jeans. *I will*, I thought.

Chapter Nine

On Thursday, I left camp right after lunch. Abby's Volvo cruised down Georgia 400 like a schooner on glassy water. Curious about her, I looked around the interior of the car. Her CDs were stacked inside the console along with a tube of lip gloss, loose change, a felt-tip pen, and a small cloth-bound notebook. A stained cardboard cup from Caribou Coffee sat upright in the drink holder. Inside it was a tangle of dental floss. Now we had something in common to talk about when I got back to camp: I wondered if she used her knees on the steering wheel like I did? Did Joan of Arc ever floss on horseback?

On the backseat was a book by Cormac McCarthy with a crow feather as a page marker. Next to it sat a hardback dictionary. I smiled. I, too, read McCarthy with a dictionary close by. Sometimes it felt like I was reading the dictionary with McCarthy close by. I reached down on the floor to see what I kept kicking with my heel. A pair of old running shoes was partway jammed under the seat. Each of her possessions whispered of some facet of her life and reminded me that I was a guest, admitted into this space on trust. I liked the thought of somehow having gained Abby's trust. Maybe I had Troy to thank for that.

For the next half hour, I thought through my plans and inventoried my supplies: sleeping bag, rope, camo clothing, one of Old Bill's sports coats, presentable sweats, and some of my canoeing clothes. In a cooler, I'd packed two-days'-worth of sandwiches plus a patty of raw ground beef in a Zip-loc. I also had a prescription bottle of tranquilizers I'd borrowed from the tack room. Bobby Whitehorse's idea. When I reached a point where I could plan no more without actually seeing Tyler's house and the exact lay of the land around it, I relaxed and enjoyed the scenery. The verdant fields that rolled into the piedmont north of Alpharetta were my last glimpse of sanity before entering the fray.

When the traffic began its subtle swell, I began to encounter those meaningless bottlenecks that slowed all lanes then mysteriously cleared. During one of these congested lulls, I reached into the console and picked at random one of Abby's CDs. It was Aaron Copland. Beginning to rethink my position on omens, I pushed in the CD and relaxed against the headrest as the string section swirled around me like a benevolent eddy stirred by the wings of angels.

If memory served me, Abby Parrish was up to six gold stars. I could think of a few constellations with less.

I would do anything to avoid Interstate 285, the perimeter highway that once skirted Atlanta and now strangled it. I took the Glenridge connector into Sandy Springs and then worked my way through the outlying neighborhoods of the almost rich and famous into the expensive heart of the Buckhead elite. West Paces Ferry Road was a showcase of surplus money. I passed homes that could have been Federal Reserve Banks or hangars for dirigibles. The lawns alone would keep a hundred landscaping businesses in the black.

At Randall Mill, I turned and checked the first mailbox for a number; then I started paying attention to everything. Around one curve, I veered from a female jogger tethered to a svelte animal with unusually long shaggy hair that hung like a wig from its pate and tail. I was pretty sure it was a dog, though, if pressed to describe its origin, I might have to guess a hybrid cross of antelope and Uma Thurman.

The road plunged into a valley steeper than I would have expected this far from the mountains. Judging from the last mailbox, I knew Tyler's house would pop up soon, but here a long stretch of woods interrupted the chain of palaces. I slowed for the bump of the upcoming bridge. To either side, trees arched over a creek I could not see for the ugly concrete walls that framed the bridge.

Just past the creek on my right, crepe myrtle partially concealed a dry-stacked wall and wrought iron gate. Tyler's mailbox number flashed past me. As the road climbed out of the valley, I mentally reviewed what I had seen: the creek canopied by a lush tunnel of box elders; then the house set back forty yards from the front gate; and across the street a neighbor's house with a sign hanging out front—*Wyntermoor*. My spirits ratcheted up a notch. Tyler had not drawn the creek on his map. It was a passageway to dream for. My entrance into the Raintree estate.

I drove around the block to get an idea of what lay behind the house, but the block was more like a country unto itself. With the roads curving so, I had no idea when I was on the backside of the Raintree property and no real sense of distance back to Randall Mill. On my second pass by their house, I began to look for the best place to park Abby's car without arousing suspicion. There had been six signs around the block that warned people with evil designs that a neighborhood security cruiser patrolled the streets regularly. It was good to know, but nothing that would alter my plans.

I was scoping out the same kind of parking place teenagers would be looking for on a Saturday night, but there was nothing promising, so I decided to go have a last hot meal before an indeterminate stint of staking-out. Later, I might decide to jog back to Tyler's neighborhood from a distance, which was why I'd brought along my best sweats. Walking this street at dusk would draw attention to me. Jogging was my passport into the landed gentry. Even better if I had brought a svelte dog with a wig on a leash, but I could never have talked T-Bone into such an embarrassing get-up.

At a shopping center about a mile away, I found a place called the *OK Café,* where I was pleased to find on the menu a home-baked chicken pot pie and fresh vegetables and apple pie. If I had success in my mission, I decided it was only fitting that I return here for a celebration meal. If I failed, I would probably need to return here just to lift my spirits. The third possibility was ordering their take-out from jail. My one phone call.

After eating, I called Tyler's house from the restaurant. My night would be a lot easier if Mrs. Raintree answered. No such luck. A terse male voice came on the line and asked me point blank what I wanted. I thickened my voice and tried for suave and confident.

"This is Tom McKey at Pace. I'm Tyler's curriculum advisor. I was hoping I—"

"Tyler is not going to Pace next year," he interrupted. Then he hung up.

I had milked the advisor's name from Tyler during my inquisition at archery class. I had figured Beau knew little about Tyler's school agenda and might default to his wife. So much for the assumed-identity approach.

At dusk I drove Randall Mill again and met with a bit of serendipity. Across the street from the Raintree property, a line of parked cars now spilled from the pebbled drive out to the curb of the street. Apparently, *Wyntermoor* was hosting a fortuitously timed soiree.

"Let 'er buck, boys," I said quietly, borrowing one of Bobby Whitehorse's favorite cowboy phrases. A security cruiser with two patrolmen passed me in the opposite direction. Both men were talking, and neither looked at me. When the cruiser disappeared in my mirror, I U-turned, parked three cars up from *Wyntermoor,* and chuckled out loud. I was sitting behind another vintage Volvo.

Lying down on the back seat, I changed into running shorts, a dark, pullover shirt, black watch cap, and my neoprene paddling booties. I packed everything I would need for the next few hours into my daypack. I wouldn't be able to leave Abby's car here longer than that. When a car pulled up behind me, I slid to the floor and pulled a blanket over me. The couple that walked past me was very quiet, only the tap of their shoes on the pavement marking their passing.

One minute later when the front door of *Wyntermoor* opened, I heard their voices chime with exuberant animation as if their host had interrupted their buoyant approach to the house. When the voices were muffled by the closing of the door, I listened for cars for five seconds and then stepped out on the street, pressed the door shut, and loped under the lone streetlight to the bridge. One more upper-crust jogger getting a late start on exercise at the end of his busy day at the office. In a suit.

It is the unwritten law of bridges: There is always a path somewhere beside it that leads down to the water. If it's not for the homeless or for fishermen, then it's where neighborhood kids answer the call of the wild. This bridge was no exception. A worn trail dropped in rocky tiers toward the murmuring water. As I peered down into the dark, the thick unnatural vapors of an urban stream enveloped me like a dirty mask soaked in cleaning chemicals. Around the curve, headlights lanced through the night and illuminated the trees, clicking shadows in an eerie, marching chain that flickered like an old silent film.

I dropped behind the guard wall and knelt, letting some of the diffused light show me what lay down below. I could make out blackberry brambles intruding into the steep path. Lots of them. With so many briers, I would need to take this slowly. But "slow" was the name of the game tonight. After the car rumbled across the bridge, I settled into stalking mode and picked my way through the brambles. At the creek, I eased into the water and moved with the patience of a heron single-mindedly stalking its prey in the shallows.

There are few paths quieter than a creek. Avoiding the swifter currents, I raised a foot an inch clear of the surface to let the water drip from my toe before progressing. Each step required the same care. There was no cutting corners in stalking. The one hasty move a careless stalker might try was the one that might be detected.

It took a half hour to get abreast of the house, where light from an upper window broke through the foliage exposing a trail to the yard, no doubt, pioneered by Tyler in his pre-computer days. By this light I realized that much of the jungled appearance of this creek was due to a robust stand of bamboo growing along the sandy floodplain. I slipped out of the backpack, sat on a log, removed my booties, dried my feet and legs with a small towel, pulled on wool socks and dry running shoes.

Using a small Mag-loc, I opened the Zip-loc of meat, broke up two veterinary tablets and pushed them into the patty. I wrapped the meat in a torn sheet of newspaper and fastened it with a rubber band to hold it together long enough for me to toss it to the Rottweiler. Sealing the package back into the plastic, I washed my hands with sand and water, left my pack, and climbed up the bank to the lawn at the side of Tyler's house.

When I first saw the dog, he was eating from a bowl. Tyler had told me his name was "Thor." His chain rattled constantly as he devoured his food. This was one hungry dog. There was no way he would pass up my fresh ground chuck. In the filtered light escaping through a back curtain and sliding glass door, he looked like a starved bear gutting a deer. The food bowl scraped around on the brick patio like an oversized hockey puck, making hollow, scraping sounds.

I felt my way across the soft lawn by inches using the corner of the house for cover. There was enough breeze in my face to keep my scent away from the dog. From the sound of that chain, it was heavy-duty, like the kind I imagined in castle dungeons. A thick chain was good, although it spoke volumes about the potential of the mighty Thor.

In maneuvering around his bowl, the dog finally swung his back to me. I was about twenty yards away. Seizing the moment, I rose up, slipped the package of meat out of the Zip-loc, took two warm-up underhand swings with my arm, and then lobbed the package in a high arc so that it appeared to drop from above. It was my first hamburger clout shot and one to be proud of. It thudded to the bricks two feet from the Rottweiler's thick head.

Startled, he recoiled, his claws scraping on the bricks as if a gun had discharged. Then he froze and stared at the ball of newsprint. He took one look toward the house then whipped his head back with new purpose and closed on the meat.

The entire package—paper, rubber band, and all—disappeared with one scoop of his massive jaws. He chewed and swallowed with violent jerks, sniffed the bricks for any remnants, licked them clean, and then returned to his bowl. With the bowl also licked clean, he checked the bricks again, licked a few more times, then sat down to stare at the backyard. Thor remained as motionless as a statue. Bobby Whitehorse used two of those pills to get a horse to lie down. If Thor could handle two without effect, he would alter my plans significantly.

I edged close to the house and eased down to a prone position on my side with my eyes just protruding around the corner. I slipped off my pullover hat and balled it up as a pillow for my head and got comfortable. Thor was getting comfortable, too. Without breaking off his stubborn gaze into the nothingness of night, he dropped to his elbows. Twice his eyelids drooped, then slowly opened. A light suddenly bloomed in the nearest window, which I knew to be the housekeeper's room. The curtains were opaque, but I could hear humming and occasional lyrics, all in Spanish. A radio turned on, and a flurry of Spanish words began what sounded like a sales pitch. I silently mouthed three words, *Thank you, Maya*. This cover of sound could be my salvation.

Ten minutes later, Thor rolled to one side and let out a deep sigh before slipping off to canine Never-Never-Land. Hopefully not to Valhalla. I imagined explaining that one to Tyler. *Tyler, keep your bow arm slightly bent at full draw. That's better. By the way I killed your dog last Thursday night.*

There were a few pinecones raked under the shrubbery by the house. I chose one firm and prickly and lofted it like a free-throw toward Thor. It landed between his fore and hind legs and bounced away. My second shot hit him in the ribs. He didn't stir.

I figured I had about an hour left before I would need to move Abby's car. Moving quietly, I gained the big glass sliding doors that opened to the patio where Thor lay. The curtains were lit up from the flickering, blue glow of a television. As I crouched there, a shadow moved across the curtain into another room, which I knew from Tyler's map to be the kitchen. The window there was bare, so I backed away from the house and stood on the low bordering wall just a few yards from the recumbent Thor.

A tall man with a cigarette drooping from his lips stood before a counter pouring from a bottle into a large glass of ice. I heard the roar of spectators at a baseball game rise from the TV, then the announcer's nasal voice filling in the dead time.

Beau Raintree had gray-brown hair slicked back as if he had just stepped out of the shower. His rumpled white shirt was unbuttoned at the neck. Turning to look back at the TV, he plucked his cigarette from his mouth and drank from the glass. In profile he showed no hints of Seneca ancestry. Mostly, he looked like a salesman who smoked and drank too much. With the cigarette back in place, smoke rose before his face giving him a permanent squint that cut three lines across his forehead. With the glass in one hand and a bowl in the other, he disappeared from the window, and his shadow returned to the TV room.

I had never watched a baseball game all the way through. The game was too slow for me. But tonight, I was a big baseball fan, as I jogged out of Thor's domain to get a look at that lighted window upstairs on the creek side of the house.

There was a good chance that Mrs. Raintree was there, but I couldn't be sure. What if the man downstairs wasn't Beau? Or what if there was a lady upstairs but it wasn't Mrs. Raintree? *Enter it like it is more than it is.* What if the man downstairs was Edgar Allan Poe, and Pat Raintree was in the basement watching the swing of a stainless-steel pendulum sharpened to a razor edge. *You never know.*

There was no way to climb the wall to the window, so I searched the lawn for small pebbles. The manicured carpet of zoysia was great for stalking but lousy for stones. I trotted back to the creek, grabbed a handful of pebbles and returned. First, I just wanted to see who came to the window without my being seen. In that one glimpse I would need to make a judgment whether or not it was Pat Raintree?

I tossed a tiny stone no bigger than an apple seed and heard it ping off the bricks next to the window. If I'd been a real baseball fan, I probably could have put it right on the center pane. I tried again. Somehow, I must have known this was going to happen, hence the handful of pebbles. I tried underhand and heard the glass *click*, so I back-pedaled into the shadows. Nothing happened. After a minute, I moved back into the light and tried again. Another hit. I retreated again.

This time a woman stood silhouetted in the window for ten seconds. I could make out nothing of her features. She was just a black cutout against a bright background. Then, when she turned, I saw the subtle slope of her neck from her shoulders as she let her head hang. I had seen that same tragic pose in Tyler the morning I walked into his cabin.

I ran back to the creek, dug into my pack for my Swiss army knife, unfolded the saw blade, and cut a piece of cane three-fingers-thick. After easing it down, I lopped off the bushy top, leaving twenty feet of stout pole. Then I trimmed the branches, smoothed the cuts, and ran my palm the length of the cane to check for rough nubs.

Opening my notebook, I wrote with a heavy magic marker: *I am Tyler's camp counselor. I need to talk to you.* I rolled the paper into the kangaroo pouch of my sweatshirt and carried the long cane to the house.

The window was framed by an ornamental jut of brick, which gave me a vertical notch on one side to catch the top end of the pole as I leaned it into the wall. I set the bottom end six feet from the house and tested its hold at top. It felt good.

As quietly as I could, I climbed hand over hand, and my feet left the ground. Right away, I detected a problem. My body weight bowed the pole, and its upper end grated on the bricks as it scraped downward in the notch. I slowed my climb to a stalk, which was much harder. The more the cane bent, the more I felt like a human arrow about to be launched by a bamboo bow into trouble. The Orientals called bamboo "the plant of a thousand uses." I wondered if peeping into windows was on the list.

Halfway up I was able to use my feet on the wall, walking up the bricks as I pulled with my arms. A yard below the window I stopped, held myself with one arm, and jammed the note into my mouth in case she had heard the cane rattle and was waiting at the window.

My biceps felt like they were about to explode. Either I was going to make it to the sill or fall into the shrubbery or pole vault into the lawn. For inspiration I thought about the hundreds of pull-ups I had performed on white pines at Itawa. In a desperate burst of energy, I hoisted myself the last few feet and swung one cheek of my butt onto the brick sill, where I was barely able to perch. I was breathing so hard I almost chewed through the paper.

She was there, both horrified and fixated on the apparition at her window. I took the paper from my mouth, but with one hand I could not make it unfurl. She clasped a hand over her mouth and backed away. With one burning arm holding me up on the cane, I whipped the paper in the air until it opened and slapped it against the glass.

Her eyebrows knitted tightly over frozen eyes. In what seemed less than a second, I felt my balance shift. My stomach went light, and by reflex I dropped the note to grip the pole with both hands. When I was able to turn, I saw that her horror had given way to curiosity. Moving with caution, she approached the window, looked quickly back at her door, and then stared at me. She wore a tee shirt that read *If the Body Fits, Wear It!* She put a hand to her throat.

"Is Tyler all right?" she said. I read her lips more than I heard her.

"He's fine," I whispered and tried to adjust my hold. I wasn't going to be able to hang up there much longer. "We need to talk!"

"It doesn't open," she said, making a nervous gesture toward the base of the window. Frantic, she looked away from me and pulled on her fingers. Suddenly, she ran to a dresser, rummaged through a drawer, and ran back. She pulled the cap off a lipstick tube, and her hand hovered before the window as if she didn't know what to do.

The aching half of my butt was losing traction on the narrow ledge, and my arms were about to burst into flames. I was wondering about crash landings in zoysia and judging how far the pole would carry me out into the yard. Then her face set with purpose, and she scribbled red capital letters on the windowglass. The word made no sense to me. It looked like "SONAVA" but the S and N were backwards. If the next word was "bitch," this was going to be one disappointing rendezvous. Then I realized that she was not taking the time to write for my perspective. It was "AVANOS."

What the devil is "AVANOS"? I wanted to shout to her.

Beneath it she wrote "MP1" with the "P" backwards. When she wrote the third line I transposed it immediately. It read "BATHROOM" backwards. She drew a hasty circle with a cross hanging below it, leaned toward me, and mouthed "tomorrow."

At this moment, her head whipped around, and she spoke to the door. When she turned back to me, she appeared terrified. She closed the curtains, leaving me in semi-dark. The last thing I heard her say was, "I told you I'm not hungry!"

Asking my arms for three more seconds, I pushed off the wall with my legs and rode the end of the pole, carving a blind arc through the whistling night air until I collapsed on the spongy grass and rolled like a paratrooper. Dragging the pole with me, I scrambled to the edge of the lawn, lay very still, and kept watch on her window. If Beau Raintree opened the curtains and read the lipstick, the game was up. In fifteen minutes, a yellow slit widened in the curtains, and I saw Pat Raintree raise a bottle and blur the glass. She wiped circles with a towel until the lipstick markings were gone. Cupping her hands to the window, she tried to see out. I didn't move.

I gave it ten minutes, waiting to see if Beau Raintree might appear prowling around his yard with a handgun or shotgun or, for all I knew, a Seneca war club. When nothing happened, I moved quietly back to the house, raked the grass with my hands then probed under the bushes until I was forced to use the Mag-light. I found the paper hung up in the bushes.

No sooner had I killed my light than I heard the whir of a motor at the front gate. The metal wings squeaked open, and a car pulled quietly through the entrance up the drive. A long black Lincoln with dark-tinted glass stopped at the intersection of the drive and the curved front walkway, idled there for a full minute, and then shut off. No one got out. I could see the pinpoint red glow of a cigarette flare and dim in the driver's seat.

The driver's door opened, and a heavy-set man got out. A bald spot on top of his head reflected light from the front porch. From the back seat he pulled a suitcase, and then he sauntered up the walkway, flicking his cigarette in a red arc out into the lawn.

When the doorbell chimed inside, the radio and ballgame died, and a vacuum of silence swallowed the house until the front door opened. The low murmur of voices was soon shut out by the slam of the door.

I wanted to sprint back around to the patio and put my ear to that glass door, but I had Abby's car to think about and a date tomorrow that should give me the information I needed. And there was Thor. I had no way to know how long he would be out of action.

I slid down the slope to the sandy beach, changed back into my wet suit booties, and retraced my route downstream. Slow. Just like a heron. *Enter it like it is more than it is. Leave that way, too.*

After drying off and changing into my clothes, I drove Abby's car into the Raintree driveway to turn around. With the headlights trained on the Lincoln, I peered through my binoculars through the windshield and front gate and memorized the tag number.

Then I headed for a big motel out near the interstate where I could park overnight unnoticed and sleep in the Volvo's backseat.

Chapter Ten

A little after noon on Friday, I walked across a shopping center's sunbaked parking lot toward a thin script of blue neon in a window that read *Avano's*. Feeling refreshed after a clandestine swim in the motel's pool, I hopped up the curb and checked myself in the window reflection. Wearing Old Bill's sport coat over a black T-shirt, I hoped I might blend in among north Atlanta's elite. After finger-combing my hair, I entered the dark, plush ambience of the restaurant.

The blood red carpet was as soft as the moss at the top of Rainbow Falls. Entombing the anteroom were black marbled walls streaked with veins of cream white, jagging like bolts of lightning against a night sky. Beyond this room and through a dark hallway was the candlelit dining room. From there I heard the soft tinkle of forks and plates and floating cubes of ice, all underscored by the murmur of canned piano.

"May I help you, sir?" The smiling receptionist was very young for her glistening, low-cut dress. She wore more makeup than a Lakota warrior going into battle.

"Yes, I am a bit early for my party. Do you have a bar where I could wait?"

"Of course," she said, ramping up her smile as if I had just cured her of a fatal disease. She walked me through the hallway until she could point out the bar. "Our bartender is Maryanne. She will take good care of you." There she left me, and off I went into the chamber of plenty and recorded music to be taken care of by Maryanne.

Just before the main dining area another hall branched off to my left with a restroom sign above the foyer. This hallway did not offer much privacy for a clandestine meeting. I assumed Beau would accompany Pat to the restaurant. The position of their table might be critical to our rendezvous in the side hall.

After passing the foyer, I stopped on a dime, frowned and backed up. My stomach sank. There was a courtesy telephone at the end of that hall. If things were like I thought they were between the Raintrees, Beau would never allow her down that hall by herself.

Only a few tables were occupied. To my left, the dark cherrywood bar extended the length of the room. Lined up in front of it was a row of backed wooden stools with cushions to match the maroon carpet below. Behind the bar a long mirror gave the illusion of expanding the size of the room. A galaxy of inverted glasses glittered in a neat line from a wooden rack. If Maryanne really was a bartender, I thought she was supposed to be twisting a towel inside a shot glass like they do in Bobby Whitehorse's Westerns. Instead, she was reading a book.

Since Avano's was expensive, my plan was to nurse a five-dollar ginger ale for as long as I could stretch it and hope for a tolerant bartender. Maybe Maryanne had a burning desire to learn about medicinal plants. Or archery. Or a thousand and one uses for bamboo. I sat down quietly without getting her attention. That would get me extra points from the start. I would be so unoffended and obliging when she realized she had overlooked a customer, it would make it harder for her to push me to keep ordering more drinks. I pretended to study the wine list printed on a paper stock card. About five minutes later, Maryanne dropped her book and hurried over to me.

"I'm so sorry, sir. Have you been waiting long?"

"Actually, I'm early to meet some friends here. I hope you don't mind if I kill some time at your bar. Could I just have a ginger ale?" I smiled and snapped tight the front of Old Bill's coat. "I've got to have a clear head for this lunch meeting."

"One ginger ale. Coming up." She flipped a small towel over her shoulder. Aha! She had seen some Westerns.

I spun my seat and looked over the room. There was a threesome of middle-aged men who were having a good time reminiscing about something. Over by the window a charming white-haired lady of about ninety was talking such good sense that her two companions were hanging on her every word. One other table hosted a man and woman more interested in eating than conversation.

"There you are, sir." Maryanne fanned a napkin down in front of me and set a glass on it. Submerged in the amber bubbles were two red cherries. *Two*! I was in solid with Maryanne.

I nodded toward her book in the corner. "What are you reading?"

"Oh, I think it's Berry or something like that. It's for school." She looked back at the book and wrinkled her nose. "It's about some old guy on a farm."

She started to turn and I said, "Wendell Berry? *The Memory of Old Jack*."

Her face brightened like a polished glass. "Yeah, that one."

I lifted my glass. "Enjoy. This will do me until my friends arrive. Thank you."

At one o'clock the only thing left in my glass were two cherry stalks. The piano tape had looped once, and I was now able to predict each piece before it began. I was wishing I'd brought my own book to read. At ten minutes after one, a group of five men clustered next to me at the bar and recapped their morning golf game. Their enthusiasm dominated the room. I watched the door in the mirror and wrestled with the problem of how to rendezvous with Pat Raintree in the women's restroom.

If Beau Raintree would not let his wife go alone into that hallway because of the telephone, I wasn't going to be able to follow her down that hall. I considered standing at the phone pretending a conversation in the receiver while waiting for her to enter the restroom. If Beau saw the phone in use, he might leave her alone then she could talk to me through the cracked door. But what if he didn't leave? That left me with only one more option that I didn't like: waiting for her inside the women's bathroom. Maybe hanging on a bamboo pole with one arm might not end up being the toughest part of my trip.

At fourteen minutes after one, they walked in. The receptionist led in Pat Raintree, followed by her husband, who was followed by the heavy, semi-bald man who had arrived at their house late last night. This was not the same frazzled Pat Raintree I had seen through a glass darkly last night. This version of her was stunning—blonde, high cheekbones, and trim. She could easily have been a model. But her walk was stilted, and, even with the smile she put on for the room, her expression was dead. She reminded me of Tyler when he had stepped off the bus on the first day of camp.

Beau walked with a lot of shoulder rotation—as if he had just bought out Microsoft. He wore a politician's smile, gray suit, peach tie, wrap-around shades, and hair that had been digitally mastered.

The heavy man with him had been a bodybuilder once upon a time. He carried enough bulk to suggest that he had beefed up on steroids in his warrior days. His face showed a distorted combination of oversized lips and drooping eyelids, giving him a strangely melancholic expression. He was overweight and breathing through his mouth as he crossed the room. He was a guy who had missed the brass ring in life and knew it, taking the last of the ride with only a vestige of resolve. He wore an off-the-rack suit that accentuated the sag of his flesh. He would look oddly disjointed wherever he was.

As she waited to be seated by her husband, Pat darted her eyes all around the room until she saw me. I stood up and dug into my hip pocket for my wallet. Behind her, Beau seemed to sense her gaze and eyed the gathering at the bar. I lowered my head to my wallet, fished out a five and two ones, and weighted them with my glass. I smiled at Maryanne, shrugged as if my friends weren't going to show, and started for the bathroom foyer.

I'd been watching the entrance to the bathroom corridor for fifteen minutes and keeping tabs on all the females in the dining room. I was ninety-nine percent sure the ladies' lounge was empty. I turned right down the foyer, pushed the ladies' room door open six inches, and listened.

"This is the management!" I said quietly. "Anyone in here?" My airy question echoed off the tiled walls like some charlatan's eerie voice at a séance. I pushed the door halfway open and repeated the question. My hollow echo floated around the room again. I walked quickly past the sinks and entered the last stall, locked the door, and waited. Trying not to feel like a perverted voyeur on a bold mission, I stood as far back in the stall as I could so my 10 ½ shoes weren't visible under the stall door.

The piano music suddenly grew louder, and I realized the restroom door had opened. Heels clicked across the tiled floor toward the sinks and mirror. The footsteps stopped, and then for a long time nothing happened. It was so quiet, I could imagine someone out there leaning down and staring at my feet. I was barely breathing.

Then I heard the exasperated whisper of a word that I could not catch. It was that awkward, cathartic surrender to misery from a person unaccustomed to inconvenience. Very quietly I stepped up on the toilet seat and rose up to peer over the door. Pat Raintree leaned against the sink on stiff arms, her head sagging between her shoulders as if she were trying to throw up.

"Mrs. Raintree," I whispered.

Her frightened eyes came up in the mirror. Then she spun to me like a person expecting to be assaulted. I stood straight up and repeated her name. Her mouth dropped open, but otherwise she didn't move.

"I'm Stoney . . . from Camp Itawa."

She threw a hand flat against her chest, sagged back into the counter, closed her eyes, and took in a deep breath. When she opened her eyes, she checked the restroom door and then looked back at me. I motioned her over, stepped down, unlocked the door, and opened it. She had not moved. In three seconds, she made up her mind and came toward me like an unstoppable force. I backed up, but she lost her momentum at the entrance to the stall.

"Stoney St. Ney," I said, holding out my hand. She took the last step and grasped my hand—hers like a bundle of thin sticks wrapped in damp cellophane. It occurred to me that this might be the first male-female handshake in a bathroom stall in the history of the world. "You'd better come on in and lock it," I said.

While she secured the door, I couldn't help admiring her body—probably a product of good genes and aerobics classes. When she turned to me, tears welled in her eyes.

"Tyler is doing great," I said.

Her tears stalled and then ran down her cheeks like the first drops of rain on a windowpane. She buried her face in her hands, leaned back into the door, and sobbed so hard that the door rattled. I waited. I thought it would be awkward to give her my shoulder to cry on . . . in a bathroom stall.

When she collected herself, she sniffed and looked up at me with wide, red-rimmed eyes that bled darkly with streaks of mascara. I handed her some tissue from the roll.

"Thank you," she whispered. She patted her eyes carefully in a futile attempt to salvage her make-up. "I miss him so."

I nodded. "I think he's liking camp just fine."

Her eyes distorted with new tears. "I can't call him or write. My husband—"

The bathroom door opened, and high heels tapped into the room beneath the swish of fabric. Pat Raintree's face froze like a deer caught in headlights. As the shoes stopped at the sink, I carefully stepped up onto the toilet seat and crouched. Pat dabbed at her eyes and daintily blew her nose.

The shoes clicked into another stall, and we had to share our third party's entire soundtrack of locking her door, unzipping, and peeing. We remained absolutely quiet and had no choice but to listen to every pitter and patter and drip. I took out a pen and the wine-list card and wrote on the back until the woman in the other stall had finished. She washed her hands, put in some time at the mirror, and then left. We waited until the door shut.

"Exactly what is going on, Mrs. Raintree?"

She cut her eyes to one side and frowned. "My husband. I'm trying to leave him. I can't use the telephone. I can't get out of the house unless I'm with him." She set her jaw and looked in the direction of the hallway. Her nostrils flared a little. "And now there's that big moron . . . Perry."

"Is somebody out in the hall now?" I asked. "The big guy?"

She nodded. "That's Perry."

"And he's there so you can't use the telephone?"

"Beau knows I've been trying to call my lawyer."

"Who is Perry?"

"He works for Mr. Dimateo and now—as of last night—he's staying in our house. I guess he's on loan or something. Beau says he's a bodyguard." She hissed air through her teeth. "Beau likes to feel important, so he pretends that Perry is *his* bodyguard. I think Perry is watching Beau." Her eyes clicked back and forth in tiny increments as she threw this information at me. She had squeezed the tissue into a tight ball.

"Can you tell me what is going on so I can understand all this, Mrs. Raintree?"

She took a deep breath but held it when the bathroom door unexpectedly pushed open again. I was still squatting on the seat doing my best to look semi-dignified.

"You in there, Mrs. Raintree?" The voice was weary . . . or bored. She looked right at me when she called out to answer him.

"Of course, I am! Do you mind?!"

"Just checking," the voice said. I heard him take one step into the room, hesitate then turn back. Before the door closed, he spoke in a quieter voice to someone in the hall. "No windows in there. She's not going anywhere." The door thumped shut.

"My husband is out there with him," she whispered. She made a caustic laugh and shook her head. "This is so absurd. Beau is watching me. Perry is watching Beau. God! It's like a prison inside a prison!"

"Tell me," I said evenly, trying to get her calmed down enough to be coherent.

This time when she shook her head, she closed her eyes so tightly that a web of lines fanned across her cheekbones. "This man named Dimateo came to the house two nights ago. I think he controls Beau, but of course Beau won't admit it."

"What kind of work does your husband do?"

She laughed with a snort. "A year ago, I would have smiled dutifully and said that he brokered peanuts, oranges, things like that." Her face soured. "But you don't associate with people like Dimateo if you are a legitimate produce broker." She closed her eyes. "I've never trusted Beau. I don't know why I ever—" More tears squeezed from her eyes.

By the way that the cynicism was crusting over her words, I could almost read the tracks of her history. My guess was she had been a prisoner of classical good looks who had socially and emotionally pin-balled through life based upon what she had been taught her beauty could do for her. She had probably jumped through the debutante hoops, driven by the heirloom pressure that was always trying to lift her up to some standard she did not recognize when she looked in the mirror.

"Tyler is afraid his father will find him and come get him," I whispered.

Her eyes were like molten metal, now solidifying into cast iron. "His father will not find out from me where Tyler is." Her teeth clenched like a steel trap. I believed her.

"Would you say that your husband is dangerous?"

She held the hard look and nodded. "And so are these other men. Perry scares me, but Mr. Dimateo terrifies me. He is so creepy."

"Does your husband ever hurt you or Tyler, Mrs. Raintree?"

She looked down immediately. I could hear the piano tape outside recycling through its repetitive tunes. Looking through a thick lens of tears she nodded again.

"He tries to control me by threatening Tyler. I don't think he actually hurts him."

I waited for her to meet my eyes. "I can call your lawyer for you. He can get the police to come out to your house."

I was surprised to see fear leap back into her face. "Not the police." She pinned me with a desperate stare. "The courts would force me to bring in Tyler. Beau would get him."

"Not if you and Tyler testify about the abuse," I said.

"Tyler would never admit his father hits him. Then it's my word against Beau's."

"Tyler can be held in a child custody center where he would be safe," I said, but she only frowned and looked down at the floor again. "I think we have to consider doing this, Mrs. Raintree. Tyler feels certain his father will find him at Itawa. It's no good living with that fear. Maybe your lawyer can work with a judge and make Itawa the safe haven Tyler needs. We've done that before. But the camp owner needs to know right now what we can or cannot do legally if your husband shows up."

She lowered her head into her hand and squeezed her forehead, her thumb at one temple and her fingertips at the other. "I know, I know. It's not right to put you at risk. But you don't understand."

"What exactly is that risk?"

She looked at me with a strange calm. "Tyler was right. His father is dangerous."

I didn't want to ask her if Beau was known to use a gun as Tyler had intimated. If she didn't already know it, it might push her right over the edge.

"How so?"

She chewed on that one for a long time before giving in. "Beau shot someone." She crouched forward slightly, as if a drawstring had been tightened along the length of her body. As she bent, one arm wrapped across her stomach. The elbow of the other arm propped on her wrist as the free hand pinched the bridge of her nose, trying to stanch her tears. "It's complicated," she said. Tears squeezed out around her fingertips.

Because I knew we couldn't stay in the bathroom much longer, I cupped my hand to the top of her arm and gently squeezed. "Let me call your lawyer."

She shook her head and made a wet sound in her throat. "I can't believe I'm telling you all this. I don't even know you."

"Probably what makes it easier to tell," I said.

"You don't understand." Her eyes couldn't hold on mine. She stared at the blank metal wall to my left and then made a long exhalation that drained out all her resistance. Her head came back to me, and her eyes became a plea. "I fell in love with someone. That's who Beau shot."

I looked at the misery in her face long enough to see that her life was coming apart like rotted fabric. "Your husband killed someone you loved, and you're going to hold back on that?"

"He didn't kill him. And I could never testify why Beau shot him. It would be grounds to label me an unfit mother." Her face darkened. "Beau has been screwing around for years with who knows how many little tramps, but I really fell in love." She reached out as though she might squeeze my arm but only touched the sleeve. "He could get Tyler. He's got proof about me and Thomas."

This story was so crazy I wasn't sure what I made of it, but she looked dead serious. "Thomas is the one who got shot?"

She nodded. "We love each other."

I pivoted my head away from her and focused on the other wall of the stall. My forearms rested on my knees and my fingers were laced together. For a brief moment, I saw the panoramic view from Standing Bear Dome and imagined Tyler there next to me as I pointed out the two valleys of the Etowah and the Chestatee and named all the mountains between them. It was *really* hard to believe I was perched on a toilet in a women's bathroom as I took confessions.

"Mrs. Raintree, what if your husband shows up at our camp? Without a court order we would have to let him take Tyler."

She wouldn't look at me. Neither of us had an answer for that. And *that* was my reason for coming down here to pole-vault off houses, sleep in a car, and sit at a bar for an hour so I could hide out in a women's bathroom stall.

The door to the room banged against the wall. "Pat! What the hell are you doing?!"

It took her less than a second to deliver her comeback, and it was a good one. "I'm having my period. Just leave me alone." Our little confessional was getting more and more intimate.

"Christ!" he hissed and slammed his hand against the door. We heard him relay that tidbit to Perry before the door closed. I wondered what the chances were that charming, old Beau would shoot a guy he found in a bathroom stall with his wife? Pretty good odds, I'd say.

"I've got to go," she whispered with some urgency. "If he were to find you—"

I handed her the wine list. "This is the sheriff in our county, and that's his number." Below the number I'd written: *This is an emergency. Call Lumpkin County Sheriff Canaday and just say the word "Stoney" and keep this money for your trouble.* I folded the card and slipped in a ten-dollar bill. "If you change your mind about getting the law involved, try to get this to somebody. The sheriff is a friend of mine. I'll let him know you might call."

"Why the sheriff? Why not the camp number instead?" she asked.

"The call might be made at night when no one is in the camp office. Someone is always on duty at the jail. And this message has more clout with a sheriff's name on it."

She gripped the card tightly and looked at me with a smile that I thought was going to bring tears again. "Thank you," she said and took that last step and hugged me. "Thank you, Stoney."

When she stepped away and unlocked the stall door I said, "What about you? What do we do about your situation? This doesn't feel right to leave it this way."

"Just give me a few days. I'll figure out something." She started through the door.

"Mrs. Raintree? If I don't hear from you by Tuesday, I'm calling the Atlanta police myself and have them come to your house. Will you at least tell me the name of your lawyer?"

She pulled in her bottom lip with her teeth and looked right through me. Then her eyes came back into focus, and she nodded.

"Arthur Scroggin."

The next thing I knew, I was alone in the women's bathroom again. I had planned to ask about Thor, but at that moment I really didn't care.

Chapter Eleven

With a few hours of daylight remaining, I left my cabin with my gear loaded on my back and started for Standing Bear. The air in the forest was pungent with new growth and the incense of the earth stirred up by the boots that had come before me. It wasn't often I had this luxury of a quiet afternoon walk in summer. I could imagine the parade that had preceded me. The signs of the Outriders were as subtle as a herd of migrating buffalo.

The moon was still in its first quarter and so high at dusk that it dropped a cool green phosphorescence on the trail that snaked up the mountain. It was almost dark when I reached the top, and I paused behind a laurel thicket just outside the loose circle of tents. The kids were quiet and intent on their jobs.

Tyler stacked squaw wood under a gnarled pine. Bobby Whitehorse stepped down from the rock dome, where the moonlight bathed the high barren point into a moonscape itself. He carried a water bag filled from the spring that seeped out of the other side of the cliff. I knew that it took a half hour to top off the bag from that trickle, so I was pleased to see how well everything was going in Bobby's absence.

I stepped from the shadows into the outer reach of the campfire's halo. When my name was called out, the campers clustered around me, welcoming me with that sense of family that had eluded me as a boy.

"How come you didn't hike up with us?" P.J. asked.

The whole crowd waited, expectant. I shrugged off my pack.

"I had some business to take care of out of town. I hope I'm in time for supper. I could eat a bear."

"How would you like that?" Troy asked with a straight face. "Rare . . . medium?"

"Over easy," I said.

Troy raised an index finger, bobbing it beside his head as if remembering my epicurean preferences. Every day he moved closer to Bobby and me as a peer, peeling away the years between us with no visible effort.

Amanda and two boys sliced something into a pan. She held up a rippled slab of orange and yellow fungus that I recognized with a pang of delight. *Chicken of the woods.*

"Look what we found on the way up, Stoney. We're cooking it with the noodles."

I bared my teeth in a wolfish smile and slapped a hand to my stomach. "Better than bear."

"And easier to catch," Troy was quick to add.

Bobby Whitehorse was arranging fist-sized rocks in the coals as a pedestal for the cooking pot. I knelt across the flames from him and watched his strong hands work as if they were made of asbestos. Without looking up, he spoke quietly.

"How did it go in the land of plenty, Gray Eyes?"

"Not exactly what I had hoped for, but I did talk to her."

Bobby balanced the pot on the triangle of stones and dragged coals around it with a stick. Dane Saxe brought over a bag and stood behind Bobby. When he bent to pour in the noodles, Bobby cleared his throat and spoke casually.

"Remember how you hated those noodles we had last summer, Dane?"

Dane stopped and made a face at Bobby. "Yeah, they were yucky."

"They were mushy," Bobby corrected.

Dane stared at Bobby and then at me, but I was no help. "Okay, they were yucky and mushy."

"They were yucky *because* they were mushy," Bobby said evenly. Then he looked at me and chuckled. "Sounds like we're speaking Inuit." He turned back to Dane. "Let the water boil first."

"Oh," Dane said. "Yeah, I forgot." He straightened up, stared at the pot, and hugged the bag to his stomach.

Tyler dropped a load of sticks by the woodpile, and when he saw me, his face became animated. "Stoney!" he said with an actual melody in his voice, "I found the 'first arrow' today. Bobby Whitehorse said I could be the 'keeper of the arrow' and return it to the office." As he talked, he backed toward his tent. I waited. He returned with the arrow cradled in his curved palms. Percival and the Holy Grail. "Bobby Whitehorse told us all about how you shoot it every year. Troy said he found it his first year at Itawa and that he and I were the only ones to ever do that."

I looked at Troy by the fire and caught the flicker of a smile as he stared at the slices of fungus he pushed with a spatula, and by that lone gesture I knew that he had played a part in Tyler finding the arrow. Tyler looked down at the ceremonial shaft as if I weren't there—like a kid who had just taken his favorite Christmas present back to the privacy of his room. "And look what else," he said excitedly. He pushed a hand into his pocket and came out with a quartz arrowhead and a smile as bright as the ivory keys on my piano.

"Where'd you find that?" I said, letting a little awe-struck laughter slip out. Either Troy was working overtime on "Project Tyler" or the angels of lost souls were with us.

"Right here . . . just after we got here. It's a real Indian arrowhead."

I nodded and picked up the stone from his open palm. A quarter inch of the tip was missing, but, otherwise, it was a work of art.

"I just wish it wasn't broken off at the end," he said.

"Well, why don't we make a whole one?"

His face came up slowly. "You can make one of these?"

I smiled. "Want to make one tonight?"

"Sure!" he said, getting about four musical notes out of the one syllable. He started to run back to his tent with the arrow then slowed his pace as if trying to contain his feelings. When Tyler zipped his tent back up, I pointed at the woodpile.

"Collect all that by yourself, Tyler?"

"That's my job," he said. "I'm in charge of firewood. And guess what? I hit three bull's-eyes from fifteen yards yesterday."

I canted my head. "Three out of—?"

"I don't know, maybe twenty." He was speaking faster than I had ever heard him talk. "And a lot of the other shots were either in the red or blue."

Troy set a kettle on the coals. "He's got the release down, Stoney. Wait'll you see him."

All I'd said to Troy before I'd left was to keep a special eye on Tyler. He didn't ask for details. He had simply nodded.

"Amanda is the one who taught him," Troy explained, "and he soaked it up like a sponge." Troy nodded at the firewood pile. "And check that out."

Tyler didn't look at us but smiled uncontrollably. Troy raised his eyebrows at me. I wondered if Tyler had ever been given a chore around his house. Most kids I knew didn't have household jobs and seemed crippled when I gave them one. Then some, like Tyler, jumped at it as if they had found the missing ingredient in their lives.

We were in no danger of running out of fuel for this trip. Or the next one when we returned here.

I traded my boots for my camp moccasins, set up a small tarp, stretched out on top of my sleeping bag, and watched the Outriders at work. Tyler was now helping with the cooking. He was a bird loosed from its cage, soaring upward to a rarefied stratum of the atmosphere he had never before dreamed existed. He and Amanda were pals now, probably bound by their shared finesse with the bow. I couldn't hear their words, but their conversation was melodic and natural.

I laughed to myself, remembering my first attempts to crack Tyler's shell of misery. The right forces were now at work—the magic of the mountain, the yellow dance of the fire, ancient stone points emerging from the earth, and steady young hearts like Amanda's and Troy's lending a hand where it was needed.

After the dinner clean-up, we gathered wordlessly on the open dome. The moon was descending to Nickajack Ridge, ceding over the dark sea of the night to the slow migration of stars floating above us. They were as thick as dust and lightly tethered into old familiar patterns.

Against this tapestry of winking diamonds, Bobby Whitehorse told the story of Standing Bear, the giant she-bear who found her lost cubs atop this very mountain and curled over them to protect them from an early blast of winter ice and snow only to turn to stone. From time to time, I would see one of the kids touch one of the islands of moss scattered about the massive outcrop upon which we sat, searching for some vestige of the thick ursine coat that had once covered it.

Tyler and I sat a little apart from the others and worked on a flake of chert that I'd stored in my pack as a back-up cutting blade. Pinching the rock inside a patch of leather, I chipped at it with a small tine of antler, showing Tyler the angles to apply pressure to achieve an edge. Without missing a word of the story, he watched with rapt attention and eagerly took over when I handed him the materials. He worked the point for another hour after the story ended. When he carried it to his tent, he thanked me three times.

With the campers zipped up in their bags and their voices fading to whispers, I stoked the fire and put on a kettle of water. On a trip like this, Bobby and I flip-flopped our ritualistic coffee hour to a late night sit around the hot coals. There was never enough time in the morning. I pulled out the deerskin pouch of dried roots I carried whenever we hiked out of Itawa. Bobby opened his foil of coffee but kept his eyes on me.

"What do you think about when you hold that pouch, Gray Eyes?"

I rubbed my thumb along the velvet nap of the bag. "The one who wore this skin," I said and extracted a root. Using a slab of bark as a workbench I began to score it.

Bobby nodded. "And what do you think about when you make those little cuts in that ginger root?"

I paused in my work and pictured the hillside of ginger I'd found with leaves as large as both my hands held together. "Noontootla Valley," I answered.

Bobby nodded again. I waited to see where he was going with this. He glanced over his shoulder at the cluster of tents, and, when he turned back to measure his coffee, he lowered his voice to the barest of whispers.

"At lunch today . . . down at the creek . . . Joey Andrews was bad-mouthing everybody about owning TVs and DVD players and stereo systems made in Japan. He preached a pretty good sermon on buying American." Bobby huffed a quiet laugh through his nose. "We were eating on that rock shelf at the crayfish hole, dangling our feet in the water. Later, when we were pulling on shoes for the climb, I sat down next to Joey and asked where his new boots came from." Bobby chuckled. "So, Joey shrugged and said his mom bought them at Lenox Mall. So, I said, 'But where exactly did they come from?' He said, 'Macy's.' I kept at it and said, 'Before that.' He just squinted at me like I'd asked him to stop the flow of the creek. At my suggestion he pulled off the boot to read the label."

"China?" I said.

"Where else?" Bobby replied.

I looked at the moccasins on my feet, and again I thought about that first deer I had killed on Sassafras Mountain. I had stalked it for four hours to get a clean shot.

Bobby's eyes smiled, and for the thousandth time I considered the level of dedication he had employed when I had been his project a decade ago. I had brought so much pent-up, violent energy to Itawa that taking me into the forest must have been like trying to endear the trees to a chainsaw.

Now I watched Bobby's hands arrange sticks on the fire as though the flames could not burn him. He proceeded to tell me all about the ascent up Standing Bear and how each of the Outriders had performed.

When the water was hot and we poured our drinks, Bobby sat back for the night's tacit feature attraction. Stirring my tea, I began relating the details of my venture into the big city. Throughout my discourse he was like a propped-up corpse unless he raised his cup to his lips. By the time I had finished my story, I knew he may as well have been there by my side wading up the creek, skulking around the Raintree's house, or hiding in the bathroom at Avano's. He could take in words and paint a picture on an eidetic canvas like no one else I knew.

"What if she doesn't call by Tuesday? You calling the law?"

"I'll call the lawyer," I said. "We'll let him call the police."

Bobby nodded. "You get a number off the car that came to Tyler's house?"

I nodded. "Sheriff Canaday is checking on it for me."

Bobby lay back on one elbow and raised his face to the stars. "Always better to know than not know."

The night wind was cool for June. I sipped my drink in small doses, enjoying the warmth that gathered in my stomach. Bobby began that deep chuckle in his chest that rumbled like a distant freight train. He started to take a sip of coffee but stopped the cup an inch from his lips.

"Never been in a bathroom stall with a woman before." He stopped the cup again and cocked his head. "Or anyone else, for that matter."

"Well, if you ever do, I can tell you that it's a lot roomier if one of you stands on the toilet seat."

He was barely able to swallow before he coughed up a laugh. "If we ever formally go into business, that would make one hellava photo for our brochure." He held up one hand and set an imaginary line of type in the air. "St. Ney and Whitehorse, wilderness trackers. 'No matter where you go, we'll flush you out.' "

"We?" I scoffed. "There wasn't room for you in that stall, too."

"Thank God," he said. The fire reflecting in his dark pupils looked like tiny dervishes dancing in dark caves. He raised an index finger and tried to look serious though he didn't quite pull it off. "That reminds me." He pushed himself off the ground and walked over to his pack. In a moment he carried back a foil package about the size of a hardbound book. "Somebody sent you a little present," he said. "I told her I didn't have any more room in my pack, but she insisted."

I felt a tingle in my stomach. The prospect of Abby thinking of me while I was gone was pleasantly surprising. When I had returned her car, she was busy with a class, so I had left her key in her office mail slot along with a thank-you note.

"I think it's brownies," Bobby said, testing the heft of it. "Feels like enough for two." He set down the shiny package between us.

I opened it to find eight brownies stacked in a rectangle, four on top, four on the bottom. "Nope," I said.

"It's not brownies?" Bobby said a little too quickly. I knew he would have already sniffed out this contraband. I left the foil open as he peeked. The firelight sparkled off the aluminum like diamonds. The brownies inside looked rich and delicious.

"Yeah, it's brownies," I said. "It's just not enough for two."

For two beats, he looked at me with his best poker face. Then, quick as snake, he scooped up a brownie and bit off half. As he chewed, he leveled an appraising stare at the remaining piece in his hand. Then, slowly, his eyes widened, and his head turreted to me.

"They're chewy and crusty," he whispered. We had agreed long ago that the best brownies were chewy *and* crusty—a viewpoint we had tried for years to sell to Mrs. Old Bill, whose caky brownies crumbled at the touch of a fork. I looked around to make sure tents were still closed before joining in on the first brownie assault on Standing Bear Dome. "We've got to find out how she did this," Bobby said.

I lifted a brownie and took a bite. "Tell me you brought along a gallon of ice-cold milk."

Bobby sighed, looked out over the dark rolling sea of mountains and shook his head. "White man is always wanting more than what he has." He leaned over the brownies and studied them. "I wonder what my freight-hauler's fee should be?" He picked up three more brownies. "We learned from you it is more blessed to give. I'm helping you feel blessed."

I was glad Abby was not here to see two grown men vie for her brownies like chess strategists. "Any message come with this?" I said. "Maybe I should take her car out for exercise more often."

Bobby's eyes locked on mine. It was the same expression that froze on his face whenever he heard one of the Outriders misidentify a plant. I stopped chewing.

"These are from Gwendolyn," he said, his voice both gentle and merciful.

I swallowed and looked down at the remains in the foil. "Oh," I managed to say.

Bobby looked out into the night and did not move for a long time. When he spoke, his voice sounded as disembodied as a ghost's.

"Uh, oh."

We spent one more night on Standing Bear then moved our camp to lower ground. In a dark grove of hemlocks we pitched tents on the flood plain of Noontootla Creek. It could not have been more different from our wide-open aerie on the dome, but its mystery was equally powerful. Last night we'd slept wrapped in the windsong of the high country. Here a smooth tongue of green water broke the stillness of the valley, funneling between boulders and sluicing into a white froth that fringed our swimming hole. For the sake of tent morale, bathing and laundry were first on our agenda.

The kids swam for hours, oblivious to the cold water, unless Bobby or I intervened at the sight of blue lips, in which case we would banish that camper to land and fifteen minutes by our fire. Tyler looked like any other kid laughing, splashing, hunting the shallows for crayfish. On a dare he swam out into the rapid to be pounded under like a pale towel cycling through a washing machine. He came up desperate for air and laughing all at once. I watched him a long time and wondered how much of this liberation of spirit he could hold onto for the challenges that would arrive in his life soon enough.

But that was weeks away. For now, Itawa had Tyler. One session at camp might give him what he needed to face the dismantling of his family—if that was all there was to it. But I was pretty sure it wasn't.

Before dark, Bobby Whitehorse pulled three trout from the creek. We cooked them with four crayfish supplied by P.J. and her cohorts. As the night settled in, I watched Tyler arrange sticks on the fire. Yellow waves of light fluttered across the creases of concentration that lined his brow, but his single-minded focus seemed peaceful and cleansed from within. It was the kind of day when your thoughts could not climb out of a green valley to dwell on things unseen. For the moment being an Outrider was a full-time occupation.

Chapter Twelve

We returned to Itawa before supper on Monday. I was hopeful when I saw a message in my mailbox in the office. More than anything else, I wanted to know that Pat Raintree had changed her situation and given us some legal stand for holding on to Tyler should someone come for him. But the message was from the sheriff's office. The DMV records showed that the tag number I had given Sheriff Canaday was registered to a Victor Altoré Dimateo with an address in the twenty-five hundred block on Peachtree Road, N.E. The suite number was in the eight hundreds, so I assumed it was an apartment in one of the imposing high rises overlooking Buckhead.

Sheriff Canaday could be a very thorough man when he set his mind to it. I supposed the rest of what was on the note was a little payback for last February, when I had pulled a cold all-nighter to find three kids who had run off from New Horizons. Thinking back on that night, the note in my hand seemed a meager down payment. When I had found those boys, they had been soaking wet and close to hypothermia, and I wasn't far behind.

The sheriff's note went on to disclose Victor Dimateo's business. He owned The Sunbelt Mortgage Group. There was a business address also in Buckhead on Maple Drive. The last line of the message was cryptic for the sake of whoever had taken the message in the camp office. I didn't know who that was; I didn't recognize the handwriting. The message read: *I'll keep an ear out for your lady friend in Atlanta.* Pat Raintree still had one more day. If she didn't call by tomorrow, I was definitely going to call her lawyer to suggest that he send the police to her house.

I hung around the office for a while, hoping for a phone call, but my vigil was short-lived, when I detected the aromas wafting across camp from the dining hall. I never knew how much I missed Mrs. Old Bill's cooking until I moved back into the reach of its spell. There was cobbler in the air—cherry, I thought—and a little adrenaline surged through me. Only once in the last few years had I been so late to dinner that I missed out on cobbler. I had been stoic about it, but, when it comes to cobbler, stoicism is not all it's cracked up to be. Giving up on the call, I jogged to the dining hall.

The Outriders were sitting together at a table in one corner, so I grabbed a tray and joined them. Abby Parrish was four tables down. She looked up as I set down my tray. I waved, and she gave me about half of the Joan of Arc smile. When she looked away, I felt my own smile frozen in place like a line drawn on the face of a scarecrow. Then before I could think too much about the chill in the air, Gwendolyn appeared on my left, tray in hand. As she stopped, her hair—which had flowed behind her in an ethereal wake—came to rest about her shoulders like a veil. Her skin seemed even darker than I remembered. And her eyes whiter.

"Thanks for the present, Gwendolyn. Bobby Whitehorse and I are ready to pay for your recipe." I was careful not to use the word "brownie" within earshot of the brownie-deprived Outriders. I was also careful not to look at Bobby. Gwendolyn smiled like the goddess of summer newly arrived to awaken the seasonal wildflowers. I could feel a little snap of attention from the whole table. I knew all eyes were on her.

"Mrs. Wellborne let me use the oven in the kitchen. I'll make you some more."

I had one leg between the table and the bench. "Were you going to sit here?"

"I'd love to," she said as if the idea had never struck her.

Before I could extricate myself from the bench, she was sliding in next to me as Dane and Jamal squeezed toward the end of the table, almost forcing Troy off the end of the bench. Amanda rolled her eyes and looked at Tyler as if to say: *Don't ever be like that*. As I tried to make some space, I looked down the other direction of the table to see if everyone had enough room and, against all better judgment, stole a glance at Bobby Whitehorse. Only I would know that he was wearing a smile. It was the subtle curve that made his cheeks dimple slightly. He stared at the casserole on his tray. He knew I was looking at him, and to his credit he simply chewed his food and swallowed.

"Well, was it a good trip everybody?" Gwendolyn asked the table at large.

To my surprise, it was Tyler who spoke up loud and clear. "You should see the stars from on top of Standing Bear Dome—especially when Bobby Whitehorse is telling the story. Did you know that every star is a campfire built by somebody who's dead? They were trying to keep the bear warm. As long as the bear would stand up and watch them, she could scare them into building those fires hotter and hotter. But she finally gave in to her cubs and lay down to cover them up from the cold wind that was coming in. So now one by one the fires go out. We saw one go out and fall out of the sky." Tyler carried his bright eyes to Bobby as if he might be convinced to retell the legend. "It's a great story. You should hear it."

"I think she just did," Amanda said in her driest voice.

"We ate fungus," Jamal reported, scrunching up his face with disgust. "And worms!"

"They weren't worms," P.J. said. "They were beetle larvae."

Jamal looked at her and raised his upper lip almost to his nostrils. "Man, they was worms . . . all white and wiggly."

"You didn't eat any anyway, Jamal," Amanda said.

"Did, too. Ate part of one." It had taken us fifteen minutes to talk him into trying a single cooked larva, and now his chin was thrust up with pride, and he was not to be denied his place in the food chain.

"Ate more than that," Bobby Whitehorse said quietly.

No matter how loud a room was, when Bobby spoke, his voice cut through the din like the first subtle tremor of an earthquake. Jamal's head turned and waited for more from Bobby, but the answer came from the other end of the table from Troy.

"Remember the night we ate the sulfur shelf fungus with noodles?"

Jamal smiled broadly and pointed a finger at Gwendolyn. "Now *that* was good!"

"About a third of those noodles weren't noodles," Troy informed him.

Jamal's eyes fixed on Troy, and everyone got quiet. "Worms?!" he squealed.

"Hundreds of them," Troy said. "All white and wiggly."

Jamal's forearms collapsed onto the tabletop and his head dropped down onto his coffee-colored skin. The Outriders exploded in laughter. Pretty soon Jamal's shoulders began to shake. I wasn't sure if he was laughing or crying. Most of the dining hall was looking our way now, and I became even more self-conscious about how cramped my bench was. My eyes went automatically toward Abby.

There was something aquiline about her. Whether she was walking or running or even sitting in the dining hall, there was a soaring quality to her. Something of the eagle in her bearing. I wondered if Bobby Whitehorse saw the eagle in Abby, too.

Old Bill ambled across the room and handed me a folded paper. "Here are the girls playing in the male-female soccer game tomorrow. Make a list of the boys for me."

"Justin hasn't made a list?"

Old Bill took a deep breath and looked away at nothing. "No, just make me a list and leave it on my desk tonight. We want to make a poster with all the names . . . play it up a bit. Maybe make up some awards for everybody."

"You want me to come up with those?"

"Yeah, for the boys. Like what you did last year. Enough awards so everybody can get one. Abby will do the girls. You might help her out till she gets the hang of it."

When Old Bill walked off, I started to open up the paper, but Gwendolyn leaned toward me until our shoulders touched. "You'd better recruit the best boys you've got for the game, Stoney," she prodded. "The girls are going to kick some butt." She raised a merciless eyebrow. "Are you playing?"

"Counselors are playing?" I asked, a little surprised. She arched the other eyebrow and nodded. "I guess *you'll* be out there then," I said. She smiled and kept nodding. "I'd better talk to Justin and find out which of the boys can survive an ego-bruising."

She bumped my shoulder with hers. "Good idea," she said in a sly tone.

At the campfire I accosted Justin. I knew he saw me, but he kept his attention on the kids stacking sticks for the pyre. "Justin," I said and waited. Finally, I had to step into his line of vision. "Have you made up a list for the boys' soccer team tomorrow?"

He tried to look around me, but when I leaned with him he deigned to look at me, which seemed to make him angry. "What is the big deal about this stupid soccer game?" he said, hardly moving his mouth. He gave me the side of his face like a petulant child. "No, I haven't made a list. Maybe we don't want to play."

"Why not?"

His cut his eyes to me, and his chest puffed out. "Maybe we don't want to have to worry about playing all out and hurting some of the girls." He lowered his voice. "And we sure as hell don't want to hold back and play like girls."

"Justin, is this the boys talking or you talking?"

His eyes flicked away a little too quickly. He began shaking his head, showing me he was tolerating me. "St. Ney, you're not into team sports. You wouldn't understand."

"I'd appreciate your making out a list. I don't know who is best at each position."

He splayed his hands on his hips and glared at me. "We don't want this game, St. Ney, okay?"

"The game's going to happen. Are you saying the boys won't play?"

He scowled. "I won't," he said. "I'm not gonna hold back for a bunch of girls."

I stared at him for a few moments, hoping he would hear the echo of his own callow response. "Justin, you are head of the boys' camp and in charge of boys' sports. Exactly how do you justify getting out of this?"

"Easy," he said and leaned closer. "I'm in charge, and I don't have to help organize some stupid competition that I think is . . . stupid." He tried for a smirk, but he had lost whatever script he had prepared for this confrontation. "You used to run everything. You do it," he said and walked away.

When all the campers were seated on the benches, Troy laid out his fire kit. It was his first public attempt with the hand-drill. He had insisted that, the first time I see him do it, should be in front of everyone. That was Troy—willing to lay it all on the line. As he said his prayer to the fire-making trees, the campers became still, some of them staring with embarrassment, others with admiration. He knelt into position and began spinning the drill with dogged determination, but the task soon became a struggle. No one laughed or jeered. His face was a multi-faceted stone, his breath a dying engine. I knew his hands must be blistered by now and his arms and chest screaming with pain. The crowd's attention began to wander. Finally, he looked up at me with a strange mix of humility and perseverance.

"Do it with me, Stoney?"

"I'd be honored," I said and made my way toward him.

As I knelt opposite him across the fireboard, I heard Amanda shush the antsy campers. I spit in one hand and rubbed my palms together as Troy did the same with what little saliva he had left. He started again and twirled the spindle until his hands had traveled down to within six inches of the fireboard.

"Take it," he wheezed.

I made my pass on the drill, and then we alternated, working as a team. Within seconds the smoke thickened, and I increased pressure and speed. "Give it five more on your own," I said, standing and backing away. It was his last five ounces of strength, but he held form and coaxed fire out of that slab of wood. The crowd cheered and applauded as Troy positioned the burning tinder under the pyre. Then he surprised everyone by raising his arm like a cop stopping traffic.

"Please don't applaud!" he yelled, his flushed face composed even though he was still breathing hard. Everyone got quiet. "I make an oath tonight," he began in a quieter voice. "I will keep trying this each night until I succeed. Until I do, I ask that you not applaud. Tonight's applause is for my teachers." Troy nodded to me and then to Bobby Whitehorse, who stood in the back leaning against the stone wall.

In the intense silence that followed, Troy gathered up his kit and walked to his seat. I looked at Bobby. He nodded once to me. We both knew that we had in Troy a new link in the chain of our legacy. The Outriders' support for Troy was like a collective muscle that tightened our circle. Amanda stared at the side of Troy's face then turned to Tyler with a look that said: *Be like that.*

I didn't see Justin, so I went ahead with my part of the announcements. "Tomorrow is the Soccer Battle of the Genders. How many of you guys are interested in signing up?" The boys started woofing and howling like a kennel of hounds watching a cat stroll past their cages. When it got too loud, I raised my hand. "Okay, as I understand it, counselors are playing, too." The boys' howling veered off into jeers, claiming they didn't need us. "It's only fair to warn you guys," I said. "I've been told the girls are taking no prisoners." The noise swelled again from a crossfire of challenges and retorts.

"We tear out the livers of our enemies and eat them!" yelled big Ben Souther.

"That explains a lot about your breath!" Amanda yelled back.

I had to laugh, and, of course, this prompted more outbursts. I raised both arms and waited, but the war of the words had too much momentum. I felt like a ship at sea raising a handkerchief to catch the wind, so I walked over to Stephen Beasley, who was manic with verbal violence, took his upper arm in my hand and led him back to center stage. Then I did the same with Amy Littlefield. I stood between them like a referee before a boxing match, holding each of them by a wrist.

When it was quiet enough to be heard I said, "This is a male." The Beez struck a pose and flexed his skinny biceps. The jeers almost picked up again, but I cut it off. "And this, of course—" I raised Amy's arm, ". . . is a female. We are now going to condense the current debate on gender supremacy into a word, and each word will stand. Anyone else who speaks during this abbreviated debate will forfeit his or her right to play in the game."

That got them. We were now playing to a morgue.

"Beez and Amy, each of you may choose one word to summarize your feelings about tomorrow's game." The Beez's eyes shone as he dug into his reservoir of crudeness. Amy's gears were better oiled. I sensed something sinister taking shape inside her.

"I've got mine" Stephen said. He waited for total quiet then screamed, "*Carrion*!"

Muffled laughter cut off when I warned the crowd with my eyes. Then I gestured to Amy. She took her time, sniffed and casually raised her chin.

"*Gwendolyn*," she said matter-of-factly. The word was like a death knell tolling from the dark. The boys were very still and their faces pale in the firelight. Then, as if pulled to magnetic north, their heads turned to Gwendolyn's luminescent blonde hair in the front row. Amy walked off the stage triumphant. The Beez slunk away.

"Thank you for your attention," I said. "I think Justin and Abby have some announcements. Don't forget . . . after we break up here, I need to see all the boys who want to play in the game."

Justin and I passed each other in a mute changing of the guard. I walked up the aisle near Abby and leaned to her.

"Can I talk to you before you leave the fire tonight, Abby?"

Justin had already started his announcements, so she just nodded then gave him her attention. I joined Bobby at the rear, leaned my back into the stone wall, crossed my arms over my chest, and became a model listener. Bobby's shirt scraped against the rocks as he leaned toward me.

"Looked like the lynch mob scene from Costner's *Wyatt Earp.*"

"Thanks for all the help," I said and then added, "*Deputy.*"

Bobby shrugged. "Costner handled it by himself. I figured you'd want to do the same."

When the meeting broke up, twenty boys swarmed me and demanded their preferred positions on the field. I was still writing it all down as the kids filed off to their cabins. When I looked up, Abby was sitting on one of the benches, staring at the lake. The bed of coals pulsed with the breeze and reflected off her dark silky hair. Off in the distance, several of the counselors were trying to curb the rekindling of the gender-supremacy debates, yelling threats that can only be learned by a cabin counselor who knows the meaning of a sleepless night. I walked over to Abby.

"Hi," I said. She smiled, looking through me to some other place. I sat down backwards on the bench in front of her. "Thanks again for the car."

"Sure," she said.

I smiled. "I filled it with gas when I got back."

She nodded once, keeping her eyes fixed on the night.

"I talked to Tyler's mother."

Abby nodded, her interest seeming lackluster. I looked down at the list in my hand and took in a deep breath.

"Old Bill asked me to talk to you about these soccer awards."

"I've already done them. Here's the players list for the girls." She handed over a folded paper.

Off in the dark, Stephen Beasley's laugh carried through the trees from his cabin like the cry of a jungle bird. Two counselors called his name in unison, and silence gradually crept back into the fragile space between Abby and me.

"Everything go okay the last few days?" I asked.

"Yes."

I nodded. It was pretty clear that Abby was not up for a conversation.

I folded up my paper. "Okay, I just wanted to make sure you understood how the awards work."

"I do."

I looked at her, and she looked back at me for several seconds. There was nothing hostile or challenging in her expression, but I couldn't see a thread of the connection I thought we had made.

"Abby, we've got a few free hours this Saturday when Old Bill shows the movie. Would you like to go into Dahlonega for some dinner?"

Her forehead creased with lines. "No, I don't think so." She stood.

I looked up at her. "Well . . . okay . . . see you tomorrow."

She made a move to walk off, thought better of it, and faced me. "You do know that Gwendolyn and I share the same cabin, don't you?"

"Sure," I said.

Abby just stared at me. "And she and I are becoming friends."

I nodded. "That's great."

She pulled in her lips, making her mouth a thin line. When she opened her mouth, her lips made a little popping sound.

"Gwendolyn is kind of excited about going to the movie."

I waited to see where this was going. Abby just stood there as if expecting me to say something. She looked so deeply into my eyes, I thought she might be reading a flawed genome of my DNA.

"Good night," she said.

"Good night," I said to her back.

I watched her become a dark blur that blended into the night. Then her silhouette emerged again under the light of the dining hall. She walked in her typically smooth gait across the lawn and disappeared around the corner of the building. Like an eagle returning to the sky, putting distance between us.

I sat down next to the fire pit. The warmth rising up into my face was a pleasant feeling after the chill of Abby's enigmatic stare. I stirred the coals with a stick and watched sparks race upward to the sky. It reminded me of a story Bobby Whitehorse liked to tell about Trickster Rabbit replacing the stars that fell from the sky.

Old Rabbit had been here tonight, toying with Abby and me. I threw the stick on the coals and wrote off tonight as a visit from the Old Trickster. But I was not going to write off Abby Parrish.

In the office I got out colored poster boards and markers, hoping for the off-chance phone call from Pat Raintree. It was still before ten o'clock. I sat at Old Bill's desk then looked up at my mailbox, where a folded paper showed in the shadowy recess. I got up, walked to the mailbox, and opened the paper.

Stoney,

I just wanted to thank you for all that you have done for me since I started camp. I was a little naïve about some things when I got here. I feel like you saved me a lot of grief by the way you "suggested" I be careful with certain people. I have heard enough from Mimi now to know that Justin has a reputation, and I see how you were trying to protect me. So I just want you to know how much I appreciate your sense of honor. And I am honored that you asked me to the movie on Saturday. I hope it will be the beginning of a good friendship for both of us. You can't back out on the movie now, even if we girls beat you in the game!

Gwen

P.S.: And we <u>will</u> win.

I let my arm fall by my side, and the paper slapped against my thigh. My head turned toward the front window, looking for wider open spaces, but all I saw was a reflection of an almost twenty-year-old guy holding a love letter that might have fallen out of a middle school girl's locker. Old Trickster Rabbit was probably outside laughing, rolling in the grass, kicking his feet at the stars.

I sat down at the desk and stared at the blank poster board for about a minute before digging into my pocket for my list of players. I read over the boys' names and then opened Abby's paper to compare numbers. Something in the slant of her letters jumped out at me. I flattened the paper on the desk and pulled from my other pocket the note containing the sheriff's telephone message I had gotten before supper. It was the same handwriting. Abby had taken that message.

I reread the sheriff's words, hanging up on one sentence like I'd been snagged by a fishhook. *I'll keep an ear out for your lady friend in Atlanta.* I frowned at the papers in front of me, then closed my eyes, and shook my head.

"Great," I breathed and then couldn't help but laugh. I picked up a marker and started working on awards. It was the typical array of silly recognitions: "Best Accidental Goal", "Bloodiest Player", "Dirtiest Player", "Smelliest Player", "Loudest Yeller", "Best Pass to a Teammate", "Best Pass to an Opponent", and so on. When I had finished I printed up one more that read *Rabbit Bait*, pinned it to my shirt, and walked out into the cool night heading for my cabin.

Chapter Thirteen

The grass should have been singed wherever Gwendolyn put on a burst of speed. She was, in the camper vernacular, "awesome"—moving the ball as if it were tethered to either ankle by a short invisible rope. Whenever big Ben Souther chased her, I was reminded of a warthog stumbling and grunting in the wake of a cheetah. Even the best players among the boys never took the ball away from her. She was electric on the soccer field.

If Gwendolyn had a weak spot, it was vainglory—always going for the dazzling play rather than the safe one. Sometimes this cost her a goal. But the percentages were with her. She seemed tireless. Following her down the field with my eye was like watching a thunderstorm from the top of Standing Bear, waiting for the brilliant streak of unexpected energy to split the molecules of the air.

Abby was in at halfback, playing a conservative game that would hardly be noticed with the blonde fireball of Gwendolyn blazing across the field, but I found myself watching Abby more often than not. When she took possession of the ball, she usually made little progress toward the goal before passing off to one of the girls who called out from an opening. Once, when Abby accidentally kicked the ball right to Jamal, she looked up to the heavens with outstretched arms, laughed, and trotted past one of her young teammates saying something that made the camper laugh, too.

At halftime the girls were up four to one. Ben Souther and Dane Saxe walked over to me at the sideline with sober glares. They looked like two miniature CEO's about to enact a corporate takeover. Ben was slick with sweat and breathing hard. Dane looked like he had tried to eat the liver of his enemy and found it rancid.

"You gotta play, Stoney," Ben said in a peremptory monotone. "Nobody can keep up with Gwendolyn."

"Come on, fellas, you've got Jimmy Dale Vickers and Andy out there already."

Dane looked as dead-serious as I'd ever seen him. "They've got Gwendolyn," he said.

"Center-fold Warrior Princess from Hell," Ben murmured. Neither boy laughed.

I motioned them over to the shade under the white pines where the rest of the boys milled around the lawn spigot. In the pall of pending defeat, we grouped together and devised some sound ploys that might take advantage of Gwendolyn's propensity for the daring play. For the thousandth time everyone promised to pass more and not hotdog the ball down the field.

"Pass away from her every time she approaches the ball," I said. "But not too far away. We want her to go after it. To tire her out."

Big Ben hissed air through his teeth. "Tire *her* out?"

I ignored him. "And if we don't fall for the same stuff ourselves, if we hold our positions and play a patient game, we've got a chance of pulling this off."

The boys looked at me with hope draining out of their pores. They were spent, both physically and mentally. They wanted a magic bullet. They wanted Andy and me to team up on offense and make some miracles happen like we had against Camp Choestoe's staff last year. I think they would have paid us if they'd had any cash.

"Why don't we put somebody fresh at right wing," I suggested.

"Like who?" Dane asked.

I looked at Tyler and tried to read his face for this enlistment. His eyes took me back to the days I'd hidden from my father in my closet.

"Tyler, want to try?" I suggested.

Ben Souther looked at Tyler with a dismissive wag of his head and stepped toward me. "Stoney, this is serious. We've got to live with this the rest of the camp session."

Tyler looked relieved that Ben had interrupted, so I didn't push it. "Try the plan, guys. Just don't get so obsessed with handling Gwendolyn that you abandon your position. If you win or lose, you can do it with some grace."

"'Grace' is a girl," Ben huffed.

"If this doesn't work, Stoney, we're going to plan B," Stephen Beasley said. I knew I would not want to know the Beez's plan B, but since I was sort of coach-for-a-day and I was responsible for my team, I asked. Stephen pointed to Ben, who lifted a can of pork and beans from a brown paper sack. "We're feeding this to Bill Columbine and putting him at fullback," Ben said. I looked around at the ring of faces. They were serious.

Thankfully, plan A actually worked. At least, it cut down on the scoring by Gwendolyn. They held her off through the third quarter, and the more she was shunted from the glory of the goal, the more recklessly she played, and the more the boys teased her with evasive passing. But I didn't think she was going to wear down. If anything, she was faster than she had been in the first half. Either that or every other player on the field was dying faster. With two minutes left in the quarter Jamal scored and that pushed the boys into overdrive. They sensed the turning of the tide, until Gwendolyn rocketed a shot from midfield and caught Troy off-guard. The score was five-two . . . girls.

Privately, I loved it, but I openly commiserated with the demise of the boys' image of themselves as athletes not to be trifled with. Gwendolyn's performance aside, the girls were outstanding, playing a smart game. I stood by Tyler as the teams returned to the field. Ben

Souther was in conference with Bill Columbine, and both of them looked toward the grocery bag on the sideline.

"How'd you like to get out there, Tyler?" I said. "You and I could team up at center forward and right wing a while. Worse thing that could happen is we make complete fools of ourselves and get banned from team sports for life."

He looked tentatively at the players taking their positions. "Do I have to?"

"Of course not," I said, and then I lifted an eyebrow. "But a true Seneca would never walk away from *this*."

Though finding no humor in my logic, he reluctantly agreed and jogged out onto the field behind me. Tyler traded off with Jamal. I switched with Andy. For the first thirty seconds, Tyler and I watched Gwendolyn at the far end of the field as she stole the ball and blazed zigzag trails our way. It seemed like half the boys' team had gravitated to the fullback positions in a last stand.

Then Bill Columbine stepped unexpectedly into Gwendolyn's path and connected with a solid boomer of a kick that bounced off Jimmy Dale's head and shot high back to midfield. When Dane looked up, the ball was practically on top of him. His instincts kicked in, and he headed the ball with a whip of his neck so that the ball made progress my way. I scooped up the ball and dribbled toward the girls' goal. In the corner of my eye, I saw Tyler run toward me.

"Stay out to my flank, Tyler, about ten yards out and watch for my pass." I slipped past Amanda, the first fullback. The center full, Dorian—who had some moves I knew to respect—came for me pulling herself out of position. Like a pro, Tyler filled that spot. It was one of those sports moments when things started to click.

When I passed to him I sprinted wide to give Brittany, the remaining fullback, too much territory to cover. She had no choice but to go for Tyler and the ball. By now Amanda had recovered and made a beeline for him, too.

Tyler was not confident with the ball, scooting it along in tentative, uneven kicks. But at the perfect moment he passed to me, splitting the difference between Amanda and Brittany and then it was just me, Mimi, and the goal.

That was when I heard cleats churning the sod behind me. The tear of grass came on like the methodical ripping rhythm of farm machinery. The Center-fold Warrior Princess from Hell had crossed the field and arrived at my back door, her blonde mane flowing behind her like a war pennant. I wound up for a kick and whipped my leg toward the ball as Mimi dove into its intended path. I heard Gwendolyn start her sliding tackle around me where she would hook the ball with her foot soon after it left mine. But I had no intention of taking the shot.

I feinted, slipped my toe to the side of the ball, and lifted it in a slow gentle arc over Gwendolyn's leg toward Tyler. I leapt up into the air, trying to avoid the crash of flesh and bone, and watched the ball lob in slow motion like a beach ball headed right to Tyler.

In their various poses of kamikaze collision, Mimi and Gwendolyn twisted their heads to watch, too. But they were out of it. Now it was Tyler, the ball, and the empty goal.

With the ball dropping right on him he instinctively put out his hands to catch it, but a jolt of reality reminded him that this was soccer, not kickball. I was pretty sure he had never headed the ball in his life, but it was all he had now, and he seemed to know this. He flexed his face into a web of wrinkles, closed his eyes, and smashed his nose squarely into the ball. It bounced weakly to the grass and rolled only two yards as he stumbled forward onto hands and knees. Seeing the ball stop short of the goal, he scrambled forward and dove headfirst at it like a human billiard stick and popped the ball into the goal by the crown of his head.

A roar went up from the boys who were all running to the goal. Ben Souther threw Tyler over his shoulder like a duffel bag and pranced around the goal-box screaming. The other boys tried to slap Tyler's hand, but he was bouncing so violently that very few found the mark. Meanwhile Mimi, Gwendolyn, and I were heaped together with me on top. I tried to ease my weight off them gingerly while they were assessing limbs and joints.

"Somebody's bleeding," Mimi reported.

"I think that might be you," Gwendolyn said from the bottom of the pile. "I'm afraid I may have kicked you in the head."

Mimi laughed. "I'm okay."

Gwendolyn managed to turn herself around enough to wince at what her cleats had done to Mimi. "Yuk! You really *are* bleeding!"

Mimi laughed again, gently probed the skin above her eyebrow with her hand, and then frowned at the blood on her fingertips. "You think this looks bad . . . wait till you see the Blood Mountain film. A guy gets attacked by a bear! They must have poured a gallon of catsup over him."

I gave Mimi a hand, pulled her up, and took a look at the cut on her forehead. I called to Andy for a clean towel, ice, and a first aid kit. The game came to a halt while I cleaned up and bandaged the wound. Gwendolyn stood by looking contrite as Mimi tried to minimize the drama by describing more about the Blood Mountain film.

"Speaking of which," Mimi said and gave me a comic grimace of dread. "Stoney, do we have to sit through that movie each session?"

"Nope. Old Bill gives the veteran counselors a little time off during the showing. He knows that no counselor would want to see it twice."

"Thank God," she said. "How many times have you seen it?"

I grimaced. "As a camper I had to watch it every session. To see it again, I'd have to be tied to the mast of Odysseus's ship." I glanced at Gwendolyn, who had traded contrition for confusion. "You ought to see it at least once though. You'll get to see some of the places where the Outriders spend time on their trips away from camp."

The boys were still milking every ounce of glory out of Tyler's goal by parading him around the field. The girls, anxious to exact revenge, huddled together and talked strategy at midfield. Gwendolyn stood looking at nothing, her glazed eyes devoid of the sparks that had possessed her on the playing field. I walked over to her.

"I invite everyone to the movie, Gwendolyn. I apologize for not being clearer."

Her mouth tightened into a humorless smile. "So, you're not going?"

I shook my head. When she looked away, I was afraid she might be starting to cry. I stepped a little closer.

"I don't think we make a fit, Gwendolyn."

She turned her head quickly, and her blonde eyebrows pushed low over her eyes. "God, Stoney, I'm not asking you to marry me."

I smiled, looked down at the grass, and nodded. When I brought up my eyes, her flash of anger had passed.

Feeling like a scriptwriter for a B-movie, I said, "We could be friends."

She exhaled a long sigh. "I know. You've already been a friend to me about . . . you know . . . Justin."

"Don't give me too much credit there," I admitted. "That was like warning someone about quicksand."

"But you did it in such a good way."

I looked at her radiant beauty and tried to imagine forging through life with her looks, trying to recognize integrity in the people who hovered around me. "You have something pretty extraordinary, Gwendolyn. You'll have to handle it a little differently than most."

Now her eyebrows knitted together with a question. Before she could gather any words, the girls kicked off, and the ball was in play.

"Uh oh," I said. "I think I'm a little off-sides."

I looked for Tyler at the half-field line but couldn't find him. Checking the sidelines, I saw Old Bill standing with two men in dark suits—their presence completely incongruous in our crowd of grass-stained, sweat-soaked campers. A little spark ignited in my gut when I recognized the two men.

Beau Raintree and the bodyguard named Perry kept their eyes trained on Tyler, who moved toward them in a slouched, funereal march. When Tyler was close enough, Beau Raintree tousled his son's hair. Tyler looked at the ground and endured the touch as if he had been kissed by a witch. I jogged to the sideline under Bill's unblinking stare.

"What's going on?" I said.

"This is Mr. Raintree, Tyler's father," Old Bill said.

As if he had not heard, Beau Raintree gave me the side of his face. With his eyes hidden by wrap-around sunglasses, he grinned at the game in progress, as though amused that such nonsense went on in the make-believe world of children. He looked like a harder version of the man I had seen at Avano's. Though his air was congenial, his movements were controlled and affected, as though he were covertly telegraphing another message. He finally turned to me and smiled, his expression saying, *I am smarter than you.* My instincts were telling me that he knew exactly who I was.

Neither of us offered a hand. His hair was thinning on top and his cheeks jowly. Nothing about his appearance suggested any lineage to Native American blood. When he turned back to the game, I studied the bodyguard.

Up close his size provided a wakeup call for anyone who might choose to disagree with him, but his stature lay less in muscle mass than the breadth of his frame. Except for his cannonball stomach testing the buttons of his suit coat, he was raw-boned and angular. His eyes seemed sculpted from disappointment, so that the pervading aura emanating from Perry was one of tragedy. The skin on his face reminded me of biscuit dough.

Perry studied the game impassively, sighed, and stuffed his big-knuckled hands into the pockets of his coat. With the coat stretched by the weight of his arms, a bulge showed just below his left armpit, and I knew he was armed.

When Old Bill introduced me by my given first name, Tyler looked at me as if I had been described as a carrot. "Come for a visit, Mr. Raintree?" I said, my voice sounding as flat as Amy Littlefield's.

"I've come to take Tyler out of camp. We're heading back today. In just a few minutes, actually." There was not a trace of the South in his accent. If I had to guess, I would have placed his beginnings in Minnesota or Wisconsin, but my experience with dialects was limited, based solely upon campers I had known from various parts of the country.

There was no regret or apology in his voice. Beau Raintree seemed the kind of man who would never feel the need to explain himself. He still would not look at me.

Tyler stared at the grass between his sneakers. His body had wilted, and once again I saw that sag in his spine that he had brought to Itawa a week ago.

T-Bone had followed Old Bill from the office and now was sniffing Perry's leg, looking up at him with a lot of white showing around his dark canine irises. Perry felt the touch at his calf and over-reacted with an awkward sidestep that made T-Bone tense and lower his head. Man and dog backed away from each other in a comical *pas de deux*. T-Bone slunk back to Old Bill with his body curved as if going and coming at the same time.

"It's a shame to take Tyler out of camp," I said looking at Raintree's profile. "He's just been voted into a special group called 'the Outriders.' He's made lots of friends. They would miss him."

Tyler's head shot up. "I'm an Outrider now?"

"Absolutely," I said. "You were voted in last night." I didn't mention that I did the only voting, and that no one who wanted to be part of our group was ever turned away.

Tyler's first response was to turn to his father with this new rationale to stay at Itawa, but as soon as he saw his father's face, his enthusiasm dissolved. Raintree kept his eyes on the field and made a little *c'est la vie* turn of his wrist. His voice was as smooth as butter, but the glare of his dark glasses was cold as steel.

"Well, you know how it is," Raintree said. "We can't always do what we want to do. That's what life is all about. We make little adjustments. Right, Tyler?"

Tyler's stare tunneled into the earth again. Perry looked at me without moving his head. He slowly blinked. Then he rotated his massive body and fixed an impatient glare on Raintree.

"How about getting your things together, Sport," Raintree said. "We need to get going."

Tyler never raised his head. Silently, he obeyed a law whose penalties I could only guess, as he turned toward his cabin and shuffled away in the slow march of the condemned. T-Bone was sniffing

Raintree now, who showed more cool than Perry and lowered a hand for inspection. T-Bone backed away and leaned into my leg. I scratched him behind the ear—a reward for discriminating taste.

"I have a dog," Raintree offered offhandedly. He considered T-Bone and smiled. "More like a tiger really. Rottweiler." I supposed that was meant as an insult to our camp hound, but T-Bone seemed to take no offense. By Raintree's tone, I assumed that Thor had not OD-ed on the tranquilizers.

High-pitched screams erupted from the boys' goal, pulling our attention to the field. The girls had scored again and were dancing around the numbed boys as they returned to center field. Show horses prancing among zombies.

Old Bill's eyes flicked my way briefly, and then he spoke in a casual tone as he watched the players take their formation for a new kick-off. "Rottweiler. That's a watchdog, more or less, isn't it?"

For the first time since he had arrived, Raintree took off his sunglasses and looked me in the eye. The air around us seemed to compress into an electric hum. With his mouth frozen into a tight smile, his lips barely moved when he spoke.

"More or less."

I felt the heated rush of violent possibilities surge through me like an electric current. My father's face tried to surface through the puffy skin of this man, and I could taste the memory of blood in my mouth.

"Why don't you go up and help Tyler pack," Old Bill said, his eyes bearing down on me like two white flares sending a private warning.

I looked out on the field, seeing no one . . . just an abstraction of bodies in motion. I nodded and without a word jogged to the office to check for a message from Pat Raintree. My mailbox was empty. I sat at Old Bill's desk and called Tyler's home. As the ringing became a monotonous dirge in my ear, I stood up with the phone and stepped to the window to watch the two men standing with Old Bill. They looked malignant out there on the freshly mown hill of homogenous green, as if they might infect the innocence of everything around them.

When the phone had rung at least twenty times, I hung up and took down from the mantle an old *Buffalo Rock* ginger ale bottle that had gathered dust for years. I laid the bottle in the trashcan and smashed its midsection with my archery trophy until the thick bottom was relatively free of sharp points. From a shelf littered with nests, bones, rocks, feathers, turtle shells, and just about every other nature artifact you could think of, I grabbed a spike buck's antler and ran to Tyler's cabin into *déjà vu*.

Still in his soccer clothes, he sat on his bunk with the tragic sag in his spine. His gear was assembled on the floor around him. I walked around it to face him, but he wouldn't look up at me.

"I talked to your mother last Friday, Tyler. She couldn't give me any legal way to—" I closed my mouth and then my eyes. I knew that, for him, my explanation was meaningless. All he knew was that he was leaving. Nothing that I was going to say would change that. A tear welled in the corner of his eye. I wrapped the bottle glass and antler in a rag I had lifted from the kitchen clothesline and dropped it into the mouth of his open bag.

His head came up and his eyes locked on mine. "You said you wouldn't let anybody take me away if I didn't want to go."

I looked into those liquid eyes and saw all the broken promises of the world reflected in my image. The screams and urgent calls from the soccer field carried to us as if from a far-off place.

"I don't want to go," he said.

"I can't stop him, Tyler. He's your father."

He looked at me another ten seconds and then stood up slowly like an old man. "What's this?" he said, pointing at the folded rag I had laid in his bag.

"For arrowhead-making. Glass and a napping tool."

He closed the bag and strained to lift it. I leaned forward to take it for him, but he pulled back sharply.

"I don't need any help." He hefted the bag and penguin-walked out of the cabin, punching the screen door open with his duffel. The door slammed, and I stared at the depression left on his neatly made bed. When his footsteps crunched on the gravel in front of the dining hall, I cursed under my breath and hurried to catch him.

Before he could resist, I scooped up his duffel and hoisted it to my shoulder. "You've got to call me, Tyler. I need to know what your situation is. And your mother's, too." He trudged up the trail, showing no sign that he had heard me. "You've got to memorize the camp number and find a way to call me." I recited the number twice. He looked at me like I was crazy, never slowing his plodding trek toward the field. I repeated the number again. "Say it back." He stared down at the path and kept walking. His father and Perry were fifty yards away approaching from the soccer field. "Say it!" I whispered.

Reluctantly, he did. I kept my eyes on his father and spoke quietly to Tyler. "Every night I'm going to sit in the office at exactly ten o'clock and wait fifteen minutes for you to call. Do you hear me? You are not alone in this, Tyler."

"Right," he quipped, his voice dry and raspy.

"Ten o'clock," I said, "every night until I hear from you."

"Ready, Sport?" Raintree said, stopping before us. Perry lifted the duffel from my shoulder. Raintree made a token try for Tyler's smaller bag, but Tyler held onto it.

Old Bill stood behind them looking at me. He made a slow shake of his head that meant: *We have no recourse . . . stay cool.*

"That was a nice goal you made, Tyler," Old Bill said.

"You make a goal, Sport?" Raintree asked in a lifeless monotone.

Without a word, Tyler started toward the parking lot. Perry turned to follow, but when he had gone only a few steps he stopped, turned and looked impatiently at Raintree. We followed Perry through the stone terrace to a black BMW parked in the turnaround.

"Well," Raintree said to no one in particular, "I'm sure Tyler has had a very nice time."

Tyler dropped into the back seat of the BMW, slumped forward, and stared between his knees. Perry tossed the duffel into the trunk, walked to the driver's door, and stood looking at us over the roof of the car. He had the vacant gaze of a man waiting out a traffic light.

Raintree put out his hand to Old Bill, who took it automatically as he had with thousands of parents. With his glasses back in place, he turned to me with an amused expression and slipped his hands into his pants pockets. Then something changed in his face, like a shadow lifting away to reveal an animosity that had been hiding there all along. When he spoke, there was a new edge to his voice.

"Aren't you going to say goodbye to Stoney, Tyler?"

And there it was. He knew me. And he wanted me to know it. His lips parted enough to show the edges of his teeth. This was, no doubt, the look he used to threaten people. I wondered how many times Tyler had seen it.

From the corner of my eye, I saw Tyler lift his face. He raised one hand as a token farewell gesture and then resumed his captive posture. I kept staring at Raintree as he opened the front passenger door. Before he got in, he snorted a quiet laugh. I would have missed it if I had blinked. He sat and closed the door. The window powered down, and again he spoke without looking at me.

"Well, good luck with your little Rough Riders and all that."

"Outriders," I said.

"Whatever." He pulled off the sunglasses again and turned to let me see the smile in his eyes. Still watching me, he powered up the window. When Perry pushed his bulk away from the roof, the car shook as though buffeted by a strong wind. When he got into the driver's seat, the car sank two inches and the shocks squeaked. None of them looked at us again as the car glided down the drive in an unhurried exit that seemed to flaunt power.

Old Bill stepped up beside me, and we watched the BMW cruise through the dappled light and shadow beyond the gate. Dust rose in the vacuum of the car's wake and hovered in the sunlight as a pink cloud over the road until the breeze swept the air clean. My body tingled with unspent adrenaline. My tongue was coated with the bad taste of a promise I had not been able to keep.

Far down the road Bobby Whitehorse walked toward camp leading a bay mare by a rope. He stopped and looked at the car as it passed. Then, through the swirling dust, he stared at Old Bill and me. From the sports field a shrill collective cry of females filled the camp like the ululations of the Sioux women after Little Bighorn. The game was over. We could hear the mass stampede for the lake, where the players would celebrate and commiserate and cool off.

"Wasn't a thing we could do," Old Bill said.

For a time, we just stood there, staring down the road. The rhythmic *clop, clop* of Bobby's horse made me think of someone endlessly knocking on a door that I could not open.

"I promised I wouldn't let anyone take him from camp."

Old Bill grunted. Usually when we found ourselves alone somewhere on the grounds, we let our eyes roam across the landscape in a tacit appreciation of the world we had chosen to inhabit. If we spoke at all, it might be about some project that lay ahead of us—like a new paddock or replacing some roofing on the barn . . . things that seemed less of a job to us than opportunities to spend time together in the improvement of a place we loved.

Old Bill kicked at the gravel, mumbled something I could not understand, and marched back to the office like a soldier who had been stripped of his hard-earned rank. I looked over the office roof at the bold, stone-capped knob of Standing Bear Dome. I closed my eyes and imagined all the night stars falling out of the sky at once and the world set ablaze. I saw panicked animals charging through the brush heading for lower ground. Deer bounding through the laurel. Squirrels leaping from tree to tree. Hawks screaming and soaring into the open space over the camp. And a lone snake with hourglass patterns carving a wavy incision across the smooth skin of the lake.

Chapter Fourteen

For two days I went through the motions of being a camp counselor, trying to focus on someone's paddling form on the lake . . . or release and follow-through at the archery range . . . or teaching the Outriders about medicinal plants. But my mind was constantly on Tyler. I kept seeing his slumped back as he sat on his bunk. His last few sentences echoed inside my head with a haunting timbre that I could not shake. For two nights I had waited in the office from nine-thirty till eleven. I sat there like a hawk perched on a power line and watching for a vole in the weeds. I stared at the telephone, willing him to call me.

Each night when I left the office for my cabin, I paused at the canoe dock where Bobby Whitehorse smoked his pipe and listened to the nocturnal sounds of the forest. Each time I approached him, he turned to check my face, and each time I just shook my head and went home to bed. If I had entertained any idea that Abby might help to balance the depression festering inside me, I quickly learned to abandon that hope. She avoided me with effortless grace.

On Thursday morning I ran harder than usual, testing the limits of my endurance. I increased my upper body work on the pines and swam sprints back and forth between the two docks until my lungs burned. When Bobby stopped by for coffee, we never mentioned Tyler, but the unspoken thought of him hung in the cabin like a third party. Bobby eased his words carefully around the dark places in my head and coaxed me into planning the river trip on Saturday. The wisps of mare's tail clouds that quilted the sky at dawn promised rain within thirty-six hours, probably sooner, which meant that the Etowah would be running high on the weekend. The water would be pushy.

After lunch, some boys gathered on the dining hall deck for an impromptu game of *Sting*—the hand-slapping duel that had probably been handed down from the dawn of man. Bobby Whitehorse may have been responsible for its reprise. For him it was the surrogate showdown of the Western gunfighter exhumed. I had finally beat Bobby at it when I was fifteen, and, still, I was the man to beat.

"Here's 'the kid,'" Bobby said as I pushed out of the door.

"I challenge you, Stoney!" Ben Souther boomed. He stepped before me, spread his feet, and rocked from side to side on his big rectangular frame. "You can go first," he said.

Keeping his eyes on mine, he brought his hands up in slow motion, his palms together in front of his belt buckle with the fingers pointing toward me. There his hands waited like a cornered animal, its entire being focused on escaping my slap.

I waited. This wait was compulsory if I wanted to win this without his raising the cry that he hadn't been ready.

"Are you ready, Ben?"

He stared at my right hand with such intensity that his face appeared as hard as rock. "I'm ready," he replied and then swallowed.

Keeping my face blank, I waited nine heartbeats and swatted his hands with a loud *smack!* At the smart report, the group of onlookers recoiled involuntarily. I hadn't even bothered to lead him by swinging where his hands would be when he scissored them apart. No need. Ben was not a top gun in *Sting*.

"Ow!" he squealed, shaking his hand in the air as if trying to cool it off.

"Were you ready?" I asked, holding back a smile. He gave me a look and didn't answer. When he got over his defeat, I said, "You can try me now." He looked at my hands—already positioned for him—

and for a moment he seemed to entertain a longshot hope for revenge. But then doubt crept back into his eyes, and he shook his head.

I spent the next ten minutes defending my reputation by stinging the Beez, Jamal, and Troy. All of them walked away red-handed.

"How come you're so good at this, Stoney?" Jamal asked.

All heads turned my way to hear my secret, but the answer came from Bobby Whitehorse, who had been witnessing all this carnage as he leaned back against the rail with his thumbs hooked in his belt. "It's the only acceptable way he can practice camper abuse without you guys even knowing it."

Finally—as I knew it must—the inevitable duel materialized when the boys called for Bobby Whitehorse. He smiled at me and started to approach, but Abby appeared out of nowhere and stepped in his way.

"Can ladies play?" she asked, her voice like a cool breeze.

The boys got quiet. Abby looked very serious, but I was in a quandary. I wasn't sure if I could bring myself to slap her. It was an all-or-nothing game, no way to play at half-speed. As I delayed, Bobby quietly whistled the theme from *The Good, the Bad, and the Ugly*.

When Abby raised her hands as the target, I shook my head. "You challenged," I said. "So, I get to choose."

I brought my palms together before me, and she lowered her hands to the sides of her legs. Her no-nonsense gaze made me think of an assassin looking through the scope of a rifle. It seemed less a game now, and the air between us was charged with anticipation. No one spoke or moved, and this stillness stretched out for almost half a minute.

Then the air crackled between us, and my left hand tingled with surprise. When everyone realized what had happened, all eyes turned to Abby. Her face was like a wood carving. The silence was so complete, I expected to hear the blood rush back into my hand.

Abby held out her hands to reciprocate, but my heart was not in it. I enveloped her hands in mine for a brief moment, bowed my concession, and stepped back. Holding her stoic expression, Abby walked around me and down the stairs, each step as sharp and punctuated as a notch carved into a gun handle. I looked at Bobby, knowing he surely must have had a Western line for me.

"There's always somebody a little faster, Kid." He mumbled something about Henry Fonda and Anthony Perkins as he, like everyone else present, watched Abby stride across the lawn. For a full minute, we stood mutely on the deck like unexpected witnesses in the aftermath a violent crime. My hand still vibrated like a struck tuning fork.

I didn't have an afternoon class; and with the film scheduled for right after supper, it was a good time to escape. I needed to vent some frustration over my obsession with Tyler and my unexpected distance with Abby. I asked Old Bill if I could take off to scout the river for downed trees. We went through our typical debate: his obligatory protest at my going on the river alone and my gentle assurances that all would go well.

As always, our script avoided the tacit understanding that it was just something I needed to do. Though he never admitted it, I suspected he had done the same when he was younger. It wasn't about being on a daredevil's edge. It had to do with intimacy. To engage the river alone, to enter the roaring silence that comes with a total presence of mind, unfettered by the joys, apprehensions, or expectations of another human being. It was, for me, a transcendental experience, and, on this day, I needed some transcending.

"Scouting for deadfalls" was nothing more than a password between Old Bill and me. I needed the spiritual ablutions that only a wild river could provide.

Thirteen years were invested into my relationship with moving water. As a child I had made model boats from scrap wood and followed their scaled-down voyages for miles on the creek that ran from my neighborhood into the uncharted territory of undeveloped woods behind a community golf course. Though the experience was miniaturized on the creek, I must have soaked up the principles of hydrodynamics pretty well, because the first time I knelt in a real canoe as a camper at Itawa, I seemed to know what to do. During the next few years, under Bobby Whitehorse's tutelage, I felt like I'd found my home in whitewater.

The power, the swell of a wild river, its changing personalities, its immediacy . . . all these things were as natural to me as the flow of blood inside my body. Bobby Whitehorse joked that whenever I donated to a blood drive, somewhere someone in a hospital would enjoy a little jolt of whitewater rush along with all those red corpuscles.

I held no illusions about the other side of that relationship. The river did not look out for me. But at the same time, it was not heartless. It simply demanded that I live up to both our expectations. I had almost drowned once a few years ago, and, at the time, I was struck by the nonchalance of it all. There was nothing malevolent in the experience. There had simply been a statement of fact about my shortcomings.

The river cannot afford to take pity on someone who chooses to enter its swollen fury. That would negate the whole definition of wild waters. But it was that near-death experience that made me wonder if angels were assigned to us. I knew no other way to explain my salvation.

Before I dropped off my canoe at Nimblewill Bridge, the sky blackened and rain dappled my windshield in fat dollops that popped on the glass. By the time I met Bobby Whitehorse at the take-out below the Narrows, a deluge of water was coming down.

I left my truck and jumped into his, and we drove back through the storm, both peering through the temporary swaths opened up by the wipers, neither of us talking until we'd stopped at the bridge where my canoe waited.

"What did the gauge read?" he asked.

"One-six," I said.

Bobby's lower lip pushed forward, and he looked over the metal guardrail at the growing surge of current. I strapped on my helmet and stepped out of the truck. The rain glued my nylon shell to my skin and thumped off my helmet and lifejacket like falling pea gravel. As his engine idled, Bobby gazed through the curtain of rain at the rapid below the bridge.

"What's she read now?" he said.

Moving to the bank I squinted through the rain at the gauge. "Two feet," I yelled.

He made a circle with his lips and might have whistled, but I couldn't hear it. I stepped back toward him, and we looked at one another the way warriors once must have when they parted in these hills. I knew he understood what I was doing. And he was wise enough to be quiet, even though there had to be half a dozen Robert Duvall-*Lonesome Dove* lines appropriate for the moment. Using the Indian hand language that he had taught me, he made the signs for "heart" and "strong." Then he ratcheted into first gear. As I climbed down the bank, his truck rumbled across the wooden bridge.

I unzipped my lifejacket pocket and carefully removed the bundle of fur, foliage, and feather I had put together. I had first seen a medicine bundle at thirteen, when Bobby Whitehorse had tied it to the knife sheath that he had given me when I left for my first solo survival trek. It was an Indian ritual that made sense to me, and as a young teenager I had adopted its use as easily as I had learned to say "thank you" as a child when someone gave me a gift. Bobby said the medicine bundle was a way to say "thank you" to the Earth . . . and the river . . . and all the gifts from the Maker of All Things.

I tied the bundle to an overhanging bough of hemlock and spoke over the water that roared and spit under the bridge. In the steady drone of rain, my voice was soft but clear, and these were the last words I would hear for the next few hours.

"Clear the way. In a sacred manner I come."

I untied the bow rope, stepped into my boat, and knelt into the kneepads, feeling the rush of the river hum beneath the hull like a massive flow of electricity. When I dipped my blade into the swift current, the bolt of power that telegraphed up the shaft was immediate—a lightning rod in reverse. Peeling out into midstream, I positioned myself for the first rapid and locked into the keen trance of reading the river with total concentration, sparks jumping every synapse in my brain, but contained . . . addressing the matters at hand while assessing what lay next.

My eyes scanned the broken surface of the water, and I made navigational decisions in split seconds, decisions that did not allow hesitation. For the span of the trip, not once did I think of Tyler, or Itawa or tomorrow. Not even Abby. I dealt only with currents and routes as I rose and fell on the swell of waves and accelerated through chutes of foaming water.

It was like stepping off the edge of the world and flying. The ecstasy of participating moment to moment in this world was balanced by the fierce strokes and raw power needed to maneuver each rapid. I was fully engaged in the act of living in the present tense, for there was no way not to. The water came up another half a foot before I was halfway to the Narrows. It was an afternoon that would take its place in the whitewater hall of fame in my memory.

It was almost dark when I returned to camp. The rain had tapered off, leaving the valley dripping and subdued. When I saw Old Bill inside the office gathering up the projector and film, I stuck my head through the door to let him know I was back. Then I hit the shower house. I'd missed supper, so I went straight to my cabin to heat up a can of soup before it was time for my telephone vigil.

Ironically, the sanctuary of my home was accentuated by the noise floating across the lake from the dining hall, where the antsy campers awaited the movie. It felt good to be alone inside walls that I had hewn and stacked and chinked with my own hands. There is no coziness like an earned one.

It was too warm to light the stove inside, so I built a small fire outside in my circle of stones, put on the soup, and stood listening to the first whip-poor-will of the season as it cranked up its insistent but dulcet song in the hollow. The bird's call got me thinking about musical onomatopoeia, until I found myself back inside seated at my piano toying with the whip-poor-will's theme, coaxing it into a melody. I lost all track of time and let my hands follow new patterns on the keyboard.

Soon, I had abandoned the birdsong and transitioned into a river theme. As I searched for the liquid notes to interpret the flow of the Etowah, I could still see the waves and crosscurrents and boulders and hydraulics coming at me. My fingers skirted through these textures of the waterscape and reached for the song that throbbed inside the heart of the river.

A light shape in the open doorway lifted my hands from the keys. Abby Parrish stood there holding my saucepan of soup. She wore a white long-sleeved blouse tucked into worn jeans, no belt, sandals, and a tentative smile.

"It was starting to scorch," she said lifting the smoking pot before her like an offering plate.

Taking the oil lamp from the piano, I stood, walked to my counter, and patted the flat stone I used for hot things. "Just put it here." When she tapped down the pan, I lifted the lid to survey the damage. The vegetables made a cityscape cemented to a common foundation of congealed broth. A ring of black crust clung to the inside walls of the pot like cooling lava.

Abby's smile was merciful. Full-bore Joan of Arc. I raised a finger as a warning.

"Don't tell me what you had for supper tonight."

She closed her mouth and pressed her lips together tightly, but not soon enough to hide the upgrade of her smile. On the counter, I opened the waxed paper on a column of crackers and popped one in my mouth.

Her eyes traveled around the room. "You built this, didn't you?"

"Bobby Whitehorse and I."

She studied the things I had on my walls so intently that I began to look at them, too, seeing them through her eyes. Across the lake came the heavy warbling minor chord that marked the distorted intro to *Survival on Blood Mountain*.

"Is that your mother?" Abby said walking toward the picture on the mantle.

"Yeah," I answered and lighted another lamp in the main room. Abby stood quietly before the photo as if introductions were in order.

"She's lovely," she said, then turned toward me on impulse and stared. "You've got her dark eyes." She cocked her head. "Why does Bobby Whitehorse call you 'Gray Eyes'?"

I finished the cracker I was munching on and shrugged. "Indians used to call their Anglo oppressors 'white eyes,'" I explained. "Maybe Bobby is letting me off the hook a little."

She touched her tongue to her upper lip. "Bobby Whitehorse thinks a lot more of you than *that*." She looked back at my mother's picture. When she turned to me again, her slate blue eyes softened, reflecting the flame from the oil lamp behind me. The serenity that spread through the room seemed to emanate from her skin. "Do you mind that I came down here?"

I shook my head and thought about the transformation of the room. My cabin was always serene. I had never thought that adding another body to it could increase that sense of peace. But it did with Abby.

"Want to sit?" I said pointing to my best chair. She walked to it, folded a leg underneath her, eased into the chair, and started a new survey of the room that ended at the piano.

"What was that you were playing?"

I sat on the hearth and worked on another cracker. "I don't know yet. Something about the river."

She looked at me for several seconds then nodded slowly. "I think I made an embarrassing mistake with you."

I stopped chewing and raised my eyebrows. "That seems to be this year's theme."

She smiled without humor, bent her knees to one side and tucked the other foot beneath her. The denim of her jeans smoothed across her thighs.

"Yes, it does, I suppose. Gwendolyn got a little confused. She's sort of chosen me as her confidant, but she hasn't talked to me for a couple of days . . . until tonight." Abby tilted her head and shrugged one shoulder. "I thought . . . well . . . *she* thought you had asked her out and—" Abby came close to squirming. "Then you asked me and—" She smiled, shook her head and laughed. "Well," she laughed again, "I thought I was all through being a teenager."

"How old *are* you, Abby?"

She gave me a look. "Don't you know you're not supposed to ask a woman that?"

I nodded, shrugged, and then smiled. "So, how old are you?"

"Twenty-two," she said, and by the way she said it I knew our age difference meant nothing.

"Gwendolyn is younger than she thinks she is," I said. "Probably hard to grow up with all those good looks."

"I think so," Abby said. "She's had all the boys lined up since she was in kindergarten."

"Well, not all of them. Ben Souther called her 'the centerfold Warrior Princess from Hell.'"

Abby had a genuine laugh that easily circled back to her serious nature. "And you," she said. "You didn't get in line."

I looked up at the far corner of the ceiling. "Well . . . Gwendolyn and I . . . we're not on the same page." I checked Abby's face to see if that lame answer would suffice. I shrugged. "Or maybe not in the same book. Different values, I think."

"Still, you gave her something important. Maybe she'll know better what to look for now."

I tried not to blush.

"From what she told me," Abby continued, "it could be the first time a man wasn't working an angle on her."

"We're not all that bad, Abby." My little testimonial in defense of men came back to me a little preachy, so I added, "Take T-Bone. He didn't try to put a move on her. Not that I know of anyway." I tried for a curious look. "Did he?"

She laughed again and sat forward. "I'm sorry about my presumptions. I wish now we'd had dinner together tonight."

"The offer still stands," I said and tossed her the package of crackers.

She caught the pack, and her smile went beyond Emmy Lou Harris. It was almost like having electricity in the cabin for a split second. Abby took out a cracker, toasted me with a twist of her wrist, and bit off a piece. I watched her chew and again thought how nice my cabin looked with her in it.

"Is 'Stoney' your real name?"

I related my given name, and she didn't even flinch. After I had told her the whole story about my first day at Itawa, about Barbie's florid handwriting and Old Bill's flawed reading of it, she laughed and let her head rest back on the chair. Hearing the joy in her voice was like listening to a song. When she stopped laughing, her face seemed to default to earnestness.

" 'Stoney' fits you fine," she whispered.

"What about you, Abby Parrish? Lots of religious territory in that name."

She gave me a tired nod as she finished a cracker. "It's Abigail. Not so clerical when you spell it all out."

"Well, Abigail. I've got to go up to the office to wait on a phone call. Come on, I'll walk you to the other side of the lake."

Outside, my little fire was dead, and the persistent whip-poor-will was enjoying an intermission. Abby and I walked the trail side by side, our footsteps like a clock ticking off our time together. Up the hill I could hear the worst actors in cinematic history surviving on Blood Mountain.

"Did you drive back into Atlanta today?" she asked. "You were gone a long time."

The images of the Narrows filled my mind. I could hear the crash of rapids and smell the freshly churned silt that had dominated my senses all afternoon.

"I took some time off by myself." With anyone else I would have left it at that, but Abby was like a warm wood stove that you opened your hands to on a cold night. "I've been dealing with something a little new for me." She waited politely. "I guess I'm a little depressed."

She frowned and cocked her head to one side. "About?"

"Tyler."

"Is he not coming back?"

"I have no idea what's going to happen to him. He didn't want to leave."

"Can't you call him?"

"No. I'm going up to the office hoping he will call me."

"What about his mother? Can't you talk to her again?"

"It wouldn't be easy for a next time." I huffed a cynical laugh. "It wasn't easy the *first* time. I've been waiting for her to call me or the sheriff for almost a week."

Abby stopped and turned to me. Against the sheen of the lake, she was a faceless shape cut out of black paper.

"The sheriff?"

"Yeah, Sheriff Canaday is listening out for me. He's easier to reach than I am, but I don't think it's going to happen."

Abby still had not moved, and it dawned on me what was going through her mind. *I'll keep an ear out for your lady friend in Atlanta.* I guess I had been acquitted on both counts now.

"I've got to go, Abby . . . in case Tyler calls. It's almost ten." I turned to jog to the office.

"Stoney St. Ney?" I stopped like a relay man waiting for the baton. "Thanks for dinner," she said.

"My pleasure, Abigail Parrish."

She stepped toward me and lifted my left hand. I watched dumbly as if she were doing a magic trick. When she carefully pressed her palm to the skin she had slapped earlier, I understood and smiled. I'd seen contrition and mischief try to mix like oil and water on children's faces, but on Abby it somehow worked. I pointed at her as I backed toward the office.

"We might have to have a rematch one day."

She lifted both eyebrows and gave me a crooked smile. "We might," she said.

At the back door of the office, I looked back. Abby moved in her smooth eagle glide up the hill toward the dining hall. She would make it in time to see the survivors stumble out onto highway 19 and hail a chicken truck for their salvation. I knew that she was going to help out with shuttling campers off to their cabins after the film.

I sat in the office for an hour. No Tyler. But when I walked back toward my cabin and passed Bobby Whitehorse with the redundant news, I wasn't quite as down as I had been on previous nights. He asked me what I was whistling, and I realized it was the piano theme I had been exploring when Abby had appeared in my door. It was sounding more like an eagle theme to me now.

Chapter Fifteen

The female voice on the telephone hummed with a jaded drone, no doubt designed to cull out unimportant calls. I had expected this with a lawyer's office, but I had no intention of being daunted by it. Plan A was courteous directness. If that failed, I was prepared to up the ante. Anything was better than waiting every night for Tyler to call me.

"Good morning, my name is St. Ney. I am calling on behalf of Pat Raintree. It's urgent that I talk to Mr. Scroggin."

"What is this in regard to, sir?" Her query was more of the jaded drone.

"Pat Raintree is a client of Mr. Scroggin," I reminded.

"Yes, sir, but exactly what is this in regard to?"

Plan B involved courtesy with references to legal ramifications. "Mrs. Raintree's safety. And her son's. Technically, this may have to do with kidnapping."

"Are you saying that she or her son has been kidnapped?"

Her voice was guarded now. It occurred to me she might think this was a ransom call from the kidnapper.

"Maybe."

Three heartbeats of silence. "Sir, perhaps you need to call the police."

Plan C: courtesy with implied threats. "What is your name please?"

"Ms. Emily Broussard." Her words were clipped and defensive.

"Ms. Broussard, I'm guessing your job is to screen out superfluous calls . . . to make appointments . . . and generally tend to Mr. Scroggin's agenda. This is not superfluous. The situation does not give us the luxury of waiting for an appointment. And this will most definitely be a big part of Mr. Scroggin's immediate agenda. Yes, I agree the police should be called, but your boss needs to make that call, and I need to explain to him why. If *you* don't give him that option, this will eventually fall back on your shoulders, and you will be asked in a court of law why you kept this message from Mr. Scroggin."

I gave her a moment to let that sink in. I couldn't hear her breathing over the line.

"So, I'm asking you now, Ms. Broussard, to put me on hold, tell Mr. Scroggin who I am, and tell him that his client and son are probably being held against their will. If you are not willing to do that, then you bear the responsibility of what happens to her and to Tyler. I have a busy day and I will be away from a phone. So . . . this is the moment that I ask you to do the right thing."

I waited for all that to wash over her and settle. Ten seconds ticked by.

"Just a moment, please," she said in a subdued voice. Her line clicked off and left me with a golden oldie radio station suddenly alive in my ear—Celine Dion belting out a chorus amid a swell of strings. Scroggin picked up before Celine could climb to her climactic high note.

"Arthur Scroggin," he said with enough impatience to let me know that Emily Broussard had briefed him on my questionable methodology in breaking to the front of the line.

"Mr. Scroggin, my name is Stoney St. Ney. Pat Raintree gave me your number. I work at the summer camp where she sent Tyler, her son."

"What can I do for you? My secretary mentioned something about a kidnapping."

I took a deep breath and dug in. When I had completed the story, I could hear him breathing as if he was already working up a sweat just thinking through the legalities.

"We have a problem, Mr. St. Ney." He shuffled some papers. "Here it is," he mumbled. "Last Monday Mrs. Raintree withdrew her intent to file for divorce. All the legal work was terminated."

His words whirled inside my head like a machine I could not shut off. "You talked to her? In person?"

"No, it was done over the telephone, but I'm certain it was she. We have talked on the phone many times."

"But not lately, I'll bet, until this."

"Well, that's true. Nevertheless, it is out of my hands now. Reconciliations do happen."

"So does coercion."

He was quiet. I could hear something tapping. A pencil maybe.

"If you have something tangible—some kind of proof—we can go to the police with this. Otherwise, I have to consider my liability."

"What about Tyler's liability? And Pat's? What if they are being held against their will? If you and she have talked about the reasons for her divorce, then you must know this is exactly the kind of power play that her husband would use."

"Again, we must have something to take to the police. I can't call up the authorities on hearsay or a hunch."

I dredged up all the patience I could muster. "Okay," I said pleasantly, "Mr. Scroggin, would you at least go out to the house to check on them. You know her. It's a reasonable visitation. Don't you have some form that needs signing to close her file for divorce?" I heard the pencil stop tapping. "For the sake of liability," I added.

He hesitated, and I knew this could go either way. It all hinged on his good will and conscience. I had more pep talk ready, but this would work better if he initiated it. He exhaled heavily into the phone.

"I suppose I could stop by with a document," he said weakly. He cleared his throat. "I have to tell you that I have had some worries about all this myself. Your input is not entirely a surprise."

"Will you call me?"

"Give me a day to set this up, and I'll call you. What's a good time to reach you?" I told him, left the camp number, and we hung up. If he followed through, I might have to work on upgrading my stereotype concerning lawyers. Then again, I might receive a bill for a telephone consultation that could wipe out my income for the year.

We carried the canoes just above the Nimblewill Bridge rapid, where the Outriders planned to spend the day using the local swimming hole as a training area to get accustomed to current. They would need this adjustment time before coming back to run the river. The water level had dropped to one-point-three and would be perfect by Saturday.

This session provided the veteran students an opportunity to help the new campers understand the unrelenting nature of moving water. Many times in the day, tandem teams had to step out into the river to drag their canoes upstream after being swept down toward the bridge. No one washed over the first rapid, which was intimidating enough to inspire no-nonsense action on the part of the paddlers, but at lunch Troy and some of the more confident kids took turns as demonstrators, showing the others the mechanics needed in running the rapid. Eventually everyone had a go at it and was smitten by the roller coaster thrill of whitewater.

The first-time campers had arrived at the river full of apprehension. Now they were screaming such nuggets of Southern prose as "Yee-haw!" and "Bring it on, Bubba!" as they dropped through the chute. We honed our skills until we felt ready for tomorrow's trip. Then we loaded up the canoes on the trailer and returned to camp.

Introductions were complete, and now the river no longer loomed quite so large as an unknown in these young minds.

That night at dinner, Abby and Gwendolyn sat together with all the girls who had played in the soccer game. I had heard rumors about a rematch without counselors. The way the girls all leaned in toward Gwendolyn's monologue, I was pretty sure their table was serving as a war room for the next gender-driven contest on the field.

With the dessert being instant pudding, I left the dining hall early and strolled down to the stables where Bobby Whitehorse was tossing hay from the loft. He saw me but kept up his rhythm with the pitchfork.

"Are your river rats ready, Gray Eyes?"

"Yep," I replied. "Everybody ran the rapid below the bridge a few times. After one of those runs, Jamal turned around to Amanda and yelled, 'It don't get no better'n this, Bubba.'"

Bobby climbed down the ladder, took off his crumpled black hat and wiped his forehead with his sleeve. He chuckled soundlessly.

"Amanda have anything to say to that?"

"She told him she was a 'Bubbette, thank you.' The water level should be down to one-one tomorrow."

Bobby nodded. "What time do we pull out?"

"Nine o'clock."

He latched the barn door and joined me at the fence, where I watched four horses in the paddock dine on their entree of seasoned hay. A cream-colored Arabian mare approached us, hooked her head over the top rail, looked right at Bobby, and nickered. He stood eye to eye with the big mare and put on an exasperated face.

"I'm going to the dining hall," Bobby said as if explaining himself. "I got to eat, too." The Arab withdrew her head and sauntered away, which I guess Bobby took as equine acquiescence, because he started up the path toward the dining room. I fell in beside him and matched my longer strides to his shorter ones.

"I talked to Pat Raintree's lawyer. He's going to go by the Raintree's house to check on things." The combined sound of our footsteps on the dirt track was no different than mine when walking alone. Bobby was always quiet when he moved. I never understood how he managed that in cowboy boots.

"What do you think are the chances that lawyer will be able to talk to her alone?" he said.

I nodded back toward the paddock. "About the same chance that mare has of eating in the dining hall," I replied.

He nodded. "You already eaten?"

"Yeah."

"Okay, see you at the fire tonight." He continued his smooth stride up the hill, and I watched him move across the rise as if there were no hill at all.

"Bobby," I called out.

He stopped and turned, his unhurried movement conveying the thread of the present tense that ran through his core. He tucked his shirt into his jeans, and then his thick square frame settled like a boulder. "If you had to say . . . what animal do you see in Abby?"

"Eagle," he said, his response instantaneous and clear, yet spoken with the respect he afforded that bird. He looked at me, waiting.

"Yeah, me too."

At the evening program, Troy did not make fire, but something beautiful happened. I asked Amanda to take my spot in the team, and together they produced a flame. A few people forgot and started to applaud, but that was quashed by the peremptory turn of Amanda's head. I made a final announcement about the canoe trip and left the meeting early to put a final coat of varnish on my paddle before dark.

At my cabin, after finishing the work, I built a fire in the outside pit and hung the paddle close by to dry. The campers had retired to their cabins, and the woods around me were quiet, so I put in time on my piano and experimented with that eagle theme.

Just as I started for the office to wait for Tyler's call, I heard something across the lake. Walking out to my small landing, I saw a dark shape lumped on the swimmers' dock fifty yards away. My best guess was that it might be a pile of lifejackets or towels, but the waterfront staff was always sharp about putting things away. I stared at it for a full minute. There was no hat brim, which ruled out Bobby. A tryst? No. Sound travels incredibly well over a smooth lake, and there was no sound at all. I didn't think the dark shape was big enough for two anyway. I cupped my hands around my mouth and whispered softly over the water.

"Name, rank and serial number." I lowered my hands and listened. There was a faint shuffle of fabric and a slight movement.

"I am not a prisoner of war. I am a listener." The whisper was completely generic. I didn't know if it was male or female, camper or counselor. For all I knew, it could be the Lady of the Lake taking a breather on the dock

I raised my hands like a megaphone again. "Listening to what?"

I stopped breathing to hear the reply. "The music of the spheres."

This wasn't a camper—which was a good thing, since all the kids should have been in their bunks.

"It was a piano," I whispered. On a whim, I waxed poetic. "Are you an eagle?"

Twenty seconds passed. "Maybe," the voice said.

"Eagles are not nocturnal," I reminded.

I waited for a snappy comeback, but the voice just said, "Oh."

By the time I moved back into the trees, walked around the lake, and reached the dock, no one was there. I walked out to the end and felt the boards with my hand. They were still warm. I looked across the water toward my cabin and imagined the dark shape of me over there. If this had been a movie, I would have found a matchbook with the name of a nightclub printed on it . . . or maybe a glass slipper. For the moment it would have to remain a mystery. My most fervent wish was that it was not Gwendolyn.

A little before eleven, I joined Bobby Whitehorse on the dock, lowered myself onto my stomach and lay on the old warped boards with my chin propped on the backs of my hands. He didn't need to ask. He knew Tyler had not called. I could see the stars in the lake's surface as if I were lying on my back.

Our moment of reverie was interrupted by an unexpected series of deep, throaty hoots from a barred owl at the feeder creek. We were very still, waiting for an encore, when the owl floated along the far shore, wove into the trees, and was lost to us. We waited another five minutes without talking, not wanting to infringe on the spell the bird had cast upon the night.

"My people believe the owl is the messenger of death," Bobby said.

I turned my head to him even though I couldn't see his face. "You believe that?"

Bobby took a draw on his pipe, and the red coal in the bowl illuminated the angles of his cheekbones. "That old owl don't know any more about death than the rest of us. I like him. Sweetest sound in the night." He tapped his pipe against the dock, and smoldering tobacco sizzled in the water beneath the boards. "How're you doing, Gray Eyes?"

I propped up on my elbows and frowned at the darkness. "Hard to leave this thing about Tyler unfinished."

"We're not finished," Bobby said with quiet conviction. Sitting with his back to a piling, he slipped his pipe into his shirt pocket. "We're just temporarily inactive. Use the waiting time to think about what we'll do when we're back in the picture. If the lawyer doesn't come through, it's up to us. There's nobody else. And who better for the task? You ever see the Lone Ranger and Tonto screw up?"

I huffed a short airy laugh through my nose. "Always positive, aren't you?"

"Better than negative. With negative, we lose from the start. With positive, we got a chance. You know where I learned that?" I looked away. I knew his answer but didn't feel I deserved the rating. "You're too close to this one, Gray Eyes," he said.

"You trying to cheer me up?" I didn't expect an answer to my rhetorical question, so I lay prone again and closed my eyes.

"Just until you let that eagle perch in your tree," he remarked.

My eyes opened at that. Bobby's head was tilted back, taking in the swarm of stars above. "She's a solid lady," he said. "Best thing to come around here since that Alabama lady who did the storytelling."

"Shannon Hardiman."

"Yeah. She knew more Cherokee legends than I did."

"How come you didn't . . . you know . . . get to know her better?"

Bobby was as still as the piling on which he leaned. "I did," he said.

My eyebrows lifted at the lost chapters of the Bobby Whitehorse story. "Oh?"

He made a deep hum in his chest that let me know he still thought about her. "She was walking the thin line between getting married to an Auburn professor and falling head over moccasins in love with a good-looking Cherokee stable hand. I came in second on that one."

It touched me that Bobby could muster his romantic forces and woo someone. It was hard to imagine him finding the time. He was the heartbeat of Itawa, keeping the gears running smoothly by a thousand deeds unseen. A lady so lucky to win his attention would have to understand that. And she would have to like the smell of horses.

"That eagle lady has something for you, Gray Eyes."

From anyone else I would have interpreted that as innuendo. But I knew how Bobby meant it. He knew me better than anyone. He would see what part of Abby would lift me to become more than I was. He could probably see me rising on the great wings of an eagle. I stood up and stretched until my back cracked.

"She is special," I said quietly. "She's almost three years older than I am."

"Shannon Hardiman's professor is thirty-five. She's forty-three." Bobby stood and together we gazed out over the lake. "She still writes me. She's happier than a 'possum in a Dumpster."

"She tell you that?" I asked.

Bobby shook his head. "Not in those words. But she's happy." After a time he added, "Older the violin, the sweeter the music."

I started home, but I stopped after a few steps and turned. "Did she tell you *that*?"

Bobby shook his head again. "Robert Duvall. *Lonesome Dove*."

Chapter Sixteen

By the time we reached the Narrows, the Outriders were nicely tuned to the rhythms of the river. Tandem teams were starting to click, calling out navigation commands and catching eddies to scout downstream rapids. Not only were they executing timely strokes and reading the currents well, but they were discovering the soul of the river.

At the bend below Beaver Tooth rapid, we surprised a doe crossing at a rocky ford. When she panicked and plunged into a deep pool, the kids instinctively backpaddled to give her room. No one spoke throughout the drama.

As far as their routes through the rapids, I had left the campers to their own designs. But now at the Narrows, that would change. Above this storied series of cascades we beached our canoes and climbed along the left side of the gorge for a view. There were six rapids: "Heaven's Gate," "Pinball," "Broken Thumb," "Regurgitate," "S-Turn," and finally, the blatantly dangerous one—"Hydrophobia," a seven-foot drop into a monster hydraulic, which we always portaged. From our precipitous sideline on the cliff, the campers looked down at the watercourse reduced by distance and tried to imagine how they fit into the scale of things.

The crash of the water carried up the smooth stone walls, reminding some of the kids of that perpetual hiss of traffic on the freeways near their homes. Both sounds carried the same signature of danger, and that was good. The Narrows was more challenging than any other stretch of the river, especially with "Hydrophobia" waiting below like an open pair of aquatic jaws. Since it was a well-known fact that many a kayaker and rafter had run into trouble in these rapids, the kids were very attentive to my instruction.

At this water level, the Narrows was not as dangerous as it was demanding. Though I knew that, to the campers, this gauntlet of boiling water had the feel of trial by whitewater. The difficulty of the Narrows was enhanced by the proximity of the rapids. Taken individually each would be challenging but not necessarily intimidating. Bunched as the rapids were, a canoe team had to position itself for the next rapid while busy with the one at hand. This put the margin for error close to the gunnels.

Bobby and Troy set up safety ropes on two boulders in the large pool below *S-Turn*. While the campers spectated from their ledge above the sunline, I climbed back down into the cool shadows of the gorge to run the rapids, so that they could see for themselves the maneuvers we had talked about in detail.

From where I knelt in my canoe, the kids looked small and vulnerable against the great slab of stone. I remembered so well watching Bobby Whitehorse make this demo-run for my maiden voyage here a decade ago. He had made it look so easy, as if he had somehow formed some kind of mystical alliance with the wild currents. But when I took my turn with my partner, it had felt like we had stumbled into a war with an enemy who could not be defeated.

Ten years later, campers were saying the same thing about me—that I enjoyed some kind of secret pact with the river. I suppose that's as good a way to say as any other, but I never forgot what it was like that first time, so I always chose my words carefully to help the first-timers handle the fear they carried inside them.

When I'd finished my demonstration run, the campers marched in varying degrees of determination and dread back to their boats. I lined my boat back upstream, rock-hopping through rapids so that I could serve as an escort to anyone who got into trouble. At Pinball, I knelt in my boat and waited in an eddy, where I had a good view of the first four rapids. Once they got to S-Turn, I knew they were safe with Bobby and Troy.

Each time a boat appeared around the entrance boulder of Heaven's Gate, I saw wide eyes and mouths agape with uncertainty. But their arms moved, performing strokes inculcated into them from our lessons. If nothing else, the kids had learned that a canoe would not go where they wanted it to go by itself. That was the paddlers' job.

I found myself looking for Tyler's face in these emerging boats. I had wanted this trip for him so badly. The reality of the river can wash away a lot of the extraneous details of other realities and make a person focus on what is immediately important. When a paddler is sideways in a rapid and heading for a ledge, getting the boat straight is a lot more important than anything going on at home. And somehow, when one walks away from the river at the end of the day, he takes some of that new perspective with him.

I didn't pretend the river could solve all Tyler's problems. It couldn't fill his spiritual cup and drown out all the bad stuff in one fell swoop. To a child of Tyler's age, too many things were immutable. But it could give him a new cup. Perhaps one made of stone carved out by centuries of swirling water.

The last boat was Jamal and Dane. As they shot through Heaven's Gate, I peeled out into the current and followed them to Pinball. There the main current divided around a jumble of rocks that required a lot of maneuvering. It was rare for a canoe to make it through without bouncing off one or two boulders.

Jamal and Dane hit the first one head-on. At impact they tumbled forward all over the bow-plate and thwarts, and the canoe pinwheeled out into the current sideways. The next rock banged them alongside the bow, spinning them backward as they accelerated toward Broken Thumb. They were disoriented and scared. Jamal grabbed the gunnels and became paralyzed. Then Dane did the same. The boat began a slow pivot that would position them sideways at the drop. They looked at me as if I were their Angel of Mercy.

There were priceless times to let students figure out their best course of action. This wasn't one of those. I yelled out the strokes they needed, and their arms went into action robotically. Then Jamal dropped his paddle. It drifted away from his reach, and he turned again to his angel. I knew I couldn't reach them in time to bump their bow with mine to point them downstream, so I yelled out instructions for Dane. He put in two good strokes, but it was too much weight for one person.

The canoe dropped over the ledge and crashed into the white foam below and flipped instantly. As I shot over the little falls, I whistled a signal to Bobby Whitehorse then spun my boat to face the capsized canoe. Dane washed out, sputtering and looking around wildly. I spoke to him in a calm voice.

"Get on your back with your feet up in front of you and watch for the rope. Bobby's got you."

As he had been taught, he lay back and let his feet surface. Then he angled toward shore and stroked with his arms like a water strider on amphetamines. He made good progress, so I focused on the boat bucking upside down in the hole like a giant green fish that had been snagged in a net. Jamal clung to the hull with his armpits over the V of the bow, the water pounding his back. His eyes were like floodlights fixed on me. Behind me I heard Bobby whistle his all-is-good signal, and I knew Dane was in safe hands.

Putting in three powerful strokes, I nosed my boat closer to Jamal. He could have stood up there, but jackknifed as he was and with the power of the waterfall behind him, his feet flailed helplessly under the boat.

"Let go and swim out, Jamal. I'll get your boat."

His eyes glazed over, and I knew I may as well have called out a recipe for larva soup. Sometimes the Angel of Mercy is all there is. I hopped out of my boat and got my footing as the current tore at my legs. Holding my boat behind me, I reached with my free hand to Jamal, but he would not release the chokehold he had on his boat.

"Take my hand," I yelled over the roar of the water. He remained glued to the jostling canoe, his eyes big as quarters. "Jamal, let go!"

He just gawked at me through tears, so I carefully inched toward him. When I was close enough, I pried his fingers loose and pulled by a wrist, but he didn't budge. When I pulled harder, I saw his boat climb a couple of inches out of the hole, and I realized that something on the canoe had snagged him. I had no choice but to get in there with him. I pushed my boat up on the shore and made a lunge for his boat.

When I got my footing, I probed underwater along his lifejacket until my hand plucked across a taut line thrumming with tension. The noise of the thick sheet of water folding into the hole was thunderous. I put my mouth close to Jamal's ear.

"It's okay. I'll get you out. I'm going to take out my knife, so don't make any quick moves." Jamal seemed to be concentrating on breathing and blinking and maybe a little bit about the afterlife. Falling water pummeled his back as his boat bumped around in the hole. When I cut the rope, Jamal scrambled over the hull to me. I sheathed my knife. "We're going to swim out," I yelled.

At the word "swim" he kicked off the boat and clawed at the water like a Labrador retriever. The slight recoil of the boat took the gunnel under the falls and the boat spun violently in my lap. The other gunnel flew up and cracked me in the chin, and all the stars above

Standing Bear Dome soared in blue streaks across the black curtain of my retinas. I crashed back into the water with the sustained ring of a hammer struck on an anvil still pealing in my head. When I surfaced, I was sluggish but coherent. I could see Dane standing next to Bobby on a boulder. Bobby was leaning back, anchoring himself against the weight tugging on his rope in the water, and I knew he had Jamal.

The white foam around me looked so muddy, I thought I had stirred up something from the bottom. But when I stood up I realized a bright stream of blood was oozing down my lifejacket, staining the bubbles pink where they lapped at my waist.

I worked my way back and tugged the grumbling canoe out one side of the hole until the current pushed it free. I went under, lifted the boat on my shoulders and flipped it right-side-up onto the water with a hollow *splat!* There was a spare paddle still tucked under the airbag, so I made a little wave to let Bobby know I was okay. Then I paddled the boat downstream.

The rope I had cut was tied to the front thwart. The knot was inexperienced and redundant. When I stepped out on the rock where Jamal stood, I saw a similar knot tied around his waist. I couldn't believe what I was seeing. I curled a finger in the air toward my face, and Jamal walked to me, his contrition turning to horror when he saw my chin.

"You tied yourself in?" I said, keeping my voice calm and without accusation. When he looked away, his eyes filled with tears, and he nodded. "Why?" I asked.

His eyes spilled over. "I was scared I'd fall out and drown."

I looked downstream toward Hydrophobia. A man had drowned there two years ago, because he had tied himself into his raft. He had flipped in the hole, and his "lifeline" became a deathtrap. When Jamal looked back at me with fearful eyes, I nodded.

"I never told you about how tying yourself in can be dangerous, did I?" He kept his huge wet eyes fixed on me and shook his head. I nodded again. "I should have thought of it."

He took no comfort in my confession. I doubted I could ever get him on whitewater again. And his resolve might be infectious. Others had seen the event. Those that didn't see it got an eyeful of the gash in my chin.

"Well," I sighed, squeezing his shoulder, "there's no one better to teach it than you. Will you tell everybody about it?" He was so surprised at my request that he nodded.

When we finished the portage around Hydrophobia we gathered around the canoes and listened to Jamal describe his brush with danger. Everyone was quiet as he dug into his soul for the right words and tried to exhume some of his trademark athletic bravado for the telling. When he finished, I stepped beside him and faced the group.

"When you turn over . . . if you are free from your gear . . . you're as free as a leaf floating down the river. But feeling yourself stop and having all that current pound on you is scary. You can't imagine the power of it till that happens." I looked downstream of Hydrophobia at the class-one rapid that rippled the water at the next bend. "I want someone to go out there and capsize and swim away from your canoe so you can see what it's like to be free in the water."

A few hands went up, but I ignored them. I looked at Dane and prayed he would come through for me. He studied the small rapid for a few seconds and nodded.

"I'll do it," Dane said."

I kept staring at him, willing him to take it a step farther. "You'll need a partner."

He looked around when hands went up again, and, as I hoped, his eyes lingered on Jamal, who looked like an orphaned puppy washed up on shore. "Jamal," he said.

Dane's name went immediately on my private Camper Hall of Fame list.

Jamal's face wrinkled into a map of misery as he looked down at his feet. "Let somebody else do it."

Dane looked to me for a cue, but I said nothing. Finally, he looked back at Jamal.

"Jamal, I've been paddling with you all day. We're a team. I'd feel better with you out there." Now I was conjuring up a Camper Medal of Honor list. "Come on, Jamal," he said. "Let's do it."

Jamal looked out at the river and frowned. Bobby Whitehorse ambled down from the rock and knelt by Jamal on the sand. Bobby tossed a rock casually into the water, and then he spoke very quietly out of the side of his mouth.

"Get back on that horse, little man."

Jamal took in a deep breath, walked to his boat, and stepped in. The Outriders actually applauded, and a chill ran up my spine.

Just as I knew it would, the demonstration went without a hitch. Dane forced the capsize, while Jamal instinctively fought it to the last instant before hitting the water. He came up gasping and wide-eyed and was the first to grab the rope that I threw. Bobby's rope found Dane, and Troy took my solo boat to retrieve the loose canoe.

At the take-out, Bobby and I lifted boats onto the trailer as the kids brought them to us. Bobby did most of the work, as I was busy pressing gauze to my bleeding chin.

When the campers were out of earshot Bobby said to me, "Better get you to the emergency room. That cut looks bad."

"It'll wait," I said. "The lawyer is going to call me at five. I'll go after that." My voice sounded hollow to me, like words heard through the wall of an adjoining room in a cavernous house. I stared off at the rapids upstream and thought about Jamal's brush with danger through his perspective.

Bobby pulled a knot tight and waited for me to look at him. "You can't tell them about everything that could go wrong, Gray Eyes. No way we could know somebody would tie himself in." On the beach the kids were searching for skipping stones. Bobby held his stare on me. "You were *there*, you know . . . right where you needed to be."

I nodded.

Amanda screamed victoriously, and I looked to see her hold up ten fingers in front of Troy.

"What if I hadn't been?" I mumbled to Bobby.

From where I stood the river had lost its lambent transparency. It was as opaque as the eye of a snake before it sheds its skin. The stones skipping across the water complicated the surface with a maze of colliding concentric rings.

"But you were there. You always are." Bobby leaned on the trailer and followed my gaze. "The river hasn't changed, Gray Eyes. If we're going to do what we do, the river's just got to count on you and me. And we came through. You did what needed doing." He twisted around to face me. "Don't think you improved your looks any though." He laughed as he tied another rope. "We've got to have a class on knots soon," he said. "What Jamal did with that rope is embarrassing. Two double-grannies." Bobby walked around the trailer testing each rope with a pluck from his finger. Then he stopped in front of me. "Let's just add 'Don't tie yourself in' to the rules. Now let's move on." And I knew exactly what he meant.

At ten minutes before five, I sat on the corner of the office desk while Old Bill gently removed the sterile pad on my chin. Soreness was creeping in, both in the tissue and the bone. He tilted his head back to look through the bottom half of his glasses.

"That's gonna need stitches," he said. "A lot of 'em." Then he retracted his head an inch more. "God! It looks like an extra mouth."

"Hey," Bobby said from the armchair. "With two mouths, maybe Stoney can teach twice as many classes now."

I angled my eyes toward him. "And eat twice as much cobbler."

Bobby pointed at my wound. "Bleeding again."

I pressed a new pad to the wound and, for something to do, got up and walked to my mailbox. All of it was junk mail except for one small piece. My name was scrawled on a dirty wrinkled envelope in a rambling, fragile cursive. The camp address had been kept to a bare minimum. No box number. No zip code. There was no return address. The postmark read *Metro Atlanta*.

I looked at my name again. It was the same loop-the-loop handwriting I had seen on Tyler's camp application. I tore the envelope with my teeth. Inside was a sheet of lined notebook paper folded four times. I read it twice. When I looked up, Bobby Whitehorse's eyes had narrowed, trying to read my face. Old Bill put down his coffee cup and became still. Without preamble I read aloud.

"Dear Stoney, I don't know if this will get to you. I'm going to drop it down to the parking lot from the deck and hope somebody picks it up and mails it. It's a long way down. I hope it lands in a good place. My father won't let me see my mother. She is in another room. I think he hurt her and that's why he won't let me see her. The fat man is mean. I'm afraid of him. We are at a diffront place. I'm not sure where it is.

Everybody said your speshalty is tracking. Can you come get us? Your friend, Tyler Raintree."

When I lowered the paper, Old Bill stared at me with the little shadow that rippled his jaw when his teeth clenched. Bobby had placed his fingertips together and was staring at the little tipi he had made with his hands. We remained frozen in this devil's triangle until the telephone rang. I glanced at the clock. It was one minute after five. Old Bill answered in a hoarse voice, never taking his eyes off me. He listened for a moment, held out the phone to me, and nodded.

"This is Stoney," I said. "Thank you for calling on time, Mr. Scroggin."

"Mr. St. Ney, I have been by the Raintree house twice and telephoned many times. They appear to be gone. There is a 'For Sale' sign at the gate."

"Did you go up to the house itself?"

"Yes, the first time. I walked around the gate."

"Could you see anything through the windows? Furniture, boxes?"

"I really didn't look," he said.

I sat on the edge of the desk and looked at Tyler's letter again, not really seeing the words but taking in the whole piece of paper like an impressionistic painting of despair. "What about a dog? Did you go around to the back?"

"I went to the side door. I don't know about a dog. I didn't see one."

My arm was getting tired of holding the bandage so when Old Bill moved to the window I walked around to his chair and sat. "Mr. Scroggin, do you know of another home the Raintrees have? In Atlanta?"

"No. We didn't get far enough along in the divorce proceedings to list all the assets."

I flattened the letter on the desk in front of me and read it to him. When I finished, he was quiet for a long time.

"Mr. Scroggin, can you take this to the police?"

He took in a lot of air and purged it. "I don't see how," he said.

"Can't you file a missing persons report?"

"Not for a family. A family can go anywhere it wants." His voice was starting to whine a little. "And I can't act on the hearsay of a child. I have to be sensitive to the potential for libel." He tried to stabilize his words by encasing them in the safety of his professional jargon. His sentences rose and fell like the hum of a bothersome insect.

"What about the potential for child abuse ... and spousal abuse?" I said.

He cleared his throat. "I'm sorry. I would need solid proof of that."

I laid down the bloody gauze, closed my eyes, and pinched the bridge of my nose. "Did Pat Raintree tell you about a man named Thomas?"

"Thomas?" Scroggin repeated. "I don't think so. Is that a first or last name?"

"First, I think. He might be her love interest."

"No, I know nothing about that," he said quickly.

"Mr. Scroggin, do you have any lead that will help me locate them?"

"I really don't know what else I can do. I went to their house twice, you know."

"I appreciate your trying, sir. I have a feeling we'll be talking again."

"Well," he said, his voice smoothing out for the conversation's end, "you know how to reach me." He cleared his throat again. "Goodbye then."

When I hung up, the air in the office was so still and fragile, I could hear the tap of spoons in cooking pots from the dining hall. "You better get to the hospital and get that gash sewn up," Bill said. Then I guess you two will be wanting a day off." He moved to the window and sipped from his coffee mug, keeping his back to us.

"Probably need two days," Bobby said. "Hard to get information on Sundays. Might need to talk to some people at their workplaces."

Old Bill held his coffee mug at half-mast for a time and then made a decisive nod. "Get Troy and Amanda to take over your classes, Stoney." He turned to Bobby. "Dorian can take care of the horses."

Bobby and I sat quietly for another half minute; then he and I got up and walked to the door. "You be careful," Old Bill said, stopping us at the threshold. He looked at us now like a military commander who demanded success in our mission.

Stepping out into the late afternoon, Bobby and I lingered by the little stone amphitheater behind the lodge. "You going to eat before you go to the doctor?" he asked.

"You go ahead. See if you can wrap up something for me to eat on the way. I'm going to get some things together at my cabin." I looked down at my shirt. The bloodstain on my belly had hardened to a dark crust. "Looks like a snake's head, doesn't it?"

As soon as I'd said it, I felt a little twinge of alarm in my gut—that feeling you get when you hear a substantial twig snap outside the light of your campfire. I looked at Bobby Whitehorse and I assumed my face mirrored his look of concern.

"I thought we didn't believe in omens," Bobby said.

"Not us," I said, turned, and walked to my cabin.

When I came back around the lake with my daypack, Gwendolyn was sitting on the canoe dock slowly stirring the water with her feet, her shoes beside her. When she saw me, she stood and moved to intercept me on the trail.

"I heard about your chin. Is it bad?"

"Just needs some stitches and an antibiotic."

She bent at the knees to look up under my chin, and she winced, even though I kept the bandage snug against the wound.

"Jamal told me all about how you saved him."

"How did he sound when he told you?"

"What do you mean?"

"Did he enjoy telling you or did he sound scared or humbled or angry?"

She angled her eyes off to the treetops for a moment. "He laughed a little. He seemed proud that he got back in and turned over on purpose at the last rapid."

I nodded. "Maybe I haven't lost him," I said more to myself than to her.

"I doubt you lose many, Stoney."

In my mind I remembered the iron refusal in Tyler's voice when I tried to help him carry his duffel. Before I could reply, Bobby came out of the dining hall and glided down the stairs carrying an overnight bag and a brown paper sack.

"Bobby is driving me to the hospital," I said to Gwendolyn. "I'd better go."

"Good luck," she called out to my back.

With his hat pushed back on his head, Bobby was behind the steering wheel engrossed in a book when I stowed my gear in the back of his truck. When I took the shotgun seat, he closed the book and stored it between the seats.

"What are you reading?"

"Western," he replied. "Only this one takes place in the East."

"So, it's an Eastern," I ventured.

He shrugged his head to one side. "Maybe an Eastern Western." He looked at my wound. "You're not going to bleed in my truck, are you?"

When I laughed, it made my chin hurt. I remembered a rainy day when Bobby had stopped to give me a lift up the mountain. His passenger seat was piled with half a dozen dead rabbits while the hunting dog he had borrowed stood in the bed of the truck.

"After we get you sewn up, we'll head on to Atlanta. Got some tribal friends where we can bunk for the night." He slipped his key into the ignition. "In Vinings . . . just a few miles west of Buckhead."

His eyes came to rest on something outside the truck, and I followed his gaze. Abby walked through the amphitheater, up onto the turnaround circle, and headed straight for us. Bobby took his hand off the key and sat back.

Abby put a hand on the windowsill and squinted at the bloody bandage that I still pressed to my chin. She relaxed her face and looked squarely at me.

"You're going after Tyler, aren't you?" She knelt to include Bobby in the conversation. He adjusted his hat and tipped the front of the brim for her.

I nodded. "His mother, too, if we can pull it off."

"Have you heard from him?"

"I got a letter. Tyler's situation is not good."

Abby looked so deeply into my eyes, I felt like a lock opened by the turn of a key.

"What can I do for you here while you're gone?"

"Troy and Amanda are taking over my classes. You might drop in on them now and then . . . for a little moral support."

"I'll move up the soccer rematch for tomorrow. That way you won't be missed as much." After a few seconds, she leaned right to better see Bobby. "Take care of each other," she said and then gave us both her Joan of Arc smile.

She straightened and backed away from the truck, her movements both graceful and strong. Standing at the curb she seemed to radiate a contained dignity.

I let my forearm swing outward, hinging at the elbow, and I extended my index finger. Abby stepped forward and touched the tip of her index to mine—a scene right from Michelangelo's palette. Then she walked back to the amphitheater and disappeared behind the office.

When I looked at Bobby, he was leaning forward and nodding with a solemn expression on his broad face. "Eagle," he said and started the engine.

Chapter Seventeen

On a bright Sunday morning, Bobby Whitehorse and I ate eggs and biscuits at a *Huddle House* on the outskirts of Vinings. I was leafing through the yellow pages of the Atlanta telephone book under "Health Clubs," looking first at the large ads and their slogans.

"Here it is," I said. " '*The Body Elite*. Three-eleven East Paces Ferry Road. *If the body fits, wear it!*' " I looked up at Bobby. "That's the tee shirt she had on."

"Open on Sundays?" Bobby asked over his coffee cup.

I finished reading. "Yeah, nine to four."

The clock above the counter read seven-fifty. Bobby wiped his mouth with a napkin, pushed his plate aside and crossed his big forearms on the table.

"I'm going back to the Raintree house while you check out the club. How long will you need?"

"A lot of people sleep late on Sunday. Give me four hours."

He slipped from his pocket a small bar of the soap he made from yucca and hemlock bark. "Let me go wash off this scent in case that Rottweiler is at home."

Bobby retired to the bathroom while I paid the bill and returned to the truck. By the time he joined me I was wearing my best sweats and running shoes. He slammed the door and looked me over, stopping at my chin.

"If you didn't have that bandage, you'd probably blend right in."

"It'll make a good conversation piece . . . help me circulate around the club."

"Careful on the chin-ups, Gray Eyes," he said.

Bobby dropped me off one block from the corner where *The Body Elite* sprawled across the ground floor of a two-story building between a stereo store and a *Smoothie City*. Huge windows in front afforded passing motorists a generous view of bodies evolving toward elite-ness, but at nine-o-five only one elderly woman cruised at a fragile pace on a stationary bicycle near the back wall. The gray-carpeted room was brightly lighted and packed with rows of glistening machinery, vinyl-covered benches, and blue gym mats. I carried my nifty exercise bag to a receptionist, who sat behind a counter stacked with towels.

"Good morning, I'm in town for a few days and you've been recommended to me."

She was pleased as punch. "Excellent, sir. So you've never visited us before?"

I smiled and shook my head. She was tall and skinny and striking with her dark eyes, sharp nose, and rolling mane of midnight black hair. She reminded me a little of a young Cher. I knew she had been selected as the store's false front, because she was the perfect testimonial for what a body without fat could look like, but I was willing to bet that her stringy muscles had never pulled one of these cables or pushed a bar or sweated on a mat. Her skin lacked color, and her posture was stooped. She reached below the counter and came up with a clipboard and a smile.

"If you'll fill out this information form for us." She flipped the page. "And this is a liability waiver. Read this over and sign at the bottom." She sort of bobbed to attention and her voice went flat. "My name is Sonya. Anything you need, let me know."

"Stoney," I said. I offered my hand, and we shook. On the wall behind her were tee shirts, sweatshirts, and headbands all sporting their slogan, *If the Body Fits, Wear It!* As I stood at the counter filling out the forms, Sonya leaned over some paperwork of her own and tapped a pencil eraser against her lower lip. When she swiveled to answer the telephone, I peeked over the counter and saw the big Sunday *New York Times* crossword puzzle. It was about ninety per cent blank. The title of the puzzle read *"Grrr, Like What?"* All the theme clues were in Italics—animal adjectives—and I memorized a few.

She looked over my form and said, "It's twenty dollars for a day. But you can get a year's membership for two-hundred and thirty."

I forced a smile and managed not to look startled. "Just the day will do."

As I opened my wallet she asked, "Who recommended you to us, Mr. St. Knee?"

"It's St. Ney," I explained. "Like a horse's 'neigh.' Sort of an equine name." Sonya didn't catch the crossword clue I dropped her. "It was Pat Raintree. Do you know Pat?"

"No, sir, I'm pretty new here." She filed away my papers, took a key from a pegboard, and reduced the towel stack by one. "The men's locker room and showers are in the back to the left." She started around the counter.

"Sonya, you don't need to show me around. I know how everything works."

She stopped as if I had rained on her parade. "Oh . . . all right. If you have any questions—" She hovered beside me with her hands on her hips.

I looked over the varied instruments of muscle building. "Wow, a fellow could get pretty ursine in this room." She looked at me as if I had just divined her birth date and favorite flavor of ice cream from a line in her palm. "Or maybe even *taurine*," I said.

"Ursine," she mumbled to herself and frowned.

"You know, 'like a bear.'"

Her eyes snapped to attention and riveted on me. "What was the other one?"

"Taurine . . . 'like a bull.'"

She smiled like a surprised child and walked swiftly behind the counter. In seconds she had fallen deep into crossword catatonia.

An hour and a half later, I was pumped up and feeling that nice exhaustion that accompanies lots of torn down muscle tissue. During that time Sonya had cautiously approached me twice about other animal adjectives. When I told her I had been feeding her clues for her puzzle, she laughed, and we were old buddies. She returned three more times.

Since it was difficult not to eavesdrop in the almost vacant room, the older woman working out—her name was Vivian—soon got into the game, too. Then we were three old crossword buddies. By eleven, only two other people had joined our ranks in the quest for fitness. Both were women battling post-middle age. Like Vivian, neither of them knew Pat Raintree. Both of them did, however, like crossword puzzles. We were becoming a lexical army.

When my workout pals asked about the bandage on my chin, I tried for a semblance of the truth. "Oh, that? Just a little accident on my boat. You know that command 'All hands on deck?' I used my chin instead." They laughed.

At eleven-forty-five a good-looking blonde woman who had definitely won the battle against anatomical mediocrity strode into the room wearing a lavender body suit over black stretch tights. She was about five-four and so shapely and colorful that, in her outfit, she looked a little like a comic book super-heroine. Wonder Woman's little sister. She moved in a relaxed, bouncing gait, letting each leg straighten at impact to thrust a hip upward as if she was using only bone and no muscle. She was either trying to emulate a matador or saving herself for the treadmill.

Her eyes were large and set wide apart, and the carefully groomed lashes curled like the tines of an old-fashioned horse-drawn rake like the Amish people still used. As she passed me, those lashes lowered—seductively, I thought—and her walk smoothed out as if she were thinking about appearing more feline. Which she did.

Large dimples flexed in and out of her firm buttocks. The taper of her thighs and outward flare of calves were decidedly beguiling. Vivian and the other women, I discovered, were smiling at me and raising eyebrows. I smiled and lay back on the bench for my sixth set of bench presses. With my new friends watching, I managed to punch out three more reps than my last set. Ah, vanity—the mother of sports excellence.

I rotated to the quadriceps lift, the lat bar, and the elevated abdominal crunch seat as the blonde woman stretched and eased into her routine. She used very light dumbbells in a variety of full-body aerobics steps then switched to flies on the bench, curls, some shoulder work, and then *Stairmaster*.

I thought her performance was dandier than a chorus line revue in Las Vegas. Twice we passed within speaking distance, but so far I had ventured only a polite smile. She smiled, too. But whereas mine felt like the innocent smile Charlie Brown gave Lucy just before a go at kicking the football, hers seemed more practiced and goal-oriented—the kind of smile that might be accompanied by a smoky voice at a cocktail bar: *I'm having a gin and tonic . . . how 'bout you?*

I was on the pull-up bar waiting for her to finish up on *Stairmaster* when Sonya returned, walking blindly with the folded newspaper in front of her nose. "What's a five letter word ending in a 'y' for 'crespuscular?'" she said and then lowered the paper to show me her confused face. "Isn't that … like … a red or white blood cell or something?" Vivian and the others stared at me and waited.

"Dusky . . . maybe misty," I said lowering myself from the bar in slow motion. She wrote one of them down. The blonde clicked off the *Stairmaster* and stepped down. She stood ten feet away and stared at us as she patted her face with a towel.

"Okay," Sonya continued, her face still buried in the puzzle. "How about . . . wait . . . here it is . . . a one-two-three-four-five-six-seven-eight-nine-ten-eleven-letter word for 'next to last.' I think it has 'u-l' in the middle."

"Penultimate," I said and dropped from the bar to the floor.

"Yes!" Sonya hissed to the paper, writing as she walked back to her post.

The blonde woman whipped the towel over her shoulder and put her hands on her hips as if she were about to deflect bullets. "Are you the new *Body Elite* reference book?" she purred.

"I charge extra for words more than three syllables. What word did you need to know?"

She laughed hoarsely, propped a foot on a rack of free weights and bent to tie her shoe. I didn't think her shoe needed tying, but her pose seemed calculated to enhance the scenery.

"I think I know all the words I need to know," she hummed.

And I was betting she did. Now that she was talking to me, I felt the full force of her animal magnetism. Her movements were fluid and self-conscious, upgrading her persona from feline to colubrine.

"This is my first time here," I said. "Sonya may not let me leave until she finishes that puzzle. Can a man work-out to death?"

She made the husky laugh again. "There are much better ways to die."

I might have blushed. I looked at Vivian and the girls, but they looked away.

"I think I can talk Sonya into releasing you into my custody," she suggested.

I walked over to her. "Do you know Pat Raintree?"

The change in direction flustered her for a milli-second, but then she gathered herself back into the image of Circe and answered in an affected nonchalance. "Sure."

"I'm a friend of hers," I said.

A light turned on inside her head and she looked at me through a new lens of inspection. "Are you—?" She pointed a finger at me as her mouth hung open.

"Thomas?" I said. I smiled and modestly lowered my eyes.

Her analytical gaze scanned the length of me down to my running shoes. "My God, she didn't tell me you looked like this." She wagged her finger at me.

"Is that good or bad?" I asked.

She laughed a single note from deep in her chest and looked me over again. I guess that meant my question was rhetorical. Maybe she was into chin patches.

"Oh, that Pat! No wonder she—" She stopped in mid-sentence and looked at me as if she had laid an egg in her tights. "But wait . . . you were—" She bent at the knees to get a better view of my chin. "Oh, my God! Is that where you got shot?"

Across the room, Vivian and the girls got very quiet. My new workout friend stepped closer and gently gripped my arm. "I thought you were shot in the leg."

I tried to shrug just like one of Bobby Whitehorse's Western matinee idols. "It was just a scrape." Just above the hem of my gym shorts I had a fresh scab on my left thigh where Jamal's bow-plate had raked across my leg. It didn't look anything like a bullet wound, but if pressed I thought it might do. "I've got to talk to Pat. Do you know where I can find her?"

"I haven't seen her for a while. It's been weeks. She was a regular here for a time. We used to go out for a smoothie sometimes after a work-out." She pushed away from the weight rack and struck a new pose. "I'm Kathy," she said in the tone she had used before she learned I was Thomas. She raised her eyebrows, clearly expecting me to recognize her name. "The one who chases men and likes to dance?"

"Ah." I nodded knowingly. "Kathy, did Pat ever tell you about another house she and Beau own in town?"

She frowned down at the carpet for two seconds. "No, I don't think so."

"Do you have any clue where she might be? She's not been at home for a while."

Kathy pushed out her lips and slowly shook her head. "No, she sometimes calls me; but I haven't heard from her in . . . like . . . two weeks? Maybe three?"

"Is there anyone else in this club she was close to? Someone who might know?"

"Not in *The Body Elite*." She leaned closer and lowered her voice. "Pat and I kind of stuck together because we're . . . well . . . we're the ones in here who don't have body parts sagging to the ground or noses stuck up in the clouds, if you know what I mean."

I smiled. "How much did she tell you about me?"

"Ooh," she giggled. "Everything." She bumped her shoulder against mine.

"Did she tell you what kind of work I do?"

"Oh, sure." She fanned a hand toward me in a dismissive way. "Listen, honey, you shouldn't feel bad about that. Selling cars is as good as selling anything else, and we're all selling something, aren't we?"

"Did she tell you what kind of cars I sell?"

She spread her hands and leaned back. "And see, that's the other thing. You're marketing the most prestigious car around. I mean, everybody wants a Beamer." She ducked her head and spread her hands an inch wider and froze with the obvious. "You're selling to the big dogs in the yard."

If I *had* been Thomas, my self-esteem probably would have spiked. "Thanks for the support." I rolled my shoulders to work out the tension from some exercises I had not done in a while. "I'm going to hit the showers." I offered my hand. "She already told you my last name, I guess."

Her grip was strong. "No. I'm Kathy Landis. I'm all done, too. Want to go for a smoothie?"

"I have to get over to the dealership," I said. "We have a Sunday sale going on."

She shrugged elegantly. "Want me to tell Pat something if I see her?"

"No, I'm sure I'll see her soon. But thanks."

Dressed in my sweats and clean and refreshed from a hot shower, I felt the endorphins swimming through my body in narcotic waves. There was no relaxation like the post-workout relaxation. Unless it was the post-Kathy relaxation. Thankfully, she was still in the shower when I re-entered the room. I was willing to bet she had multiple definitions for a "smoothie," and though I enjoyed the idea of spending more time with her, I knew it wasn't in me—especially since I was posing under an assumed name. And Bobby was waiting for me outside. And there was an eagle waiting in the mountains.

As I thumbed through the yellow pages, I helped Sonya with the last blanks of the crossword puzzle. I found *Buckhead BMW*, memorized the phone number and address, and left before Kathy emerged from the locker and pressed her "smoothie" offer again.

The day had warmed considerably. Bobby was parked in shade near a small park half a block away. He looked sound asleep under the tilt of his hat. After I got in and slammed the door he remained in repose and spoke with hardly a lip movement.

"You think she might want to come back to Itawa and be a sports counselor?"

"She knows Pat Raintree," I said.

He opened his eyes and turned toward me. "She know anything?"

"Pat Raintree's boyfriend probably works at *Buckhead BMW* on Roswell Road. What did you find out at Tyler's home?"

"Nobody there. No dog in the back. Furniture still in the house. Water's on. Power's on. Air-conditioner is still running. 'For Sale' sign out front. I called the realtor and got a recording. Office is closed till tomorrow." Bobby sat up and straightened his hat. He stretched an arm out to the steering wheel and hooked a limp wrist over the top. "Want to go buy a Beamer?" he said.

"Yeah, let's go see if Thomas works Sundays."

As we passed *The Body Elite*, Kathy came out in a cream-colored pants suit carrying a satchel strapped over one shoulder. Bobby leaned forward to watch her.

"You think she'd go to the drive-in with me?" he said.

"They don't have drive-ins anymore, do they?"

"Got one over near Clarkesville."

I turned to see if he was serious. "That place has been closed down for years."

"So?" he said and looked back at me. His smile blossomed and disappeared.

We sat in the truck and watched the BMW lot for ten minutes. In that time two customers had gone into the office and then walked the lot with two different salespersons. The third salesman who appeared was a good-looking guy in a powder blue suit and sunglasses with tapering sides. He walked with a marked limp.

"Hel-lo, Tho-mas," Bobby said under his breath.

When Thomas waved goodbye to a lost sale and limped inside, we got out, crossed the lot full of beaming Beamers, and followed through the front door. After we had milled around the air-conditioned lobby for several minutes, an energetic young man in a white shirt and red tie saw us through a glass partition. He promptly came around to meet us.

"How are you gentlemen today?" His greeting could almost be measured in dollar signs. By his smile alone, he appeared most eager to relieve us of our combined life savings as a down payment and a reasonable monthly plan that we could pay off over the next eighty years.

"We have an appointment with Thomas," I said.

"Tommy? I'll let him know. He'll be with you in a moment." To his credit, the young man left as upbeat as he had arrived. He returned to his glass cubicle, picked up his desk phone, and punched two numbers.

In less than a minute I heard someone limping down a hallway. When Thomas rounded the corner, he did his best to put weight evenly on each leg. He had black curly hair and a square jaw with a dimple just like Kirk Douglas's. Without shades, his eyes were like blue stained glass.

There was a generic clean-cut quality about each of his features—small nose and W-shaped mouth. I'm pretty sure his hair was dyed. He reminded me of someone who might have aspired to be a movie star but settled for being a game show host. His eyes went from Bobby to me and back to Bobby before they lost their charismatic twinkle. His pace slackened, and he seemed to be deciding whether or not he was going to cross the lobby or make a run for it.

"Thomas," I said, "I'm Stoney St. Ney. I'm a friend to Tyler and Pat Raintree."

His eyes stayed on Bobby, but he seemed to be talking to me. "Listen, I haven't seen her again." He took a step back and made a quick glance toward the glass cubicles. "You can go back and tell whoever sent you that I'm out of it."

"Thomas," I said, stepping toward him, "we're on the other side of that equation."

"What do you mean?" he sounded a little desperate and tried to cover that by clearing his throat and starting over. "I don't know what you mean."

"We're trying to find Pat and her son. We think they may be in trouble."

His humorless laugh was almost a cough. "Tell me about it," he quipped. His mouth was crooked with sarcasm. He could not keep his eyes off of Bobby. He raised his Kirk Douglas dimple at Bobby. "Who's he with?"

"This is Bobby Whitehorse. We're both from Tyler's summer camp."

"Tyler's the kid, right?" He checked behind him again, stepped closer, and slid his hands into his pockets. "I can't talk about this stuff here. I don't know where she is."

His nametag read "Tom Sabine." He looked to be in his mid-thirties, but the dyed hair could have thrown off my estimate by five years. He had been fit at some time in his life, probably a high school athlete who started the downslide in college and fought back on weekends to preserve something of his self-image.

"Mr. Sabine," I said, "look, I know you don't know us well enough for me to ask you the things that I need to ask you. So, maybe we can just get past that. Pat and Tyler need help. I figure you would want that for them, too."

His eyes darted to the floor. Guilt was written all over his face.

"Well, yeah. I mean, hell, she's got a husband who goes around shooting people."

"Why didn't you file charges against him?" Bobby said.

Sabine stopped breathing for a moment and stared at Bobby, then he looked back at me to answer. "Because he'd come back and shoot my brains out, that's why."

"Mr. Sabine," I said, "do the Raintrees have another home in Atlanta?"

His face tightened like a fist. The question seemed to anger him for some reason.

"I don't know anything about what they have."

I kept my voice as non-invasive as I could. "When you and Pat got together, was there a place she provided for the tryst?"

"The what?"

"Where did you meet?" I said. "Was it in a house or apartment or a motel or what?"

"No." Indignation resonated through the lone syllable. "That's none of your damned business." The young man behind the glass peered at us and frowned. When Bobby glanced his way, he turned his attention back to the papers on his desk.

"I agree," I said. "But the fact is I need to know."

"What you need is not my concern," Thomas whispered.

"Maybe it is," Bobby said with that knife-edge voice never heard at Itawa. Bobby hadn't moved a muscle, but somehow, he seemed to loom larger in the spacious room. Sabine kept his attention on me as if that made him ineligible to receive Bobby's threat. But he held the knowledge of it in his eyes, and he swallowed involuntarily.

"Mr. Sabine," I said, "I assume you care something for Pat."

"We had a good time," he said defensively. "I don't have to spell it out to you."

"So that was it? A good time? She seems to think more of you."

"Yeah, well, things change." He glanced at his leg. "It's easier to detach from things when some guy walks up your doorstep and shoots you in your own house."

"Look," I said, "I don't really care to be judgmental about your feelings or motives. We've all operated on more hormones and less conscience. All I want to know is where they might be staying. I'm pretty sure they are somewhere in Atlanta. You've spent enough time with her that she might have told you about another place. Maybe you've even been there. I just need to know, then we drop out of your life, okay?"

When I ended my little speech, I could see that Thomas was struggling with what to do or say. The fellow behind the glass was overly absorbed in his work.

"I don't know about any place." Thomas said, pouting like a child.

A heavy man with a handlebar moustache and big beer gut lumbered down the hallway and watched us through the glass until he turned the corner and swaggered up beside Sabine. "Problem, Tommy?"

Sabine spoke too fast, his manner too jittery. "No problem, no problem."

The four of us stood in an awkward tableau until Sabine stepped toward me and took my elbow in his hand to turn me to the door. "Look, Raintree—Pat's husband—is a customer," he said in a fast whisper. "He looked nervously back toward his colleague. "If the management finds out about this, I'm out on my butt. You know what I mean? That's why I didn't press charges."

I stopped and resisted his tug on the door. "I thought it was because Beau threatened to kill you," I said.

"Well, that too." He gripped my upper arm to convince me of his misery. Look, it was just one big screwed-up mess. The best thing was for me to bow out. I wish her well, you know? But she married the creep. Why the hell would she marry a guy like that?"

"Or be with a guy like you," I added.

He looked back at his friend and back at me and sighed. I looked at his hand until he let go of my arm.

"Just come outside with me a minute, will you?" he pleaded.

We stepped into the city heat and the intermittent static of Sunday traffic. God knows what Bobby and the big guy were doing.

"So, you're not going to help her?" I said.

His face paled to a sickly gray. The jet black of his hair fared badly in direct light. It looked like he had been inverted and dipped into a vat of paint.

"Look, I got a family, too. I was damned lucky nobody was home when that maniac shot me. If I knew of the place you're talking about, I'd tell you. But I don't. Pat and I always met at a motel."

I stared into Tom Sabine's face hoping to discover a new inroad to his sense of loyalty to his lover. I wasn't sure what to ask. Maybe he had leveled with me and knew nothing about a second home.

"I'll come back later to see if you have remembered anything."

"Don't come here," he said quickly. "There's nothing else I can tell you."

I was so tired of his sniveling that I just stared at him. He looked toward his friend inside, then at the traffic on Roswell Road, and then at his watch.

"Thomas, I told you I wasn't going to be judgmental with you. But I've changed my mind. You make me want to scrub my hands with Clorox." He stopped fidgeting and angled his eyes away from me. "I'm going to find her. When I do, if I find out you've lied to me, I'm going to come back here and raise a big stink about your affair. I'm going to go to your home and talk to your wife and children. I'm going to find out how you avoided the police in getting your gunshot wound treated by a physician. I'm going to make Beau Raintree's potshot the most innocuous thing that's happened to you lately."

He tried for an indignant expression. "You can't talk to me—"

I reached up, wrapped his necktie in my fist and snapped it taut, stopping him in mid-whine. "I wasn't finished," I said. "I'm also going to satisfy my primordial lust for swatting things that annoy me. If you are lying, I promise you I will do this."

"Listen, dammit. I've told you everything I know—which is nothing. I don't know about a house except the one on Randall Mill. So just leave me alone, all right?"

I let the crumpled tie fall, rapped on the glass for Bobby, and walked to the truck. After I climbed in, I watched Bobby and the big man shake hands at the door. Sabine was gone. Without speaking, Bobby got in, started the engine, pulled out into traffic, and drove south.

We said nothing as we cruised with the light traffic. Ten minutes later we wheeled into the parking lot of *The Old Corral* steakhouse and Bobby cut the engine.

"You believe him?" Bobby said.

I shrugged. "I think most of what comes out of his mouth is not to be relied on."

"He's a salesman," Bobby said and straightened like a plank in his seat to stuff his keys into his jeans pocket. "Maybe we should follow him for a while." A dog barked at us from the next car, and we both turned that way.

"No," I said. "The one thing I did believe from him was that he's not going to risk Beau's gun. He's done with Pat."

The dog barked tirelessly, one racking *yap* after another, as though it had been trained to count to a hundred. I couldn't imagine any throat—lupine or vulpine or drill-sergeantine—that could keep up such an abrasive racket.

Bobby stared at the dog. "You think he's too hot in there?"

The dog thrust its head forward with each painful bark, smearing its nose on the glass. It was a mongrel with some boxer and probably a little terrier.

Bobby studied the manic animal, "You think he's trying to tell us something?"

As the dog slobbered against the glass, I thought of Thor. "Bobby," I said, "Tyler dropped that letter from a high window to a parking lot. Which probably means he's in a high-rise apartment or condo. What are you going to do with a Rottweiler when you move into a place like that?"

Bobby's black eyes flickered with light. It was like the moment when smoking tinder burst into a flame. He smiled and touched a finger to the brim of his hat.

"Tonto is proud to ride with Kemosabe." He turned back to the dog and gave it the same salute he had given me. "Mighty obliged, little fellow."

When I opened the door and got out, the heat rising off the asphalt was cloying. The dog's performance escalated into a frenzy. Bobby put his hand on the roof of the car and shook his head.

"Must be ninety degrees in there." Oblivious to the dog's aggressive snarls, he peered inside. Then he walked to the back of the car and checked the tag. "Let's go eat."

Inside the restaurant, I hunted up the trusty yellow pages while Bobby strode directly to a booth where a short balding man with two children ate their meal. After a few seconds of conversation, the man got up and walked outside. The kids stood in their seats to watch through the window. I alternated scanning through veterinary kennels and watching the man open up the car for the dog.

After writing down all the kennels' numbers in the Buckhead area, I joined Bobby in a booth to look over the menu. As soon as we had ordered, the bald man returned and nodded to Bobby. The kids stared unabashedly at us then leaned over their table to whisper to their father. I counted twelve other parties eating in the room.

"How'd you know who owned the dog?" I asked.

Bobby's dark eyes danced with victory. "There are always tracks, Gray Eyes."

I threaded my fingers together and set my hands before me like a basket on its side, and I waited for my lesson.

"The rearview mirror angle that accommodates someone short, a coloring book, and the dog hairs on the little boy's pants."

"T-Bone will be proud of you," I said. "I'm glad you didn't have to sniff everybody in the room."

"Well, that *was* my final verification. Up close I could smell that dog on them."

I narrowed my eyes. "Even with all this steak aroma in here?"

Bobby made an amused smile. "Dogs don't smell like steak, Gray Eyes."

After ordering, I started calling the vets on my list. After the fourth one, I watched the waitress put down our plates. I dropped one more quarter into the telephone and reached *Pet North Veterinary Medicine*, using the same line I'd used with the others.

"Good afternoon, this is Beau Raintree. You're keeping our dog, Thor, while we are away for a while. I believe I left you the wrong telephone number where you could reach us in case of an emergency. Would you check to see what number I gave you?"

"Certainly, Mr. Raintree. Just a moment."

A little burst of fireworks went off in my chest. In less than a minute, the woman came back on the line and read off a number.

"No," I said, "that's our home number. We left you another number, didn't we?"

"Let's see," she murmured absently as papers rustled. "I'm here just on weekends, so—" Her voice tapered off. "Oh, here it is!" She read it off and I wrote it down.

"Well, that's right. Sorry to bother you. How's old Thor doing?"

"Is he the big Great Dane?"

"Rottweiler," I said.

"Oh, he's asleep. But he's doing fine. I'm taking him for a walk in a little while."

"Well, thank you so much." I hung up.

Oddly, I thought of my third-grade teacher, the one who had denied me a good part in our class play. I wished she could see me now. This was my second effective thespian role in the same day. First

Thomas and now Beau Raintree. One more call got me through to Sheriff Canaday's office back home. I looked at Bobby. So far, he had left the food on my plate alone, but I knew not to dally.

"We don't usually accept collect calls, Stoney," said Miss Maxie the dispatcher. "We have to justify all our billing at the end of the month, so I'm writing this up as a call from the sheriff in . . . where are you?"

"I'm in Atlanta, Maxie. Thanks for accepting. I'll pay you back when I get home.

"I've heard that one before." Miss Maxie was a thirty-eight year-old firecracker of a deputy sheriff. She told me once that if she was fifteen years younger, she'd commit a crime and run into the National Forest just so I would track her. "Let me put you through to Harte," she said, and by the tone in her voice, I knew she didn't mind this call at all.

"Sheriff Canaday." His voice always reminded me of a cement mixer.

"It's Stoney. Remember the lady I told you might be calling?"

"Sure."

"I've got to find her. All I've got is a telephone number. Can you help me?"

Silence. I guessed he was weighing the balance of which one of us owed the other. I was hoping for more mileage out of that hypothermic episode last winter and was prepared to ask him the question again but this time with a little shiver in my voice.

"Let's have it," he said.

I gave him the number and told him I'd call back in a half hour. When I joined Bobby, he was well into a huge T-bone steak and showed no sign of slowing as I related my news about Thor and the sheriff. He nodded and scooped baked potato into his mouth. He chewed with the unvarying cadence of a horse with its nose in a feed bag.

"You sure take good news in stride," I said.

He kept chewing and shrugged. "No surprise. You and I are the best trackers in the state. Hell, we're mystical trackers." He nodded toward the parking lot. "Animals talk to us and give us clues."

I started on my sandwich and stared at his plate. I probably should have ordered a steak, too. My muscles felt like they had been ripped from my body, squeezed through a wringer, and tied back in place with rusty wire.

"What in the world were you and the big Beamer salesman talking about?" I asked.

"Karmic relationship between the salesman and the needy customer. A little Dale Carnegie, Karl Marx, and Jean Dixon." Bobby beamed. "He was fascinated by me."

Bobby finished his steak, picked up his plate, and slurped the amber juice that had oozed from the meat. A woman with her family looked our way and turned back before I could give her a commiserating smile. Bobby set the plate down and stared at me.

"I always heard the Indians let no part of an animal go to waste," I said.

Bobby pushed out his lower lip and nodded thoughtfully. "True,' he said and pointed at my half-eaten sandwich. "You going to eat that?"

"Yes," I said.

He stared at my plate. "Going to lick up the juice, too?"

I looked down at my meal. There were, at most, three drops of brown juice dappling my plate. Most of the drippings from my sandwich had been soaked up by the bread.

"Probably not," I replied.

Bobby shrugged and looked out the window. "I can wait."

Chapter Eighteen

Armed with new information from Sheriff Canaday, Bobby and I arrived at the Dogwood Towers, which, in spite of its plural moniker, was a single obelisk of apartments stacked to the sky. It rose out of the trees along Piedmont Road like a huge, rectangular, blunt-nosed missile set to take off for another galaxy. Its chrome and glass fascia was busy with the reflecting and refracting of light.

If the crystalline monolith had been wired with solar panels, it probably could have run all the electrical needs of every home in Atlanta. But it wasn't. Behind the building, giant air-conditioning units hummed, their oversized fans forcing tree limbs into a relentless dance of thrashing leaves—all this to balance the invasive rays of the afternoon sun through all that glass. The South did rise again . . . but not with efficiency.

Somewhere on the twenty-seventh floor was Tyler, sequestered with his family in an apartment owned by Victor Dimateo. The security was tight with a doorman, two guards who covered the grounds on modified golf carts, and three valets in the garage. Several security cameras were perched strategically around the premises.

Bobby and I sat in his truck across the street in the parking lot of a colossal cathedral. There we had a view of Dogwood Towers's main lobby door and driveway. We decided to wait to see if the Raintrees might come out. We had no idea if or when that would happen, but waiting and observing is never a bad idea. As a last resort we had their phone number and might think up some ruse to get them out.

Sheriff Canaday had discovered fourteen other addresses under the name Victor Dimateo. It was my guess that this was one of many mortgage foreclosures. Maybe he had loaned one to Beau Raintree while the Randall Mill house sold. Whatever the reason, it proved to be a formidable castle keep. It was a wonder that Tyler's letter had fluttered into someone's path and not out into the street where it would have been ground into litter by the endless current of traffic.

Bobby and I spent hours naming every movie we could for certain actors. Because we kept score for who would buy dinner, I had to outlaw Westerns from the competition. If not, it was like playing *Jeopardy!* against Messrs. Rand and McNally if the category were "Highways."

Just as twilight settled in, Perry stepped out the door and spoke to the doorman. Behind him appeared a man, a woman, and a boy.

"There they are," I said.

Bobby cranked the engine. In seconds, a black BMW zoomed off the garage ramp and rolled to a stop at the front foyer. A valet jumped out and do-si-doed with Raintree. Perry sat at shotgun next to Beau. Tyler and his mother slid into the back.

When the BMW pulled out into the northbound traffic, Bobby shot out of the church driveway and ran a gauntlet of horn blowing until he bulled his way into the far lane four cars behind the Beamer.

We followed them to a restaurant on Pharr Road called *Dem Bones*. It was an expensive steak house with standing lanterns all around and valet service for parking. Out front spinning in a bright cone of floodlight was a huge mobile of over-sized white metallic bones. We passed by the restaurant and pulled into a strip of stores attached to a gas station and parked. As I dug into my pack for some slacks, I looked at Bobby's jeans.

"Did you bring anything else to wear?"

"Got a tie in the glove box. Clean white long-sleeved shirt under my seat."

"Clean white shirt under your seat? Isn't that an oxymoron?"

He pulled out the shirt, crisply folded and wrapped in plastic. I was impressed.

"We're going to have to look like we didn't just fall off of the cabbage truck," I said. "This is an upscale place."

Bobby gave me his deadpan expression. "So . . . no war paint?"

We changed in the cab, keeping an eye out for pedestrians. When I would eventually call Old Bill, I didn't want it to be about bailing us out of jail for indecent exposure or a supposed gay tryst in a public parking lot.

"You think normally we look like cabbage-truck rednecks?" Bobby said.

"I don't think Indians can be considered rednecks. I think you're redskins."

"Cher'kees got rednecks, too," he assured me.

"You're not going to wear that, are you?" He turned to me with a question on his face and saw me looking at his hat. "Bobby, how long have you had that?"

"Same hat I was wearing when I met you." He propped it on the gear stick then tucked his long ponytail down through the collar of his shirt. He stopped the motion of his arms and stared at my bandage. "You're not going to wear that, are you?" he said.

"You don't think it's a good disguise?"

"I think it's kind of like having a whipped cream pie thrown in your face and hoping nobody will notice."

I leaned to the mirror and pried up a corner of the tape. When I ripped it off it felt like an electric sander had done a U-turn on my chin. Scowling, I looked at Bobby to see if he was happy.

"Now it looks like a centipede is sucking your blood," he said.

"Centipedes don't suck blood," I reminded him.

He shrugged and got out. I looked in the mirror. It did look like a centipede sucking my blood. I dabbed at it with the shirt I had just taken off, and then I got out. We walked around the back of the restaurant and entered the main door from the valet area. In the lobby, two tastefully dressed women hovered over a wooden podium studying the reservations book. One of them came around to greet us.

"Good evening," she said through a row of brilliant teeth.

"Well, I hope yours is good," Bobby said. "Our car broke down."

The hostess took on a tragic face. "Oh, I'm so sorry." Then she noticed my chin and leaned in for a better look. "Oh! Were you hurt?"

"Yes," Bobby answered for me, "but he's very stoic." She frowned at my stitches, but Bobby gave her no time to comment. "We'd like a table," he explained, "but I've just been tinkering under the hood of my Jag and need to wash up first." He gazed out the window at Pharr Road as if he might spot his broken-down XKE by the curb. Then he looked at his hands and brushed his palms together.

"Of course, sir. Do you have reservations?"

"No, is that a problem?" Bobby said and gave her the stranded motorist's appeal-for-mercy smile.

She responded with her there's-no-setback-that-the-cuisine-at-Dem-Bones-can't-alleviate smile. "I believe we can accommodate you. The restrooms are through there." She swept an arm toward a dark hallway hung with impressionistic paintings of bones. I noticed a pay phone attached to the wall there.

"Thank you," Bobby said and walked alone to the bathroom. At the threshold of the dining room, I surveyed the tables. White linen glowed and silverware sparkled with candlelight in the darkened room. A thin woman with a train of long red hair played a piano on a raised platform in the center of the eating area. A long polished wooden bar covered most of the wall on the left. The bartender had his back to the room, but I could see his face in the mirror that stretched the length of the bar. He sported a brushy handlebar mustache and the sagging eyes of a basset hound.

It took a few seconds to adjust to the light and spot Perry and company in the back right corner of the room. Tyler and his father had their backs angled to me. Pat was scanning the menu. Perry had an elbow on the table, propping up his tired head by two fingertips and a thumb on one temple. When Bobby appeared by my side, the hostess approached us with menus.

"I wonder if you have a table near the front window," I said before she could start talking. "We'd like to keep an eye on our car until the wrecker comes."

Her mouth formed an O, and her eyes slanted with compassion, as though she had just received devastating news. "So, you weren't able to fix it?"

"No," I said, "looks like it needs a computer reset."

Her head canted to one side, and she ramped up her look of concern. "Oh, no."

"The Jaguar people will send someone over though," Bobby assured her. "Part of the package, you know. We decided to make the best of it and dine here while we waited."

She smiled at our prudent decision and returned to her friend at the podium. They ran their fingers over the schematic chart of the dining room as if they were double-checking a nine-step equation they had just completed for nuclear fusion.

"Good news," she announced and led us to the empty table at the front window.

As we followed her, I whispered to Bobby, "Back right corner."

Crossing the front of the room we found much to be interested in to our left, giving the Raintree party only the backs of our heads should they look our way. The warm notes of the piano filled the room with classy major ninth chords that reflected the mood of the city at night. The tinkle of glasses and silverware fit perfectly into the piece. I wanted to see the pianist's hands, but instead I studied the abstract sculptures of bones on the wall.

At our booth I slid all the way to the window in the seat that faced the room, while Bobby sat down catty-cornered to hide me from view. The hostess dealt us the menus and informed us that our waitress would be Holly. While we looked over the menu, I glanced at Tyler's table. Perry was still half-asleep on his fingertips.

"How much money you got on you?" Bobby said.

"I think I can afford some water and the rental of the napkin and silverware if you go in halves with me," I said.

"How long do you think they're gonna let us sit here and sip water?"

A college-aged brunette appeared at our side and didn't quite suppress her smile at our diagonal seating. She looked at her writing pad, wrote something down and came up with a new smile for a fresh start.

"Hi, I'm Holly. I'll be your waitress tonight."

"It's his legs," I explained.

"Sir?" She looked innocently at Bobby, whose chest barely cleared the tabletop.

"His legs are very long," I explained.

"Yes, sir," she said smiling. "Are you two gentlemen ready to order?"

"If you don't mind, we're waiting on a third party. We'll order later."

"Certainly, sir. What about something to drink while you wait?"

"You have qualla?" Bobby said.

She raised one eyebrow, and a wrinkle check-marked her forehead. "Sir?"

"Qualla," Bobby repeated.

She wrote on her pad. "I'll ask the bartender." She brought up a doubtful look at me. "And for you, sir?"

"Ginger ale," I said. "*Buffalo Rock* if you have it." She wrote that down, too.

"I'll be right back with your drinks and another menu for your friend."

Halfway to the bar she stopped, turned around and returned to us. "I'm sorry, sir, how do you spell 'koala'? Is it like the bear?"

Bobby smiled. "A koala is not really a bear. It's a marsupial. I'm asking for 'qualla.' It's a Cherokee drink made with sumac berries." He spelled it. "If you don't have qualla, well . . . I suppose ginger ale will have to do."

When she disappeared across the room, I waited for Bobby to look at me. "How many restaurants have you known that serve qualla?"

Holding a poker face, he winked. "You may learn something tonight, Gray Eyes."

I shifted my attention to Tyler's table, where Beau was ordering. When their waitress left, Perry took a long pull from a tall glass of beer and looked around the room with a bored expression.

"So, who are we waiting on to join us, Gray Eyes? In case the waitress asks?"

I gave him a look. "You get to choose. Whom would you like?"

He gazed out the window at the evening traffic. "How about Clementine Carter?"

I frowned and shook my head—my version of a raised white flag.

"Doc Holliday's lady in *My Darling Clementine*."

"That's an old one, isn't it? Is she still alive?"

Bobby shook his head. "Gives us a good reason to wait here indefinitely."

I peeked at Tyler's table. "Have you got a plan how we're going to do this?"

Bobby gave me a knowing nod but said nothing as he watched Holly set down two green bottles before us. Then she placed two chilled glasses on the table and posed as the picture of contrition.

"I'm sorry, sir," she said looking at Bobby. "Our bartender doesn't know how to make a qualla." She turned her disappointed face to me. "And we don't have the brand of ginger ale you wanted." She tried for a commiserating smile. "I hope this brand is okay."

I started to put her at ease, but Bobby kicked me under the table.

"So," she continued, "Rick—that's our bartender—he said these drinks are on the house. But he wants you to drop by the bar and tell him how to mix a qualla."

Bobby poured a shot into his glass, downed it, and made a muted grunt deep in his chest. "Tell him 'thank you.'" When she left, Bobby gave me another wink. "Free drinks," he gloated and emptied the bottle into his glass. "Now, tell me about Perry."

I peered around Bobby's shoulder and looked at the moody man as I spoke. "He's an inch shorter than me and a foot wider. Once upon a time, he put in a lot of hours in a weight-room and guzzled steroids. Probably weighs two-seventy, two-eighty. Most of that is in his gut now. My guess is . . . he had an edge once . . . might remember a few moves if pressed. He always looks like he's regretting something—like going to thug-school instead of med-school."

"You talked to him at Itawa, right? Anything up there besides steroids?" Bobby tapped the side of his head with his forefinger.

"I doubt there is a Phi Beta Kappa key on the mantle at home. He didn't talk."

"And the gun is in the left armpit?"

I nodded. "Yep."

Bobby sipped from his glass and set it down. "Now tell me something bad about him."

"What do you mean? I don't know him."

"Okay, tell me what you *do* know."

I stared out the window. "Well, Tyler is afraid of him. Tyler's mother, too. He carried a gun to camp. How's that?"

Bobby nodded. "Can you see what he's drinking?"

I leaned for a better look. "Looks like he is working on his second glass of beer."

"Okay, I want you to let me know the instant you see him start to get up?"

"What are you going to do?"

"We've got to quietly de-activate Perry," he explained. "I'll take care of that. You think up a plan about how to get Tyler and his mother away from the father."

I'd been thinking about that ever since we had entered the restaurant. "How long will Perry be de-activated?"

"How long do you need?"

"Long enough to get to the pay phone in the lobby and call the restaurant. I'll be Victor Dimateo asking for Beau. The hostess will go get him."

Bobby casually turned around to study the room. The Raintrees seemed not to be having much fun. Tyler's head was slumped in its trademark sag of misery. Pat Raintree had her hands folded in her lap and stared at her wineglass while her husband kept up a running monologue. Perry guzzled beer and looked around the room.

Bobby leaned on his forearms and laced his big fingers together like a corral around his ginger ale. "When Raintree leaves his table to get the phone call, go to Tyler and don't hesitate. Take them out the fire exit door. Go right through that stand of junipers at the side of the lot. I'll know you're out when the alarm sounds."

"Where will you be?"

"In the bathroom with Perry." He leaned to one side, dug his keys out of his pocket, and set them in front of me. "Drive out the far entrance of the gas station, turn right and right again on Peachtree Trail. Pick me up on the backside of the block."

At the mention of a neighboring street, I wondered at what point Bobby had started making his plan. "How are you going to handle Perry? Even if he is past his prime, he's a moose."

Bobby's face was as serene as if he were smoking his pipe on the canoe dock studying the curve of the moon. "Every man has one weak moment. Every moose, too."

Holly appeared with a menu for Clementine Carter and two more ginger ales. "Are we all right?" she asked and smiled hopefully. "These are complimentary, too."

"Thank you," I said. Bobby winked twice at me.

"When she left, he tapped a finger on the front of the menu. "Here's the number for the restaurant. You got coins for the phone?"

I committed the number to memory and set a quarter on the tablecloth. Without looking I recited the number. Bobby nodded.

"Okay," he said, "now we wait for the beer to run its course."

"What if *I* have to tinkle?" I said.

Bobby shook his head. "You don't get to tinkle," he replied with a crooked smile and hitched his head sideways toward the room of diners. "Keep watching him."

Ten minutes passed before Perry finally pushed his chair back. "He's getting up," I said.

Bobby was already in motion, gliding out of the booth and walking toward the bathrooms without turning his head. Perry stood next to Beau Raintree with his hand out, waiting. Raintree said something angry to Perry, but it was like a fruit fly trying to disagree with a Kodiak bear. Perry wiggled his fingers, and Raintree grudgingly forked over a ring of keys. Perry pocketed them and came up the aisle past the piano player.

Bobby had disappeared. I followed in Perry's wide wake and wasted no time making the call from the phone in the little hallway. The telephone behind the podium rang, and I watched the hostess who had welcomed us to the restaurant hurry to pick up.

"Dem Bones. This is Lisette." I heard her in stereo—live in one ear, through the earpiece in the other. I turned my back to her and lowered my voice to a soft mumble.

"This is Victor Dimateo. I have an urgent call for one of your customers—a Beau Raintree." I twisted at the waist and watched her check her list and seating chart. The assistant hostess left her station and walked past me into the other restroom.

"Yes, he is here. I can have a phone taken to his table. Just a—"

"No, wait!" I scrambled for a rationale. "The news I have is very bad for his wife. He needs to hear this alone so that he will know how to prepare her. Just have him come to your phone. It's Victor Dimateo."

"Of course, Mr. Dimateo. Just a moment."

At our table I had slipped two sugar packets into my pocket. I wedged them under the receiver cradle, gently replaced the phone, and followed Lisette back into the dining room. As I left the lobby area a dull thud rocked the walls. It reminded me of the pipes knocking in our old steam-heated grammar school when I was a kid. The sound came from the bathroom. Undoubtedly, Perry had just met Bobby Whitehorse.

Lisette made a beeline for the Raintrees. I veered around the piano for the bar and slowed to a loitering gait, admiring the woodwork around the big mirror. As soon as Beau was on his feet, I was sidling toward his table. As Beau made his way toward the lobby, I noticed he had a big purple bruise on one cheek.

When Tyler saw me, he sat up as straight as a sourwood shoot, his eyes wide and zeroing in on my chin. "Stoney!" he whispered. His mother's face paled. She looked like she was having trouble drawing a breath. As I sat down in Perry's seat, I put a hand on Tyler's shoulder and gave it a squeeze. I addressed my question to Pat.

"We don't have long. Are you two being held by duress in the apartment?"

Pat Raintree's eyes filled with tears, and her face pinched with pain or embarrassment or both. "We can't go anywhere without Beau, and he can't go anywhere without Perry."

"Are you saying that your husband is as much a victim in this as you two?"

"No," she huffed. "He has his problems, but our problem is him."

"Do you want to get away?"

Pat faltered. She looked toward the lobby where she had last seen her husband.

"Tell him, Mom," Tyler whispered forcefully. He gave her five seconds then faced me. "He hurts her, Stoney."

I leaned toward her and gripped her arm. "You've got to tell me right now, Mrs. Raintree. Do you want to get away?"

"Mom!" Tyler pleaded.

As she looked at her son, a deep sadness crept into her eyes. "Yes," she said.

I stood, lifting her by the arm and taking Tyler with my other hand and whisked them toward the back emergency exit that read *FIRE EXIT ONLY! ALARM WILL SOUND!* I leaned into the push bar with my hip and a loud buzzer cut off the music and conversation in the room. It was like the ratcheting of a giant insect that had invaded the restaurant. Once we were through and running across the lot, the alarm abruptly shut off as the door slammed. I kept a firm grip on Pat and Tyler and rushed blindly through a wall of nine-foot-tall junipers. The scent of the foliage was tart in the night air. For a brief moment, I saw it as a cleansing ceremony delivering us from the evils in their lives that we had just left behind.

When we reached the truck, we piled into the front seat, pulled out of the gas station lot, turned right and right again on a darkened road with no streetlights. Just as Bobby said, it was Peachtree Trail. I slowed and looked for Bobby to emerge from the row of houses that backed up to the business section. After one pass I turned around in the last drive and started back. No sooner had I let out the clutch than I felt the truck list gently to my side. I peered through the rear window and saw Bobby lying in the bed.

"What was that?" Pat Raintree said.

I rolled down my window and called out softly. "Everything okay?"

"Drive out to Peachtree," Bobby instructed. "Find a gas station."

I smiled and U-turned. "That," I said, finally answering Pat Raintree's question, "is Robert Steals-the-White-Man's-Horse."

We turned on Peachtree and headed north, just a couple of cabbage farmers in a produce truck heading back to the mountains . . . with two people they had just kidnapped.

I pulled into a Texaco station and got out to pump gas. Pat and Tyler had been very quiet during the drive, but now I could hear them talking in hushed voices. I couldn't hear what they were saying but by the tone of it I guessed Pat was feeding Tyler motherly assurances that everything would be okay now. I hooked the nozzle in the tank and locked the handle at full-throttle. Bobby now lay on his back with his hands clasped behind his head.

"Never rode back here before. Pretty nice. Sort of like a redneck limo."

"Everything go okay in the bathroom?"

"Went okay for me. Not so good for Perry. You leave a tip for Holly?"

I shook my head. "I was in a hurry."

He frowned. "Guess we won't be going back to *Dem Bones* anytime soon."

"How did you handle Perry?"

Bobby's eyes could smile when nothing else on his face moved. "I locked two stalls and waited in the third so he would have to stand at a urinal. When I heard him unzip and start, I stepped up behind him. It's the most vulnerable moment in a man's life. He's got both hands preoccupied, he's facing a wall with his back to the room, and his most delicate possession has come out of hiding and he wants his privacy. Plus, his whole body is relaxed so he can empty his bladder. My daddy used to say 'the weasel is out of his hole and his eyes are closed.' "

"So what did you do?"

"Put my hand on the back of his skull and introduced his forehead to the tiled wall. Hard!" He smiled, closed his eyes, and sang, "Pop-goes-the-weasel."

I wondered if I'd ever be able to relax at a urinal again. I pictured Perry's head ramming the wall like a wrecking ball. That explained the sound I'd heard in the lobby.

"How'd you know how hard to push without killing him?"

"Practice," he said and looked at me with his don't-ask-me-any-more-questions look. He rolled his head back to the bright lights of the station's plastic colonnade and shrugged. "To tell you the truth, I was more worried about the wall. You were right. He is a moose. But he looked pretty human lying on the bathroom floor wetting himself."

Pat was quietly holding Tyler as he watched me over her shoulder through the back window. I gave him a wink and a reassuring smile, but he didn't acknowledge me. I think he was still in shock.

"Hey," Bobby said, "did you see that bartender? Looked a little like Bat Masterson?" Bobby closed his eyes and smiled. "Bet if I'd worn my hat he would have whipped up some qualla for me."

I leaned my forearms on the sidewall of the truck and studied Bobby's peaceful face. I had never seen him hurt another human being, but I knew he had the potential for it. It was what had earned him a year in prison. And he'd survived a war. I wondered: *What if there had been a third person in that bathroom?* I saved that one for another time.

When the gas pump kicked off with a loud *clunk*; I capped the tank and holstered the nozzle. "You want to drive?"

Bobby shook his head. "Just hand me my hat. Then find a restaurant with a drive-through and we'll eat on the road."

"Fast food?" I said.

Bobby shrugged. "When you're a kidnapper, Gray Eyes, you have to compromise your nutritional standards."

When I reached into the cab for Bobby's hat, Pat Raintree was hugging Tyler and staring at me through a thick lens of tears. "Thank you," she whispered. "Thank you both. We were so scared in that apartment. Perry, the big man, is an animal. He said he would break one of our fingers if we tried to leave or use a telephone."

It was probably good Bobby hadn't heard this before entering that bathroom.

"He hit my dad, Stoney," Tyler said.

For a moment I thought I was hearing a vestige of compassion that Tyler still held for his father, but then Tyler's face darkened. "Whenever he hit my dad, Dad took it out on Mom."

Pat took Tyler's chin in one hand and turned his face to hers. "No, Tyler, we—"

Tyler gently but firmly took her hand from his face. "He hit you, Mom. I heard it through the wall." He looked out the window and lowered his voice. "He hit me, too."

She pulled Tyler closer, squeezed her eyes shut, and began crying again. By the bright overhead lights of the station, I saw for the first time a dark bruise surfacing beneath the tear streaks in her make-up.

Chapter Nineteen

Pat Raintree, Tyler, Abby, Bobby Whitehorse, and I sat with Old Bill in the office before breakfast. T-Bone's head, with eyes narrowed to contented slits, lay across Tyler's thigh as Tyler stroked him. T-Bone always knew which hand to approach for unlimited attention. If Tyler hadn't been there, it would have been me.

I was feeling better than when I woke up. The lactic acid build-up from my marathon workout felt like I had walked through a high-density radiation field and, regrettably, lived. The cobwebs in my joints that I sometimes had to tear apart in the mornings had been icicles when I'd started my run at dawn. By the time I had pushed through a hard quarter-mile swim, I was well-oiled and serviceable again.

"Tyler already has a place here," Old Bill said. He had been talking to Pat but now he looked right at Tyler. "You just take your old bunk, and we'll fix you up with the clothes you need. We've got enough lost-and-found to open a Salvation Army branch." Old Bill poked a thumb at the adjoining office where Mrs. Old Bill was talking on her telephone. "Mrs. Wellborne will get those for you."

"Bill," I said, "maybe Tyler should stay with me."

Old Bill stared out the window at the empty sports field where Beau Raintree and Perry had stood. "All right. How do we keep a low profile on him during the day?"

"He sticks with me. I'll be his radar."

"That means I get to do a lot of archery!" Tyler said in a rush. He dug into his pocket and held out his hand, revealing a crudely roughed-out arrowhead. "I worked on it some from the glass you gave me."

"That's a good start," I said and turned to Old Bill. "What about Mrs. Raintree helping out with riflery. It's low visibility, in the woods, on the far side of camp."

Pat's eyes widened. "I don't know anything about guns. I'm afraid of them." In her expensive dinner clothes and jewelry, she did seem an odd candidate.

"That is an excellent qualification," I said. "Our first concern over there is safety. You don't have to know how to shoot. Just teach the kids how to shoot without a flinch, which is probably more a feminine thing than male. Justin Kent will teach you all the technical stuff." She looked unconvinced.

"It's the safest place for you if someone shows up unannounced," Bobby explained. "You'll be remote and well-armed."

Her face froze in shock. "I could never shoot anyone."

Bobby gave her a kind smile. "Could if someone wanted to shoot you." She started to protest, until Bobby added, ". . . Or Tyler."

Pat closed her mouth and fixed her worried gaze on her son. Finally, she nodded.

"You'll need a new name," Bill suggested.

Three beats of silence passed until Bobby Whitehorse spoke again. "Phoebe Anne Moses." Everyone in the room turned to Bobby's placid face. Three more beats ticked by. "Annie Oakley's real name," he explained.

Old Bill arched his eyebrows at Pat. "How 'bout it, Miss Moses?"

She turned a silver bracelet on her wrist. "I don't want to be any trouble."

"You'll earn your keep," Old Bill assured her. "Abby, you've got room for another counselor in the staff cabin, don't you?"

"We have plenty of room," Abby said and smiled at Pat. "I've got clothes you can wear."

Bill held a serious eye on Abby. "I figured you ought to know what we're doing here, but I see no need for anyone else to know."

Abby nodded and produced a smile that was neither Saint Joan nor Emmy Lou. Mother Theresa, maybe. They all looked good on her.

Pat bowed her head and sniffed wetly. "I'm so grateful to you all."

Old Bill opened a drawer, pulled out a sheet of paper, and slapped a pen on top of it. "All right, Miss—" he looked at Bobby and waited with his mouth open.

"Moses," Bobby said. "Phoebe Anne Moses."

"All right, Phoebe, I'll need you to fill out this employee form so if somebody comes looking for Pat Raintree, I can say she's not here." Old Bill dropped his elbow on the desk, settled his chin in the cup of his hand, and stared at Tyler. Without moving his head, he angled his eyes to me. "Any ideas on this one?"

"Tyler," I said, "do any of the other campers know your last name?"

Tyler thought for a moment and shook his head. I pressed a little harder.

"You didn't tell anyone about your being part-Seneca and talk about your name?"

He shook his head again. Without breaking eye contact with Tyler, I could see in my peripheral vision that the Seneca connection was news to his mother.

"Changing your first name would only draw more attention to you. No one will remember your last name from the first day's roll call. How about 'Tyler Hood.'" I checked Bill's face for consensus. "Troy says he is Itawa's next Robin Hood."

Tyler's smile stretched across his face like the first cut into a watermelon. When Pat saw that, she couldn't help but smile.

"Tyler Hood," Old Bill said. "I want you to start using that name around camp."

Tyler nodded with enthusiasm. Bill turned to Mrs. Old Bill, who stood expectantly in the doorway of her office.

"See if you and Tyler can round up some clothes that'll fit him."

We watched in silence as Tyler rose and left the room. Old Bill turned his attention back to Phoebe Moses and lowered his voice.

"Meanwhile, I want you to get hold of that lawyer of yours and start the ball rolling on getting your husband behind bars, where he can't get at you."

Before she could respond, I asked her, "Does Beau know who your lawyer is?"

"No!" she said emphatically. "I got his name from a friend at the health club."

We were quiet for half a minute, listening to Tyler choose his wardrobe with Mrs. Old Bill. Through the doorway I watched him pull off his tee-shirt. The mark I had seen between his shoulder blades on the first day of camp was smaller and less colorful. I turned to see if Pat Raintree had seen this, but she was smiling out the window—both hopeful and determined. There was a positive feeling in the room, and I decided not to break it.

"Explain to me again why this guy, Perry, is staying with you," I said.

Pat's face paled. She sat back deeper in the sofa, closed her eyes, and exhaled a long breath.

"It's worse than I told you," she admitted and wrung her hands in her lap. "When Beau started working with Victor Dimateo, all they talked about was shipping schedules, so I assumed they were working together on produce imports. Since Beau already had all the freighter contacts, he acted real important around Mr. Dimateo, but I could tell that it was Dimateo who held some kind of power in the arrangement. He always had this smug smile on his face that left no doubt as to who was in charge."

"Mr. Dimateo arranged for Maya to come work for us. She's the maid from Guatemala. She doesn't speak much English, but I was able to learn from her that she is an illegal and came to America with her family on a ship filled with oranges and bananas and avocados. That's all they ate for seven days.

"As I got to know Maya better, I learned that she, her husband, and both her children were forced to tape bags of white powder to their bodies. I tried to tell Beau, but he got livid and wouldn't talk about it."

She gazed out the front window, her eyes glazed like ice. "Somehow—I guess through Beau—Mr. Dimateo found out I knew about the drugs. About that same time, he found out what an idiot Beau was, because that's when Beau shot my—" Her eyes lowered to her hands. "Beau shot a friend of mine." She shook her head angrily. "I think Mr. Dimateo must have taken care of that by providing a doctor. From that point the facade of partnership was gone, and Beau was clearly the one taking orders."

She raked her hands through her hair. "Then Dimateo sent *Perry*." She pronounced the name painfully, the way a shy, grammar school, science teacher might say "penis." "He's like a bodyguard or something. Beau pretends Perry is guarding *him*, but it's pretty clear that Perry is watching *us*, as if we might cause Dimateo some kind of trouble."

We were quiet, digesting her story, until Bobby laughed quietly. "I'm betting old Perry won't be running to his boss to report in till he's got things under control again."

Old Bill glared at me. "Could he know you're the ones who took them?"

"Perry and Beau never saw us, but they might ask questions and figure it out."

Bobby shook his head. "Being in business with someone like this Dimateo . . . and owing him money. That's not good."

"Beau has always owed money," Pat bemoaned. "He'll find a way to squeeze it out of someone."

"Is that why you're selling your house?" I asked.

The blood drained from her face, and she stared at me with vacant eyes. "Selling our house?"

When I didn't reply she slumped forward, putting that curve of misery in her spine. "Dear, God!" she whispered and started to wrinkle up for a new cry. But she checked herself and turned to the sound of Mrs. Old Bill talking to Tyler, who was holding out his arms like a forklift, amassing a stack of clothes as she sorted through piles.

"Mrs. Raintree," Old Bill said, "uh . . . Phoebe . . . you two can stay here as long as it takes. Don't worry about the other stuff. That's what your lawyer is for."

"That sale can be barred while your divorce is underway," Abby offered.

"I don't care about the house," Pat sniffed. "It's full of horrible memories." She buried her face in her hands and broke down. Each of us found some other place to focus our attention. I chose the window and the view of Standing Bear, wishing I was up there right now with Tyler, where the wind could sweep clean a cluttered mind.

Old Bill handed Pat a handkerchief, stood, and patted the back of his chair. "Come on . . . sit here at my desk and call your lawyer," he said. "Everybody else, let's go get these kids up for breakfast. And—" he said, stopping us. "It would be best for Tyler not to acknowledge that you're his mother. As far as the camp is concerned, he's back from a short leave of absence and you're a new employee. All right?"

As the others filed out the door, Old Bill stepped close to me. "So, you think these buzzards might show up here?"

I could hear the worry in his voice. "Better to be ready than not."

Bill pinched the bridge of his nose and walked away muttering something I couldn't hear. When he entered Mrs. Old Bill's office, I left for the dining hall.

At the edge of the soccer field Abby was pointing, telling Pat how to find the staff cabin and about the clothes she would put out on the spare bunk. I lingered nearby simply because I liked hearing Abby talk. She was so kind to this stranger dressed in expensive formal wear, it made me wish I'd been kidnapped and left in a basket on Abby's doorstep.

"You're sure I won't be crowding all of you in the cabin?" Pat said.

Abby laughed. "I've been teaching classrooms of thirty eighth graders for the last year. Compared to that our cabin is monastic. Besides it will be nice to have someone to talk to about anything other than sororities and rock concerts."

Pat started up the hill toward the staff cabins. When Abby came over to me, she bent at the waist to inspect my stitches. This was a smile I'd not seen.

"That just might turn out to be a sexy scar," she said, lifting an eyebrow.

I lifted an eyebrow, too. "Bond," I said, in my English accent. "James Bond."

She straightened and cocked her head to one side. "How in the world did you manage to whisk away Tyler and his mother like that?"

"Whitehorse," I said, keeping the accent. "Bobby Whitehorse."

She tilted her head the other way and gave me a smirk. "Right. And if I asked Bobby he would put on the same modest face and say it was all you."

"This is not my modest face, Abby. It's supposed to be my James Bond face. I'll tell you all about it later when I have more time to impress you."

"Too late for that, double-o-seven. I'm already impressed."

I felt like wagging my tail, saying "Woof!" and following her around to all her classes. "You don't look old enough to be a veteran schoolteacher, you know."

Her eyes held on mine with something bordering on mischief. "Remember the time I told you that asking a woman's age was the wrong thing to say?"

"Yep."

"Well, the thing you just said? That's the right thing to say."

I smiled.

"So how old *do* I look?" she said, testing me.

I could have gone for the easy score, but I didn't want all our conversations to be banter and riposte. "It's complicated. You can look at a person before you really get to know them and answer that pretty easily. Once you see who they really are, it all gets mixed together—the physical and the spiritual. You know what I mean?"

Abby folded her arms across the Itawa logo on her sweatshirt and gave me a smile that made her eyes shine like flakes of mica.

"You know, you seem older than you are, Stoney. You move in an economical way. You're well-read. You speak well. You know how to be quiet. You're very good with the children. And maybe best of all, you know how to share your knowledge without stuffing it down someone's throat."

I probably should have blushed, but all I could think about was how Bobby Whitehorse had played the vital role in shaping who I was. I couldn't imagine what I would be right now if I had never met him. Unless it was less literate about Westerns.

"So, it comes down to this," Abby said, laying her right index into the palm of her left hand. "A. You're younger but seem older." Two fingers in the palm. "B. I'm older but seem younger." She opened both palms to the sky. "A plus B equals—?"

Abby's smile just about loosened every joint in my body. I shrugged and said, "Somehow it seems like that equation evens out nicely."

"It does, doesn't it?" she agreed. "Come on, I'm hungry."

Side by side we started for the dining hall, but we both stopped at the same moment. The morning sun sent a shaft of light through the trees that illuminated the camp like the opening of a play. Together we admired it without the need for words. When the ray of light dissolved into the general illumination of the morning, Abby turned to me.

"That was a good thing you two did in Atlanta."

"It's not over," I said. "We'll need to keep our eyes open."

Three sleepy girls came down the trail from the cabins and clopped up the steps to the dining hall. Abby and I fell in behind them like the lagging members of a cortege.

As she held the door for me, I stopped at the threshold and faced her. "Abby, the folk dance at Sautee is Wednesday night," I said. "We all go over in buses . . . the whole camp. There's always a waltz at the end. Sort of the special dance of the evening."

She lowered her eyes and made a little smile that I had not seen before.

"Would you save it for me?" I asked.

Her slate eyes met mine and brightened. "I will," she promised.

Chapter Twenty

Abby and I sat across from each other at a table that was dominated by male sports talk. The boys had won the soccer rematch and already accepted a counter challenge from the girls. The table was buzzing with new strategies, which left Abby and me in a vacuum of semi-privacy. I wanted to know how she spent her free time, about her reading preferences and her teaching career. Mostly I just wanted to hear her talk, which was a challenge amid the oceanic mix of conversations in the room.

She spoke with a quiet confidence, her words always following a contemplative pause. She sat very straight without seeming stiff and nodded to me to emphasize points that needed emphasizing. Her graceful neck was a sculptor's dream. Even perched on a cafeteria bench, the eagle in her was not to be denied. Her aquiline bearing did not alter as we arrived at her unhappy childhood.

"My father left when I was seven. Most of what I remember before that was Mother and Father screaming at each other."

"Were you ever close to either of them?" I asked.

She closed her eyes and shook her head. "I guess they tried to be parents in the token ways they had been taught as children—just minimal supervision—but there was no substance to it. After he left, Mother sought solace in a bottle. I never had any friends over. I was too embarrassed. Alcohol didn't make her mean or loud like it does some. It just fed her melancholy. Her defeat was like a black hole. It pulled at everything around her. For a while I got sucked right in."

Abby forked up eggs and chewed, the tendons in her jaw rippling like water. In that simple motion I caught a glimpse of the resolute little girl who had been forced to forsake childhood too early.

"But you made it out of there," I said.

She laid down her fork and looked me squarely in the eyes. "Yes." She said the word softly, and I knew I was one of precious few people who had heard this story. "I pretty much raised myself. I am not my mother . . . or my father. I'm who I want to be."

I smiled. "Congratulations."

She picked up a piece of toast and bit off a corner, and we worked on our breakfast in silence. When she caught me watching her eat, she pointed her fork at me.

"What about you, Stoney? What got you where you are?"

"Bobby Whitehorse."

"And what were you before Bobby Whitehorse got hold of you?"

I finished off a strip of bacon and cleaned each finger with my napkin. I felt her eyes on me like a spotlight.

"I didn't have a father either," I began. "Only he was there in the house instead of running away. He never knew me. Never liked me. I used to wish he would leave."

I busied myself by spreading Mrs. Old Bill's muscadine jelly on a biscuit.

"He hit you, didn't he?" Abby asked quietly. Her voice was like a key turning in my chest, and I knew I was going to open up to her just as I had with Bobby.

"Yeah," I said, "he did."

I propped my elbows on the table and enclosed one fist with the other hand. "I think he was trying to beat out of me whatever it was that he disapproved of in me."

Abby nodded. "How was he to your mother?"

I pushed my tray aside with the biscuit untouched. "She died when I was seven. I remember her always bending to his dictatorial rule. If he hit her, I never saw it."

I watched Abby stir her tea and lay down her spoon. The swirl of dark water slowed to an aimless drift, like planets relaxing from their orbital laws. The movement was hypnotic and peaceful, in complete contrast to the memories buzzing through my nerves. My father's wooden face materialized inside my head. He was streaked in red, and my fists were slashing at him like dismembered entities that I could not control.

"Were you afraid?"

"Of him? Hell, yes. He was strong. I was just a kid, meek and nervous. And then when I was about eight, I went sullen. By then, Bobby Whitehorse had me for the summers. Bobby began smoothing out some of the wrinkles, but my fuse was lit."

I looked out the screen to the lake and balanced what I was about to tell her against not telling her at all. Out of the corner of my eye, I saw Abby's patient stillness. I knew she could wait for whatever time it took.

"When I was fourteen the whole thing blew apart at the seams. I'd started getting into fights . . . preparing for my father, I think. Even trained for it pounding on an old duffel I'd filled with sawdust and hung in the backyard. When the day came I almost . . . well . . . the neighbors had to pull me off him. I haven't seen him since."

Abby frowned. "He left?"

I shook my head. "I left. I hitched a ride up here to Itawa and stayed."

"He didn't come looking for you?"

I shook my head again.

Abby sipped her tea and quietly set down her mug. "And Mr. and Mrs. Wellborne just took you in?"

"And Bobby. Old Bill called my father, of course. He never told me the contents of that conversation. I never asked."

"And you finished high school up here," Abby asked.

"Yeah," I replied and gazed out the screen door at the hemlock trees beyond the lake. "But my real education came from Bobby. He saved me, really."

Her eyes scanned the room and settled on something, and I knew she was studying Bobby Whitehorse.

"On a good day, in some small way," I said looking around the dining hall, "maybe I can do that for some of these campers."

Abby wiped her mouth and laid her napkin in her tray. "I'm betting you have a long record of good days, Stoney. From what I hear, you're the teacher the kids will remember." She canted her head. "Maybe you were born for this?"

I shrugged. "I think what makes a good teacher is simply your memory of the age you're teaching. You hear your own words the way the children are hearing them, because you remember what it was like to hear words spoken that way."

I knew by the way she was smiling that she had arrived at a similar insight through her own history. "Mimi says you were the head-counselor for the boys for the last few years. What happened?"

"I was spending too much time orchestrating camp events and not enough teaching classes. So, I stepped down."

She pursed her lips and raised her eyebrows. "So, you've not bought in to climbing the ladder of success . . . even here at Itawa."

I shrugged. "I guess everybody's definition of success is not the same."

Again, by the way she smiled, I knew I was not telling her anything new.

"What would you call a success?" she asked and stacked her forearms on the table as she waited to hear my answer.

I counted off on my fingers. "One, seeing a camper in the forest, alone, kneeling before a plant, speaking to it, before taking. Two, watching a tandem team work in sync down the Narrows. Three, finishing my cabin."

Her smile grew wider at each example. She nodded toward the lake.

"Was there a reason you chose that spot for your cabin?"

I nodded. "With the amplification of sound off the water, I can hear just about everything that happens from the office to the barn and back to the staff cabins."

"Mr. Wellborne told me you were the Itawa security system . . . year-round."

I pushed an airy laugh through my nose. "It's funny. My father did give me something valuable. He kept me alert. I needed a radar to let me know what was coming next. He was so unpredictable. I think that alertness has paid off. Bobby told me I—"

I looked down at my cold biscuit and shook my head. "I'm babbling, aren't I?"

She laughed. "Stoney, I don't think you would know how to babble if you were holding the official how-to manual on babbling."

"Okay, maybe I'm bubbling. Is there a difference between babbling and bubbling?"

Abby wasn't going to let me off so easy. What we had shared this morning ran deep in our blood. I felt privileged in the exchange, and I did know better than to dilute it with humor.

"You're lucky to recognize your place," she said. "You and Itawa are right for each other. Most people brush right up against their 'Itawa' but think they're supposed to keep climbing toward something else. They leave behind the best place they could be."

Like a reverse baptism in mountain springwater, a cold tingle ran up my spine. "Yeah," I agreed. "I'm one of the lucky ones."

"Or one of the alert ones," she countered.

I looked into her eyes, and she looked right back. When I slid my hand to mid-table and extended my forefinger, she did the same and our fingertips connected.

The dining hall was almost empty. I looked at the clock on the wall.

"Hey, we'd better get to the morning meeting. Troy is trying for fire this morning." I stood, holding my tray and hesitating, wanting to say something that acknowledged the sanctity of our conversation. 'Thank you' wasn't enough.

"Thank you," she said.

It sounded just right when she said it. She cocked her head, and a feathery lock of chocolate brown hair dropped over one eye. The subtle smile on her face was one I'd not seen. I wasn't sure what it meant, but I liked it.

"I'll help Phoebe settle in," Abby said. "We may be a little late to the meeting."

I stacked her tray on mine and walked to the tray-return window, trying to remember how Abby had looked to me the first day I had met her. It was interesting to connect that person to the Abby I knew now. And I wondered how I had fared with her, now that I had pried the lid off my dark side.

Chapter Twenty-One

After announcements, Troy made fire. I felt the heat of it rise inside me like a mercury of pride. I watched him receive the gift of fire-making with that strange mix of victory and humility that was his cachet. Unabashed, he hugged me. It was the first time we had ever connected with more than a handshake or a slap on the back. By the squeeze of that embrace, I could see he had strength to spare.

Frozen in that grand moment, I looked over his shoulder at the crowd of campers applauding, yelling war cries, and hoisting fists into the air. Bobby was in the back by the wall, kneeling to Tyler, explaining something. Beyond the jubilant campers starting to disperse to my right, my vision locked on a silhouette alien to this setting. Beau Raintree, dressed in a gray suit, strode confidently up the stone walk. I averted my eye and whispered into Troy's ear.

"Go tell Bobby Whitehorse to take Tyler out to the rifle range. Then I want you to run like a deer to the women's staff cabin. Tell Abby to have Phoebe stay put."

"Phoebe?"

I disengaged from him and squeezed his upper arm. "Do it now, Troy!"

The situation got worse when Perry loomed into view around the curve of the path. He wore an ill-fitting sports coat of blue, a bright red necktie, and khaki slacks. The big overweight bodyguard came plodding up the path into a splash of morning sunlight that illuminated his face. A dark ugly bruise, like the cap of a rotted mushroom, was centered on his forehead. A white bandage ran horizontally across the bridge of his nose. He stopped at the outer edge of the benches where Beau Raintree stood and bobbed around on his toes trying to see each of the faces in the crowd.

As Justin rattled off last-minute announcements, I checked the place at the back wall, where Bobby and Tyler had been standing. It was empty.

In the mass exodus to first activities, the campers parted around Beau and Perry like water flowing around two bridge abutments. Beau's ferret-eyes checked every camper that passed. Behind him, Perry had risen above his trademark melancholy to look all-business. His eyes picked apart the crowd, too, but I had a feeling he was looking for someone who could have made an imprint of his face in the bathroom tiles at *Dem Bones*.

As they passed Perry, some of the kids looked back, their mouths open and their eyes wide with curiosity, as if they had just walked past the last of the prehistoric woods bison. Perry turned slowly until his broad back was to me.

To play this right, I knew I should break into a smile and ask them if they'd brought Tyler back, but I couldn't make myself enter into a performance. I walked over to the two men and spoke in a flat tone to their backs.

"What can I do for you, Mr. Raintree?"

When he turned, his eyes were cold as ice. "Where is he?" Raintree hissed.

He'd made no mention of his wife. Maybe it was like Pat had said. If he controlled Tyler, he controlled Pat, too. Perry stood to my left and glowered beneath his bruise, which now contained the purple of eggplant. In their coats and ties they looked ridiculously overdressed among the retreating campers in cut-off jeans and running shorts and tee-shirts. Perry eyed me from head to toe then spoke quietly, devoid of emotion.

"The bartender described you with a goatee." He smiled at the stitches on my chin. "That threw me at first."

Raintree looked impatiently at Perry. "Is that all you're going to do . . . talk about what threw you?" Perry smiled indulgently as Raintree spewed air through his teeth. "You're supposed to be a goddamned professional. Or at least used to be." Perry's smile dissolved into a dead expression. He turned his head to Raintree. It was a warning.

I waited for Beau to look at me, but I kept my peripheral focus on Perry. "I'll have to ask you not to use profanity here, Mr. Raintree."

His face flushed until I thought the veins in his neck might burst. I wasn't too worried about Beau, but I sensed something winding up inside Perry. I bent my legs slightly and eased my weight over the balls of my feet. The façade of amenities was about to snap.

"Stoney, why aren't you down at the lake. Your class is waiting on you." Old Bill sounded angrier than I had heard him speak to me in years. He stepped within two feet of me but would not meet my eyes. He was like a novice actor on a stage, concentrating on his part. He tilted his head back to look at our visitors through the bottom of his glasses. "Mr. Raintree, what brings you here?" he said, his voice brusque and businesslike.

Raintree's wrath cooled a bit. "I'm looking for my son."

"Run away?" Bill asked without a hint of compassion.

One corner of Raintree's mouth curled into a smirk. "Or taken away."

"What do the police say?" Old Bill said.

Raintree hesitated just a beat too long, and I knew before he spoke that he would be lying. "They're doing what they can. So am I." He glanced at Perry. "We," he corrected with more than a hint of smugness.

"Well, we'll call you if something comes up," Old Bill said.

Justin wandered up behind them, his face compressed with a question. He set his softball gear on the wall. Standing next to Bill, he eyed Perry, and his chest puffed up, causing his arms to levitate a few inches from his sides.

Raintree scanned the grounds down to the lake the same way William the Conqueror must have surveyed the fields at Hastings from his flag ship in the channel. Beau was the kind of man who assumed he was in charge wherever he went. He smoothed the front of his coat and sniffed.

"We'll just have a look around." He made a tight V-shaped smile. "Just in case."

"No, sir," Bill said flatly. "Camp's not open to visitors today."

And there it was: the law as laid down by the landowner. Old Bill could sound like the final word on Judgment Day when he wanted to. My eyes must have widened when Abby jogged up the trail, because Raintree spun to look. I could only pray that Pat Raintree was not with her. Abby circled our visitors until she stood between Bill and me. By the nod she gave me, I knew Pat was safe.

"Kiddie camp's open, Pops," Perry said and gestured with his hand as if to say: *because I say it is*. "It's a long drive so we're gonna walk around a little." He leaned into Old Bill's face. "You got a problem with that?"

When Perry bent forward his coat opened enough to expose a dark nylon holster strapped under his left arm. Old Bill saw it and stepped closer to Perry.

"You bet I got a problem with it. You're trespassing and you're carrying a firearm at a children's camp. That's a bad combination."

Perry chuckled. "But there's not much you can do about it, is there?" He reached up with his right hand and lightly patted Bill on the left cheek. I had never seen Bill move so fast. He swatted the offending arm with the back of his forearm. I shouldered between them and felt Pandora's Box crack open inside me. I slapped Perry's fleshy cheek so hard my hand buzzed like a hive of bees.

Bill's arms reached around my chest, and he pulled me back with a strength that surprised me. Justin started for Perry but stopped when Abby stepped in his way and stood in front of Perry, glaring at the big man with her fists clenched.

"You two men are leaving right now," Bill said over my shoulder.

I could have broken out of Bill's arm lock, but I didn't want to struggle with him.

Perry showed his teeth in an ugly smile and laughed at Abby's appearance on the front line of battle. Casually, he pulled open the left side of his coat. The butt of a gun jutted from a nylon rig under his armpit.

"We're gonna look around, boys and girls" Perry said, holding his pose for effect.

Abby's hand moved so fast it was a blur, striking like a snake inside the loose opening of Perry's coat. It was the same quickness I had seen when she had stepped into the game of *Sting* with me. Now the gun was in her hand, and it seemed that the world stopped turning on its axis. The voices of campers down at the canoe dock floated up to us both distant and disconnected.

The gun was some kind of clip-fed automatic. It shone in the morning sun like a dark crystal ball prepared to read our fortunes. In the dreamlike stillness, Bill's hold on me relaxed. I reached over and gently lifted the gun from Abby's hand. My thumb found the safety and clicked it off, the sound crisp and clear. Everyone heard it.

Perry took an involuntary step backward, as if, instead of a gun, I held a red-hot poker that might singe his coat. Raintree retreated, too.

I knew I wasn't going to use the gun, but the potential of it held everyone in a tableau of uncertainty. I held the muzzle pointed down in the vicinity of Perry's feet. He alternated checking my grip on the gun and my eyes for intent. I expected him to be enraged by the turned tables, but a sadness crept into his face. He closed his eyes and sighed.

"You damned moron," Raintree snapped. I wasn't sure if he was talking to Perry or to me. Justin stepped forward and wrapped his fingers around Raintree's upper arm. Beau was livid now. "Get your damned—"

Justin shook him so hard that Beau almost slipped in the dew-wet grass.

"You were told to watch your mouth," Justin growled into Beau's ear.

Raintree tried to jerk his arm free, but Justin wouldn't let go. "I'll have all of you brought up on charges," Beau spat.

Old Bill's fists were clenched into white marble, but he managed to steady his voice. "You've got one minute to get off this property or I call the sheriff."

"I'm not leaving here without my gun," Perry said.

He took a step toward me, and I pointed the gun at his thigh. "Yeah . . . you are," I informed him. It was the first time in my life I had pointed a weapon at a man. Oddly, I felt an irrational anger toward the weapon. In a reaction that surprised even me, I popped the clip, turned, and threw it as hard as I could out into the lake. It cleared the shore by fifty feet. The water took it in with a sharp, sucking sound.

At the dock Troy and my paddlers turned to the sound and then looked up the hill at us. Stephen Beasley started walking up the lawn, curious, until Troy called him back.

There was either a round in the chamber, or the gun was now empty. When Perry still didn't move, I knew the answer to that riddle. I ratcheted back the slide and a bullet somersaulted through the air and thumped into the dirt. Perry watched it roll to a stop then looked up at me, his breathing quieter, his face transformed with the new possibilities of an even playing field.

My old demons slithered out of their holes, and my chest tightened like bands of steel had replaced muscle. In my mind I saw my father raise his folded belt into the air that last time. The flame that lived at the core of me was just about to erupt and ignite at the surface of my skin. I stuffed the gun in the back of my belt and faced Perry.

"You can pick up your gun at the sheriff's office," I said.

"I'm gonna chew you up and spit you out," Perry whispered through his teeth.

I don't know how long Bobby Whitehorse had been standing there. I hadn't seen or heard his approach behind our visitors. His dark hat bobbed up over Perry's right shoulder as his hand came around to Perry's shirtfront. After one short step toward me, Perry straightened and jerked backward like a rug had been pulled out from under him. For a moment he went airborne and scrambled to get his hands behind him, but he slammed heavily on his back, forcing a rough wheeze from his lungs. His eyes were glazed over. Raintree tried to step away as if he might get his shoes dirty from the fallout of dust, but Justin jerked him back to his side like a puppet.

Bobby knelt behind Perry's prostrate body with Perry's necktie still doubled around his fist. The tie had served like a hangman's noose dropped over his head, and Bobby had leveled the brute with a powerful jerk from behind. It was a move Bobby had probably used dozens of times on unbroken horses. The big man lay very still on his back, his face so florid now that the bruise on his head showed less contrast against his skin.

"It always amazes me," Bobby said quietly, "that people like you will walk into a situation like this with a noose around your neck." Bobby shook his head. "Dumb."

Perry's fingers tried to dig beneath his tightened collar. He made a sound much like T-Bone when the dog was trying to cough up something that had snagged in his throat.

"Hard to be tough when you can't breathe," Bobby remarked casually, but Perry was not listening. He looked like a man tasting the air for the first time.

"Your time is up, Mr. Raintree," Old Bill commanded. "Get off this property!"

When Bobby released Perry's tie, the thug sucked repetitive deep breaths. Then, in a surprise comeback, he lunged at Bobby, who was squatting behind him. In a deft sideways hop, Bobby avoided the attack and delivered a quick punch to Perry's forehead. Perry's hands flew to his head but did not touch. The dark bruise had burst open and a bright ribbon of blood oozed down into his face.

Raintree, still dangling in Justin's grip, pointed a finger at Old Bill. "If you've got my son here, I'll have the law all over you."

"Not today," Old Bill said.

Raintree turned his glare on me. He didn't say a word, but I knew that he knew I had taken his wife and son. When Justin released him with a little push, I stepped toward him, and he backed away a step.

"The owner has asked you to leave," I said. "I suggest you do that."

Beau turned and walked aggressively back toward the office.

"Get up, big man," Bobby said and tapped Perry's head with the side of his boot. "You're gonna miss your ride."

Bobby gripped Perry's coat and helped him up. Then he turned the ailing man and got him started down the trail. About twenty feet away, Perry stopped and looked back at us.

"This ain't over," he said, his constricted throat humming with menace. "That gun cost me a bundle."

Bobby Whitehorse sidestepped to the wall where Justin's glove, bat, and ball lay. He picked up the bat by its thick end, flipped the handle to his hand and tapped the end on the ground next to his boot in a move as neat as a Charlie Chaplin choreography.

"You want that nose broke again?" Bobby said. "I can run up your medical bill to make that gun look like a gift from your grandma."

Perry tried to resurrect some of the swagger he had brought here and followed Beau out to the parking lot. He jerked a towel off the railing at the office and dabbed at his head as he went. Old Bill started off in pursuit, but Bobby touched his arm.

"We'll give him that one. I'll replace it with one from lost-and-found."

In seconds, we heard the car start. Tires squealed, and the car tore down the road spraying gravel until it was but a distant whisper. The canoe class stared at us from boats that followed a slow drift from the faint breeze on the open water.

Old Bill set his jaw and looked at me. "Let's get to work," he said. "We've got a camp to run." He turned and strode down the trail, walking the way he does when the world is not running according to Itawa standards. Bobby and I had straightened out that walk many a time, but we had some distance to go on this one. I picked up the bullet in the grass and pocketed it.

Bobby stepped before Abby, his eyes shining with admiration. "That was damn quick, Abby. Did you get that from Kurt Russell in *Tombstone*."

Abby was shaking, so I put an arm around her shoulder. "I can't believe I did that," she said. "But when he handled Mr. Wellborne like that—"

Bobby and I looked at one another, silently acknowledging the boost of Itawa's female force. Justin turned to leave, and I called out to him.

"Justin. Thanks."

He raised his chin to me. "Yeah," he said. He took the bat Bobby offered, snatched up his glove and ball, and walked off.

Bobby and I watched Justin's back. "Might be a little nugget of gold in that dirt clod after all," Bobby mumbled. He turned to me. "That was a pretty nervy game you played with the big man's gun, Gray Eyes."

I looked down at the crash site where Perry's dead weight had rocked the earth, and I thought about that day Bobby had lifted a tractor off Boyd Justus. The two acts must have had their similarities.

"They'll be back," I said.

"Sure," Bobby said, as if I'd predicted a thundershower within the next month. "And we'll be ready."

"More so than today, I hope."

"Better," he said. "Now we know the gauntlet is down." He smiled. "You and Abby just keep confiscating the enemy's artillery and I'll practice my rodeo skills and we'll do fine . . . as long as the bad guys wear neckties." He reached behind my back and extracted Perry's gun from the waist of my jeans. "I got to go to the feed store today, I'll take this shooter to the sheriff."

Someone stayed by the office front window all day. We ran an extension from the bell rope through the back window and decided on a code of three pairs of rings, which meant "unwanted visitors." I set up a camo tarp for myself about ten yards from my cabin, so that Pat Raintree could move into my home with her son. Tyler stuck with me through the day. When Pat—a.k.a Phoebe—was not at the rifle range, she was inside the cabin. Both took their meals there, too, catered sometimes by Bobby Whitehorse and sometimes by Abby. I took my supper out to my small dock and ate cross-legged as I kept watch over the camp grounds. At night I slept with my strung bow tucked under the edge of my blanket.

Arthur Scroggin was slow to get the legal process into gear. He said he had to start from scratch since the previous attempt at filing for divorce had been terminated. He was "looking into the most prudent methodologies" for addressing an arrest for abuse. The main problem was that Pat Raintree had never filed a report with the police. She had never even talked to a friend about it. Scroggin promised a courier would be up in a day or two with papers to be signed.

Tuesday and Wednesday ran smoothly. But, more and more, Bobby Whitehorse and I stood guard in the shadows of the bordering forests. Justin was vigilant, too, but he was determined to re-establish distance from me and refused to take part in any organized plan of sentry duty. His personal problems with me took on a new slant, as he traded sarcasm for a brooding aloofness, but his attitude was not high on my list of problems.

When it rained all Wednesday afternoon, we amended our schedule and bumped up the second river trip to Thursday. The Etowah would rise enough that we could launch our canoes farther upstream at Black Falls. Instead of a day trip, we planned a three-day camping excursion that Andy and I would lead. Not even Chingachgook could track us over water. Tyler would be safer on the river than at camp.

While we would be away, Abby was to move into my cabin with Pat, and Bobby would take over my tarped outpost. On Saturday, Bobby would drive over to Nimblewill Bridge so we could load our camping gear into a van. There he would join our river trip, taking Andy's place for the more demanding final section of the river, which included the Narrows.

After supper, as the rain let up, the whole camp pulled out of Itawa in three buses headed for Sautee's community center. The old building where dances were held had once been a barn, then a school gymnasium, and now a rustic venue for craft classes and potluck dinners. The walls of rough-sawn oak had stood for a hundred years, while the floor sported a wood strip finish for a basketball court from the 1950s.

We arrived in time to see the musicians tuning their instruments on the raised stage at the far end of the spacious room. Uncertain of their involvement in this dance, the Itawa campers filed in and retreated to the bleachers, hiding their embarrassments by quietness or loudness, depending upon personality.

The band was called "The Playin' 'Possums." Two guitar players—one male, one female—faced one another and warmed up with an impromptu medley of Stephen Foster tunes. A thin, bearded man in coveralls sat motionless with a banjo resting in his lap. Behind him a Paul Bunyan of a man thumped on a standup bass sending deep throbs out into the room beneath the conversations of the waiting crowd. A willowy, dark-eyed woman with long black hair that swayed back and forth across her back, ran a bow across her fiddle like a magic wand and delivered flawless melodies that I remembered from my earliest days at Itawa.

After a few community announcements, the caller talked the crowd through the particulars of the first dance. Mimi and I were the groundbreakers for Itawa, dancing in a fishbowl to prompt the campers to join in. We'd played this part before and knew to ignore the giggles and catcalls. After we had learned the steps from the caller, the band launched into a rollicking Irish piece, and we on the dance floor reigned. As always, it became obvious to the spectators that the participants were having all the fun.

When the second dance started, half the Itawa campers had climbed down the tiered seats to mill about on the periphery of the dance floor. Mostly, this was the result of Amanda's spontaneous pairing of partners. I danced with Abby twice in the first hour and twice again in the second. When I wasn't with her, I enjoyed catching a glimpse of her twirling and promenading with Justin or Andy or Jimmy Dale Vickers. Once, as I danced with Gwendolyn, I spotted Abby in a do-si-do with Old Bill. She held a mysterious smile on her face as if she were somehow connected to the metaphysics of dance. She swayed and tilted her head to the enchanting call of a poetic netherworld, the way an eagle might dip a wing and bank in the rapture of flight.

Three different times I heard Pat Raintree introduce herself to some of the locals as Phoebe Moses. And though she shuffled through the steps with reticence, by the end of the evening she had discovered the catharsis of mountain music and dropped most of her inhibitions. Once, when the music seemed to lose its bottom, I looked over to see the bass player swinging her in his massive arms, his crinkled eyes smiling into hers.

The kids laughed and stumbled through the dance patterns. When they strayed into missteps, they endured their momentary lapses among strangers in good form. The locals seemed to enjoy them even when they got lost, giggled with embarrassment, and looked for help.

A guiding hand would send them back into the flow of the dance until terpsichorean harmony was restored.

It was the kind of night that only a Sautee dance could divine, and it helped me to believe that the world beyond Itawa might still be a kind one. It was good for kids like Ben Souther, the Beez, and Amy Littlefield to meet and talk with people like Homer Rider, Duffy Grizzle, and Callie Sullens—country people with truthful eyes that shone with appreciation for life from the leathery landscape of their sun-hardened faces.

These old mountain folks knew how to be tender with their callused work hands. The practiced turns of their body spoke of countless hours with a hoe or bales of hay thrown over a fence or brushing the muck off their livestock. Their voices chimed with the Appalachian charm that gave these mountains one of their enduring songs.

In any other setting, our media-battered kids might have written them off as irrelevant and dated. But here in this old barn, the locals ruled the night, and the campers stumbled to keep up, sensing the value and gratification of mastering such an arcane art.

I bought two lemonades and grabbed Abby just as the big bass player was homing in on her for the next dance. He stopped and propped his hands on his hips like Papa Bear discovering someone had eaten his porridge. I gave him a wink, and he pointed a finger at me. "Good luck" was written all over the smile that broke across his square-jawed face. Before I turned away, he had already adjusted his sights for Gwendolyn.

The caller's voice became a blur as we stepped out into the night under the huge pecan trees that spread like black lace against the stars. Last year's nutshells mashed under my shoes into the soft, wet ground. The night air liberated my sweat-soaked body with its cool touch.

Abby stopped and looked up at the night sky. "Do you think these kids feel the magic here, Stoney?"

"Yeah, I do. Once they get over the fear of asking someone to dance." I motioned back toward the barn with my cup. "These boys will discover something in the girls tonight . . . something they had no clue about before."

Abby canted her head. "Like what?"

"Well, maybe Bill Columbine probably thought Darcy Greyfield was just a skinny kid who lived on a horse, never swam more than ten feet from the dock, and shut her eyes when she tried to head the soccer ball. Tonight, she's a fairy queen floating on invisible wings. She's got something he doesn't quite grasp, so he's watching her from a new angle."

Abby stared at me a moment, smiled, and nodded her agreement.

I looked across the road where a rolling wet meadow caught moonlight like a giant crystalline wave swelling out of the land. A lone black silhouette marked an abandoned barn that crumbled away by secret increments between my visits to this place. It rode the wave like an abandoned ghost ship stranded without a mast.

"This kind of magic is getting rare for these kids," I said.

She nodded. "The world gets tougher and tougher to grow up in."

I held out my cup, and we tapped the cardboard rims and held them poised for my toast. "But we've got them for a while. And tonight, the music has them. They're dancing through the turns and patterns handed down from centuries past."

We drank, and the world outside the barn became our private domain. Abby tilted her head the other way.

"You remember that first night when you were here stumbling and gangly, don't you?"

I breathed in deeply, and, as I exhaled, I whispered, "Mary Lou Deschene."

"Aha," she said with a melody of her own. "Smitten at the dance?"

"Smitten, emboldened, and liberated."

"By Mary Lou?"

I nodded and turned back to the Flying Dutchman barn across the road. "Mary Lou was kind. She tolerated me as I chased her beguiling smile and tried to keep up with her on the dance floor. She was sort of a milepost for me. She was something I'd discovered that had nothing to do with my family back home. She was all mine. And she was something that reached into me as deeply as all those roots I was tearing away from."

"And?"

"And . . . she was seventeen and a counselor. I was nine. We still write."

Abby lowered her head, smiling, no doubt, at the little boy that was once me. "The magical years," she said wistfully. "You've made some good memories at Itawa."

"As we speak," I said and brushed the rosy spot on her cheek with the back of my fingers. When the surprise melted in her face, she looked at me the way I once wished Mary Lou Deschene would have, taking my words as if they carried substance and were connected to a string of truth that unraveled from the center of me.

The music stopped, and now the caller was announcing the last waltz. He was telling all the gents to go find that special lady. Inside the dance hall, I knew, the farmers were taking the hands of their wives and some of the campers were building up their courage to ignore their peers and follow their hearts' desire.

"I believe this is our dance, sir," Abby said.

"Yep." I touched her elbow and started to escort her to the room, but she didn't go. I turned to see what was wrong, but she just held her ground with an unreadable face. The music started, and I could hardly believe the band's choice. It was *Ashokan Farewell*—a lilting waltz that tugged at anyone whose memory lingered on a face once courted. I had first heard it the night I watched one of the male counselors glide Mary Lou Deschene across the ocean of the dance floor, as I stood on the shore and soaked up every note of the last song of the evening into my constricted heart.

Abby raised her left hand to my shoulder, held out her right, and waited. I took the hand and slipped my right into the small of her back. Poised like this, we did not move at first, but looked at one another and breathed in the scent of wet pecan leaves.

"Smitten, emboldened, and liberated," she said. "Here in the magical years."

We waltzed beneath the pecan tree and out beyond its shadow into the moon's baptismal light, turning and sailing on an ocean that had waited for our crossing. It was the turning that seemed to keep us afloat. With our arms locked into the shape of gunnels, we made a sturdy ship—one that might weather just about anything the sea had to offer. My socks grew damp from the wet grass, and that felt just right.

In my turning I caught glimpses of the dilapidated barn across the road and entertained the strange idea that it was watching me, marking this time for me. I imagined the faint strains of the waltz reaching across the field to the old barn's open loft window and lopsided door. *All things must pass*, the music seemed to say. But here I was with Abigail Parrish. In the magical years.

Chapter Twenty-Two

As Troy and I loaded the canoes and the Outriders packed the van, Pat Raintree came out of the office and stood under the big hemlock. Fingering the drawstring of her sweatpants, she divided her attention between me and the stone terrace where the Outriders were sorting out gear. When I approached, I could see the worry in her eyes.

"My lawyer called," she began. "He sent someone to serve the papers on Beau at the apartment and found another family living there. So, he called the owner, Mr. Dimateo, and he claimed not to know Beau. Mr. Scroggin filed the assault report with the police, but I have to go down to make the charges formal. He's sending up his aide today. It will take a few days. I have an aunt in Atlanta where I can stay."

"Don't stay there. That's too easy. Ask your lawyer to put you up somewhere?"

"Well, maybe I could stay with Thomas," she said hopefully.

"I've met Thomas, Pat. He won't take you in." Her face ran the gamut from surprise, through hurt, to resignation. "Get a motel room," I said.

Her eyes tracked off with something she did not want to say. I excused myself and walked into the office. When I came back out, I gave her an envelope with eight twenty-dollar bills. She looked inside it and back at me.

"It's a loan," I said.

Her whole body sagged, as if she was burdened with the knowledge of too many things gone wrong in her life. Her expression reminded me of Perry's face when I threw his ammunition clip into the lake. I waited. Behind me Troy and Amanda herded campers into the van, Tyler among them. Andy jogged up the steps from the stone amphitheater with several lifejackets. He checked my face and gave us a wide berth.

Pat exhaled in a long breath and busied herself with her drawstring. "One of Beau's brokerage partners dropped out of the firm last year. He's a decent guy, and I had introduced him to a friend of mine—Kelsey—and they hit it off. Kelsey tried to tell me last Christmas in little hints, but I wouldn't let myself listen. I called her this morning."

She looked away and shook her head as if a fly were annoying her. "Victor Dimateo smuggles in and farms out Hispanic families to work in sweat shops. He houses them in the homes foreclosed by his mortgage business until he finds a buyer for the workers." Pat's mouth tightened into a false smile. "Beau bought into it all the way. Kelsey said he liked the danger of it. I remember when he bought a gun and showed it off to me. God, he was just like a little boy . . . playing gangsters. I couldn't believe it when he shot Thomas."

"Does Beau know that his ex-partner and your friend Kelsey know all this?"

"No, the partner figured it out and bowed out on some other pretext. He knew Beau well enough that he couldn't talk him out of it. Beau was quite taken with his new image. I could see that at home, even though he would not tell me about it. He liked to drop hints that he was into something so profitable that 'only the big boys could play the game.'" She rendered the phrase in a husky voice and wagged her head from side to side. "He must have known about the drugs, too. The partner did."

The more I listened to her story, the more this guy Dimateo worried me. I didn't want to add to Pat's problems, but I was beginning to see that Dimateo had more than one reason to keep Pat quiet.

"I've seen the way Beau and Perry are around him," she said, "especially after Beau shot Thomas. I don't think they will tell Mr. Dimateo how they've screwed up here. They'd do anything to keep from facing him with that news."

"Do you still have the sheriff's number?" I asked. When she nodded, I stepped closer. "I want you to call him before you go to Atlanta."

She recoiled and frowned, and her eyes filled with fear.

"Pat, you've got to stop worrying about being an unfit mother. What you did is not in the same ballpark with what your husband is into. Tell the sheriff everything you told me. Tell him about what happened out here Monday morning. He knows the county sheriff in Atlanta, and maybe that can get the ball rolling in our favor. I would imagine the federal people will have to get in on this with the alien thing and the drug trafficking. Do you have any qualms about turning in your husband?"

"No," she said without hesitation. "I don't think I could ever feel safe again unless he is behind bars."

"Don't go anywhere your husband would know to look for you, all right?" The van was getting rowdy, and I needed to leave. "And before you go, I want you to tell all this to Bobby Whitehorse."

"All right," she said, her voice trembling. I squeezed her arm and walked back to the van. When I climbed in, the screaming tapered down a few decibels. Peering out the back window at his mother, Tyler sat by himself. I settled into the driver's seat.

"Everybody ready for three days in paradise?" I yelled, looking in the mirror.

The Beez piped up before anyone else. "We're going to Gwendolyn's cabin?"

The van filled with female groans and male snickers. As I turned around to give him a look, I felt a nudge of pressure on my left hand. Abby was standing outside my window with her hands clasping the window frame.

"Don't worry about Phoebe," she said. "We'll be fine."

I leaned out the window and kept my voice low. "She's going to Atlanta. You'd better catch her in the office and let her tell you about it."

Abby's forehead wrinkled. "She's going alone?"

"She'll tell you. Maybe it's best that she and Tyler are away from Itawa for a while."

Relaxing, Abby nodded once. "Okay. What can I do while you're gone?"

"Make Itawa a wonderful place for three days until I can come back and help you."

Her serious expression dropped away, and she gave me a veiled smile. "Full moon on Saturday night," she said. "A good night for waltzing."

I wasn't sure what to make of that, but I liked the sound of it. Waltzing with Abby had been inducted into my pantheon of all-time best memories, and I hoped there would be many more such nights.

"I would dance with you anytime, anyplace, little lady," I said in my best buckaroo-cowboy dialect, the one that always made Bobby Whitehorse smile.

Abby raised an eyebrow and folded her arms before her. "Oh, really?"

"Really!" I said and opened my door, but she ran for it around the back of the van toward the office. "Bawk!" I squawked in my best Rhode Island Red dialect.

Black Falls made for an ominous put-in. The kids could not keep their eyes off the seventy-five-foot cascade of water that plummeted into the pool where our journey would begin. As they carried their boats to the river's edge, the roar and mist enveloped them like a sustained blast from a bomb.

The geologic fault that had created the waterfall was singular and severe, but there would be only one major rapid downstream of here until we hit the last section on day three. I knew this. The kids did not. Whenever they asked what the up-coming rapids were like, their voices were restrained with humility and their faces prepared for bad news.

"Just be ready for whatever the river offers," I answered each time.

Finding a moment of privacy before we disembarked, I tied a medicine bundle to a bough of hemlock and whispered my prayer to the river. Then I added one more prayer for the children and the gift they were about to receive.

With their boats packed to the gunnels with gear, the kids adjusted to the new weight and, within the first mile, got the hang of maneuvering a heavy canoe. It was good training, like wearing leg-weights for running. When we would shed this gear above the Narrows, these young canoeists would feel Herculean in their ability to move their lighter boats along their chosen routes.

This far upstream, the river was only thirty feet wide in most places, with hemlocks that leaned over the water to make a steepled, green vault. There was an intimacy about this size of stream I had always been drawn to, and though the campers could not articulate it in words, I knew they liked the scaled-down proportion, too, as if this part of the river was a better fit for them.

The water was deep green in the pools and darker still beneath the shaded border of rhododendrons that bunched along the banks. The verdant colors, the shearing song of folding water, the smell of galax and rotting wood and the textures of moss, sand, and stone worked its way into our senses until we were as much a part of this wild land as the steady glide of the water itself. The Etowah had taken us in.

At about mile three, we canoe-stalked for an hour. Not a word was spoken, and only a few times did a paddle shaft tap a gunnel. At a deep shady pool, two otters gamboled in the water, pirouetting and somersaulting until the front boats were within twenty feet, at which point the surprised otters dove to safety. We watched their bubbles rise in staggered bursts downstream like the footsteps of a gigantic, invisible wading bird.

We had lunch by the otter pool and swam for an hour. Though not as graceful as otters, the Outriders lacked none of the otter-enthusiasm, especially Tyler, who seemed immensely grateful to be back at camp. He was probably safer here than almost anywhere outside a witness protection program, which was exactly where he and his mother might end up.

We camped a mile upstream of Wahsega Bridge on a needle-carpeted floodplain beneath some of the largest white pines and hemlocks in the county. The river was placid here but for one riffle that seemed to grow louder in the dark. Hours later, zipped up in sleeping bags, we fell asleep to this sound. It had been a perfect first leg of the trip.

In the morning with mist still rising from the river, we passed under the bridge and entered the long stretch to Nimblewill Bridge above the Narrows. About a mile downstream, a beaver dam spanned the river. Most of these campers had never seen one up close. As they portaged over it, all marveled at the solidity of the construction.

P.J. chewed on one of the sticks just to see what it took to gnaw through one. The Beez tried pulling one of the larger sticks out of the mass of woven wood in hopes of seeing the beaver come out of their lodge to plug the leak. I smiled as I watched him strain. The stick didn't move.

"It's just the work of a little thirty-pound rodent, Stephen," Troy said. "And a stick!"

"Yeah, but he's got that flattened tail," the Beez complained, "That probably helps."

Troy climbed down off the dam mumbling something to himself about flattening Stephen's tail. He looked up and caught my suppressed smile. I placed my hands together prayer-style—our sign for patience. He cracked a smile and knelt down into his boat. If someone did decide to "flatten the Beez's tail," I didn't want it to be my counselor-in-training.

The river went through a huge meadow where we floated lazily under the sun. The heat lulled us into the mentality of driftwood. At a large swimming hole, we ate lunch in the shade of a sycamore, from whose largest limb hung an old rope swing with a thick knot tied at its end. I lay back against my folded life jacket to watch the campers' youthful antics on the swing. It got pretty rowdy with lots of male bravado that terminated in many a bellyflop or back-smack.

A competition evolved for performing gainers off the rope, but none of the boys could master it. As Amanda said, they were "more lip than flip." Amanda was a gymnast with a flare for timing. When the boys were exhausted from their aerial frolics, she climbed the bank with rope in hand, stepped up on a sycamore root and leapt up to gain a higher grip. With toes pointed she sailed downward, arched her back at the bottom of the swing and whipped her legs forward and up on the upswing. Airborne, her body somersaulted majestically and spun on an axis as she pirouetted through a full gainer with a full twist, her arms outstretched like a human crucifix.

When she surfaced, I held up ten fingers. The boys were quiet, especially the Beez, who, on Amanda's downswing, had been yelling something about "suicide by rope swing." But Amanda had unleashed an aerial performance that closed the Beez's mouth and left him in awe, staring at the barely disturbed surface of the river after Amanda had made a clean incision into the water.

There was more than one way to flatten a beaver's tail.

When the river left the meadowlands, it grew wider with the input of several creeks and began to snake around the bases of steep mountains to carry us into wilderness again. We ran Buckhorn Shoals without incident and then encountered a few rapids that were made difficult only by the weight of the gear-laden boats.

Whenever a team got stuck on rocks, they had to step into the water to lighten the load and push the boat free. By the time the sun sank into the trees, the group was tired. Andy and I decided to pull out and make camp early to give everyone plenty of rest for the demands of tomorrow's appointment with the Narrows.

At twilight a few boys fished in a placid pool using lines and hooks from our first aid kit. Tyler followed a more atavistic calling and fashioned a spear of rivercane to which he lashed his napped glass point. I had never seen him so focused and intent as he stalked the edge of the river.

In five minutes, he returned to shore holding a pointless cane. "I broke my point on a rock," he said. "The stupid fish wouldn't hold still."

I showed him how to split the end of the cane, wedge it open, and serrate its inner edges with barbed teeth that pointed backward, just as Bobby Whitehorse had taught me. When Tyler finished the binding, he seemed to have forgotten all about his broken glasswork.

"Cool," he said. "Thanks for helping me, Stoney."

"Helping you is half the bargain," I said. "Your half is to honor the fish."

He stared at me as if I had broken into an aria. "What do you mean?"

"When you hunt, you enter into a sacred pact between the hunter and the hunted. It doesn't matter what animal it is. A deer or a rabbit or a fish. You are taking a life. And even if you're not successful, you carry that sanctity because you have entered into the pact."

When he still looked confused, I continued. "What happens to a fish after you eat it, Tyler? What does it become?"

He frowned. "You mean like . . . part of me?"

I nodded. "And what if you've killed a *stupid* fish? And you ate it?"

He pulled in his lips as he thought about it. "Part of me is stupid?"

The Beez screamed that a fish had stolen his bait. We watched him scowl at his bare hook, and then we turned back to each other.

"Hunt with dignity, Tyler," I said. "Yours and the fish's." I hitched my head toward the others by the water. "They need to learn this from you."

He frowned. "How do I do that?"

"Sometimes when the Indians went off on an adventure, when they returned, they shared their story by dancing around the fire."

Tyler's eyes widened and fixed on me. He appeared to be at the edge of panic.

"You want me to dance?"

I shrugged. "Or just tell the story."

He looked upriver where the last rays of sun slanted across the valley in broad spears of light. "What if nothing happens? There wouldn't be anything to tell."

"Things always happen, Tyler. It might not be catching a fish, but—"

He looked back upstream and strode away without a word, walking around the bend with purpose. I imagined him entering a time tunnel to connect to something as old as these ancient hills. I knew he stood only a small chance of bringing back a fish . . . but a fairly good chance of securing his place in the real world.

Just as it got dark, as I was about to start upriver to search for him, Tyler entered the halo of warmth surrounding our fire and planted the base of his spear on the ground. His face was smeared with mud. Above his head a small trout writhed between the tines of his weapon. He inverted the spear and added the fish to the bounty that Amanda was preparing for the skewer. She laid the fish on a log and raised her eyes to Tyler.

"You catch it, you clean it," she said. Tyler slanted his eyebrows into a peak, pinched his upper lip with his lower teeth, and looked uncertainly at me. "Go wash it off," Amanda said, "and cut off its head. I'll be right there." She looked at me, and together we raised our eyebrows.

After supper I asked if anyone had a story to share at the fire. Ignoring the Beez's raised arm and manic gyrations, I looked at each face in our circle.

"Tyler?" I said, surprising him. He thought for only a few seconds and then slowly rose. After fetching his spear, he stood before us all and stared into the flames, his spear planted in the sand beside him like a wizard's walking staff. Slowly, he began moving through his story like a mime. Taking his time, he re-enacted the patience of his stalk and the long, frozen moments when he dared not move. His silence was commanding. Throughout the performance no one spoke. All mouths hung open, and all eyes tracked him as he orbited around the fire.

Amanda began tapping together two pieces of firewood, creating a drum rhythm. One by one the others found something percussive and joined in: a hand on a log, two rocks, a hat slapped against a pack. The unified beat seemed to empower Tyler, and his footsteps bit into the sand with quick decisive punches.

After building toward the climax, he thrust the spear toward the earth and lifted an imaginary fish into the air. As if the moment had been choreographed, the Outriders' musical hands fell silent, and the murmur of the river returned to remind us of its constancy.

Tyler sat down and looked at me. The bargain had been sealed. I raised my hands, palms outward, and rotated them slowly in the Cherokee sign for approval. Then, everyone else did the same. I believe this was the moment that Tyler stepped upon the true path. The sacrifice of one trout had been a fair price, I thought.

Chapter Twenty-Three

As we rounded the last bend above Nimblewill Bridge, I saw several cars with roof racks perched on the bluff. Multi-colored kayaks lay spilled out in zigzags across the riverbank, and a group of teenagers pumped up a raft on the sandy beach below the bridge. Bobby Whitehorse leaned against the front bumper of a camp van with his arms folded below his chest. He turned his head to one side and spoke, and someone sitting against a hemlock trunk stood up and shaded her eyes with a flat hand. It was Pat Raintree.

When we beached our boats, Pat walked without hesitation to Tyler and hugged him. I looked at Bobby to see what was up. He gave me a two-finger salute from his hat that told me everything was okay. When everyone got busy unloading camping gear to stow into the van, I climbed the bank to where Pat and Tyler were talking.

"How did it go in Atlanta?" I asked.

Pat's eyes locked on mine as if she had not heard me. "I think I saw Beau's car in Dahlonega this morning. I want to take Tyler back to camp."

I shook my head. "He's better off out here. Beau knows camp. He doesn't know this river." As soon as I had said it, I made an involuntary glance up the road and wondered about the possibility of the van being followed out here.

Beyond the parked cars the dirt road disappeared around Sadie Mountain. On the other side of the river the road climbed up a steep grade and wound out of view. As far as I could see, no one was lurking about in a car.

"*She'll* be better off out here, too," Bobby said. "I brought along a raft. I'll go with her."

Pat frowned at the river. "I've never done this. Is it dangerous?"

"We walk around the part that is," I said. "It's beautiful. And you'll get to see something of Tyler you've never seen before." She looked at Bobby, and he nodded.

She considered the river again, her eyes taut with worry. "All right," she finally said.

Bobby pushed away from the van. "I brought everything she'll need for the river."

We walked around the van and Bobby opened the passenger door. My bow and quiver lay on the seat.

"That's for later when we go back to camp. I'll drop you three off before we get to the gate. You can walk to your cabin the back way through the woods." He nodded at the bow. "Thought you'd like to have some firepower . . . just in case."

"You never know," I said.

" 'You never know,' " he repeated.

The group of kayakers had most of the Outriders hypnotized. Compared to our big, cumbersome open boats, their sleek kayaks looked specialized and mysterious. All the talk among these paddlers was about Hydrophobia, the most notorious rapid on the river. There were war stories, close calls, the farcical attempts that failed or succeeded, and the loss of equipment that the rapid had claimed—including kayaks and canoes.

Jamal turned at the waist and gazed at me with big questioning eyes. I walked over to him and knelt to his level.

"We're not running Hydro, Jamal. Period."

Relief flooded through his face. "How come they do?" He glanced toward the kayakers.

"First," I began, "they have enclosed boats. Kayaks can crash through anything without taking on water and extra weight."

"Isn't it dangerous?" he asked. "Couldn't they die in that rapid?"

"Yes, it is dangerous. And, yes, they could die. People have drowned in Hydro before."

"Don't they know that?" Jamal asked with that ring of intelligence that I admired.

"When you're young and strong and all your friends are watching you and you've watched enough TV shows with happy endings . . . you're immortal."

"I'm young," he said, apparently worried that he fell into that demographic.

I knelt beside him. "And strong. But you've felt the power. You know what's out there waiting for you if you mess up. You might know it better than they do."

"What if I mess up again?"

I smiled. "We'll all mess up again, Jamal. We just won't do it in Hydrophobia. We'll be carrying our boats around it just like before."

Andy yelled from the van. "Justin's here to run shuttle with me. I'm headed for the take-out. Got everything?"

As I gave Andy an "okay" sign, I saw a second car crest the hill and stop. I climbed halfway up the bank with a bad feeling stirring in my gut.

Justin rolled to a stop in the camp's green van, turned down the blast of the radio, and leaned out of his window. He slapped the side of his van twice.

"Let's go, Andy!" he yelled. "I gotta get back for my sports class!" He looked at me as if he might speak, then slapped the van again, and backed around in a checkmark turn. "I'll be at the take-out. Let's go!" He pulled out and roared up the road.

Andy and I studied the car up the hill. "What do you think?" he muttered.

"I think that's Beau Raintree. Drive the shuttle as planned. Call the sheriff as soon as you can and tell him to send one car to the take-out and one car here."

Andy fired his engine. The black car started our way. It was a BMW.

"Go!" I said and ran down to the beach and called Bobby's name with an edge that turned everyone's head my way. "Black Beamer pulling up!" I gave the Outriders a no-nonsense command to shove off, and within thirty seconds five boats launched into the current like a precision military unit.

The BMW slid to a halt. Its wake of trailing dust washed over the car and drifted toward the beach. I cupped my hands around my mouth and called out to Tyler's canoe. "Amanda, lead the way! Now! The rest of you follow! It doesn't matter the order." I met Bobby's squinting eyes and made a sign to lower Pat to the bottom of the raft. Trying to keep a low profile behind the knot of kayakers and rafters, I stepped into my solo boat, pushed out into the stream, and herded stragglers toward the first rapid under the bridge.

Bobby and Pat floated through the drop with ease in the raft, and the others followed. As soon as I'd shot through the flume, I counted heads, and my stomach tensed. Pat Raintree was alone in the raft flailing at the water with little effect. I was about to call out to her when I caught a motion to my left. I saw Bobby gliding through a thicket of sumac trees up to the road, moving with the grace of a cat, making no sound that I could hear.

Perry shuffled down the bank toward the kayakers, tripped face-down onto the beach, and pushed himself up like a man doing his last pushup. Every person on the beach was staring at him. He got up brushing sand off his sports coat and then he glared at me.

Around the first bend, I called for Amanda to hold up in the shadow of a hemlock on river-right. Troy helped nose the raft to shore with the others. From the eddy where I had turned, I could see that Beau Raintree and Perry had singled out one of the kayakers. As they talked, the kayaker pointed and motioned his arms like he was giving directions. Beau checked his watch, and he and Perry climbed back up the bank, and I knew they had just learned the route to the take-out.

The roar of the bridge rapid drowned out all sound from the put-in, but I strained to hear the BMW start up. I decided our best bet was to pull out here on the opposite side of the river and wait for the sheriff.

I heard Bobby's thrush-whistle and looked up to see him lope down the hill and return through the trees the same way he had gone up. I ferried across the current, picked him up, and returned to my shaded eddy just in time to see Perry reappear on the beach and approach the teenagers who were still inflating their raft with a foot pump. Raintree stepped beside Perry and reached into his breast pocket. For one horrible moment, I thought he might pull a gun . . . but it was a wallet.

"What were you doing back there?" I said to Bobby's back.

"Ham-stringing their pony." He turned so I could see his smile. "Four flat tires."

I watched the negotiations on the beach and realized Beau was probably trying to get transportation to the take-out. But the young kids were pushing their raft into the water, trying to extricate themselves from Perry, who stepped into the water and grabbed the raft's rope. The kids backed away and stared at him.

"You don't think they'd follow us in that raft, do you?" I asked Bobby.

He didn't answer. We watched Perry and Beau step into the raft. One of the kids stepped toward them in obvious protest but stopped when Perry pointed his finger at him and growled something I could not hear. With paddles in hand, Raintree and Perry headed for the drop under the bridge.

"Yeah," Bobby said, "I believe they just might follow us. That big un's got a burr under his saddle." He turned in the canoe to look at me. "That's three times we've made a fool of him. If he didn't have that raft, I think he'd be swimming after us." Bobby turned back to watch the raft. "His job is to have Pat and Tyler and Tyler's father under wraps, but that's pride we're seeing coming at us."

They hit the ledge at the wrong spot but bounced through in the forgiving way of rafts. Beau picked himself up from the floor of the raft and cursed. It was the first audible word I had heard from them. They immediately ran up on a partially-submerged rock.

"We're only as fast as our slowest craft, Gray Eyes. You think Phoebe and I should pull out and double back for help?"

"No, if they spot her, they'll pull out, too. Plus, she won't leave Tyler." I weighed our options. "With you in the back of her raft we're going to be faster than they are. We're better off on the river putting distance between them and us. Let's just get to the take-out. The sheriff should be there waiting on us."

I delivered Bobby to the raft and asked Pat about the restraining order. "It's drawn up and ordered by the court, only Beau hasn't received it officially. No one knew where to find him, but it was made public through his firm and through Victor Dimateo and even in the newspaper." She swallowed and lowered her voice. "Is that Beau back there?"

"Yes," I said. "And Perry."

"What will they do? Go to the place where we get out and wait for us?"

I gave her a believe-it-or-not look. "They're in a raft."

Her face went numb. "They're on the river . . . chasing us?"

I closed my eyes. This was like a bad movie and its requisite chase scene.

"They can't catch us, Pat," I said, keeping my voice confident. "All we have to do is move on down the river. They *can't* catch us."

"How do you know they can't. Perry is strong, isn't he?"

"Strong doesn't matter. It's knowing how to do this. I'm betting he doesn't know."

"But neither do I!" Her desperation put a little screech into her voice.

"Bobby does. He'll tell you everything you need to do. Just listen to him."

She wasn't sold on it, but when I yelled to the group that we needed to hustle downriver, our flotilla jumped into a momentum that carried her along with it. I moved to the lead to pick the best routes. As long as we negotiated the rapids efficiently, our progress would be steady, and we would outdistance our pursuers. But a quarter mile into the trip on a long straightaway, I looked back to see Perry and Beau not only in sight but sitting side by side on the air compartments of the raft and stroking in unison. Beau's stroke was typically novice, but Perry's wasn't. When Bobby saw them, he made a little cock of his head and an amused smile, acknowledging the unexpected.

Though she tried, Pat Raintree contributed little to the progress of her raft. I considered different combinations—like abandoning the raft, putting Pat with me in my solo boat, and Bobby taking over the stern of one of the other boats. The more I thought about this the more I liked it, so I turned into an eddy and signaled everyone over.

My plan shattered like a key snapping off in a door lock. As the Beez and P.J. approached the drop of the rapid, Stephen's paddle blade jammed between his boat and a submerged rock and held fast like a steel post rising from the river. The bow of the boat caromed off it and pivoted sideways until the paddle broke. When the boat slapped into the small hydraulic at the bottom of the drop, it filled with a gush of cascading water.

The partially submerged boat then thudded against the side of a boulder, jarring the campers. The boat looked like it was made of rubber as it jackknifed around the unyielding stone and pinned.

P.J. and Beez washed out with horror-stricken faces, their eyes already searching me out with contrition. But this was my fault. I was hurrying them. They were doing the best they could while knowing that something was wrong . . . but not knowing exactly what. Troy towed P.J., and Bobby jerked the Beez out of the water by his swimsuit.

"Whoa!" Stephen screamed. "Wedgie!"

Everyone gathered in the eddy and stared at the bent canoe in the rapid. "P.J., you're the lightest. Get in the middle of Troy's boat. Beez, switch places with Tyler. Do everything Amanda tells you to do. Tyler, get in here with me."

When I checked upriver, Perry's raft was three hundred yards away. The group of kayakers had passed him, their svelte boats gliding effortlessly with the steady windmilling of their double-bladed paddles. They looked like a swarm of lazy insects with wings out-of-sync.

As Tyler climbed into my canoe, Bobby and Pat led the group through the next rapid. "Take the spare paddle," I said to Tyler. "You and I are a team now." Two of the kayaks pulled into our eddy. One paddler sidled up to me and nodded.

"Stoney St. Ney, right? I remember you from a race in North Carolina."

"That's right," I said.

He nodded upstream. "Are those guys back there in the raft in your group?"

"No," I said, keeping an eye on the raft's progress.

He seemed unsure how to continue and he, too, looked upstream. "They asked a lot of questions about you guys. The big one sort of strong-armed those high school kids into using their raft. Actually, he just took it from them, and the other one gave them some money. Do you know who they are?"

"One is a parent with a restraining order against him to keep him from his son." I nodded to Tyler's back. "You guys should stay clear of them. We're doing the same."

He looked at the pinned boat, then at Tyler crowded into my solo boat. "What can we do to help you?" He had the warrior's eye. I knew that he would do whatever he said he would do. "Want us to slow 'em down?" He patted the knife clipped to a plastic sheath on his lifejacket. "Rafts are pretty easy to disable," he said and smiled.

I gave him a look that erased the smile. "At least one of those guys has a gun." He frowned and looked upstream. "You have a cell phone?" I asked.

He nodded. "Yeah, but there's no reception until we get past the Narrows."

"Best thing you could do to help us is get your group to the take-out," I said. "If the sheriff is not waiting there, call him; tell him the situation. Mention me by name."

He nodded again. "You got it, Stoney." He did a pivot turn, gathered his friends together, and after a brief conference, led them downriver at a racer's pace.

Over the next hour, we put more distance between Perry and us, but the kids were tiring and begging for lunch. I waited for the next long straightaway and chose a beach at its far end, where we pulled out and opened up the dry bags to search for food. All the while, I kept watch upriver, descrying the yellow raft and the odd couple chasing us. No sooner had we sat down than the raft appeared around the bend. Perry was sluggish but still working hard.

"Sorry, guys," I announced. "We've got to load up now. I know I owe you an explanation for this, and you'll get it. But I don't have time now to explain. We can eat while we float. I'll make it up to you at dinner. I promise."

I was pretty sure the secret was out. More than likely, the Beez had filled everyone in. He had seen better than anyone the episode at camp when Abby snatched Perry's gun. Most of the kids were looking upstream with varying stages of concern creased on their faces. Tyler was quiet. He sat near his mother on one of the raft compartments and stared at the current.

When Tyler looked up toward his father, he reminded me of myself when I had gotten old enough to replace the fear and hatred I had for my father with the sad and lonely loathing of loss of what might have been. But I'd reached that place only last year.

The beach evacuation impressed me, and, for the first time, I was sure we were going to make it off the river before Perry caught up. Maybe the Beez had instilled into the Outriders the fear of God . . . or the fear of Perry. Whatever their inspiration, they wasted no time getting back on the water.

Tyler stood beside a ring of rocks that held the ubiquitous cache of trash that local fishermen expected to be carted off by the Garbage Fairy. He stared into the rubbish like he wanted to crawl into it and hide. I didn't blame him. I walked over and stood by him, thinking what to say. In the blackened heap of charred aluminum cans and melted plastic was a reddish-brown beer bottle. I pulled it out. He needed something to think about besides his father.

"Ever see an amber arrowhead, Tyler? You can make a beauty out of this."

A sound in the woods brought me up alert. Two shirtless fishermen clad in camo overalls made their way toward the beach. I didn't know them and didn't see any way they could help us without putting themselves in harm's way, so I nodded a greeting and then showed Tyler how to break out a triangular shard from the bottle.

For a napping tool we found a twenty-penny nail that had been burned out of a driftwood plank. As the fishermen stood motionless watching us chip glass, one of them pulled a pack of cigarettes from a pocket. With it came a small piece of paper that he let sail to the ground.

Before we cast off from the lunch spot, by habit, I picked up the fisherman's litter—a receipt from a bait shop—and slipped it in my back pocket.

After passing our group, I paddled as Tyler leaned over the gunnel to flake the glass. In his hands, the nail and glass seemed like trauma therapy. After a mile, he put the materials away and turned to me.

"Stoney, I've gotta go pee real bad."

I didn't want to linger. We were at the sharpest bend in the river where that raft, if it were to appear, would be less than a hundred yards from us. At that moment we were actually a very short distance from Perry and Beau on a hairpin turn that put only an eighth of a mile between us. Without a map, however, they couldn't know that.

"Okay, go pee. But you need to hurry."

His bright orange lifejacket disappeared into the woods. When the Outriders came through the shoal and turned into my eddy, I told

Amanda to continue downstream with them and gather in the next big eddy to wait for Bobby. Tyler and I would catch up.

I yelled for Tyler to hurry up. When Bobby and Pat drifted by, she sat up and, with hollow eyes, looked inside my boat for Tyler.

"He's watering a tree," I said and looked at Bobby. "The Outriders are waiting for you at the big eddy at Mooney Creek."

As they drifted on, Bobby called out, "We've got about a half mile on them."

I nodded, took off my lifejacket, and lowered myself in the water to cool off. When I surfaced, I thought I heard my name. I stilled myself to listen over the sounds of the current.

"Stoney!" came the same yelp. Tyler's voice was high-pitched and weak.

I tied the boat to a shrub and rock-hopped to the edge of the forest. "Tyler?" I called out.

I heard a scuffling noise up ahead about thirty yards away. Here the white pines were enormous—giant wooden columns towering up into the sky. When I saw him, he was standing in a bath of sunlight next to a large boulder. His face was frozen. I bent under the limbs, careful to check for a snake that might have paralyzed him. There was an inordinate amount of scuffs marks in the dirt for a boy relieving himself.

When I looked up, Perry stepped from behind the boulder, one hand locked on Tyler's wrist, the other holding a shiny automatic pistol. Perry extended his arm to point the gun at me, but when he saw me slightly crouch as if I might bolt, he quickly swung the gun to point at Tyler's head.

"Don't you hate it when you lose?" Perry said and allowed a gloating smile as I straightened up and raised my hands to the height of my shoulders.

Chapter Twenty-Four

Perry's coat and tie were gone, and his rumpled shirttails hung over his bulging mid-section like a huge, mud-stained toga. He was wet from the thighs down. Thick beads of sweat clung to his flushed face. The soiled bandage on his forehead had peeled partway off, showing that his bruise had turned pale green. He stuffed the gun under the shirt into his waist band, which, I guess, was meant to be an insult to me.

"The kid's going with his father. I don't give a goddamn about the mother." He made a snide laugh. "Or am I not supposed to use that kind of language out here?"

I took two steps toward Tyler. "Are you okay?" He looked at me as if I were his last possible hope of surviving this day. When he squirmed in place and pressed his free hand into his lower abdomen, I knew he had not had a chance to urinate. I moved another step toward him and calmed my voice. "Tyler, go ahead and pee." I pointed beside the boulder. "Just go right there. I'm not going anywhere."

Tyler's forehead tightened, and his fearful eyes fixed on mine. "I can't," he replied, his voice so meek I barely heard him.

"He can piss in his pants for all I care," Perry said, holding fast to Tyler's arm.

"There's a restraining order on Raintree to stay away from Tyler," I said.

Perry's shoulders shook once as he snorted a laugh. "Restraining order's a joke."

"There's something else," I said. "I'm going to pull a paper from my pocket, all right?"

Perry's hand disappeared under his shirt. When it returned, his gun reentered the equation, its muzzle pointed at me. I took this as his assent for me to continue. From my pocket I removed the bait shop receipt.

In a past decade, Perry might have been an arsenal unto himself, but I knew he had lost a few steps over the years. He had slid a long way down the fitness scale, and I had to assume that both the physical and the psychological edges he had once carried were now dulled by the years. His baleful eyes could not mask his curiosity at the paper in my hand. I took a step forward and held it out.

Just as he lowered the gun and reached for the paper, I kicked him in the crotch as hard as I had ever kicked anything. I used the flat top of my foot, so as to cover a maximum area for impact. It was a good kick, but I knew, if I had somehow missed his jewels, I would probably be shot in the next second.

Perry doubled over as if he'd been hit in the belly by a cannon ball. I put my hands on his shoulders and drove him backward the same way I would push a stalled car. He tripped and crashed into the snapping limbs of a downed tree.

I grabbed Tyler's arm and broke through the underbrush with him dangling beside me like a limp marionette. We had gone only a short distance when I heard Perry crashing through foliage behind us. I hadn't expected this. I wondered if it were possible that his history with steroids had encased his testicles in a wall of muscle.

"Take off your lifejacket, Tyler!" I whispered as we rushed through a stand of doghobble. When he unclipped the belt, I slipped the bright orange preserver off him. "I'm going to stash you somewhere. When I do, I want you to become as still as a rock. Like when you stalked the trout. When you hear me do a crow call, go get in my boat, put on my lifejacket, and get to Bobby Whitehorse!"

When he just stared at me with those big bright eyes, I gripped his shoulders. "You know how a crow sounds, right?"

He nodded, but the whites of his eyes shone like fluorescent lighting. "I'm gonna be in a canoe by myself?"

"Sit toward the stern. You'll be fine. There are no rapids until the Narrows. Bobby will be waiting for you." As I was saying it, I felt doubt well up inside me, but I could see no other choice. I wanted distance between Tyler and Perry.

He swallowed and licked his lips. "I've still got to pee real bad."

I pulled him to the backside of a boulder where a crescent-shaped depression cut into the rock midway up. "Do you think you can squeeze in there?"

Pumping his knees with his thighs clamped together, he bounced up and down while holding his crotch. "I've really got to pee, Stoney!" he whispered.

I picked up Tyler by an arm and a knee and stuffed him horizontally into the cavity. "Lie there and pee on the side of the boulder so it will be quiet," I instructed. He showed no qualms or embarrassment as he began positioning his body to relieve himself. While he was busy, I snapped off a big branch of laurel, stabbed it into the ground, and leaned it against the boulder to cover him. "Don't touch this branch, Tyler. Stay absolutely still until you hear my call."

And with those instructions, I left him.

I held Tyler's orange lifejacket at my side and kept up a running monologue of commands as I ran noisily through the thick woods. "Stop stumbling, Tyler!" I barked. "Get your feet underneath you!"

Fifty yards later, I stopped and looked back. Perry was still coming. He had passed Tyler's hiding place, and I said a silent prayer of thanks.

A Copperhead Summer

After another thirty yards, I turned and waited until I saw Perry bulling his way through a web of grapevines. I knelt, tilted back my head, cupped my hands around my mouth, and dredged up the raspy call of a crow. When I looked back at Perry, he was leaning on a tree trunk with stiff arms, heaving to suck in air, his head slumped below his shoulders. Now I was afraid he might turn back and find Tyler pushing my canoe out into the river for an escape.

"Tyler!" I yelled out into the woods, keeping my voice low enough so as not to be heard by Tyler but loud enough to draw Perry toward me. "Where are you, Tyler? Walk toward my voice!"

Crouching in a stand of huckleberry bushes, I peeked out at Perry. He straightened from the tree and started my way again. Staying low, I moved through a fern bed and past a thick beech tree where I broke into a sandy clearing where a circle of stones was filled with charred wood and scorched food cans. A pile of firewood was stacked nearby. I ran across the sand in choppy steps, trying to simulate the tracks of two people scrambling across the little clearing. Tossing Tyler's lifejacket a few yards down a path, I circled back and picked up from the stack of wood a hefty, three-foot-long rhododendron club with which I planned to knock a home run on Perry's tender forehead.

As I returned to the beech tree, I tiptoed through the ferns and almost stepped into a small bowl-shaped depression about the size of a kitchen sink. In the shadow of the bowl a copperhead lay coiled in the ferns. My back leg reflexively propelled me over the hole, where I landed lightly and pressed my back into the beech tree. I settled my breath and waited, willing myself to be part of the tree. When Perry was so close that I could hear the wheeze of his breathing, I gripped the club with both hands and slowly cocked it back like a baseball bat.

I saw the gun first as it inched into view. The hammer was cocked. Silently, I pivoted and adjusted the angle of my swing until I held the club above me like a splitting maul. When I had a clean shot at his wrist, I came down with a sledgehammer blow.

The gun went off just before he screamed. I saw his hand open up, and the gun spun in the air before him as though defying gravity. By reflex, I swatted upward at the hovering automatic and connected with a sharp *clack*. It arced across the clearing into the ferns.

Another rough scream of pain tore from Perry's throat. I'd never heard a grown man cry out like that. Stepping around the tree, I wound up and delivered my next swing at Perry's head, but he caught the stick in his left hand and held fast. I tried to jerk it free, but he was too strong. His sweaty face was compressed into a mask of determination.

Letting go of the club, I turned to run, but Perry was quick and kicked my feet out from under me. When I hit the ground, I rolled sideways, and the rhododendron club whirred through the air, spinning like a tomahawk. It hit the sand next to my head, gouging a hole like a deer print. I scrambled to my knees and, with my hands cupped into a bowl, threw a pound of sand into his face.

Spitting and squinting, Perry charged me as I turned to run. He crashed into my back and took me down, his massive weight on my back, grinding my face into the sand.

"Might be your jungle, Tarzan," Perry said, panting like a steam engine, "but this is *my* game." His breath was hot on the side of my face, and I felt little, warm droplets of spittle spray my cheek in a fine mist. "Yell for the kid to come back, or I'm gonna tenderize your kidneys into pudding. You'll be pissing blood the rest of your life."

When I made no reply, he jammed an elbow into my side with brutal force. It felt like I'd been gored by a bull.

"Call him, you little sonovabitch!"

"I can't yell with all your weight on me," I said in a wheezing voice.

He elbowed me again—a vicious blow in the same place, and the pain shot to the core of me. He lifted his weight off me long enough to put his knee into my lower back. Then he put his weight on that leg, and I thought I might break in half.

"Yell to him, goddamnit!" he growled and bounced on my spine.

I nodded. "Okay, let me up, and I'll call him."

For a moment Perry didn't move. Then the pressure on my spine eased up. In the next moment, he whipped his belt free, made a lasso of it, and slipped the noose over my head to tighten around my neck like a leash.

"Get up and start yelling for the kid," Perry ordered.

When I pushed myself up on my hands and knees and looked back at him, I saw the end of the belt doubled around his fist. Apparently unhappy about my hesitation, he jerked me to my feet, and the vertebrae in my neck popped like a string of muted firecrackers.

"This is not going to help me yell," I rasped.

Perry pulled the belt tighter. "Why don't you try."

"Tyler won't come if he sees you," I said and pointed toward the beech tree. "Let's stand over there at the edge of the clearing, so you can hide behind the tree."

He kept the belt taut as he pushed me through the ferns where I had seen the copperhead. The leather dug deep into my throat and triggered my choke reflex. I coughed spasmodically and had to work at getting my words out.

"I'm . . . going to . . . throw up!" I gasped and dropped to my knees before the little sinkhole. If he pulled me back, the game was up. But he didn't. I leaned forward, and some vestige of decency in Perry gave me enough slack to get my face just above the ferns.

Forcing a wet gurgle from my throat, I simulated the vomiting sound I had heard countless times from Stephen Beasley.

Carefully, I parted the greenery and saw the copperhead coiled exactly as I had last seen it, the head lying on top of its body. I knew better than to try to pin the head against its own flesh. Too dangerous. I tapped the snake's flank with my fingertips, and its head rose up an inch. Making a free-hand grab at that head hovering in the air was also too risky. I knew how quickly this snake could strike.

I gave it another tap on its thick section, and the snake lengthened out for a slow slither up the far side of the bowl, which is exactly what I needed for a safe catch. Retching again for Perry's sake, I flattened the fingers of one hand on the snake's head, gently pinning it to the ground. With my free hand, I took a firm grip just behind the jaws.

As I turned to Perry, I rammed the snake up his shirt front and pressed its head flat against the clammy skin of his round belly. As he backpedaled through the ferns, I went with him, until he collided with the trunk of a big pine. With my free hand flattened on the outside of his shirt, I replaced my hold on the snake's head and retracted my other hand from inside his shirt.

Walleyed and mouth agape, Perry looked down to see the squirming tail of the snake flexing and curling at the hem of his shirt. His face was transfixed with terror.

"It's a pit viper," I said. "Venomous. If I let go with my hand—" I didn't need to finish the threat. He couldn't take his gawking eyes off the snake's writhing tail. I whipped off the belt over my head and threw it behind me."

"Don't let that thing bite me!" he blurted out in a voice that had risen to a falsetto. His face was the dull gray of dishwater.

With my free hand I tugged at his waistband until it pulled away from his stomach a few inches. "If I let it go, this snake is dropping right into your shorts."

He began to show the first signs of panic. "Don't!" he pleaded.

"Give me your left hand," I said.

"What!? What for!?"

"Do you want a dose of venom so close to your heart?" I asked.

"Hell, no, I don't!" His inflection suggested that I was crazy.

"Give me your hand," I repeated. "I need you to help me hold it."

He let me take his hand but resisted when I guided it toward the snake. "What the hell're you doing!?"

"Press right here," I said and guided his reluctant hand to the snake's head.

"I ain't touchin' that!" he whined.

In its writhing, the snake worked its tail down into his pants. Perry inhaled quickly, his breath shuddering as if he were braving a sleet storm.

"We're going to switch," I explained. "You're going to press on the snake so it can't bite."

"The hell you say!"

I gave Perry a merciful smile. "One way or the other, I'm letting go. It's your choice what happens next."

However tough Perry had once been in the prime of his career as a thug, he was now the picture of surrender. When his hand flattened on the lump under his shirt, he winced as if he'd been stabbed.

"That's the neck," I said. "Slide to the head as I slide away.

Perry's face drained of all color, and tears welled in his eyes. The snake shook suddenly, as if all its muscles had fired at once as it tried to escape my grip.

"I can't do this!" Perry hissed, his voice so desperate that his words rushed together like a burst from an air hose.

I waited for the snake to calm down, and then I whispered, "Be still! Don't move!"

His forehead creased from temple to temple. "Did it bite me?"

"Stand still!" I ordered him. "I'm taking my hand away now! You'd better press his head down or you *will* be bitten!"

I eased away my hand and felt his big fingers roughly take the place of mine. Taking a step back from him, I slowly pushed my palms toward him.

"Be still," I warned.

Perry's face wrinkled in disbelief. "What the hell do I do now?"

I considered returning the insult of the light slap to his face, but instead I leaned in and whispered, "I suggest you don't move. It's not your game anymore, Perry."

I picked up Tyler's lifejacket and left Perry to his dilemma of hara-kiri-by-copperhead and made my way to the river. When I saw that my canoe was gone, I felt a surge of relief. Rock-hopping and scanning the downstream horizon I hoped for a glimpse of Tyler, but there was not a craft to be seen on the river.

Behind me, I heard a crashing in the woods and turned to see Perry burst into the open light of the shoreline. With his shirt open at the front, his big belly bounced like a water balloon as he struggled over the boulders. The dark tufts of hair splotched over his plump torso made his pale skin appear sickly. He was breathing so hard that his head rose and fell like a pump handle. When I saw that his hands were empty, I assumed that he had not found his gun, so I turned and continued downstream.

When I looked back to check on my pursuer, I saw that the larger rocks had slowed his progress. His arms levitated from his sides for balance as he lunged from one rock to another. I couldn't help but think of the dancing hippo scene in Disney's *Fantasia*.

I knew it would be easy to stay ahead of him. I established a pattern of jumping from rock to rock for ten yards then turning to check on him. After fifty yards of this, a hand reached up from the backside of a rock and pulled me down to the sand. Squatting low, Bobby Whitehorse dragged me behind a boulder and turned me so that our faces were inches apart. He was bareheaded with his ponytail unleashed into a mane of black that splayed over his shoulders. I almost asked him where his hat was.

"Is Tyler okay?" I whispered.

"Yeah. Everyone is waiting above the Narrows. Tyler told me about Perry. He said he heard a gunshot." His eyes traveled over my body. "You okay, Gray Eyes?"

I nodded. "Perry's lost his gun. He's about a hundred yards behind me."

"I know," Bobby said and eased his head above the top of the rock. When he spoke again his voice carried an amused lilt. "Looks like he's done. He's going back . . . probably to look for Raintree." He chuckled. "These guys are worse than a Three Stooges Western. Let's get to the Narrows, Gray Eyes."

When Bobby and I emerged from the trees into the roar of the open gorge, the Outriders were just returning from their scout along the rim with Troy and Amanda. Pat Raintree and Tyler sat on the side of the raft talking. When they spotted us approaching, their eyes filled with questions. I walked to Tyler and put a hand on his thin shoulder.

"How was your first solo paddle?"

He gave me a serious nod. "Different," he said. "But I sorta got the hang of it."

"Here," I said, handing him his lifejacket. "Let's trade."

As Bobby talked to Pat, I called out to the group, "Who's ready for the Narrows?!"

Stephen Beasley was the loudest to reply, but I saw a positive look on each face. I was especially interested to see how Jamal would feel about his second visit to the Narrows, but he was already in good hands. Dane had wrapped an arm around Jamal's shoulders, and their heads leaned together, the top of their foreheads glued to one another as Dane gave a private pep talk that had Jamal nodding with a solemn expression on his face.

"Let's be smart and strong," I said amid the pumped-up revelry. "Let's do it!"

The group moved to their boats like a cavalry responding to a command to "mount up!" I looked upriver. Still no sign of Beau and Perry.

The Outriders maneuvered through the Narrows with precision. Jamal and Dane came back at Pinball with a vengeance and shot across the drop of Broken Thumb with squeals of victory. The gorge echoed with triumph for this forced march and grand finale. These kids were probably more physically worn out than ever before in their lives, but they were still operating with finesse and proving to themselves that presence of mind was even more important than strength.

As we gathered the canoes on the shore above Hydrophobia, Bobby and Pat surged through the last chute of S-Turn and paddled their raft into our eddy. Relaxing from our vigil, Troy and I coiled up the throw-ropes, and I felt relief begin to seep into me like the warm touch of the sun. I looked around at the campers, who might never know how close this trip had come to disaster. Tyler sat on a rock, head down, industriously chipping away at the amber glass.

A Copperhead Summer

I watched Bobby climb to the top of an eight-foot-high boulder and look upstream. When he turned and fixed his eyes on mine, a little bomb detonated silently in my gut. His expression said: *You're not going to believe this.*

Most of the rapids were blocked from my view by the rock on which he stood, but I could see the upper ledge of Regurgitate. I watched the water there spit upward in arrhythmic surges until a yellow raft bounced into view. Beau Raintree sat low and wide-eyed in front, both his hands gripping the rope that ran through the eyelets along the gunnels of the raft. Perry, bare-chested and frantic in his open shirt, fought the water from the stern, constantly switching sides with his paddle. I shook my head. This man had perseverance.

Facing the campers, I kept my voice steady but firm. "We're going to leave the boats here. Collect all your gear and take it to the van. Now!"

Chapter Twenty-Five

The Outriders went into action one more time, one eye on their job, the other on the raft that always seemed to portend bad news. Pat Raintree pulled at Tyler as he pocketed his glass and napping tool. Wearing a grim expression, she hurried her son across the sloped wall of stone toward the take-out, not once glancing back at her husband.

When the raft splashed into the pool below S-Turn, Perry sagged back against the stern air compartment and let his paddle drag in the water. As he glared at me, he seemed oblivious to the rapid waiting just downstream. Raintree pointed at Tyler and turned quickly to Perry to say something I couldn't hear. I think that was when Perry first heard the deep thunder of Hydrophobia.

To the uninitiated, this last rapid did not look so daunting from upstream. What they saw from the raft was a clean horizon line where smooth water disappeared over a ledge. Here the typical treble sound of other rapids was replaced by a deep and troubling rumble.

Perry stretched his thick neck high to see what was coming. Frozen for an instant, he fixed his eyes on the magnetic abyss that was drawing him closer to a horrible reality. I could see the slap of panic jar him into action. He churned the water with a series of strokes that grew more and more desperate. His paddle shaft curved like a strung bow when he started pushing water to the front. Beau awoke from his stupor, and the two of them paddled like madmen, but they weren't going to make it.

Troy ran up to me. "Stoney, should we throw them a rope?"

"Get the campers into the van, Troy," I said taking his rope." I jumped into my boat and yelled to Bobby. "I'm gonna throw from the other side." If I was going to pull these two out of this pending danger, I decided, it was going to be from the far bank, putting the river between them and our van.

I made a fast ferry right above the drop of Hydro, got out, and tied my boat to a lone basswood tree. As I readied the throw-rope, I called out Perry's name. Exhausted from flailing against the relentless current, he turned to my voice as if searching for a miracle. I threw the rope for maximum distance, and it threaded right between Beau and Perry. In grabbing the rope, Perry dropped his paddle, which bounced off the raft into the water.

When Bobby yelled from the other side, Beau perked up and caught another perfectly thrown rope. If ever I had imagined any Seneca in his face, it was nowhere to be seen now. He looked more like a child caught sleeping in class, trying to appear alert.

My idea had been to tie off the rope to the basswood and let the raft swing to river right. Meanwhile I could ferry back, and we could make good our exit while these two would be stranded on the far side of the river. Bobby Whitehorse had a different idea.

"Feed it out!" Bobby yelled to me. He let out his rope hand over hand, and I did the same until mine played out. I had no choice but to tie it off to the tree. Bobby wrapped his rope around a sturdy rock. With a lifeline to each side of the river, Perry and Beau held on for dear life fifteen feet above the roaring rapid. If either of them let go, they were going to swing over the drop into the vicious hydraulic and tumble around like a pair of sneakers in an industrial-sized washing machine. Meanwhile, their raft plowed a stationary furrow in the current, and, when water started to mound over the upstream edge, they scrambled to get their weight off that side.

I ferried back across the river above them, pulled my boat up onto the rocks, and ran to Bobby, who stood watching the raft with a flicker of amusement showing on his face.

"Must be like water-skiing at the edge of hell," he said.

"Is the sheriff here?" I asked.

"Haven't seen him."

"Let's get to the kids, Bobby."

Bobby nodded at the raft, where Perry was busy tying Bobby's rope to the gunnel rope. "Think I'll watch the show. I'll be along soon."

All the gear was packed in the trailer, and Pat and the campers were inside the van. There was no sign of the sheriff or anyone else. When I climbed in, the kids were glued to their windows, soaking up the drama taking place above the rapid. Tyler's head dropped forward and his shoulders jerked. I thought he was crying, so I started toward him. But far from crying, he was steely-eyed, chipping the edge of the red-brown glass with the hefty nail. Next to him his mother's face was buried in her hands.

Just as I placed my hand on the horn to signal Bobby, Sheriff Canaday's car crunched over the gravel into the parking area, stopping at the classic policeman's angle that announced: *I am in charge here.* The sheriff unfolded from his patrol car with his jaw set and his eyes fixed on the river. His driver, a black deputy named Cody, who was a friend of mine from high school, got out and propped one foot on the open doorframe as he leaned a forearm on the roof. His other hand was propped on the butt his sidearm.

"God-a-mighty!" Cody said, taking in the spectacle on the river.

Perry was slowly pulling the raft upstream by one of the ropes, inching his way toward Bobby, who sat relaxed on the boulder exactly as I had left him. The backdoor of the cruiser opened, and I recognized the skinny teenager who owned the raft that Perry had taken.

Sheriff Canaday squinted at me. "That Mrs. Raintree's husband out there?"

I nodded. "And his business associate . . . slash bodyguard."

Perry had pulled a third of the way up the rope. He was strong. I had to give him that. But he had a long way to go. The more he advanced on the one rope, the more the other rope pulled at the raft in the other direction. Then I understood his plan. Raintree was trying to untie the other rope attached to the raft. If he freed it, the tension on the raft would drop significantly, and with a few quick hand-over-hand pulls by Perry, the raft might swing clear of the ledge and land on the rocky shore on our side. I started running, ignoring the sheriff's call for me to come back.

When I reached Bobby, he was sitting on the rock, as if he were enjoying a colorful sunset. I noticed the rope was belayed around the rock and the end was gripped in his right hand. There was no knot. It appeared that Bobby had a backup plan.

I started to let him know the sheriff had arrived but was interrupted by a string of profanity that exploded from Beau Raintree. It might have contained every curse word I'd ever heard, all of them directed at Bobby and covering just about every aspect of his native heritage, his mother, and his personal anatomy.

Oblivious to Beau's outburst, Perry was single-mindedly pulling the raft closer to us. He had found his mission in life, grip by blistering grip. His face was a carving of determination. A rivulet of blood snaked from the scab on his forehead.

When Raintree finally loosened the knot in his rope, he laughed and spun to give us a victorious sneer. Bobby Whitehorse spoke just loud enough to be heard over the rapid.

"You boys saddled this bronc . . . now let's see if you can ride 'er."

I didn't see any movement from Bobby, but his rope suddenly went slack, and Perry fell backward into Beau. The raft immediately swung toward the center of the current until the other rope popped free of the raft's gunnel rope with a dull *twang*. Both men sat up, twisted around to face the approaching drop, and then froze like manikins. In the next second, they were gone from sight as if they had fallen off the edge of the world.

"*Conagher*," Bobby said. "Sam Elliot to Gavan O'Herlihy." He smiled. "Great line. Been wantin' to use that one for a long time."

I grabbed one of the tandem boats, flipped it up on my shoulders and jogged the portage trail over the big, slanted rock. On the sandy beach below the rapid, Sheriff Canaday and his deputy ran toward me but couldn't tear their eyes from the scene below the drop.

The raft was upside down jostling violently in the foaming hydraulic. Perry and Beau flailed in the current on the downstream side, their chests pressed against the rubber air compartment and their hands clawing at the bottom of the raft as they tried to scramble higher.

"You got a rope, Stoney?" the sheriff yelled over the roar.

I shook my head. "It's tied to the other side of the river."

"Can you get in there with your boat to pull 'em out?" Cody suggested, not understanding the folly of what he was asking.

"No way," I explained. "I brought this boat to pick them up if they wash out."

A loud thump turned our heads. The raft was right side up, but then it flipped again and slammed upside down in the hole with Perry still holding on just as he had been. Raintree had been swept downstream a couple of yards but was immediately sucked back into the hole. He windmilled his arms wildly to stay buoyant in the boiling froth until he grabbed the false security of the raft again.

Behind us, the kid who owned the raft stood transfixed watching the ordeal out in the rapid. I asked him if he had a rope. Never looking at me, he shook his head.

"Sheriff?" Cody said. "How the hell're we gonna get 'em out o' there?"

Sheriff Canaday pursed his lips and pivoted his head to me. "Any ideas?"

"They need to swim down deeper," I said, "where the current will wash them out. The raft is keeping them in the hole."

Cody yelled instructions to the two men, but he may as well have been screaming into a tornado. I knew what Perry and Beau were experiencing—a world of white panic and thundering water.

"Shoot the raft," I said.

The sheriff turned and held a hard look on me. " 'Shoot the raft'?" he repeated, the tone of his voice full of doubt.

"It's the buoyancy of the raft that's holding them in there," I explained. "Without the flotation, the waterfall will push them down and out of the hydraulic."

Sheriff Canaday studied the scene again. "Cody, what have we got in the car?"

"Pump shotgun in the trunk. That's it."

The sheriff frowned and shook his head. "That's no good."

"I can probably hit it with my handgun, Sheriff," Cody offered.

The sheriff set hard eyes on him. "You can prob'ly hit one of those men, too."

Cody sucked at a tooth and started back for the cruiser. "I'll call in Search and Rescue and an ambulance."

Above the rapid Bobby Whitehorse ferried a canoe across the river to the basswood tree where I had tied my rope. When he got out and began pulling the rope in, I saw him look beyond me toward the van, and I turned to follow his gaze. Tyler was running toward me, his teeth bared and his face streaked in tears.

"Stoney!" Tyler sobbed. "Don't let him die!"

He ran right into me, burying his face in my life jacket, his arms wrapping around my waist. He dared to look again at his father but could not bear the horror of it and pressed his face into me again.

Suddenly, he looked up at me with his tortured eyes and waited for me to produce a miracle. Bobby was still pulling on the rope, but it wasn't moving. It was snagged on something in the riverbed. He met my gaze across the deep roar of the rapid and shook his head.

Sheriff Canaday glanced at Tyler and then settled his gaze on me. It seemed that he, too, wanted a miracle.

"Take a shot at it, Sheriff," I urged him, knowing his reputation with his handgun. "It's our best option."

He seemed to consider it for just a moment, but then he shook his head. "Too risky with a pistol, especially with them bucking around in that turbulence." He tried to boost his voice with authority. "Maybe when they get tired of holding on, they'll go deep and, like you said, wash out. Then we'll pick 'em up below. Why don't you go get another canoe, and let's get ready for that."

The sheriff was not connected to this river and its power, and Tyler seemed to know that. Tyler faced me with fresh tears standing in his eyes.

"Please, Stoney," he whispered, his fists still gripping my life jacket. "Do something!"

I took his wrists and gently disengaged his grip. I saw a trickle of blood dripping from his right fist. When I unrolled his fingers, there was the finished glass arrowhead and a small cut it had made in his palm. I plucked the napped glass from his hand and tested its edge with my thumb. It was razor sharp. The look on my face must have startled him, for he took a step back. I took the point and started running for the van.

"I'll be right back!" I called to Tyler.

Cody met me on his way back to the sheriff. He stopped, and when I ran past him, he called out to me.

"They're on their way, Stoney!" When I kept running, he raised his voice. "Where the devil are you goin'?!"

At the van, I tore open my dry bag and called to Troy to bring my bow and quiver from the front of the bus. From my first aid kit, I tossed him the dental floss and opened the saw blade on my Swiss Army knife. After sawing off the field point of one of my arrows, I cut a groove into the newly squared-off end. The base of Tyler's arrowhead wedged perfectly into the slot. Troy already had a length of dental floss ready, and I wrapped the shaft and glass about twenty turns and tied it down tight, as he and Amanda strung my bow. The whole process took less than two minutes, and I was off and running for the river.

Sheriff Canaday interrupted his conversation with Cody to frown at me. "What do you think you're gonna do?"

I guess he needed to say it, but he made no move to stop me. I positioned myself downstream to get an angle on both air compartments, which came together at the front of the raft. I loaded, calmed myself, took a deep breath, and drew, aiming right across the seam between the two compartments. Feeling the familiar tension of the bow, I felt the whole of my existence funnel down into the execution of perfect form. I let my fingers relax with a downy lightness, and the arrow flew across the water and ripped into rubber.

A loud whoosh of air announced a hit, but I didn't know how deeply the arrow had penetrated. One compartment emptied fast, and the two men frantically climbed onto the other. Then the far compartment began to shrink until Perry and Beau were wallowing on deflated rubber. Suddenly, the pounding waterfall drew them closer and pushed both men under.

The three of us stood on the shore suspended in time as the rapid transformed into its former self, looking just like it had whenever I had stood here so many times before. The raft was gone. Beau and Perry were gone. The familiar soundtrack of Hydrophobia roared mindlessly through the gorge, resonating from its archive of history established long before people had come along with their inane agendas.

Perry's head popped up twenty yards downstream. Then Beau surfaced behind him. Both men sputtered and gasped for air as they slapped at the river's surface, trying to keep their heads above water. I started for the canoe and felt a tug. Tyler's fist was locked around my wrist. In his other hand he held my bow. I didn't remember handing it to him. His mouth quivered, and his eyes were like fragile, leaking dams. He reached out and flattened his free hand over my heart.

"Stoney," was all he said.

A loud *thump* and falsetto scream cut through the roar of water. It was the war cry you hear in old Westerns when the Indians attack the wagon train. Bobby Whitehorse put in four powerful strokes as he climbed up the slope out of the hydraulic and cruised downstream below the rapid. His battered Stetson was perched on his head, droplets of water raining off the brim. He wore an impish smile I'd never before seen on his face.

"God o' Mighty!" Cody said. "That crazy Indian."

Bobby continued to smile at me, and I held up two fingers spread into a V. To the others, it may have looked like a victory sign, but he knew it for what it was: the Indian sign for wolf . . . the ultimate warrior. Robert Steals-the-White-Man's-Horse nodded and held my eye, and I knew he was praising my shot with the glass-tipped arrow. I ran to the beached canoe to give "that crazy Indian" a hand.

Chapter Twenty-Six

With the arrival of the ambulance, Search and Rescue, and two more deputies, I decided to leave the canoes and get the kids back to camp. The sooner we put all this behind them, the better. As we pulled out, I told Sheriff Canaday I would stop by his office in a couple of hours. He gave me a thumbs-up and waved me on.

As we unloaded the gear at camp, Pat and Tyler walked off in deep conversation toward the staff cabin. I watched them climb the grassy hill, leaning into one another like the first support beams of a piece of architecture that would rise in time.

Old Bill came out of the office and talked with Bobby Whitehorse for several minutes. Then he walked to me and squeezed my shoulder until I met his eyes.

"You okay?" he said.

When I gave him a weary nod he smiled like a proud father.

Mrs. Old Bill appeared next to him and opened her arms to me. "Double desserts for all the canoeists, Stoney!" she announced and hugged me around my neck.

When I started back to the van, Old Bill stopped me. "Go get something to eat, Stoney," he said. "Justin and Jimmy Dale can go back and pick up the canoes."

I shook my head, climbed into the van, and started the engine. "I'd like to do it," I said through the open window. Bill looked at me with a curious grin but said not a word. He just nodded and stepped back.

The light was beginning to soften to twilight. I gazed across the meadow beyond the split rail fence. The plush spring grass had darkened to deep green and would need cutting soon. Then it would make its way to the barn in square bales that Bobby Whitehorse would spread for the horses. I nodded to Old Bill and pulled away, feeling the internal glow of a promise that all this would be waiting for me when I returned.

In the rear-view mirror, I saw Bill and Mrs. Old Bill standing next to one another, watching me, their hands at their sides. As I coasted into the shadows of the single lane that wound down the mountain, I looked at them once again in my mirror. They hadn't moved.

The parking area at the river take-out was crisscrossed with tracks. The recent buzz of excitement here—or rather its absence—gave the river a heightened sense of serenity, as if the gorge was breathing steadily again after hyperventilating over all the human folly. The crepuscular light gave the foam an internal white radiance that, though pleasing to my eye, always baffled me. How can water gather so much light out of so little?

The air in the gorge was cooler in the darkening hour. The roar of the rapid seemed louder as it always did at night. I looked into the hole and could not make the image of the raft and two men materialize. The river was as it should be, free and unsullied. It held no grudge; it forgave nothing. Neither did it commend nor condemn. The river abided.

One by one I carried the canoes to the trailer and listened to the familiar ring of the gunnels hitting the trailer rack. The sound echoed off the rock walls across the river and then died in the hushed roar of the rapid. My hands worked the soft rope by rote, tightening knots I could depend on. Each time I returned for another boat, the beach was a little less cluttered, and the river valley slowly regained all its dignity. Its integrity. Its autonomy.

With everything loaded, I walked back to the river's edge, knelt, and dipped my hand into the water that softly lapped against the shore. I raised my hand like a ladle and let the water dribble back to the river. These droplets, I knew, had fallen from the clouds, trickled down a mountain rivulet, joined the solidarity of the river, and hurdled through the violent turbulence of Hydrophobia in a moment of chaotic transition.

Now the water remaining in my hand was like the gentlest of lovers. It was no wonder we ascribed so much poetry and personality to the river. Always changing. Always the same. Maybe it was the river that helped us understand contradiction and its place in our lives.

I lived in a world where men beat their sons and wives, and, for all I knew, where some wives beat their husbands. Where little boys' souls withered under the flawed supervision of parents, whose parents before them had probably passed on the legacy. And they grew up to be the Perrys and Beau Raintrees of the world. And men like Victor Dimateo, who destroyed lives in order to feed his own disproportionate needs.

But Bobby Whitehorse was in this world. And Old Bill. Itawa and the kids. And Abby Parrish. As soon as her face materialized in my head, my stomach filled with its own whitewater effervescence. The chill that accompanied it brought me to my feet. It was time to go.

I was in the sheriff's office for three hours. My statement was recorded, as were the many questions and answers that helped to flesh out the story. From our small-town, county sheriff's office, this misadventure on the river would spread to all manner of government agencies. Eventually, I would be telling this story again and again until finally a huge net would be dropped over the illegal alien network, the drug pipeline, and Dimateo, who would be in prison for a long time.

Perry—who turned out to be Francis Lyle Perham—and Beaumont J. Raintree had been considerably humbled by their near-death experience in Hydrophobia's rinse cycle. I didn't see them at all at the jail, but Cody told me that Beau, after being read his rights, spouted out a lot of information about Dimateo. Eventually, Beau settled into a contentious pout and demanded his lawyer, but by then a lot of the beans had been spilled.

"Perry," Cody said, "was neither uncooperative nor helpful. He just seemed kinda sad and waited for whatever misery would next show up in his life."

It was almost eleven when I pulled in front of the camp office. When I cut the engine, Old Bill came out of the office wearing a robe and slippers and carrying a flashlight in his hand.

"Mrs. Raintree and Tyler are sleeping here at the office," Bill said from the walkway. "You've got your cabin back."

I waved an acknowledgement and got out of the van.

"Everything go all right at the sheriff's office?"

I pressed the van door shut with a hip. "Yep."

Bill looked deep into my eyes. "You look tired."

"Yep," I said again.

He clapped his free hand against my shoulder. "Go get some rest. You can tell me about it tomorrow."

"Goodnight, Bill."

"Goodnight, son," he said quietly. He turned and walked back to the building.

The camp was quiet. I walked past the lake knowing that all the Outriders were safe and asleep in their bunks. Pat Raintree, too. She was probably dreaming about a second life. I was pretty sure she was going to be okay. And I was almost certain that her main strength was going to be a young man named Tyler.

My cabin showed a faint glow in the front window. When I stepped inside, I found a lighted candle perched upon the cold wood heater and next to it lay a foil-wrapped plate. Bobby Whitehorse had saved me some supper.

When I opened the foil I found a heaping portion of cobbler, which I carried to the counter next to the sink. Spooning up a mouthful of cobbler, I chewed as I crossed the room to my piano and set the candle next to the sheet music stand.

Sitting on my piano bench, I let my fingers wander through the patterns I'd been exploring of late. Some of the sections moved like water and some like an eagle. Through the next half hour, I developed Abby's motif into an extended composition and jotted it down lest my tired mind forget it by morning.

Taking one more bite of cobbler, I grabbed a towel and walked out to my little dock, where I sat and pulled off my boots. The full moon played behind a gallery of gray ships sailing on a soundless sea. The lake was as smooth as glass.

I slipped out of my clothes and eased into the water. Taking a deep breath, I went under for a long time, rubbing down my legs, arms, and torso and then scrubbing my scalp briskly with my fingertips. When I surfaced, I swam a few quiet circles doing the breaststroke, then pulled myself up on my dock.

After drying off with the towel, I stood with my feet spread and laced my fingers behind my head as I looked up at the sky. Every narrow cloud that stretched in front of the moon showed a bright, fine edge of light, as if each had been framed by a superheated wire.

The sound of stirred water traveled across the lake—just the faint rippling that a muskrat might make when it dives beneath the surface.

I held my breath to listen, but the sound stopped. Staring at the swimming dock, I could just make out a single shape sitting at the edge of the boards. I lay belly-down on my landing and lowered my head over the edge close to the water.

"Someone is up late tonight lurking around the lake," I whispered.

In ten seconds, a sibilant answer traveled back to me. "I don't think eagles lurk."

"Who told you that you are an eagle?"

This time a longer silence stretched out. "A white horse named Bobby."

There was enough moonglow to see her head come up. I cupped my hands around my mouth and whispered again across the smooth skin of the lake.

"But eagles do dive into water."

My long-distance whispering-pal stood and went through a fluid motion with her arms over her head, after which she dropped a garment to the dock. Then she stepped out of her jeans. With a light spring off her legs she dove in, making a clean incision into the water. I eased back into the dark lake and swam her way.

Just shy of bumping heads, we stopped and treaded water. Abby's wet and glistening hair was swept back on her head, which made her cheekbones stand out. Her face was largely in shadow, but I could sense her smile. It wasn't Joan of Arc.

She glided the final few inches toward me until I could feel her breath on my chin. I paddled forward a stroke and touched her lips with mine. Our bodies conformed, and my hands pressed against the strong arch of her spine. While we kissed, as if we had choreographed the evening, we both took deep breaths through our noses and sank in unison.

Weightless and soundless we fell as slowly as dust motes in a shaft of sunlight. She kissed me hard, nestling her silky skin into the perfect fit that we made. When passion finally yielded to oxygen, we laughed in an explosion of bubbles and surfaced.

When my breathing settled, I whispered, "It would be embarrassing to drown tonight and be found like this at first period swimming tomorrow."

Without a response, she started swimming toward my little dock. When I caught up to her, we switched from breaststroke to freestyle and made our way side by side to my landing. She put a hand on the boards and turned to me.

"Welcome back," she whispered. "I'm glad you're okay."

"Me, too. I wouldn't have wanted to miss this."

She drifted into my arms again. "Me, too," she said and kissed me. The moon appeared suddenly at a break in the clouds and light washed over us. I opened my eyes in that moment and watched the shadow of a cloud envelope us again—our snapshot for the scrapbook of the universe complete. She backed away to look at me.

"Are you cold?" I asked.

She shook her head. "The water feels wonderful. Are you?"

"Wonderful or cold?" I said.

"I know you're wonderful. Are you cold?"

I shook my head and reached for her. She slipped her hands behind my neck, and I held onto the boards for both of us.

Long after Abby had wrapped herself in my towel and disappeared across the lawn that led to her cabin, I sat on my dock and watched the clouds skate across the sky. When I was just about air-dried, I stood up and looked at the empty swimming dock that I would now be checking nightly. The clouds thinned out, and the moon found a big hole to shine through.

Off to my right a movement pulled my eye. A dark weaving line sliced through the silvery surface of the water and set up a pattern of ripples that spread in its wake in ever-widening V's. It cut across the lake through the swimming area to the grass, its path almost a perfect reversal of the one made by the copperhead Tyler had spotted.

It had been too dark to identify, but it got me thinking about omens and curses again. I still didn't believe in them. But if that was a copperhead I had just seen . . . and if it was recanting a curse cast upon us on the first day of camp . . . and if the rest of this season went a little smoother . . . that was okay with me.

Even if all that was nonsense, how bad could a season be with Abby in it?

Here in the magical years.

About the Author

Mark Warren is a teacher of Native American survival skills in the Appalachian Mountains of north Georgia, where he lives with his wife, Susan. He is a lifelong student/historian of the Old West, a composer/musician, and an archer.

Upcoming New Release!

AWARD-WINNING AUTHOR
MARK WARREN

THE LAST REAL PLACE
THE CAMP ITAWA MYSTERIES
BOOK TWO

Stoney St. Ney learns that his new girlfriend, Abby, has met with trauma in the North Carolina high school where she teaches. Two students have gone on a shooting rampage in the school library, killing one student and critically wounding three others. Concerned about her welfare, Stoney leaves Camp Itawa to offer moral and physical support to Abby, but he soon finds himself in the unexpected situation of being one-third of a love triangle. Abby's safety becomes a top priority, when Stoney learns that she might have been one of the shooters' intended targets.

**For more information
visit:** www.SpeakingVolumes.us

Now Available!
AWARD WINNING AUTHOR
MARK WARREN

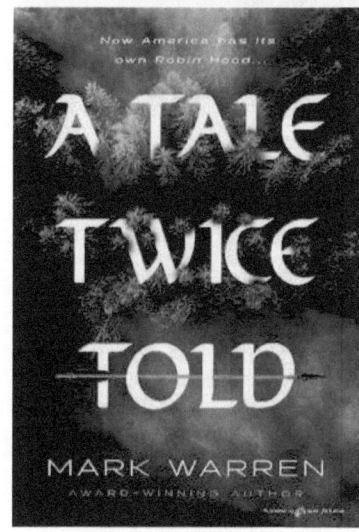
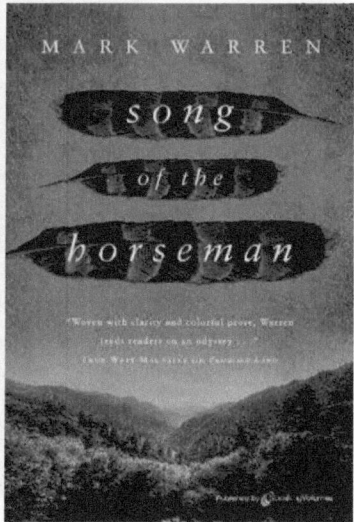

**For more information
visit:** www.SpeakingVolumes.us

Now Available!

BRIEN A. ROCHE

THE PROHIBITION SERIES
BOOK 1 – BOOK 2 – BOOK 3

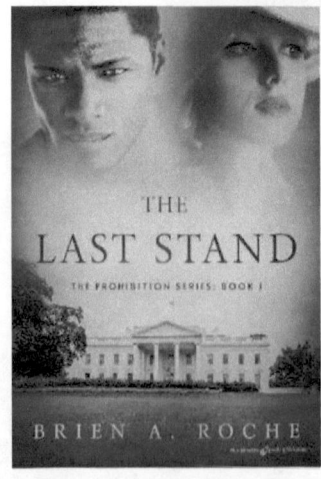

**For more information
visit: www.SpeakingVolumes.us**

www.ingramcontent.com/pod-product-compliance
Lightning Source LLC
LaVergne TN
LVHW041655060526
838201LV00043B/449